THE Love You Deserve

THE *Love in the City* SERIES
BOOK FOUR

JEN MORRIS

First edition April 2022

Kindle ISBN: 978-0-473-62370-8

Epub ISBN: 978-0-473-62369-2

Paperback ISBN: 978-0-473-62368-5

Cover illustration by Elle Maxwell

www.ellemaxwelldesign.com

For anyone who has ever felt they don't deserve love.
You do. You deserve everything.

If I know what love is, it is because of you.

— HERMANN HESSE

AUTHOR'S NOTE

Please note that this book contains sensitive topics such as parental abandonment, anniversary of a parent's death, and adoption. It also references infidelity, which occurs in the past, off-page, and not between the two main characters. Finally, this story shows a character struggling with low self-worth, and eventually seeking help. If these topics are triggering for you, please read with caution.

This book is different from the previous three in the series, because it is written in dual point of view (you get both the heroine and the hero's perspective). For this reason, it is also slightly steamier than the previous books.

1

JOSIE

There are four million men in New York and I was foolish enough to fall for my boss.

Okay, wait. It's not as scandalous as it sounds. That probably conjures images of some stuffy guy in a suit who owns a global corporation, while I'm a lowly assistant who's twenty-five years his junior, trying to climb the corporate ladder.

But it's nothing like that.

Cory Porter owns Bounce, a bar in Manhattan's East Village, where I've been a bartender for five years. I'm not twenty-five years his junior, just twelve. And I'm not trying to climb anything.

Except him.

"Bud Light, please."

I blink, fixing my attention on the customer in front of me. Black cap, brown, shoulder-length wig, black T-shirt. Even if he didn't have the *Wayne's World* text on his hat, I'd get the reference.

"Sure thing," I say, reaching for a bottle and popping the top. "*Excellent* costume."

"Thanks." He takes the beer, letting his gaze slide down to my chest. It lingers on my breasts, which I intentionally push together so they threaten to spill out of my low-cut Lycra bodysuit. When his eyes finally come back to mine, his mouth tilts in a sleazy grin and he hands me a twenty. "Keep the change, gorgeous."

"Thank you." I try not to grin too hard as he walks away, swapping his twenty in the register and adding the large tip to my jar behind the bar. I wouldn't normally dress—or behave—like this, but dress-up trivia nights are always a great opportunity for extra tips. Tonight's theme is movie trivia, and I'm giving all my tips to the animal shelter where I volunteer. If I have to dress as sexy *Catwoman* for a few hours to help one of my favorite places in the city, I'm all for it.

Besides, it's not just me. Camila also dresses sexy for the tips. Hell, she dresses like that even when it's not trivia night.

I wipe the bar, letting my gaze drift across the crowd. I love working here. It's rustic and kind of a dive, but it's fun. Cory's kept the decor pretty minimal: low, warm lighting, exposed brick walls, red vinyl booths, a long bar stretching the left side, and a small dance floor near the back. I found this place five years ago when, after foolishly following my boyfriend to the city from Austin, we had a messy breakup and I wanted to drown my sorrows. The bar owner was super nice—okay, hot—and even though he didn't need another bartender, he didn't hesitate to offer me a job when I mentioned I was looking. I might have only been twenty-two, with zero bartending experience, but he took a chance on me and I've been forever grateful. Now, I split my time between bartending full time here and volunteering at Animal Oasis, a shelter in the

Seaport District. One day, if I'm lucky, I'll land a paid job at the shelter.

"You should take a break," I hear from beside me. I turn to see Cory, all six-foot-six of him, dressed as Thor—the short-haired version. And boy, is he wearing his costume well. He's got the body armor plate, the wrist-guard things— I don't even know what they're called, but they make his biceps look damn good—and the red cape. His dirty-blond hair and short beard perfectly suit the Chris Hemsworth coloring, but trust me when I say that Cory is way hotter.

I'm not the only one who's noticed; women are trampling each other to get him to serve them tonight. Although that happens most nights, regardless of what he's wearing.

I shrug. "I don't need a break." The more time I spend on breaks, the fewer tips I'll make.

Cory's hazel eyes travel over my body, and for a split second I think he's checking me out. But his brows tug together into a frown and he shakes his head, turning down the bar to serve a group of women. I try my best to ignore the disappointment that bleeds through me.

Of course, he wasn't checking me out. Despite how I feel, we've never had that kind of relationship. In the five years I've worked at Bounce, he's treated me more like a little sister than anything, which is hardly surprising—I'm nine years younger than his actual sister. He looks out for me, worries about me, makes sure my customers don't get too rowdy. That's nice, but it's not exactly what I want from him.

A couple hop onto the barstools in front of me, and I smile at the familiar faces. The woman with pink hair is Cat, Cory's younger sister, and the bearded guy with a sleeve of tattoos is Myles, her fiancé. He used to be a bartender here before we hired Camila and Levi. I always liked him— despite the fact that he was a big flirt—because he was respectful and kind. Cory, on the other hand, took some time to warm to him.

I glance at their costumes. They've really gone all out. Cat looks awesome in a *Cinderella* dress, and Myles... appears to be in drag.

"Hey, Josie," he says, tugging off his red wig and lifting a tattooed arm to scratch his scalp. "Man, that thing itches."

I fight a snicker. "Myles, *why* are you dressed as Ariel? Why not Prince Charming?"

He repositions his wig, feigning indignation. "What, you don't think I can pull it off? Just because I'm a guy, I have to be a prince?"

Cat giggles. "Amber chose our costumes and he didn't have the heart to tell her no. Ariel is her favorite." She leans in to plant a kiss on Myles's scruffy cheek. "You can totally pull it off, baby. Amber loved it."

I laugh. It's sweet that Myles would do that for his daughter, but I'm not sure I'll ever get used to a bearded, tattooed *Little Mermaid*.

"The usual?" I ask, already reaching for the whiskey and vodka as they both nod.

"Will you be at our anniversary party here in a few days?" Cat asks.

I nod as I pour their drinks. "Yep. What anniversary is it again?"

Cat and Myles share a secret look before she says, "The anniversary of when we moved in together. One year."

I smile. I've never known anyone to throw a party for their moving-in anniversary, but that's really sweet.

"Hey, sis." Cory rounds the bar and slings an arm over Cat's shoulder in a half-hug. He looks at Myles, hesitating as he takes in his costume, and they do that head-nod thing that guys do instead of saying hello. Then he bends down under Cat's barstool, and my heart gives an excited kick. That can only mean one thing: Cat brought her dog, Stevie.

I slide their drinks across the bar and step around to the other side, dropping beside Cory. "Hi, Stevie!" The little pug abandons Cory's outstretched hand for mine, and I grin. "Hey, girl," I coo, as she wriggles out from under the barstool and lunges at my legs. I gather her up into my arms and squeeze her warm body, rising back to my feet. Then I shower her with affection, which is only returned double. Dogs are the best.

"She loves coming in here to see you," Cat says with a chuckle.

Cory huffs as he straightens up. "What about me?"

"I give the best cuddles," I joke, scratching under Stevie's chin. When I lift my gaze, Cory is watching me, a tiny smile twitching at the corner of his mouth. He's got such a soft spot for Stevie.

"Your costume is awesome," Cat says as I reluctantly deposit Stevie back under her stool and scoot around the bar again.

"Thanks." I grin, but Cory mumbles something I don't catch under his breath.

Cat glances between me and Cory. "What?"

"Well, you know." He wanders back behind the bar. "Every dude in the place is leering at her."

Annoyance prickles up my spine. This isn't the first time he's said something like that about my dress-up choices, and it seems a little hypocritical given the way he's been mentally undressed by every woman in here tonight.

"Um, Cors?" Cat gives him a funny look. "Why are you talking about her like you're her overprotective big brother?"

"Or her boyfriend?" Myles chips in, eyebrows raised smugly.

"What?" Cory's cheeks color. "I'm not. I just think, as her *boss*, that she should dress appropriately."

"You know I can hear you, right?" I wave a hand in Cory's face but he ignores me.

"Oh come *on*." Cat motions to Cory. "As if your costume isn't designed to make women ogle you. Talk about double standards." She glances at me and I send her a grateful smile. At least someone has my back.

I square my shoulders and arch an eyebrow at Cory, wondering what his comeback will be. But before he can say anything there's a tap on the microphone, signaling the start of the first trivia round.

Eddy runs our trivia nights. He's twenty-three and a pretty mediocre bartender, but he's surprisingly great at this. I think it's the only reason Cory keeps him on.

Myles and Cat turn to join in the trivia questions as a redhead in a black *Playboy* bunny costume approaches the bar. I can't decide if it's a *Bridget Jones* tribute, or if she thinks *Playboy* is a movie.

"Hi," I say, smiling. "What can I get you?"

Her gaze flits over my shoulder to where Cory is serving a round of beers. "Um..." She bites her lip, issuing an awkward laugh. "I hope this isn't weird of me to ask, but that bartender—is he single?"

Ah, here we go. This is the first time I've been asked this question tonight, but it will not be the last. We need a sign or something. Maybe I should wear a T-shirt that says, *Yes, my boss is single.* Or a sandwich board; that would make it pretty clear, right?

"Yep." I adjust my cat ears, attempting to suppress the jealous twinge in my gut. This woman is beautiful and, given half the chance, I'm pretty sure Cory would happily head home with her tonight.

"Oh, great." Her eyes brighten and she leans forward to speak in a conspiratorial tone, apparently sensing some kind of sisterhood between us. "I've been in a few times but I haven't had the chance to talk to him. He's always talking to other women. My friend said he's a total player."

I frown. I hate when women call Cory a player. He's a committed bachelor, sure. And he definitely gets through more than his share of women. But the word "player" makes me think of guys who string women along, who play them off against each other. Cory might get around, but he's not the kind of guy to mislead or manipulate women. Not like my ex.

"He's not," I say. "He's a good guy. But he doesn't do relationships."

"Fine by me." She gives a wink that makes my stomach roll. Her gaze darts behind me and I glance over my shoulder to find Cory.

Ugh, may as well get the inevitable over with.

"Cors," I say, stepping aside, "can you serve this lovely lady? I'm going to clear some tables."

His gaze swings to the redhead. "I sure can. What can I get you, gorgeous?"

"Prosecco, thanks."

He reaches for a bottle and she gives me a secret thumbs up. I return it as if we're the best of friends and I haven't just set her up with the guy I want for myself. *Why* did I do that? I should have told her he's married. With three kids.

Cory places her drink on the bar and she lets her hand linger on his. "I'm Rachel."

"Cory," he replies with a grin. "Great costume."

I ignore the sharp twist through my middle as I go to refill a few drinks and try to make some more tips. It's going to be a long night.

2

CORY

In hindsight, hiring Josie was a mistake. Don't get me wrong, she's great at her job—easily the best bartender I've ever had. But I did it on a whim one rainy afternoon, because she was sad and I wanted to make her smile.

Not my smartest move.

It took me about three weeks to realize I was way too excited to go to work. I'd wake up each morning with a giddy, intoxicated feeling, eager to get to the bar, and there was only one reason for it: the cute, funny, and sweet-as-honey brunette who'd started working for me. I might've had a reputation for taking women home from the bar, but they weren't usually as young as Josie. And they sure as hell weren't my employees.

"Please tell me you're not walking home in that." I pause in the door to the back room, folding my arms across my chest as I watch Josie rummage in her bag. The bar closed a while ago and we've finished cleaning up, but she's still in her *Catwoman* costume.

She glances up. "No," she mutters, pulling her jeans and

tank top out of her bag. "I'm going to change, obviously. Although, I'm pretty sure if I walked home in this I could make a lot more than I made here tonight."

She laughs but I don't join her. The thought of her wandering the streets in a Lycra bodysuit that hugs her tight little frame does not amuse me. It was bad enough watching every asshole in here devour her with their eyes tonight— not that I can blame them. She's five-foot-seven, with enough curves to distract any straight, hot-blooded male, but it's her smile that gets me. It's so wide, almost... innocent. It lights up her whole face, makes her green eyes sparkle.

And it makes me want to do very *not* innocent things to her.

"What are you still doing here, anyway?" she asks, gesturing for me to spin around so she can change.

"What do you mean?" I turn my back to her and rake a hand over my scalp, trying not to picture her peeling that costume off behind me.

"You seemed to be hitting it off with Rachel."

"Who?"

"The redhead." When I don't respond to this, she adds, "The *Playboy* Bunny." I hear the scrape of a zipper and turn around, assuming she's changed.

She's standing there in her jeans and a white lace bra.

"Shit, sorry." I throw my hands up and whip back around, but the image of her half-naked is now seared into my brain. I can see it plain as day when I press my eyelids shut.

Fuck.

"It's fine." She laughs, then a moment later says, "You can turn around."

I gingerly peek over my shoulder, relaxing only when I

can see she's fully dressed. The last thing I need is another eyeful of her bare skin. Five years ago I made the decision not to touch her, and I don't need the temptation now.

"I could have locked up," she says.

I stride over to change, and she glances away as I pull off my costume. "I'm walking you to the subway. You know that." Ever since there was a violent mugging near Houston Street a few months back, I've been walking her to the subway station. I can't stand the thought of her being out there alone at one in the morning. Anything could happen.

"You don't have to. I'll be fine."

I tug on my jeans and Henley, shoving my feet into my boots. She follows as I head toward the door. "We're not having this conversation again, Buttercup. Let's go."

Josie gives a playful roll of her eyes at the nickname.

It wasn't a conscious choice to call her that. It just slipped out one day. She'd been complaining about how busy we were, and I said, 'Suck it up, Buttercup.' She'd given me the funniest look, then burst out laughing. 'Buttercup?' she'd asked. When I shrugged, she gave me a grin and said, 'Alright then.' Just like that, the name stuck.

I hold the front door open and she steps through, saying, "thanks." I lock up, then we head out, walking in easy silence for a few blocks.

The city is different at this time of night. Even though it's late May, the air feels cooler, especially after working in the stuffy bar all night, and the streetlights cast pools of yellow light along the sidewalk. Almost everything is closed, except for the odd bar and twenty-four-hour deli. There's less traffic around the East Village at this hour, but I can hear a car horn and siren somewhere in the distance; that classic New York soundtrack that reminds you this city never sleeps.

Growing up on Long Island, I always knew I'd end up in the city. I moved here a year after high school and worked in bars around the East Village. In my late twenties I took some business classes online, and when the bar I was working at came up for sale, I got a bank loan and bought it with a buddy of mine, Rob. Eventually Rob left Manhattan to settle down and have kids in New Jersey, and I bought him out, renaming the bar Bounce. It wasn't quite the same without him, but I made it work. Then four years ago I bought my apartment on the Lower East Side, and now, I can't see myself ever leaving.

When we hit Houston Street, I pause and gesture to a diner, glowing brightly across the road. "Hungry?"

Josie nods, and we cross to Sam's Diner. We don't always stop to eat on the way home, but I'd be lying if I said I didn't enjoy the extra time in her company.

We slide onto the vinyl of our usual booth and I pick up the menu, even though I know what I'll order. When I finally glance up, Josie's gaze meets mine and a smile curves along her lips.

It hits me right in the chest.

I feel my own mouth tug into a grin. Now that I'm away from the bar—away from the stresses of managing dick-heads like Eddy, of watching guys hit on Josie all night—I can relax. I know I can be a grumpy bastard at work, but I care about my bar and my staff, and I'm not going to half-ass things there. Usually that means I get too serious, but focusing on the job helps to put a barrier between me and Josie. God knows I need that.

I set my menu down. "The usual?" Josie nods and I gesture to the waitress nearby, ordering for us. We watch her go to the kitchen window to place our order. She returns with two ice-cold glasses of Coke and I take mine with a nod of thanks.

"The trivia nights seem to be going well," Josie says, sipping her drink.

"Yeah." Six months ago Josie came to me with the idea to host themed trivia nights, and while I was initially skeptical, they've been a huge success. "They were such a good idea, Joze." She gives me a smile that makes my heart punch against my ribs and I force myself to glance away, taking a long sip of Coke.

Our food arrives a few minutes later. The best thing about eating at a diner in the middle of the night: almost no wait time.

I grimace as she picks up her vegan burger. "I don't know how you can eat that," I say, reaching for my own—beef, of course, with extra bacon.

She grins and takes a huge bite. She told me once that she stopped eating meat after she began volunteering at the animal shelter because she felt like a hypocrite spending her days saving animals and then eating them for dinner. That's the thing about Josie; she cares about stuff like this. She cares enough to give up meat—even though she's told me she likes it—because she thinks it's the right thing to do.

"Myles's costume was good tonight," she says around a mouthful of fries.

"Yeah." I laugh. "Never thought I'd see a grown man dressed as a mermaid."

She giggles too. "I know, but it's sweet he did that for his daughter." I nod and she adds, "Remember when you hated him?"

"I didn't hate him. I *hired* him."

"I know." She chuckles. "But when he started dating Cat—"

"Yeah, alright," I admit, polishing off my burger. I think back to when Myles started working for me a year ago and I caught him hitting on my sister. I was convinced he was bad news and I wanted to kick his ass. "I thought he was going to hurt her. She's been through a lot." I wipe my hands on a napkin. "But he's a good guy. They're good together."

"Just as well you think so, since they're engaged and all." Josie is quiet for a moment, pushing her fries around her plate. Then she looks up at me, chewing the straw of her drink. "Sorry you didn't get to go home with that girl tonight."

I frown. That's the second time she's mentioned that, and it bothers me that she assumes my goal for the evening is to take a woman home. Admittedly, I used to sleep around a lot. I'd consider it a good night if we'd met our day's target at the bar and I'd found a beautiful woman to take to bed. But the last few times I went home with a woman I found myself bored—making polite conversation, doing what needed to be done—then relieved when the night was over. Lately, I haven't felt the urge to take anyone home. I don't know if it's because I'm a year away from turning forty, or because I've spent my nights walking Josie to the subway instead of losing myself between some gorgeous blond's legs, but the thought doesn't interest me like it once did.

I lift a shoulder and glance away, draining my Coke. "You know I don't just look for women to take home every night, right?"

"I know," she says quickly.

I stare out the window onto the dark street, frustrated. I probably should be at home with that redhead right now, not here in an empty diner with my employee.

Josie pushes her plate away. "Are you going to tell me you're more than just a pretty face, too?"

I laugh, bringing my gaze back to hers. She's good at making me loosen up when I get too in my head about shit. "I'm *way* more than that, Buttercup."

She grins, her gaze lingering on mine before drifting out the window, and I steal a quick glance at her. She's beautiful, but not in a flashy or overly done-up way. With Josie it's more subtle, like the tiny heart-shaped freckle below her left ear, or the sound of her surprised laugh when you've caught her off guard with just the right joke, or the way her jeans and white cotton tank top make her look like the classic all-American girl next door.

An image flashes into my mind—the actual girl next door to me, growing up. Alice. I haven't seen her in well over a decade, but I can see her face as if it were yesterday. Josie has always reminded me of her. Alice was beautiful in a subtle way too, and so sweet.

Too sweet for a guy like me. All I did was break her heart.

I shove the memories away as I finish my meal and check the time—nearly 2 a.m. I'm exhausted, and I know Josie will get up in the morning to head off to the shelter. I pay the check, ignoring her protests about paying for herself, and rise from the table.

"You don't have to walk me to the train," she says again as we head for the exit.

"I know I don't have to, Joze. I want to." I pause at the door, turning back to her. I want to make sure she's safe, but I don't want to be some jackass who makes her feel smothered. "Do you want me to leave you alone?" I ask. But once the words are out of my mouth, I'm not sure I want to know the answer.

She bites her lip, her eyes searching mine. "No," she says, so quiet it's almost as if she couldn't bring herself to really say it. She swallows. My gaze drops to her mouth, to that full bottom lip tucked between her teeth, and I imagine what it would be like to pull her into my arms and press my mouth to hers until neither of us can breathe.

Whoa. Take a step back, buddy.

I clear my throat roughly, forcing the image deep down inside where it belongs. "I'm already going that way, anyway," I say, shrugging in what I hope appears to be a casual manner as I open the door for her. "It's on my way home."

She blinks, glancing from me to the door. After a moment's pause, she steps past me onto the sidewalk.

I make myself walk two feet apart from her the entire way to the train.

3

JOSIE

O kay, so things with Cory aren't how I'd like them to be, but it's fine. There's another guy in this city who's always excited to see me.

I drop into my seat on the J train and pull out my phone with a yawn, noticing it's not even 9 a.m. Way too early on a Saturday morning to be on a train.

Swiping my phone open, I press the photo app with a smile. Ah, there's my boy. He's got big brown eyes and an even bigger heart. He gives the best kisses, not to mention he's sweet, loyal, affectionate...

If only I didn't have to pick up his shit.

Still, that's part of being a volunteer at an animal shelter, and if the love of a stray dog is all I can get, I'll take it. Dogs love unconditionally.

Just like my mom.

Mom—as I've always called her, even though she's my godmother—had no kids of her own. She'd been happy fostering dogs and volunteering in local community projects back home. When my parents died in a car accident, two-year-old me had nowhere to go and my birth mom's best friend stepped up. She adopted me and raised me as her own, sacrificing dating and marriage so she could focus on raising me. As I got older, she started fostering dogs again, but she never dated, maybe because she worried about someone coming into our home and ruining what we had. Sometimes I feel bad that she gave all that up, but I'm eternally grateful for the sacrifices she made to raise me. I could have ended up in the foster system, passed from one place to another, but I was lucky enough to grow up in a home that taught me the importance of loving those who need it most.

Thinking of Mom sends a pang through me. She's back home in Austin, but we text most days, usually about my work at the shelter or the dogs she's fostering at home.

I return my attention to the picture on my phone: a caramel colored dog named Pretzel who's been at the shelter for a while now. He's a total mutt—some American Staffordshire Terrier, some Basset Hound, and who knows what else —and he's my favorite. At six years, he's older than a lot of the other dogs at the shelter, and gets anxious around new people. I think he might have experienced some kind of abuse or trauma in his past, but I can't be sure. All I know is that when he first arrived at the shelter, he was this scared little ball who stayed in the corner of his cage. It broke my heart to see him so frightened and lonely, and I made it my mission to spend extra time with him, to help him develop his trust in people again. The shelter manager, Gerard, says it's because of me that Pretzel has become more confident and opened up to people.

If I'm being completely honest, I've kind of fallen in love with him and I'm already dreading the day someone adopts him. I'd take him home myself if my landlady allowed pets or I could afford to move, but I stay at my shoe box studio apartment because the low rent means I can donate more generously to Animal Oasis. I only use it as a place to crash between work and the shelter anyway. If I ever manage to get a full-time job at the shelter, I might think about moving somewhere a little nicer.

I smile and send the photo of Pretzel off to my mom, knowing she'll appreciate it.

Josie: Seeing this beautiful boy today.

Mom: What a cutie! Give him a cuddle from me.

I slide my phone back into the pocket of my jeans and glance up, catching my reflection in the window opposite. The tiny diamond stud in my nose glints in the fluorescent light, and I rake a hand through my short, brunette bob. My alabaster complexion is paler than usual, my eyes puffy since I only got about five hours of sleep last night. Most nights I can survive on six, which allows me to fit in a volunteer shift at the shelter before heading to Bounce, but last night's detour to the diner stole that extra hour that makes me look a bit more human.

Worth it, though. Always worth it to spend time with Cory outside of work, because when he's not being Grumpy Boss Cory, he feels more like Friend Cory.

Though I'd much prefer Boyfriend Cory. Or Husband Cory.

I shake the ridiculous thoughts from my head. Those Corys don't exist, no matter how much I wish they did.

As the train pulls into Delancey Street station, I push to my feet. I can't wait to see Pretzel.

"Oh my God."

I break into a jog as I approach Animal Oasis, trying to

make sense of the sight before me. Animals are lined up in cages outside the front of the shelter while water pours through the door onto the sidewalk. The staff are gathered to one side and I hurry toward them.

"Gerard!" I spot the shelter's manager as I approach. "What's going on?"

"Josie, thank God you're here." Gerard turns to me, wiping a towel down his arms. His wet clothes cling to his mahogany skin. He's tall and generously proportioned, with the personality of a teddy bear. I've worked at the shelter with him for years and he's truly one of the most selfless people I've met. He reminds me of my mom in that way. "A pipe burst and we had to get everyone out as quickly as possible." I can barely hear him above the din from the animals, their cages stacked beside each other along the concrete.

I look across, instinctively searching for Pretzel. When I spot him curled up in a ball in one of the cages, my heart gives a relieved thump. I turn back to Gerard. "Did you get everyone out?"

He nods. "Everyone's fine. A little wet, but fine."

I look at the water flooding out onto the sidewalk and over the gutter. I feel so helpless just standing here. There's a stab in my chest to see the shelter I love in such a state of chaos. "Is there anything I can do?"

Gerard shakes his head. "There's not much we can do until the fire department arrives to shut off the pipes. It's going to take all night to clean this place up."

I pull out my phone, ready to call Cory and see if I can get out of work tonight, but I remember Camila is off for a few nights and she'd have to come in to cover for me. I can't ask her to do that.

Gerard gestures for me to put my phone away. "Don't

worry, we've got a team of professional cleaners coming in later today to deal with the damage."

I nod, breathing out.

"There is one thing you can do, though," Gerard says.

"Yes! Anything."

"We've found places for most of the animals overnight while we get the shelter cleaned up, but not all of them. I know you have a special bond with Pretzel. Could you take him for the night? It's been a stressful morning and I'd hate to send him somewhere that would only distress him more."

I open my mouth to agree, then stop. My landlady, Mrs. Petrovski, will kill me if she catches me with a dog in the apartment. I can't risk being kicked out of my building. I glance back over at Pretzel, who's spotted me talking to Gerard and is up on his hind legs, wagging his tail vigorously. Can I really say no to him? What would Mom do?

I know exactly what she'd do.

When I look back at Gerard's hopeful face, I find myself nodding. "Yep. I'll figure something out." Maybe it will be okay if I can sneak him in and keep him quiet. Besides, it's one night—it's not like I've adopted him. I can't be kicked out for one night.

"You're a saint, Josie. Thank you. He'll be much happier with you than anywhere else."

"Yeah," I say, knowing that's probably true. I don't like the idea of sending him somewhere new for the night. "Should I take him now?"

"It would be good if you could. The others will be picked up and taken off to various shelters across the city for tonight."

I head over to Pretzel's cage and crouch in front of it, smiling at the way his excited tail-wagging makes his entire body shake. "Hey, boy." I slip my hand into the cage and stroke his velvet ear. "You want to come have a sleepover with me?" It's almost as though he understands what I've said, because he smothers my hand with wet kisses in response.

I straighten up, thinking. I don't know how I'm going to do this, because I'll need a crate or something for him to sleep in tonight, and I'll have to get out of working at the bar for sure—I can't leave him in my apartment alone. Maybe I can tell Camila I'll work three extra shifts for her, or something. She's got a dog herself—I'm sure she'll understand.

Pretzel lets out a whine and I reach down to stroke him again. Whatever I have to do, I'll figure it out. This little guy needs me.

"It's going to be okay," I say soothingly. The cab bumps along over the Williamsburg bridge while Pretzel cowers on the backseat beside me.

Gerard found a collapsible soft crate for Pretzel to sleep in, and we stuffed some food and treats into a bag to keep him happy overnight. Everything was going fine until I had to get him into a cab. The first two cabs I tried told me they wouldn't take dogs. When I finally found a taxi that would take us, Pretzel refused to get in. I had to lift him in myself, which wouldn't be so hard considering he only weighs 25 pounds, but he thrust his legs out and fought me every step of the way. I thought a cab would be less stressful than the subway because I could have him out of his crate, but he's been unusually quiet. Even with me sneaking him treats when the driver isn't looking.

When we pull up outside my apartment building in Bushwick, my stomach cramps with nerves. I don't know how I'm going to get him inside without getting caught, but what choice do I have?

I pay the driver, adding a generous tip, and grab tight onto Pretzel's leash. It's just as well I do because the moment I open the door he lurches off the seat and across my lap onto the sidewalk.

"Pretzel! Wait!" He nearly yanks my arm from its socket as I try to gather up the folded crate and bag of food on the backseat. I slam the cab door shut with my hip. Pretzel is all too relieved when the cab peels away, turning back to me and hurling himself at my legs, knocking the crate and bag of food out of my arms as I stumble backward.

Jesus.

I drop to my knees and he puts a paw on each of my shoulders, licking my face. I know I should tell him off, but this is the most affection I've had in years. It's hard to be mad.

"Good boy," I say when I eventually pry his paws off my shoulders and calm him down. I lower my voice. "Now, we need to be quiet and well-behaved in here, okay? You're not supposed to be in my apartment, so we have to be sneaky."

I glance up at the building, looking for any signs of movement at Mrs. Petrovski's window, but there's none. Maybe she's out. I can only hope.

I scratch Pretzel under the chin. "Can you do that for me? Can you be a good boy?" He licks my wrist and I take this as a sign of agreement. "Good. Let's go."

I gather up the bag of food and tuck his folded crate under my arm, then head for the front door, keeping a tight hold on his leash. I manage to key in the code and the door pops open. The lobby is empty when we step inside, and I take a deep breath. We only have to make it up five flights of stairs and we'll be in the clear. Easy, right?

"This way," I whisper, nudging Pretzel toward the stairs. His head turns in the general direction but he doesn't move. "Come on, boy. Let's go."

Nothing. It's like he used up all his excitement outside and he's completely lost interest. If that wasn't clear enough, he lowers himself down onto his belly with a yawn.

"Pretzel," I hiss. "Get up. We have to get to my apartment." I glance nervously at the front door. If Mrs. Petrovski comes through the door right now, I'm screwed. It doesn't even have to be Mrs. P. Any of my neighbors could rat me out if they see us. We need to move now.

"Fine," I mutter, glaring down at Pretzel. But he's closed his eyes and is dozing on the linoleum of the lobby.

For God's sake.

With a grumble, I set the crate and food aside, then crouch down to scoop him up in my arms. He gives a tiny yelp of surprise, but once I've got a good hold on him, he settles against me. Then I use one arm to grab the crate and food, awkwardly tucking it under my arm as I grasp Pretzel and head for the stairs.

Fuck, this isn't as easy as I'd hoped. He didn't feel that heavy when I first picked him up, but it's like he gains a pound with every step I take. By the time we make it to the second floor, my arms are burning. He's a dead weight, and the crate keeps slipping out from under my arm, so I have to stop every few steps to reposition it before starting again.

On the fourth floor, he licks my face. I'm not sure if it's his way of thanking me, but it tickles and I begin to laugh. The more I laugh, the more he takes this as a sign of encouragement. By the time we get to the fifth floor, my cheek is wet and I'm laughing so hard I almost drop everything. Finally, I set Pretzel down to pull my keys out, and when the door opens he seems to be reinvigorated and bounds inside.

I stumble in after him, throwing down the crate and food, leaning against the back of the door to catch my breath. All the yoga I do is worthless—it didn't help me at all back there. I need to do more jogging or something.

But it doesn't matter, because we made it inside without being caught.

Thank fuck.

I leave Pretzel to sniff his way around my apartment and go to rinse his enthusiastic kisses off my face. When I return, I set out food and water dishes for him, unfolding his crate and setting it up beside my bed. I watch as he inspects the small space, and smile.

I got this place after my ex, Paul, broke up with me five years ago. I'd uprooted my entire life to follow him here from Austin because he said he "needed me," and I was so committed to our relationship that I didn't question it. I should have, though, because things were a mess from the start: we'd go through these awful cycles where we'd get close, then he'd "need space" and push me away. Each time I'd convince myself that I should try harder, that it was my fault things weren't working. That's always been my down-fall: falling too hard for a guy who doesn't want me. Paul broke it off shortly after we moved here, and I've remained chronically single ever since.

I mean, it's not like I haven't tried. I've been on dates, they just haven't gone anywhere. I guess it doesn't help that I compare every guy I meet to my boss, but can you blame me? He took me in when I was a mess—heartbroken and lost, desperate for a job so I could stay in the city I'd fallen in love with. Paul might not have been my forever, but I knew in my bones that New York was, and when I found this tiny apartment within my price range I jumped on it. It didn't occur to me at the time to ask about pets, because I wasn't ready to have one. I'm still not—I work late every night and I'm at the shelter almost every morning. I don't have the time to give a dog the attention it deserves.

When Pretzel gets bored with examining the unfamiliar territory he turns to me, tail wagging. He meanders back across the room, then pauses at the post in the center of my apartment to sniff something. When he lifts his leg, my stomach drops.

"Pretzel, no!"

It's too late. Urine pools on the wooden floor around the post and I curse, grabbing the roll of paper towels off my kitchen counter. Pretzel drops his leg and wanders off in disinterest while I dive on the pee, desperately trying to soak it up. It's a huge puddle, and I realize as I mop that it's my fault—with everything that happened this morning it's probably been hours since he's had a chance to pee. I should have taken him to go before bringing him in here.

Dammit.

It takes the entire paper towel roll and half a tub of Clorox wipes to clean it up, but once I'm done, I find Pretzel asleep in a ball in the middle of my bed. I can't even be mad at him for peeing on my floor and sleeping on my bed when he looks so peaceful like that. After the morning he's had, he deserves to rest.

I pull my phone out, ready to call Cory and tell him I won't be able to come into work, when there's a knock at my door. Dread snakes up my spine and I freeze, glancing at Pretzel. His head pops up, his ears on high alert, and I raise a silent finger to my mouth, indicating for him to stay quiet. Because of course he knows what I mean.

When the knock comes again, Pretzel launches himself off the bed, barking like mad, and I blow out a defeated breath. There's no way the entire building didn't hear that.

I trudge over to the door and open it, not at all surprised to see Mrs. Petrovski's unimpressed face on the other side. I don't even bother to hide Pretzel, who's going berserk at my side. If anything, I'm secretly pleased by his show of loyalty and protectiveness toward me.

"Josephine," she says, by way of hello. "You know we forbid pets in the building."

"I know," I mutter. How did she even know he was here? He hadn't made a sound until she knocked on the door.

Mrs. P. shakes her head in disappointment. "I saw you with him on the sidewalk and I thought, *Surely that sweet girl won't bring such a filthy creature inside.*"

I feel a surge of defensiveness for Pretzel. *Filthy creature* is a little dramatic.

"So imagine my *shock* when I came out on the landing to see you carting it upstairs."

I shrink with shame, trying to restrain Pretzel. "I'm sorry. But—"

"No buts. Rules are rules."

I glance down at Pretzel, who's doing nothing to help his case with the way he's barking and jumping at my leg right now. "It's only for one night—"

"Absolutely not. He has to go. Now. He's upsetting the other tenants."

He wasn't until you arrived, I want to retort, but I bite my tongue. The last thing I need is to be evicted.

"Okay," I mumble, stroking Pretzel's head. This seems to calm him, and I try one last-ditch attempt at keeping him here. "If I can get him to be quiet—"

"Josephine, if I break the rules for you I have to do the same for everyone. Next thing you know the building will become a menagerie of wild animals keeping us up at all hours of the night. Is that what you want?"

"I..." What can I say to such a ridiculous statement? "No."

"Exactly. So this... this... *beast*"—she gestures to Pretzel, who is now sitting quietly at my side—"has to go. I trust you'll remove him immediately so I don't have to take further action."

"Fine." I heave out a breath, trying to ignore the panic winding through me.

Mrs. P. gives a final curt nod and shuffles away, and I close the door with a frown. I look down at Pretzel, who's gazing up at me adoringly, his tail brushing back and forth across the wooden floor.

Fuck.

4

JOSIE

"Are you comfortable, sweet boy?" I crouch down to inspect Pretzel, making sure he has enough water and a chew toy. He licks my hand through the mesh window of his crate and I smile.

I've got him set up beside the sofa in the back room at Bounce. I decided there was no point in canceling my shift because we couldn't be at home anyway, and figured he could hide out here for a few hours until I come up with a plan. We took the subway from my apartment, which was marginally more successful than the cab, apart from the fact that I had to carry Pretzel inside his crate for the entire ride. Thankfully, a kind man in a suit saw me struggling up the steps and offered to help. New Yorkers have a reputation for being rude, but I seldom find that to be the case.

"This is just for a few hours," I assure Pretzel. "I'll be right out there"—I point to the door—"and I'll come back to check on you all the time."

I push to my feet with a weighted sigh. I don't love having him back here in his crate, but I don't have many other options. During the subway ride I went through a mental checklist of friends I could call for help, but for each one I decided it was too much to ask. Cat and Myles have his daughter, Amber, plus they already have Stevie. I can't ask them to take me and a dog, even if it is only for one night. My friend Harriet is working at her cafe, and I'm pretty sure her boyfriend is coming back from Houston today, so she'll want time alone with him. And I don't want to call Gerard and tell him I *can't* take Pretzel after all, because he'll have his hands full dealing with the shelter clean up tonight. I already feel bad enough that I'm not there to help.

Besides, I'm the one who stupidly took a dog home when I didn't have a plan. This is my problem to solve. I can't put that burden on other people.

"Joze!" Eddy calls from out in the bar. "I'm getting slammed here!"

With a regretful glance, I step out of the back room and close the door. I slide behind the bar and apologize to the nearest couple for the wait, my mind still on Pretzel as I mix their margaritas.

"Hey, Boss." Eddy's voice snaps me out of my thoughts and I look up to see Cory arrive. Eddy and I opened up, so Cory hasn't seen Pretzel yet. I'm not sure he'll be entirely pleased about having a dog back there, but there's not much I can do about that now.

Cory nods at Eddy as he shrugs off his jacket, then his eyes meet mine. "Hey, Joze."

"Hey." I smile, surprised when it's met with a little smile in return. He heads for the back room and nerves pinch my gut. I focus on wiping the bar down, hoping he might, by some holy miracle, not notice Pretzel's crate.

But a moment later he appears in the doorway, his

hands on his hips and a deep V between his brows. "Why is there a dog in the back room?"

"It's hers," Eddy blurts, mercilessly throwing me under the bus.

Cory's gaze swings to me, eyebrows lifted in question.

"Okay, yes. It's mine." I set the dishcloth down and turn to face him, taking a deep breath. "A pipe burst at the shelter and they had to evacuate the animals. He had nowhere else to go." I put on my most angelic expression, gazing up at Cory with wide eyes. "It's just a few hours. Please, Cors? Pretzel's been through so much today."

Humor flickers at the corner of Cory's mouth. "Pretzel?"

I nod, turning up the wattage on my smile.

He blows out a breath, examining me from under low brows. "Fine, but it's only for a few hours, right?"

"Yes, I swear. You won't even know he's there."

"I better not." Cory shakes his head and turns to serve some guys at the far end of the bar.

The next couple of hours pass in a blur. Pretzel seems happy enough with me checking on him, and I use my break to take him for a walk around the block to stretch his legs and pee. When it's time to go back into his crate, he wanders in and settles down without complaint. I'm relieved to see he's mostly relaxed this evening, despite the circumstances.

If only I could say the same for myself. It's been three hours since work began and I still don't know where we're going to sleep tonight. I could always try to sneak Pretzel back home, I suppose, but if I got caught it wouldn't be good.

I'm considering texting my mom for advice when Cat's friend, Geoff, slides onto a bar stool in front of me. His slightly chubby frame is dressed in his usual neat cashmere sweater and chinos, his dark hair closely cropped.

I like Geoff. He's kind and genuine, and has a fantastic sense of humor. He's usually in here with Cat and their friends, or sometimes with his boyfriend, Daniel, but tonight he seems to be alone.

"Hey, Geoff." I smile, wondering if he'd let Pretzel and me crash on his sofa for the night. Do I know him well enough to ask that? Probably not.

"Hey." He offers me a lukewarm smile. As he adjusts his glasses, I notice his green eyes are a little puffy. "Is Cat around?"

"I haven't seen her, sorry. I think she's home with Myles and Amber."

"Oh, right. Of course." He slumps down onto his elbows on the bar.

"You okay?"

"Not really. I was hoping to talk to Cat, but..." He lifts a shoulder and glances around, looking a little lost.

"You could talk to me," I suggest, already reaching for his usual merlot and pouring him a glass. He takes it with a grateful smile and slugs back a gulp.

"You don't want to hear my problems."

"I'm happy to listen. And"—I glance at the door to the back room, feeling that same thud of anxiety—"I could use the distraction."

He sighs. "Okay. I think..." His voice cracks and he takes another sip of wine. "I think my relationship is over."

"Oh." Sympathy weaves through me and I lean forward on the bar. "Why? What happened?"

"Daniel is moving to India to live on some ashram and study meditation." Geoff shrugs. "And I'm not. So that's that."

"Fuck," I mutter. "You don't want to go with him?"

He gives me a look that makes me laugh. "Hell no. I don't mind meditation—we even went to a retreat upstate together, but nothing could make me leave New York to go live on an *ashram*. Not even Daniel."

"Yeah, I get that." I don't want to leave this awesome city either. "And long-distance isn't an option?"

"What's the point? He's going indefinitely, and I don't want to be sitting around, waiting for him."

"Fair enough." A few customers have gathered at the bar and when I turn to look for Eddy, I find him making a tower of shot glasses on the back counter instead of doing something actually useful. "Ugh. Sorry, Geoff. Just give me one sec." I throw a dishcloth at the back of Eddy's head, which gets his attention. We both fill a few drink orders, then I turn back to Geoff.

"What do you need distracting from, anyway?" he asks after a mouthful of wine.

"Oh, well..." I explain the situation with Pretzel and our subsequent homelessness for the night, and Geoff looks regretful.

"I'd offer you my place, but Daniel is there packing his things right now." His gaze falls, and instinctively, I reach for his hand and give it a squeeze.

"I'm so sorry, Geoff. Breakups suck."

"I guess I just thought this was it," he mumbles into his empty wineglass. I grab the bottle and refill it for him, right to the top. "It felt like he was my perfect guy, you know?" He pulls his glasses off and rubs his eyes. "Now no one will compare to him."

Cory wanders into my line of sight, clearing some beer bottles from a booth, and I nod. "I know the feeling," I murmur. I let my gaze follow him as he leans across to wipe the table, his back and shoulders flexing with the motion under the thin cotton of his T-shirt. He's ridiculously tall, and I've always loved that about him. At five-foot-seven, I'm not short for a woman, but I feel tiny when I'm with Cory.

I feel a lot of things when I'm with Cory.

I sigh as I watch him work. How would my life be different if I didn't compare every guy I meet to him? Would I date more? I try to imagine myself going on dates with nice men, but the thought leaves me cold. I've done that and it's gone nowhere. There's only one guy I want.

Geoff clears his throat and I focus my attention back on him. There's a knowing tilt to his mouth, despite the sadness in his eyes, and I feel my cheeks heat with awareness.

"Have you considered asking *Cory* for a place to crash tonight?" Geoff says around a casual sip of wine.

"What? I—no." I shake my head, inching away from the bar. I only make it a few steps before a woman with short blond hair approaches me, and I'm forced to put on my best professional smile. "Hi. What can I get you?"

"Oh, I'm not here for a drink." She tucks a golden strand behind her ear, glancing past me. "Is Cory working tonight?"

I heave out a weary breath. I just want to get through *one* shift without having to run interference for women wanting to hook up with my boss.

"He's around somewhere," I mutter, all sense of professionalism gone. "Do you want me to tell him you stopped by, or something?"

She nods. "I'm Stacey. Tell him I had a great night with him, and I'd love to do it again sometime."

For a second I think she's referring to last night, and jealousy rushes hot through me at the thought that Cory went home with someone else after he walked me to the train.

Then a memory surfaces—three, maybe four months back —of this woman chatting Cory up on a particularly quiet evening. At the end of the night he left early, saying he was tired, but I saw him get into a cab with her outside. I wish I could say that was a one-off, but given the number of women who come in here, looking hopeful and asking about him, I know for a fact it's not.

I spot Cory approaching the bar and gesture in his direction. "Here he is. You can tell him yourself."

Before I can hear what either one of them has to say, I turn and head for the back room. When I slip inside and close the door, Pretzel's head pops up, his tail swishing against the fabric of his crate.

"You okay back here, buddy?" I unzip the door on his crate just enough to slide a hand in and stroke his fur. When I give him a little treat he gobbles it up, tail wagging. It makes me smile. I need to figure something out soon for tonight.

I consider Geoff's suggestion to ask Cory, then dismiss it. I've never been in his apartment and I don't want a mental image of where he lives—where he relaxes after work, where he undresses, where he takes women for the night.

Besides, I get the feeling he's annoyed at me for bringing Pretzel here in the first place. He's been grumpier than usual, snapping at Eddy and avoiding me altogether. It doesn't usually bother me when Cory is grumpy at work, because I know he cares about this place and it's hard work, but tonight his bad mood seems to be directed at me. I can't blame him—he pays me to serve drinks, not to spend half my time in the back room looking after a random dog.

Even if he is the cutest dog I've ever met.

I step back out into the bar and Cory's eye catches mine, accompanied by a frown. At least he doesn't seem to be talking to Stacey, but that hardly makes me feel better when he's glowering at me like that. He mutters something to Eddy, who's cleaning up a drink that's spilled all over the counter, and I turn back to Geoff as he stands from his stool.

"I'm going to meet Alex for a drink in the Village," he says, draining his glass. "Thanks for listening."

"Of course. I hope you feel better."

"Thanks." He takes a few steps toward the door, then glances back. "I hope you and Pretzel find somewhere to stay tonight. Good luck."

I smile, despite the unease swirling through me. Cory gives me a funny look from further down the bar, but before he can say anything, a redhead approaches him.

My gut clenches involuntarily. First Stacey and now this woman? Can't the universe give me a break, just for tonight?

As she leans over the bar, I feel a twinge of recognition. How do I know—oh, wait, that's the *Playboy* Bunny from last night. Rachel. She's dressed immaculately in a form-fitting dress, her long hair spilling over her shoulders in loose curls. No wonder he called her gorgeous. I glance down at my jeans and simple tank top, wishing I'd worn something different. She touches Cory's arm and I watch his thunderous expression morph into a grin as he pours her drink. A knife twists through my chest. I hate that I'm the one to make him scowl all night while a simple arm-touch from Rachel makes him beam like the fucking sun.

"Hey, Joze," Eddy says, sidling up to me. He pushes a hand through his shoulder-length black curls and offers me a grin that makes me queasy. "What are you doing next Friday night?"

"Um..." I open and close my mouth, uncertain about how to answer. Is Eddy asking me out? Because that is *not* going to happen.

"Oh, fuck. No." He seems to realize where my mind has gone and gives an awkward laugh. "I was just going to ask if you'd cover my shift."

Thank *God*.

But then I consider his words. I don't really want to cover his shift next Friday, because that will mean working two weeks straight without a night off. Still, I can't think of a good reason to say no.

I sigh. "Well, I guess I could—"

"No way," I hear from beside me. I glance over to see Cory standing with his arms folded as he stares Eddy down. "That's her only night off. Don't ask her to do that."

"Why not? She doesn't mind."

"I said no. It's your shift; you work it. Or find someone else." Cory moves closer to my side and gratitude glows in my chest at the way he's sticking up for me.

Eddy's gaze slides to mine. "Is this because I wasn't asking you out? Jeez." He rolls his eyes. "Sorry, I'm not into brunettes."

Although I have *zero* interest in being asked out by him, humiliation singes my cheeks.

"What the fuck is wrong with you, man?" Cory shakes his head, glaring at Eddy. "You should be so lucky."

Eddy's eyes dart from me to Cory, now standing firmly at my side, and narrow. "Oh, I get it. I guess if you're hooking up with the boss he lets you choose the best shifts, huh?"

"What?" I rear back, shocked. "I'm not—"

"Are you kidding me?" Cory takes a menacing step toward him. "That's enough. Clear those tables like I asked you to twenty minutes ago, before I send your ass packing." He motions across the room in agitation and Eddy slinks off.

My face burns. I'm so mortified, I can't even look at Cory.

I turn for the back room and slip inside, sinking down onto the sofa beside Pretzel's crate.

Why did Cory have to witness that?

The door cracks open and Cory's head pokes in. "You okay, Buttercup?"

I nod, unable to meet his gaze. Pretzel whines in his crate beside me and I wince. Tonight is such a mess.

Cory glances over his shoulder out to the bar, then steps into the room, closing the door behind him. When I see the frown of disapproval on his face, it feels like he has kicked me in the gut.

I drop my head into my hands. "I'm sorry, Cors. I know I've been distracted tonight and I don't blame you for being annoyed with me. But I promise—"

"Wait. You think I'm annoyed with *you*?" He lowers himself onto the arm of the sofa. "No. You have been a little distracted, but I can deal with that. You work your ass off, Joze. You're allowed to have an off night."

"Oh." I look down at Pretzel, nuzzling my hand through the mesh of this crate. When I bring my gaze back to Cory, he softens.

"Sorry if I've been a jerk. Eddy is driving me up the fucking wall."

I snort a small laugh, but don't say anything more. No point in dissecting Cory's horrified response when Eddy suggested we were sleeping together.

Cory twists on the sofa toward me. "What did Geoff mean about you finding somewhere to stay tonight?"

I grimace. "My landlady caught me trying to sneak Pretzel in and told me he couldn't stay."

"Why can't he stay with someone else?"

"He's funny around new people and he's had such a

stressful day. I know it sounds silly but he knows me. I need to be with him tonight, so he feels safe."

"Where are you going to take him?"

I shrug. "I'm working on that."

Concern shimmers in Cory's eyes as he gazes at me. The brown flecks of his irises remind me of a fresh glass of beer —but which kind depends on the light. In the bright light of the diner they're like a brown ale, but in the darkness of the bar they're a porter. Given Porter is his last name, it fits him well.

There's a loud crash out in the bar and Cory presses his eyes shut, his jaw tightening as he appears to count to ten. He hauls himself to his feet with the weary sigh of a parent who knows his kid has destroyed something in the next room. "I need to deal with whatever Eddy's done now. I swear I'm about five seconds away from firing him."

When he steps out of the room, I release my breath in a long stream. Pretzel has settled down in his crate, and I lean my head back on the sofa and close my eyes, wishing I could go to sleep right here and get this night over with.

Actually, hold on. Why *don't* I do that? This sofa isn't half bad, and I have keys to this place. If Cory goes home with Rachel, Pretzel and I could just camp out here for the night. Then I can walk Pretzel down to the shelter in the morning. It's perfect.

I sit up with renewed energy, leaning over Pretzel's crate and reaching in to stroke his ears. "I think we'll be okay, sweet boy," I murmur. "We can sleep here tonight."

"SHE'S WAITING FOR YOU," I say, stepping into the back room. I'm surprised to find Cory crouched beside Pretzel's crate, looking at him through the mesh.

He stands as I enter. "Who's what?"

"Rachel's waiting in the bar. You should go. I'll close up."

Cory's brows slant together. He goes to say something, then his gaze drops to Pretzel. "What are you going to do?"

I hesitate. I should probably tell him my plans, since this is his bar. He might not notice if I can get him out the door, but I don't feel good about lying to him.

"We, um…" I kneel in front of Pretzel's crate so I don't have to look at Cory. "If it's okay with you, we might just crash here."

"What? No."

Dammit. I knew he was going to make this difficult.

I swivel around to glance up at him. But he's so freaking tall that I feel like I'm looking up at the ceiling, so I rise to my feet.

"We won't make a mess, Cors, I swear."

"No way." He pinches the bridge of his nose, exhaling.

"He'll be in his crate the whole time—"

"Jesus, Josie, I don't care about the mess. I'm not letting you sleep alone in the back room because it's not safe, and it's sure as shit not comfortable. I've slept on that sofa and it's awful."

"Oh." I wasn't expecting that. I aim for a carefree laugh to lighten the mood. "That's because you're way too tall for that sofa. I'm, like, a foot shorter than you. It will be fine."

"It's not happening." Cory stares at me hard, then turns to crouch in front of Pretzel's crate, holding his hand up to the mesh for Pretzel to sniff.

Fuck. Fuckety-fuck. If we can't stay here, I am well and truly screwed.

My throat tightens, and when tears of panic press at my eyes I try to blink them away. What the hell am I going to do now?

"Oh, shit." Cory rises beside me, touching my shoulder. "No—you can stay at my place."

I suck in a surprised breath. "What? I can't ask you to do that."

"You're not asking, I'm offering."

"What about Rachel?"

"I'm not—" He shakes his head. "This is more important."

"Are you allowed pets? I don't want you to get in trouble."

"I won't."

I stare at him, feeling tears well in my eyes—this time for an entirely different reason.

"Hey." He hooks an arm around my shoulder to give me a quick, comforting squeeze, but I throw my arms around his waist in gratitude and bury my face in his shirt.

"Thank you," I murmur against his chest.

As the impulsiveness of my actions subsides, I realize what I've done. I've never hugged him before and holy fuck, every atom in my body wakes up, alert and at attention, as the smell of Cory's sweat and musky, earthy cologne fills my nostrils. His heart is hammering against my forehead, and I lose myself in that moment, pressed against him with my arms around his firm waist, overwhelmed by his kindness.

It occurs to me, after a beat has passed, that he is not reciprocating the hug. He huffs an uncomfortable, shuddering breath, and I come to my senses.

"Sorry," I mumble, tearing myself away from the solid heat of his body. "I was just—thank you. I was worried that Pretzel would have nowhere—"

"Oh, yeah. I know." Cory drops down beside Pretzel's crate again, focusing his attention on the way Pretzel is sniffing his hand. "We have to make sure this guy is happy."

I stare at the back of Cory's head. He won't meet my gaze and for some reason, the air feels suddenly thick and heavy. My arms tingle with the memory of being wrapped around him and I force myself to look away.

Staying at Cory's place might not be the best idea, but I'm out of options.

5

CORY

This is probably one of my worst decisions. What was I thinking, inviting Josie to stay? I promised myself I'd never let her near my place. There's only one reason I bring women back here and it's *not* to help them look after stray dogs.

I just couldn't stand the thought of her sleeping on that shitty couch, alone in the back room. She's been anxious as hell all night worrying about that dog, and when I saw how close to tears she was, I snapped.

Besides, it's important to me that my employees are safe. I'd do this for any of them. Even Eddy.

Okay, that's not true. Even *I'm* aware that I'm lying to myself.

I haul Pretzel's crate out of the cab and push the door closed. Josie explained that the dog didn't like being in the back of a car, and we decided it would be easier to get him in the cab if we kept him in his crate. He seemed happy on the ride, but the closer we got to my place, the more I wondered what the hell I was doing—bringing home a *dog*, and a woman I can't touch.

But as soon as Josie told me she was looking for somewhere to stay tonight, I knew this wouldn't go any other way. If I can't have her, I can at least look out for her. I was glad to tell that woman waiting in the bar that I was busy, and as I watched her leave I didn't feel the slightest hint of disappointment or regret. I felt nothing.

Not like when Josie hugged me after I told her she could stay. It took all my strength not to wrap my arms around her and hold her close, not to nuzzle my face in her hair and breathe her in. And now, as I unlock the door to my building and lead her into my ground-floor apartment, I realize I'm actually *nervous*.

"So, this is my place," I say, flicking on the light and locking the door behind us. I set Pretzel's crate down in the entryway and glance around, trying to see the place through Josie's eyes.

The space is long and narrow, with a small entryway and hall. I wander down the hall, glancing into the bathroom on the way to double check that it's clean (yes, thankfully). At the end of the hall is an open-plan kitchen and living area. The walls are mostly bare, painted a plain taupe color that was here when I moved in. The living room is taken up by a huge sectional in front of a TV, and at the far end are two doors. I quickly poke my head into my bedroom, because I can't remember if I made the bed this morning or not (I did). When I turn back, Josie is at the other door, peering through the glass, but with the reflection of the indoor lights it's hard to see into the inky blackness outside.

"Here," I say, fiddling with the lock and opening it for her. "There's a courtyard out there." I gesture for her to step outside and when she does, I take the chance to grab some dirty socks from the end of the sofa and swipe a few crumbs off the kitchen counter. Then I let Pretzel out of his crate. He bolts out the back door to find Josie and I follow.

This courtyard is one of the reasons I bought this place. It's a paved area about 30 feet wide, lined with plants and grass. It's blocked in on all sides by other buildings, but when I look up I can see the cloudy night sky. A siren blares somewhere in the distance. Some nights if I can't sleep, I'll come sit out here and stare at the sky, listening to the sounds of the city.

"Hey, boy," Josie murmurs, dropping to pet Pretzel at her side. He licks her face and she giggles. I watch as Pretzel sniffs around the courtyard, choosing a plant to pee on. Josie glances back at me apologetically but I'm smiling. I'm smiling like a fool at how sweet she is with him, at how good she looks here at my place.

Fuck.

She stands and brushes her hands on her jeans. "I can't thank you enough. Seriously."

"You don't have to thank me."

She wanders back to me with a grin. "You know, you put on this big mean guy act all the time, but you're such a softie when it comes to animals."

I cock my head, amused. "Am I?"

"Yeah. Whenever Stevie comes into the bar you're so sweet with her. And now"—she gestures to where Pretzel is sniffing around the outdoor table set—"you're giving up your bed for Pretzel…"

"My *bed*? I never said—"

"I'm kidding." She laughs as she follows Pretzel back inside and I trail after, shaking my head.

I go to the kitchen and fill a dish of water for Pretzel, then take some of the food from the bag Josie brought and put that down too. Pretzel looks reluctant and I crouch beside the bowl, holding out a piece of kibble to entice him. He wanders over to sniff my hand, tentatively taking the food. He lets me stroke his ears, then lowers his face to the bowl and begins to eat. I feel a tiny sense of triumph at winning him over in front of Josie.

"I'll make up your bed," I say, heading to the hall closet and pulling out some sheets. She might have joked about me giving up my bed, but there's no way I'm making her sleep on the sofa.

She follows me into the bedroom. "What are you doing?"

"I'm changing the sheets for you."

"What? I'll sleep on the sofa. You don't have to do that."

"If I was going to make you sleep on the sofa you may as well have stayed at the bar." I strip the bed, tossing the old sheets into a hamper in the corner. Josie watches with a funny expression on her face.

"Cors, I was kidding about the bed. Pretzel and I will sleep in the living room."

I smooth a hand across the sheet, tucking the corner in tight, and glance over at her. "You're not sleeping on the sofa. You're a guest in my house, so you get the bed." To be fair, all the guests in my house get the bed. It's just that I'm usually in there with them.

"I can't make you sleep on the sofa," she says as I throw the comforter back over the bed. "You're too tall, it will be—"

"I've slept on that sofa and it's fine." I straighten the comforter and turn to her. Before I can say anything more, Pretzel comes barreling around the corner and launches himself onto the bed.

"Pretzel! Down!" Josie reaches for him but he ducks out of her arms, prancing across the comforter. She stomps around the other side looking unimpressed, but he springs away, wagging his tail like it's the best game on earth. I muffle a laugh as I watch her desperately trying to grab him.

"Stop it!" she hisses, rounding the bed again. "Get *down*, Pretzel." When he jumps away from her, she throws herself across the mattress to grab him, emitting a strangled sound of annoyance.

A laugh bursts out of me, but I stop when I see how frustrated she is. I stride over to the bed, lifting my fingers to my lips, and whistle. Pretzel freezes, his head snapping my way. "Down," I say firmly, and he rockets off the bed and back into the living room, his claws scrabbling over the wooden floors as he tries to round the corner too quickly.

Josie rolls onto her back and looks up at me. She's pink from wrestling with the dog and her breathing is shallow. My pulse trips as her gaze meets mine. So this is what she'd look like underneath me on my bed, her dark hair mussed and her cheeks flushed with pleasure.

She'd look fucking perfect.

Stop.

I step away, wiping a hand down my face, hoping she can't read my thoughts.

"That was impressive," she says, rising from the bed.

It takes me a few seconds to realize she's talking about Pretzel, and I shrug. A loaded silence falls between us. I walk over to my dresser, desperate for a distraction. "Here." I pull out a navy-blue Giants T-shirt and hand it over. The shirt is old, worn almost threadbare in places, because I wear it for every game. I have no business giving it to her to wear and yet... I want her to have it.

"What's this?"

"I just thought, if you need something to sleep in..."

She glances down at her jeans and tank top. "Oh, okay.

Thanks." She takes the shirt and heads off to the bathroom to change, and I take the opportunity to pull myself together.

She's way too young for you, I repeat over and over as I strip down to my T-shirt and boxers. She might be in her late twenties, but it feels like we're from different generations. I once joked that waiting for Eddy to clear tables was as painful as waiting for a movie to download over dial-up, and she looked at me like I was speaking another language.

Yep. Too young.

I grab a spare blanket and set myself up on the sofa. Then I lie there, wondering if I should have offered to run out and grab her a toothbrush from the bodega on the corner.

Nope, that's too much. She'll be fine.

I'm tempted to just turn out the lights and pretend to be asleep when she leaves the bathroom, but that feels like a dick move. Instead, I throw my arm over my eyes and give an exaggerated yawn as the door creaks open. I hear her padding softly across the living room and make the mistake of lowering my arm to glance at her as she passes.

Holy *shit*.

My shirt comes to mid-thigh, hanging loosely off one shoulder, and I want to bite my fist at how fucking sexy she looks.

Her gaze meets mine and she stops in her tracks. For a second I don't know what to do. All I know is that every bone in my body wants to haul her onto the sofa and tear that shirt to shreds.

You're her boss. She's here because she was vulnerable and needed a place to look after the dog. You just have to get through tonight without touching her.

"Um, good night," she mumbles, darting for the bedroom.

"Good night," I choke out. The door clicks shut and I stare at the ceiling, resigned to the fact that I won't get a minute of sleep knowing she's in my bed.

6

JOSIE

I spend the entire night tossing and turning. When I wake, I'm hit with a fresh wave of embarrassment at the fact that Cory saw me creeping from the bathroom into his room. Why did I have to get changed in there? What was I thinking? I should have waited until the lights were out and he was asleep. Now I'll be forever haunted by the fact that my unbelievably hot boss saw me in this ratty old shirt.

It's not just that; I couldn't stop thinking about how many women he's had in his bed. I can't see any notches on his bedpost—he doesn't actually have a bedpost, probably because it's been whittled away to nothing—but the thought makes me squirm with jealousy.

There's a whine from beside the bed. I roll over to find Pretzel's nose pressed to the mesh window of his crate, and I reach for him with a smile. Cory didn't seem bothered about him jumping on the bed last night, so I let him climb up to join me. He nuzzles into my side as I stroke his caramel colored fur, and I sigh.

Being at Cory's place is weird. It's nothing like I imagined it would be. I guess I expected some kind of bachelor pad, littered with empty pizza boxes and beer bottles, the walls lined with posters of half-naked women and sports memorabilia. Besides a signed Giants jersey in a frame on the living room wall, it's pretty clean and, well, *grown up*. He has a hamper, for Christ's sake. I don't even have a hamper.

I don't know why this surprises me; it's not like Cory is Eddy's age; Cory is thirty-nine. When I think of him as the owner of a bar—as my *boss*—this place makes perfect sense. But when I think of him as the perpetual bachelor—the guy who calls women *gorgeous* and never sleeps with the same girl twice—this place seems too mature for him.

And when I think of him as my friend—the guy who worries about me getting mugged on the walk to the train, who laughs with me over burgers at Sam's diner—I don't know how to make sense of him.

He's a bunch of contradictions.

Pretzel wriggles onto his back beside me, splaying his legs so I'll rub his belly. I chuckle as I reach down to give him a scratch. If there's one thing I love about dogs, it's how shameless they are in seeking affection. Imagine if people were like that—if every time Cory looked my way I rolled onto my back and threw my legs up in invitation.

Actually, hold on. That could work.

Or not. I think back to when I was changing out of my *Catwoman* costume the other night and he accidentally saw me half-dressed. He couldn't look away fast enough. Even now, my cheeks heat with embarrassment. He has such a knack for making me feel undesirable.

I sit up in bed and pull back the covers to take Pretzel outside. He's been great, but I don't want to risk another pee incident like at my place. I'm not sure Cory would find that amusing.

I pad across the carpet and open the door to the living room, trying to be quiet. It takes me a moment to pop open the lock on the back door, and in that time Pretzel makes a beeline for the sofa. He lunges at Cory's sleeping face, licking it.

"Pretzel!" I whisper-shout across the room. "Stop!"

He doesn't, of course. I love the way this dog pretends he can't hear me whenever it's convenient for him.

There's a muffled sound from Cory as he wipes his cheek, still asleep, and I creep over, acutely aware that I'm still wearing his old T-shirt.

"Come *on*," I hiss, inching closer to Pretzel.

Cory wipes his face again and blinks awake, jerking back when he sees Pretzel so close. Then he gives a sleepy chuckle and reaches out to pet Pretzel's head, wriggling to sit up on the sofa.

"Sorry." I cringe, attempting to pull the shirt down to my knees. I should have put my jeans back on. "Pretzel," I say through gritted teeth. *"Outside.* Let's go." He continues to blithely ignore me, and I huff in irritation.

For fuck's sake. It's like he's *trying* to make this situation more awkward.

Cory is still half asleep, rubbing his eyes, and I take the chance to step forward and grab Pretzel, who at that exact moment leaps onto the sofa beside Cory. My finger catches in the loop of his collar and I'm yanked forward. I trip and fall face-first across Cory's lap, landing in the position of someone about to be spanked.

Oh my God.

Pretzel leans down to lick my face in delight, but I'm

barely aware of it. The only thing I *am* aware of is the hard bulge digging into my belly. I think my brain melts at this point, because it takes me a good few seconds to compute what I can feel. That hardness, pressing into me, right there...

Holy crap. That's an erection. That's *my boss's erection.*

I freeze, unsure what to do. If I move he might feel it, and then he'll know *I've* felt it—

My thoughts screech to a halt as I suddenly become aware of the sensation of cool air on my backside. I snap into action, lurching to my feet and stumbling backward.

Was I flashing my panties at him? Could this be any more *horrifying*?

Cory's cheeks are crimson and he shifts his weight, dragging the cushion from the sofa across his lap.

I want to die.

"I—am—so—" I can't even get the words out. My face is on fire.

"It's—" he attempts, then shakes his head and tries again. "You're—" The words stick in his throat and he grimaces, forcing his gaze to the floor.

Leave. I need to leave. Now.

I glance around for Pretzel, only to find he's apparently decided that now is the perfect time to take himself outside.

For God's sake.

"Sorry," I manage, fleeing to the bedroom. Pretzel dashes in behind me and I close the door, so mortified I can barely breathe.

I felt Cory's erection. I felt it. I mean, I know it wasn't for *me*—it's just what happens to guys in the morning—but *I felt it*. I'm not supposed to know what that feels like, and I'm quite certain *he* doesn't want me knowing that, either. I'm not sure if I'm more embarrassed for him or for me.

And then there's the fact that I may have flashed him. Granted, I'm wearing okay underwear, but still. It wasn't sexy in the slightest; it was just a boatload of awkward. Like, how-am-I-ever-going-to-look-him-in-the-eye-again awkward.

I quickly change into last night's clothes, buzzing with humiliation. Then I fold up Pretzel's crate and clip on his leash, ready to take him back to the shelter. I might be reluctant to return him, but I know it's for the best. This dog is getting me into too much trouble.

I MANAGE to sneak out of Cory's place while he's in the shower, and I feel better once I'm outside. I want to erase the entire fiasco from my mind, but I can still feel him pressing into me. It's like memory foam, imprinted on my belly. That hardness. *His* hardness.

No. I have to forget about it. It was an embarrassing mishap. Poor Cory is probably equally horrified.

I force my attention to my phone, double checking the route to the shelter in the Seaport District. Even though there's a more direct route, I decide to head out and walk beside the water on the East River Greenway. Pretzel will appreciate having more room to roam, plus it's a beautiful spring morning, and I love the views over to Brooklyn.

We have to follow South Street under the FDR Overpass, but I don't mind. I love how this city is both gritty and dirty, and beautiful and scenic at the same time. It contains so many contradictions that make me adore it.

We finally get out by the river, and I pause to take in the view over the water to Brooklyn. When I first moved to the city, I was convinced I had to live in Manhattan, but it quickly became apparent that was out of my price range. Now, I love living in Brooklyn. It's become super trendy recently, and I'm lucky I can even afford to live there. Plus, I love that we get the view of the Manhattan skyline. If I lived in Manhattan, I wouldn't be able to see the Empire State Building lit up at night. Not that I can see it from my apartment, of course, but if I walk for fifteen minutes down the road and peek between some buildings, I can. It's lovely.

We follow the Greenway under the Manhattan Bridge, then the Brooklyn Bridge comes into view. I pick up Pretzel and take a selfie of the two of us with the bridge in the background for my mom. I texted her last night in the cab on the way to Cory's, explaining what had happened at the shelter. Once I knew I had somewhere to sleep, I felt much better about sharing it with her because I knew she'd ask where we were staying and if we were safe.

I type out a text and, with a grin, send the selfie of Pretzel and me.

Josie: Beautiful morning with this guy in the Big Apple.

Mom: How was he last night?

I watch Pretzel attempt to chase a pigeon, thinking as I walk. He was great, actually; apart from when he caused Erectiongate this morning, but that... I shake the thought from my head and reply.

Josie: He was amazing. Slept so well in his crate and even got some cuddles this morning.

Mom: How wonderful that you could make that sweet dog's life better. I'm so proud of you, Sugarplum.

I glow from her words as I slip my phone back into my pocket. It buzzes again and I pull it out, expecting another text, but Gerard's name lights up my screen. I lift the phone to my ear.

"Hey, Gerard."

"Hi, Josie. I'm glad I caught you. Listen, I know you were planning to bring Pretzel back in this morning, but we have a problem."

His tone makes my stomach sink. I glance around and spot a bench, tugging Pretzel over to sit with me. "What's up?" I ask, dropping onto the seat and setting Pretzel's folded crate down beside me.

"The burst pipe has created more of a problem than we thought. I figured it would be a matter of cleaning it up and drying the place out, but some of the building's structure was in worse shape than we realized and the water caused considerable damage."

"Okay," I say, my thoughts whirling. "So, what does that mean?"

"We'll be closed for at least a few weeks while repairs are completed; maybe longer while we wait for our code compliance to come through."

"Right." I stare at Pretzel as he pulls on his leash, attempting to grab a piece of garbage blowing past. "And the animals?"

"Those that are at shelters will stay there for now. There's only a few with staff, but they're going to look after them. It's up to you what you want to do with Pretzel, but if you can't keep him with you we'll need to locate a shelter for him to go to."

A corkscrew turns through my gut. Pretzel going to a new shelter would be difficult for him, but that's not the worst thought that hits me right now; the thing I'm worried about most is what shelter he'd end up at. They vary greatly in terms of their euthanasia policies and there's a very good chance...

I look down at Pretzel, gazing up at me with big, chocolate colored eyes, and my throat tightens. I can't even let myself think what could happen to him if he goes to a different shelter.

"No," I say, resolutely. "I'll look after him."

"Are you sure?"

My rational mind reminds me I'm not allowed to have pets at home, that I work long hours and this is not a good idea. What the hell am I going to do with him for several weeks?

When I feel Pretzel's nose nudge gently into my hand, my heart knots. I'll figure that stuff out. What matters is that he's safe and loved. When I think of my mom's texts only moments ago, I know I'm making the right decision.

I PUSH open the door to Game of Scones with a sigh, relieved it's not too busy.

Cat dragged me along to the opening of this board game cafe six months ago, and that's how I met the owner, Harriet. When I tasted the vegan brownies made by her coworker, Paula, I couldn't stay away. After popping in for them a few times, Harriet made me a soy latte, and we chatted. In the early days, when her cafe was new, things were slow to take off and I would hang around and talk. It's not like that now, though, after the cafe was spotlighted on a popular local blog. Now, you're lucky to get a table. And if it's Saturday night—forget it. You have to book in advance.

I'll always be grateful for those early quiet days, because that's when I made my first real girlfriend here in the city. It's been tough for me to make friends outside of Bounce and the shelter, because that's basically where I spend all my time, and the truth is, I tend to get along better with animals than people. Especially dogs. They don't judge you; they just love you and want love in return. That, I understand.

Harriet is a lot like that, too. She's sweet and kind and easy to talk to. It helps that we're of a similar age, and both not from New York. She came here from New Zealand last year, and I've enjoyed telling her some of my favorite places I've discovered since moving to the city.

"Josie!" Harriet grins from behind the counter as I enter with Pretzel in tow. Her eyes light up when she spots him. "And who's this?"

"This is Pretzel. Is it okay to bring him in?"

She nods, rounding the counter to greet him. "Hi, Pretzel."

He ducks behind my legs, hesitating. When Harriet crouches to his level and extends a hand, he tentatively peeks around, sniffing. She waits patiently until he creeps forward to accept a gentle pat.

"He's adorable," she says, adjusting her glasses as she straightens up. "When did you get him?"

"He's not mine."

She lifts her brows. "Oh. Why do you have him?"

I puff up my cheeks and blow out a slow breath. *Don't panic. You can figure this out.*

Harriet chuckles, apparently sensing my anxiety. "I'll make coffee and you can tell me."

I nod, finding a quiet table near the back. It's a large space with a big counter area filled with baked treats. The walls are painted a sunny, golden yellow and lined with shelves stacked with board games. It's got such a warm and happy vibe, and while I'm not big on board games, it's a lovely place to hang out.

I set Pretzel's folded crate down and wrap his leash

around the table leg, motioning for him to sit beside my chair. He does, until Harriet approaches with a tray. I have to hold his collar to stop him from toppling the whole table over in excitement.

Harriet giggles as she sets the tray down, unloading coffee and brownies. She places a bowl of water down for Pretzel, which he lunges on gratefully. Then she holds up a plate with a weird-looking cookie on it.

"Is it okay to give him this? Paula makes peanut butter dog treats for some of our customers. They're vegan."

I nod, surprised and delighted. What an awesome idea. I'll have to ask her for the recipe. I watch as she holds it out to Pretzel and he sniffs it, then munches it down.

"So," Harriet says, sliding into the chair opposite me. She pulls her long, cranberry-red hair over one shoulder and picks up her coffee. "What's the deal with Pretzel?"

I take a deep breath and explain the past twenty-four hours, finishing with the call from Gerard this morning. She nods as she listens, quietly sipping her coffee. When I'm done, she nudges my mug toward me.

"Don't let your coffee go cold."

I smile and take the cup, gulping down a mouthful.

"What are you going to do? I'd offer our place, but Luke is allergic to dogs."

I wave a hand. "That's fine. I'd never ask that of you."

"Are you sure you can't go back to Cory's?"

I feel that hardness on my belly again and cringe, shaking my head. "It was weird being in his home. Super awkward. I mean, he's my boss, so..." I shrug. I can't explain what happened this morning, or I'll die from embarrassment all over again.

Harriet eyes me over her coffee cup. "Are you sure that's the only reason?"

I sigh. She might be my closest girlfriend in the city but there's one thing I've never told her. "No. I kind of... have a thing for him."

Harriet's eyebrows rise. "Yeah?"

I nod, shoving a hunk of brownie in my mouth. I haven't had breakfast and I'm only now realizing I'm famished.

"I don't blame you." She giggles. "How long have you liked him?"

I look down at Pretzel as I mumble, "Five years."

Shit. I've never actually admitted that out loud before, but when I do, it sounds ridiculous.

I glance up but Harriet is sipping her coffee, quiet.

"I know it's silly," I say. Sometimes I wonder if I should look for another job. The thought bums me out because I don't want to work somewhere else, unless I could get a paid job at the shelter. Even then I'd struggle to leave Bounce, because I love it there. Still, I'm starting to wonder if working with Cory isn't good for me.

"It's not silly. You can't help who you fall for." There's a little smile around her mouth. "Are you sure he doesn't feel what you feel?"

"Um, no. I'm pretty sure he sees me like a little sister or something." I wrinkle my nose, thinking of how he calls me Buttercup. It's sweet, but that's not what you call someone you want to have sex with. "Anyway," I mutter, taking another sip of coffee. "I don't want to stay at his place and see him bringing women home or whatever."

"Oh. Yeah." Harriet winces. "That wouldn't be cool."

I polish off the brownie, mulling this over. There's another reason I don't feel comfortable asking Cory, something I can't quite articulate. He's done so much for me—giving me a job all those years ago when I had no experience, looking out for me at work, walking me to the train—I don't want to burden him more than I already have. It's not his responsibility to look after me.

"Maybe you could stay at a hotel for a while?" Harriet suggests over her coffee. "I stayed at a great one when I first arrived in the city. I'm sure I saw people with dogs there."

I consider this. It's not a long-term solution, but it could take the pressure off me for a few days while I figure out my next move.

"It would cost you a bit, though." She stands and gestures toward the computer on the counter. "Let's see if we can find one that would work."

I unwind Pretzel's lead from the table leg and follow her. After about ten minutes, she finds me a room in a pet-friendly hotel in Murray Hill for a hundred and fifty dollars a night. With my small savings, I could manage three or four nights there, but we'd need to find a much cheaper solution for the next few weeks after that. Still, it would mean we have somewhere to sleep for now.

"Yeah, okay. That could work." I give Harriet a grateful smile. "Thank you."

"Glad I could help," she says as she walks me and Pretzel to the front door. "Are you working tonight? I'll see you at the party later?"

"What party?"

She laughs. "Cat and Myles are throwing an anniversary party at Bounce, aren't they? I thought you'd probably know about it."

"Oh." I breathe out, adjusting my grip on Pretzel's crate under my arm. "Yeah, I think Cat might have said something. I've been so stressed with Pretzel, I completely spaced."

"Well, you can relax for tonight," she says, pulling me into a hug.

I nod, squeezing her. Now I just have to hurry home, pack a bag, avoid Mrs. Petrovski, and get over to the hotel before work starts.

7

CORY

I wake up almost every day with morning wood, but after spending the night imagining Josie in my bed—and seeing the way she looked in my shirt—I was hard enough to shatter concrete.

I place the barbell back onto the rack with a frown. My daily gym sessions are usually enough to distract me from my thoughts, but this isn't doing the trick. I can't help but replay that moment when Josie fell across my lap and felt...

Fuck, I'm certain she felt it.

And then there's the fact that her shirt rode halfway up her back, exposing her beautiful ass across my lap. I tried not to look—really, I did—but I'm only human. She was wearing perfectly innocent white cotton panties, but on her they looked sexy as sin. At least I managed to keep my hands well clear of the area, even though I was dying to slide them under the fabric and squeeze—

Stop.

I grab the heaviest kettlebell off the rack and focus on doing some deadlifts. With every lift I think of her, of the way she was so sweet with Pretzel, the way she looked on my bed, the way her soft curves felt pressing against the part of myself I want to bury inside her—

Stop, stop, stop.

I drop the kettlebell and turn for the treadmill, setting it to the highest speed I can manage. Then I force myself to run for twenty straight minutes. When I'm done, my lungs are burning and sweat is running in rivers down my back.

And I'm still thinking about Josie.

By the time I hit the showers, I'm angry with myself. What the fuck is wrong with me? Why am I turned on by something she obviously found embarrassing? Sure, it was pretty damn embarrassing for me too, but my brain isn't focusing on that part—it's too busy thinking of her. And that's even more concerning. I've worked with this woman for years now, and yes, I've wanted her the entire time, but I've never felt quite so... restless. Desperate, almost. Like if she'd stayed in my place for one minute longer I would have exploded.

Having her perfect ass presented to me on a platter sure as hell didn't help.

It's not until I've rinsed off and dressed again that I realize what the problem is: I haven't had sex in three months. Shit, has it really been that long? I think back to the last time I went home with a woman from the bar and yeah, it was three months ago—before I started walking Josie to the train.

Relief seeps through me at this realization. That's what's messing with my head: I need to get laid.

I sling my gym bag over my shoulder and head off to work, feeling my phone buzz in my pocket as I turn toward the bar. My first thought is that it's Josie, and I pull it out realizing I'm actually hoping it's her.

It's not, and the disappointment that follows only serves

to reinforce how urgently I need to fix this little problem of mine. Instead the text is from Eddy, telling me he can't come into work tonight—no explanation why—and I clench my jaw in irritation. I'm so busy stewing over what to text back to the little shit I almost run smack into someone.

"Sorry," I say, stepping aside.

"Cory?"

A voice snaps me out of my thoughts and I glance up, taking in the blond in front of me. "Oh... hey," I say uncertainly. She's familiar, but—fuck, I have no idea what her name is. I cringe, knowing exactly what kind of guy that makes me.

"Bridget," she prompts with an amused smile.

"Right, of course." I force a laugh, raking a hand through my still-damp hair. I remember her now—we hooked up about a year ago. I think. "How've you been?" I ask, in an attempt to feel less like a douche. I don't know why I'm so uncomfortable all of a sudden. I run into women I've slept with all the time.

"Oh, you know." She twirls a finger in her hair. "The usual. What about you?"

I shrug. "Same." I'm about to say goodbye and continue on to work when she reaches into her purse.

"I'm assuming you don't have my number," she says, pulling something out. She hands it over and I realize it's her card. "We should catch up for drinks or... *whatever*." Her hand lingers on mine, her eye contact meaningful as I take the card. Then she heads off down the street, her hips swaying casually, as if she hasn't just propositioned me at four in the afternoon.

I stare after her. I rarely sleep with women more than once, because I don't want them to get attached. I'm upfront about only ever wanting casual sex, and the few times that

I've tried to do that with a woman more than once, it's always gotten messy. But Bridget was pretty blatant right now, and this could be just what I need to clear the slate.

Before I can overthink it, I send off a text asking if she's free when I finish work tonight. And when she immediately replies with *yes*, I blow out a breath.

This will be good, I tell myself. *This is what you should do.*

Anything to get my mind off Josie.

"You FORGOT?" Cat's hands are on her hips as she stares me down, her voice echoing through the empty bar. I'd only been at work for ten minutes before my sister came storming in.

"Sorry, sis. But I'm here. It's all good." I round the bar and pull her rigid, angry body into a hug. She and Myles booked Bounce for a private party months ago and, yes, with all the stuff happening with Josie and the dog, I forgot that it was tonight.

Myles pushes through the door, carrying a box overflowing with decorations. He dumps them on the bar, looking at us. "What's going on?"

"He forgot that our party was tonight," Cat says, rolling her eyes as we part.

"What's the big deal?" I ask, peeking into the box. Silver and white balloons, packets of streamers, and—

"Don't look in there," she snaps, yanking the box away.

I raise my hands in defense and step back behind the bar. "Whoa, okay. Why are you so pissed? I'm here and I'll help to set up." I look to Myles for support, but he reaches for Cat, pulling her into his arms.

"Hey, it's going to be awesome, baby." He presses a kiss to her pink hair. "Please don't worry."

She sinks against him, sighing. This is how I know he's a good guy—he puts up with all her shit and knows exactly how to make her relax.

"I know," she murmurs. "I'm just stressed because Mom's train was late. She's in a cab now, but—"

"Wait." I lean forward over the bar. "Mom's coming into the city? Why didn't you tell me? I would have met her at Penn Station."

Cat shares a long look with Myles, saying nothing.

"Actually—" I frown as this information sinks in. "Why is she coming all the way here just for this?"

Myles finally releases her from his arms, saying, "Just tell him."

"Ugh, fine." She turns back to me while Myles grabs the decorations and takes them through to the back room. "Tonight isn't only our anniversary party. It's also... our wedding."

My mouth pops open. "You're getting *married*? Here? Tonight?" I fold my arms over my chest. "Why didn't you tell me?"

"We wanted it to be a surprise—super low key and casual. But yeah, I probably should have told you, given I want you to walk me down the aisle."

My chest expands. I soften, asking more gently, "You want me to give you away?"

"Of course, who else? It's not like I have a father who'll do it."

I grunt in response, and we exchange a bitter look. Cat and I haven't had a father since we were kids—since he chose to abandon his family for meaningless sex with random women. I wish I could say I don't take after my old man, but I have more in common with him than I care to admit.

"Besides," Cat continues, "if anyone has looked out for me all these years it's you, Cors. You're the overprotective pain in the ass of my life. And let's face it, I pretty much had to get your permission to date Myles in the first place, so—"

I cut her off with a laugh. "Alright, I'm not that bad. But, yeah. I'd love to give you away, Cat." My voice catches and I clear my throat. She notices and wanders around the bar to pull me into a hug.

"Thanks, big bro. And I'll do the same thing when it's your turn."

I chuckle. "What?"

She gazes up at me. "Okay, maybe I won't give you away, but one day you'll fall in love and get married."

"What has Myles done to you?" I shake my head. My sister never used to be like this. She was a sarcastic cynic who took no shit.

Still. It might take some getting used to, but it's nice to see her so happy.

"Come on." She giggles as she heads toward the back room. "Let's set up."

I pull out my phone, checking the time. "Where is Eddy?" I mutter, glancing around. Then I remember his text from earlier and curse under my breath. Levi is out of town and Camila is off for a few days while her sister visits.

Crap.

I drag a hand down my face, knowing exactly who I have to call. I was hoping to avoid speaking to her until it was absolutely necessary, given how weird things were this morning. I know I didn't help by stuttering nonsense like a fucking teenager when she tried to apologize.

I lift the phone to my ear, my stomach dipping

nervously. I don't have a choice. I want this night to be perfect for my sister.

"Hey, Joze," I say, relieved when I get her voicemail. "I'm going to need you to come in early."

8

JOSIE

I'm carrying my overnight bag and Pretzel's folded crate when I push through the door at Bounce. There's a sign in the window that says "Closed For a Private Function," and the bar is empty, except for Myles in a booth with his laptop, Cat hanging streamers and balloons, and a woman who looks to be in her early-sixties sitting at the bar.

Pretzel pulls ahead on his leash, sniffing the floor. Last time I didn't let him out of his crate in here, so it's all new to him. I managed to get him back to my place to pack a bag, but I was only in my apartment for five seconds before Mrs. P. came banging on my door, asking why I'd brought "that filthy mutt" back. I explained that I was getting a bag and leaving, and she looked very unimpressed. If anything, it just reinforced that I definitely can't have Pretzel at home.

Then we were in a cab heading to the hotel when Cory called me, and I let it go to voicemail because I couldn't face talking to him. His message said that Cat and Myles are throwing a surprise wedding tonight and Eddy has let him down, and even though I was considering calling in sick—or maybe quitting, changing my name, and fleeing the country

—when I heard the desperation in his voice I texted to say I was on my way. I'd never leave him high and dry, no matter how awkward I might feel.

I tighten my hold on Pretzel's lead and head for the back room, waving at Myles on the way past. Cat spots me from her perch up a step ladder and grins.

"Hey, Josie! Glad you're here. Mom, this is my friend, Josie. She works with Cors." Cat turns back to her streamers, using a staple gun to fasten them to the wall.

The woman at the bar stands, offering me a friendly smile. Her caramel-blond hair is short with loose waves, her lips a frosted pink. "Hi, Josie. Lovely to meet you."

"You too, Mrs. Porter."

"Oh, it's Gail, please. And who's this?" She gestures to Pretzel, who bounds in her direction. I try to hold him back, but his leash slips from my hands, the crate and my bag crashing to the floor.

"Pretzel! Down!" I say, horrified. Gail is wearing a beautiful summer dress and I don't want his claws to damage it. "I'm so sorry."

She swoops down to pet him, grinning. "Don't worry about me, honey. I'm a dog person." She makes a huge fuss over Pretzel, letting him lick her hands, and I decide I might like Cory's mom even more than I like him.

"I think he can tell," I say, chuckling.

"How long have you had him?" She rubs behind his ears and he slumps against her leg in ecstasy.

"Oh, he's not mine. I'm just... fostering him for a while."

"Well, that's very good of you. He's adorable."

I grin, turning to Cat. "Do you want some help?" If this is supposed to be her wedding night, she should get dressed, have a glass of champagne, and try to relax.

She glances over at me. "Maybe, if you don't mind? Myles won't come near me when I'm holding a staple gun."

I look at Myles and he winces. "She's lethal with that thing," he mutters. "Anyway, I'm finishing the playlist."

Cory appears from the back room, his expression turning apprehensive when he spots me. "Hey. Thanks for —" His words are cut short as Pretzel lunges at his legs. Cory drops to pet him, then, as if realizing Pretzel isn't supposed to be here, he straightens up with a frown.

"Cors," Gail says, sliding an arm around her son's waist, "why didn't you tell me you work with such a sweetheart?"

Cory's eyes swing from his mom to me and his cheeks color. He goes to say something but it turns into a cough, and his gaze moves to Pretzel. "I thought he was going back to the shelter today?"

I shake my head, gathering my things off the floor so I don't have to look at him. "The shelter is closed for a few weeks to repair the water damage, so he's with me for now."

"But..."

I wave a hand, not wanting to get into all the details in front of his family. "It's fine. I've got something organized."

"Shelter?" Gail glances up at Cory from where she's petting Pretzel's head. "You're not going to let this little angel end up in a shelter are you?"

"I'll make sure he's taken care of," I say, avoiding Cory's gaze. "Now, I'm just going to get Pretzel settled, then I'll help set up." I tug him into the back room, then unfold his crate and set out food and water. He curls up inside. "I'll be back to check on you soon. Okay, buddy? I'm sorry you're here again. I didn't have a choice."

"Josie?" Cory steps into the back room, pulling the door closed behind him. "Can we talk?"

I cringe, focusing on Pretzel in his crate. "Sorry I've

brought Pretzel in again. I wasn't going to, but you said you wanted me to come in right away, so—"

"That's fine. I'm... are you okay?"

"Yup," I say, keeping my back turned to him. "I'm great."

"Okay. So... why won't you look at me?"

I draw in a deep breath, forcing myself to stand and meet his gaze. "Well, you know. This morning was kind of..." *Hideous. Mortifying. Soul-destroying.* "Bad."

He chuckles, rocking back on his heels. "Yeah. It was."

"I'm sorry," I mumble. "I didn't mean to land on your, um—I mean, not that I *felt* your—anything, but I didn't mean to *fall* on your..." I raise my hands to my face to stop myself from rambling like a lunatic.

Kill me. Kill me now.

Cory is still chuckling. "It's okay. It was an accident."

"Yes." Slowly, I lower my hands from my burning cheeks. "It was."

"I'm sorry, too. I didn't handle it very well." He rubs the back of his neck, staring at the floor. With a loud exhale, he brings his gaze back to mine. "We should just forget about it."

"Okay. I'll try." I tear my eyes away, inwardly cursing myself.

I'll try? What does that mean? For fuck's sake, you basically just told him you can't stop thinking about how hard he was.

When I risk a glance at Cory's face, his eyes are fastened on mine, dark and piercing. Crap, I think he knows *exactly* what I've been thinking about.

"I'll try too," he says at last. There's an unusually rough edge to his voice that sends a shiver through me, but before I can think anything of it, he gestures to Pretzel, changing the subject. "How long do you have him for?"

I swallow, trying to get my head on straight. "Uh, it

depends how long repairs take at the shelter, but probably a few weeks."

"And where are you going to go?"

I look away, feeling uncomfortable. The last thing I need is for him to feel obligated to offer his place again. "I told you, I've got something organized."

"Joze." He places a hand on my arm, his brow bending with concern as I look back at him. "Where are you going?"

"We're staying at a hotel. I've already booked a room, so it's all taken care of."

He opens his mouth, then closes it again. I watch his jaw work as he glances from Pretzel to me, then finally says, "Okay."

The tension loosens from my shoulders, and I offer him a smile. "Okay. Now let's go give them a wonderful wedding."

I THINK I've been to maybe three weddings in my lifetime, and this one is by far my favorite. You'd think that a surprise wedding in a dive bar wouldn't be that romantic, but it's perfect for Cat and Myles, who met and fell in love here. By the time we get all the balloons and streamers up, the bar looks awesome. None of the guests know it's Cat and Myles's wedding, and as they all trickle in and mingle over drinks and canapes, I can't help but feel excited for the couple. I hand champagne around to everyone, stopping in to say hi to Geoff, Harriet, and her boyfriend, Luke.

Gail and I help Cat get her hair and makeup ready in the back room. Then she pulls on a white, 1950s-style wedding dress she designed, with a narrow waist and flared skirt over platform pumps. Her cotton-candy pink hair is pulled back with a beautiful vintage pearl barrette on one side. But the best thing is the way she can't stop smiling.

"It's finally happening," she breathes, looking from her mom to me. I asked if she wanted me to send any of her friends back to help, but she insisted on it being a surprise. The only other person who knows is Geoff, because he's officiating.

"I'm so happy for you, honey." Gail wraps Cat in a hug, careful not to disturb her hair or dress. "I know your father and I didn't set the best example, but I'm happy you've found such a wonderful man."

"He is wonderful," Cat says as they pull apart. "I'm so lucky."

A bittersweet feeling winds through me as I watch Cat dab at her eyes. She *is* lucky. What must it feel like to have the person you love with your whole heart love you back just as much? I can only imagine.

I pop out of the back room to check everything is ready in the bar. Myles and Geoff are waiting at the other end of the room, grinning when they see me. I glance around for Cory and give him a thumbs up. He nods and turns down the music.

"Okay, everyone," he calls across the bar. The chatter settles down and they all turn to Cory. A few people notice Myles has changed into a dress shirt with a tie and begin to whisper, and when Cory announces that—surprise!—this is also Cat and Myles's wedding, a loud cheer goes up across the room.

The next thirty minutes go quickly. Stevie starts off the ceremony, trotting down the center of the room with the rings on her collar, accompanied by Myles's daughter, Amber, in a colorful dress that I'm sure Cat made. Cat follows as Etta James's *At Last* plays over the stereo, her face wet with tears, Cory at her side. When I turn to look at Myles, he's almost blubbering, he's crying so hard. He keeps burying his face in his hands, then looking back up as if he can't stand not watching Cat walk down the aisle. When she gets to the end she has to wait for him to pull himself together, and most of us are chuckling at how sweet it is. Except for Cat's friend—and Harriet's sister—Alex, who is crying so much her husband Michael has to keep stealing cocktail napkins from behind the bar.

Their vows are nontraditional, but they're perfect. When the ceremony is over, Myles toasts his new bride, followed by Cory who gives his own impromptu speech, his eyes shining as he congratulates the happy couple. Then Cat climbs up onto the bar and spins around to toss her bouquet. I grin, turning back to the bar to get more champagne, when the bouquet hits me on the head.

Like—*smack*, in the side of the face.

I stop, looking around to find the entire room watching me as I pick it up. "Throw it again," I say, holding it out to Cat with an embarrassed laugh, but she shakes her head and climbs down off the bar.

"Nope. It's yours now."

"What? I didn't catch it. I wasn't even—"

"Too bad." She lifts a shoulder, her mouth curled in a playful smile. Then she turns back to Myles, and I'm left standing with the damn thing.

I catch Harriet's eye across the room and she grins. She leans in to whisper something to Luke, and he looks over at me with a secret smile.

I shake my head, placing the flowers behind the bar with a sigh, and focus on pouring everyone another round of champagne.

As if a stray bouquet is going to solve my problems.

"Did it turn out how you wanted, honey?" Gail smiles at her daughter from her perch on a barstool.

The evening is winding down as people head home after a night of dancing and celebrating. I let Pretzel out of his crate once the crowd thinned out, and—after playing with Stevie for a while—he curled up on his pillow behind the bar with me. I wish I could do this every shift, but it would never work when we're busy.

"It was perfect." Cat tucks her face into Myles's neck. He tightens his arm around her and plants a kiss on her forehead.

"I can't believe you're my wife," he murmurs. "How did I get so lucky?"

Cory chuckles beside me. "I've gotta say, if I'd known a year ago things would turn out like this, I might not have been so hard on you."

Myles laughs, reaching for his whiskey on the bar. "I forgive you, man. I know you were looking out for her. That's your job."

"It's your job now. And I should warn you, she's a handful."

"I can look out for myself, thank you very much." Cat reaches over to shove Cory and everyone laughs.

"Last call," Cory says across the room. He wanders off with a bottle of champagne, seeing if anyone wants a refill, and I wipe down the bar. Pretzel and I will have to head to the hotel soon, and I'm counting the minutes. The stress of the past couple days is catching up with me and I'm exhausted.

"I wish Cory would settle down," Cat says to her mom.

"I'd love to see that too, honey, but I don't know if it will ever happen."

I wipe the counter, pretending I'm not listening. Pretending I'm not secretly wishing for the same thing. You know, with *me*.

"He puts on this big show of being a man whore," Cat says with an affectionate snort, "but honestly, I think he'd make a great husband." She leans forward. "You know what I mean, right, Joze? He's such a good guy."

I glance up, trying to feign indifference and failing. I knew Cory was a good man the day he hired me. Paul had just ended things for the millionth time—except this time it was finally over, and I was a mess. It was pouring rain and I had nowhere to go, so I stumbled into a bar, desperate to numb the pain. Instead of drinking my problems away, I ended up talking with the cute bar owner all evening. When I told him I was looking for a job, he offered me one on the spot. I smiled and said I'd never poured drinks before, and he assured me I'd pick it up in no time. It wasn't until weeks later that I learned he hadn't actually needed a new bartender. He was looking out for me before he even knew me, and he's looked out for me ever since.

"He's great," I murmur.

"He'd be a good dad, too," Gail adds, almost sadly. "He might not have had a good role model, but he's instinctively caring."

"Do you think he wants kids?" I hear myself ask.

"Yeah." Cat watches him across the room as he chats with Harriet and Geoff. "He'd never admit it, but I think part of him wants to settle down and have a family. You should see him with our cousins and their kids. They love their Uncle Cory." She chuckles quietly. "But, you know"—she turns back to me with a shrug—"I think he feels like he has an image to maintain around here."

I run the dishcloth through my fingers, thinking. I agree with everything they're saying: he's a caring guy who would make a good husband and father, if he could ever bring himself to settle down with just one woman.

My heart squeezes hard at the thought because, God, I want that to be me. I want to be the one he chooses to settle down with, the one he realizes he can't live without. Seeing him walk his sister down the aisle tonight only brought that ache I feel closer to the surface.

I shake my head, pushing these thoughts away. Why do I keep letting myself think about him like this? What's the point?

"Stevie enjoyed playing with Pretzel tonight," Cat says, reaching down to scoop Stevie up from her spot under her stool.

I lean across the bar to pet Stevie's head, smiling. "It was nice to see Pretzel play. He's had a hard time lately."

"Well, you're doing a good thing, fostering him," Gail says kindly. She reminds me a little of my own mom and homesickness ebbs through me. "So why are you fostering him, honey? You don't want a dog of your own?"

I sigh, focusing my attention on Stevie's tiny smushed face. Pugs are so cute. "I'd love to keep him. I'm kind of in love with him, but my building doesn't allow pets, and it's one of the few places I've found that's both affordable and not totally gross. Plus, I work long hours—both here and volunteering at the shelter." I pause, thinking about this. At least with the shelter out of action while I've got Pretzel, I'll have my days free to be with him. But once it opens again, I'll be busy again. It's not fair to have a dog if I don't have time to be with him.

"Stevie was a rescue." Cat nuzzles her nose against Stevie's fur. "She's what got me through my divorce."

"Aren't dogs amazing like that?" I say. "They're always there for you, no matter what."

This is why I'm determined to help Pretzel during this time. His love is unconditional and I want to return that, in whatever way I can, however brief it may be. I need to stop letting my crush on Cory mess with my head and focus on what's most important: looking after Pretzel. I might have the hotel secured for the next few nights, but soon enough I'll be needing something more affordable. I can't waste my energy thinking about my stupid unrequited feelings for my boss—I need to find a way to make sure Pretzel is safe and happy.

9

CORY

"Are you sure you don't want me to take you?" I lean on the door of the cab, watching as my mom shakes her head.

"I'm fine, honey. The hotel isn't far away and I know you have to clean up."

I nod, my brow furrowed. I don't like the idea of Mom taking a cab across town alone in the middle of the night, but I was relieved when she told me she'd booked a hotel room instead of taking the train back to Long Island.

"Stop worrying so much." She reaches up to squeeze my hand. "You need to let yourself relax and have fun sometimes."

"Text me when you get to the hotel?" I say through the window as I close the cab door.

"I will. Love you, Cors."

"Love you too, Mom." I tap on the roof of the cab, watching as it peels away from the curb. Something about her words—*have fun*—remind me that I have a booty call lined up for later tonight, but when I cast my mind back to the blond I ran into this afternoon, I struggle to muster the enthusiasm. It's not her fault—she's attractive, and if I remember correctly, not bad in bed—but I'm tired and, for whatever reason, not in the mood.

Still, I need to get out of this funk. I need my life to go back to normal.

I head back into the bar to find Josie mopping the floor. She glances up with a smile when I enter.

"Your mom is lovely. It was such a surprise, considering you're so…" She gestures to me vaguely and I frown. It's not until I see she's biting her lip to suppress a smile that I realize she's joking.

Shit, Mom's right. I do need to lighten up.

"Yeah, well, I take after my dad," I mumble, stepping around the wet patch on the floor. I grimace as I hear the words fall into the empty bar around us. All throughout my childhood I was told how much I was like my father: both tall, both athletic, and—as I learned later—both capable of hurting people deeply.

"Your dad…" Josie begins. I can tell she's trying to tread with care, but I tense up all the same. "Why wasn't he here tonight?"

I hesitate, then settle on the easiest answer. "He's dead." It's not a lie, at least.

"Oh," she says softly. "I'm sorry."

I'm not.

I push the thought away and step over to the sink, forcing myself to think of anything else as I stack the dishwasher. I never think about Dad, but walking Cat down the aisle made it impossible not to. The fact that he's passed is not the real reason he wasn't here tonight, and both Cat and I know it. He was a selfish asshole who chose himself over everyone else and, frankly, we're better off.

Oh well. It was a great evening and Cat was thrilled with how it went. That's all that matters.

I wasn't sure if I'd ever see my sister get married again, after she caught her piece of shit first husband cheating on her, but I'm so pleased to see her happy. She deserves it after everything she's been through. She and Myles have so much to look forward to together.

That thought stirs an unfamiliar sensation in my chest. I try not to think too much about the future—mine or anyone else's. The problem with thinking too far ahead is you get your hopes up for things that might never happen—things you think you deserve, but really, you don't. For years I assumed I'd get married and have kids one day, because that's what everyone assumes. That's how the script goes. The older I got, though, the more I realized that assumption was misguided. Now, I'm wiser. I've learned it's easier to focus on the present and take things day by day, rather than let yourself imagine a future that's not meant for you.

My phone buzzes with a text, interrupting my thoughts. It's my mom, letting me know she's checked into the hotel, and relief settles over me. That's one person taken care of for the night.

I double check the bar is clean, then step into the back room, looking for Josie. Most of the awkwardness seems to be gone between us, but I got dangerously close to telling her I haven't been able to stop thinking about the way she felt on my lap this morning.

I need to put some serious distance between us.

I find her on the floor beside Pretzel's crate, speaking to him in a soft voice, and I pause in the doorway, not wanting to interrupt. The way she treats that dog... God, any man would be lucky to have that kind of attention from her. One day she's going to make some guy really happy.

There I go thinking about the future again. Only this time, the thought makes me want to put my fist through a wall.

Just get the fuck out of here and go see... Shit, what was her name again? *Bridget. Go see Bridget.*

"Do you want me to call you a cab?" I ask, and Josie turns to look up at me.

"I think I'll walk to the hotel. It's not that far."

I force my breath out. *Don't offer to walk her.* "I'll walk you."

"You don't have to." She rises to her feet. "We'll be fine."

Somehow, I manage not to push it further. I glance down at Pretzel. "How much is the hotel costing you, anyway?"

She stifles a yawn. "One-fifty."

"A *night*? And you're going to stay there for three weeks?"

"Well, no," she concedes, shifting her weight. "But I'll figure something out."

I cross my arms, leaning against the door frame. "Why are you doing this? Why go to so much trouble for a dog that isn't even yours?"

She opens her mouth then closes it, glancing down at her hands. "Okay. You told me about your dad, so I'll tell you about my mom. My mom is actually my godmother, even though she's always just been Mom to me. My birth parents died in a car accident when I was two. I'm... an orphan."

"Oh," I murmur, feeling a tug behind my ribs. How on earth did I not know this about her? We've spent nearly every night together for the past five years, and *this* didn't come up? Well, I guess that makes sense. 'I'm an orphan' isn't exactly casual workplace chit chat. "I'm so sorry," I add inadequately. The urge to hold her is overwhelming and I press my shoulder hard into the door frame to stay put.

"Thanks," she says, meeting my gaze. "I don't remember

my parents at all. I know it's sad, but it's always been kind of normal for me. My mom—my godmother—didn't want kids, but she took me in and raised me as her own, always made me feel so loved. I learned a lot from her. She's incredibly selfless, always living in service to others, especially animals. She taught me the importance of looking after those who don't have a voice of their own—like the animals at the shelter."

I study Josie, understanding washing through me as I see her in a whole new light. No wonder she is the way she is. She's just like her mom—selfless and giving. She cares so damn much.

"But it's more than that," she says, crouching down at Pretzel's crate again. She looks through the mesh window at him. "Pretzel has no one. No one loves him, no one wants him. He's this sweet, loving little guy..." She pauses as her voice cracks, and for some reason, I feel my own throat grow tight. "But *I* love him. I see what's there, underneath all the reasons no one else wants to adopt him. He needs me right now and I won't give up on him, just because it's inconvenient for me. If I can't adopt him for myself, I can at least do this for him."

She unzips the side of his crate door and slips a hand in to pet his head. I stare at her, watching the way she lovingly strokes his fur, the way she gazes at him like nothing else matters in her world right now, and something in my chest breaks.

"Stay with me." The words jump from my mouth before I can think better of it, but I realize the second I've said them I don't want to take it back.

She glances up in surprise. "What? We're staying at the hotel."

"Don't waste your money at the hotel. You can stay with me."

She hesitates, her gaze sliding away. "I don't know if that's a good idea."

I grimace at the way she won't look at me, at the way she can't stand the thought of coming back to my place. But suddenly, I can't stand the thought of her being anywhere else.

"Joze," I say, stepping forward. I won't let myself think about the fact that having her at my place nearly drove me to my knees. All I can think about is what she said—*if I can't adopt him for myself, I can at least do this for him*—because it's exactly how I feel. If I can't have her for myself, I can at least do this for her. I *want* to do this for her.

"I can't ask you to do that, Cory. It's not your responsibility as my boss."

The way she refers to me as just her boss stings, but I guess I've spent the better part of the past five years attempting to think of her as just my employee.

I sigh. "No, it's not, but I'm not offering as your boss. I'm offering as your friend." I pause, before letting myself admit, "I guess I thought we were friends, too."

Her expression softens. "We are. But..." She scrunches her nose. "It was so awkward this morning."

I crouch down beside her, resisting the urge to reach out and touch her. "Then we just have to make it not awkward. You know, like, maybe you should wear pants when you walk around."

A laugh shoots out of her. Her cheeks turn a rosy pink, but she's smiling and I'm glad. "I can do that." Her eyes move over my face, assessing. "Are you sure? It feels like it's way too much to ask."

"You're not asking, I'm offering."

"I know, but..." She pulls her bottom lip into her mouth, wavering. "I don't want to cramp your style."

"You won't be. It's only a few weeks. Besides, Pretzel was happy there. He'd be safe there, especially when we go to work." I watch her face as she considers my words, and realize I'm holding my breath. I'm fucking holding my breath.

"Okay," she says at last. "If you really think it could work. But on one condition."

Anything, I nearly say, but I pause enough to get it together. "What's that?"

"I'm not taking your bed. I'll sleep on the sofa."

I open my mouth to protest, because no way in hell is she spending three weeks on the sofa, but she holds up a hand.

"I mean it, Cors. I'll only stay if you let me sleep on the sofa."

I grind my molars. "Fine," I say, knowing that I'll come up with something better for her, whether she likes it or not.

She releases a long breath, still looking at me. Her eyes are greener than I've ever seen them, her cheeks still rosy, the tiny stud in her nose catching the light. We both straighten up to standing, our gazes locked on one another. Her expression turns almost shy and she leans closer, and for a split second I think she's going to kiss me. "Can I give you a hug?" she asks.

I should say no. But that would make things awkward again—and honestly? I just want to haul her into my arms and melt into her.

I nod, and she slides her arms around my waist, stepping closer. I resist for a fraction of a second before I let my arms encircle her back and hold her close. Her head tucks perfectly under my chin and she smells like sweet, fresh flowers. God, she feels so good.

"Thank you," she murmurs into my shirt.

My heart is racing when she finally pulls back and I clear my throat, looking away. "You're welcome, Buttercup." I force myself to sound casual, but I'm not sure I pull it off. I grab my phone and wave it in the air like a doofus. "I'll call us a cab."

She nods, turning to fuss over Pretzel again, and I'm relieved to have her eyes off me. When I look down at my screen, there's a text.

Bridget: What time are you free?

Somehow during that conversation I completely forgot I had a hook-up planned for later tonight. I take a second to imagine Bridget spread out on my bed, but the image is immediately replaced by Josie, lying in that exact position last night, with her flushed cheeks and wide eyes. I don't know if I'll ever be able to imagine another woman lying in that spot now.

Fuck. I'm not going to let myself dwell on what that means. Instead, I send off a quick text to Bridget.

Cory: Sorry, something has come up.

What matters right now is getting Josie home safely. And she *will* be safe with me—I can help her out as a friend and still keep my distance from her. In fact, that's exactly what I'm going to do.

I feel better once I've stepped out into the bar and called us a cab. It's been a weirdly emotional night, with Cat's wedding, and thinking about Dad, and Josie—whatever that was, back there. As long as I can keep my head on straight, I'll be fine.

I wander back to where Josie is waiting and grab Pretzel's crate, hauling him up. "Come on, Joze. Let's go home."

10

JOSIE

R elief. That's what I felt when Cory asked me to stay with him. It wasn't until I woke on the sofa at his place the next morning that I began to wonder if I'd made a mistake coming back here. Let's face it, last time was kind of a disaster.

Well, it was fine at first, but then Erectiongate happened and things got incredibly awkward. What if something like that happens again? How on earth will I deal with that for three weeks?

It's not just that, though. Cory's used to living alone, and having an employee crash on his sofa is bound to get annoying. I hate being a burden like this.

I glance down at Pretzel, sleeping soundly in his crate on the floor beside the sofa. *It doesn't matter*, I remind myself. I have to make it work, for him. I'll just need to make sure I don't get in Cory's way—in fact, I'll do everything I can to make his life easier. I'll visit friends for a few hours if he wants to bring women home. I'll cook some of his favorite food to say thank you. I'll—

No, I probably shouldn't do his laundry. That would be crossing a line.

The main thing is that I don't let this destroy either our professional relationship, or our friendship. I'll just do my thing quietly in the background, and try to stay out of Cory's hair.

I sit up on the sofa with a yawn, then pop into the bathroom and get dressed, brushing my short bob and washing my face. Back out in the living room I roll up my blanket, tucking it with my pillow down beside the wall. See? It's like I was never even here.

I pad into the kitchen and peek inside his cabinets. I'd love to cook something for him, and I'll need to prepare my own food here too. One of the ways I've kept my diet affordable—and healthy—is to cook everything myself. I've been vegan for almost five years now, and while it began as an experiment after I started at the shelter, it's blossomed into a genuine love of cooking vegan food.

Before I can cook for either of us, I need to check what I'm working with. I just need a few basics: pots and pans, maybe a slow cooker if he has one. A juicer would be nice, but—

Wait, what?

The space under Cory's counter is almost empty. There are a few random plates, a couple of mugs, a toaster, and some Pilsner glasses. Baffled, I open the fridge to find only a few items—coffee creamer, leftover Chinese takeout, and what I think was once a block of cheese. Christ, I hope the takeout isn't that old. I cautiously pick up the container of leftovers to sniff the contents.

"Morning, Buttercup."

Holy—

The container flies out of my hands, landing on the counter with a thud. I spin around to face Cory, holding a hand over my stampeding heart. "You scared the crap out of me."

"Serves you right for snooping."

Heat creeps up my neck. "I wasn't—"

"I'm kidding." He chuckles as he wanders into the kitchen, scratching his stomach absently. My eyes slide down to take in his snug black T-shirt and gray sweatpants.

Fuck. Me.

I've never seen him in sweatpants before. I'd never considered that sweatpants could be sexy, if I'm honest, but I was wrong. I was so wrong.

A strangled sound escapes my throat and I snap my gaze back to his, hoping he didn't notice. But he's staring at the sofa, his expression clouded.

"I tried to put the blankets out of the way," I blurt.

Cory's gaze swings back to me. His brow tugs low and I begin to ramble.

"I mean, I didn't want you to come out here and—"

"Josie, stop." He shakes his head, examining me. "You're allowed to take up space in my home. I asked you to stay with me and I want you here. Okay?"

I open and close my mouth, feeling uncomfortable. Why did I think living with my boss would be a good idea?

"Look, this is only going to work if you make yourself at home. I know I'm your boss," he says, like he can read my damn mind, "but maybe don't think of me like that when we're at home. Think of me as a friend. Try to relax."

I take a deep breath, forcing my shoulders down from my ears. "Okay."

His gaze swings back to the sofa and his frown returns. "I don't like you sleeping on the sofa, though. We'll need to figure something out. You can't sleep there for three weeks."

There's a whine from across the room and I realize Pretzel's awake, with his nose pressed to his crate window. I stride over to let him out, dropping to shower him with kisses.

"Good morning, beautiful boy. Come on." I lead him to the back door and open it, watching as he meanders out into the courtyard. Then I turn back to Cory, who's standing and stroking his beard in thought, pondering an empty wall in the living room.

"We could put a Murphy bed on this wall, and if I move the coffee table, it could fold down here." He gestures to the space beside the sofa.

"A Murphy bed?"

"Yeah, you know those beds that fold up against the wall to look like a closet? Cat has one at her place for when Amber comes to stay."

"Cors, really, I don't need you to do that."

He spins around, giving me an impatient look, but something on my face makes him soften. "I want to, okay?"

I release a long breath. "Okay. If you really feel the need to do that... okay." I wander back to the kitchen, hunting for a coffee maker. He's bound to have one of those, surely.

But another search through his cabinets turns up nothing.

Okay, this is a real problem now.

"Cory—" I turn to find him hovering behind me and back up into the counter. "Where's all your kitchen stuff?"

"My what?"

"Your pots and pans and knives. Your *food*. What do you cook with?"

He hikes up a shoulder, leaning back against the counter opposite. "I don't cook."

"Why not?"

Another shrug. "I just... don't."

"Right." I take a moment to digest this information. An almost forty-year-old man who doesn't know how to cook. That surprises me, actually. "Well, I'd be happy to teach you some basics."

"It's not about that. I know how."

"Oh. So what do you eat?"

"Takeout, mostly."

"Seriously? You spend so much time at the gym. You'd get way better results if you cooked for yourself instead. So why don't you?"

He grinds his jaw, staring at me. "It doesn't have very good memories associated with it."

I want to ask more, but Pretzel comes bounding back inside and Cory turns to pet him—I think, because he wants the conversation to be over. And that's fine, but I still need to eat.

"Okay, well..." I hesitate, then think of his words from just now—*you're allowed to take up space in my home.* Inhaling, I force myself to ask, "I hope it's okay if I cook while I'm here?"

He looks up from where he's scratching Pretzel's ear. "Of course. You do what you need to do, Joze."

"Right. It's just... I'll need some pots and things to cook with. Is that okay?"

He nods. "We'll pick some stuff up at the store today."

"Or I can just grab the most essential things from my place. No point in buying stuff you won't use after I'm gone." I think for a minute. "Actually, I'm probably going to need more clothes, and Pretzel will need more food, too."

"Yeah, that's a good point. Let's get your stuff, then we can stop by the pet store." He stands and heads back toward his bedroom, calling over his shoulder, "I'm going to order a Murphy bed online."

THE MURPHY BED arrives in a box later that afternoon. It requires assembly, and when I ask Cory how, exactly, we are going to assemble it, he gives me another look.

"*I'm* going to assemble it. Just you watch." He drags the box through to the living room, then heaves the mattress in after. Pretzel is bouncing around, enthusiastically sniffing everything, and Cory pauses to murmur something to him about being patient and not getting in the way. Then he produces a toolbox from the hall closet and places it on the kitchen counter, popping it open. Measuring tape in hand, he sets about choosing the exact position on the wall and marking it off with a pencil.

Something strange happens then. To me, I mean. My stomach gets kind of fluttery and my heart rate ramps up. I'm not even doing anything; just sitting on the sofa with Pretzel, watching Cory work. But *something is happening to me*.

It gets even worse when he pulls out an electric drill to screw the frame together. I don't know if it's the concentration on his face, the fact that he apparently knows how to do useful man-stuff like using a drill, or the way that his shirt is straining over his broad, muscular shoulders and back as he fixes the cabinet frame together, but I'm going to need a cold shower in a minute.

"Do you want some help?" I say in a choked voice.

He shakes his head. "I've got it." Then he makes a grunting sound as he hauls the frame up against the wall and my mind tumbles into the gutter.

Suddenly I'm imagining him making that sound in a very different context—with my legs over his shoulders while he moves above me; that same look of concentration on his face, but this time it's aimed at making me fall apart beneath him.

Holy God in heaven.

"I should get ready for work," I blurt, springing to my feet. Pretzel leaps up, wondering what the hell is going on.

"It's your night off," Cory says over his shoulder.

Oh. Right. Shit.

Actually, no. That's good. I'll get a few hours alone at home—a few hours away from Cory to clear my head.

Or furiously masturbate.

Get. It. Together.

I turn for the kitchen and focus on unpacking the things we collected from my place earlier today. A big pot, frying pan, some spatulas and knives, my slow cooker and juicer. I unpack the groceries we picked up, including fresh fruit, which I unload into a bowl on the counter. Then I check Pretzel's water bowl and top up his food before unpacking the kibble and dog treats we got from the pet store. Anything to keep myself from watching Cory work with an electric drill.

"All done!"

I take a deep breath and turn to see Cory standing triumphantly beside what looks like a big closet.

"Look, it's got shelves so you can store your clothes and stuff while you're here." He gestures proudly to the unit, and when I wander over I can see what he means—there are shelves on either side of the doors.

"Wow."

He beams. "Are you ready? Watch this." He grabs the closet doors, but instead of pulling them open like a normal closet, they fold down from the top to reveal a mattress. Legs pop out, supporting the bed as it hits the floor. It sits neatly between the two rows of shelves, and I can't help but grin. I love it.

"Now," he says, pulling sheets out of the hall closet. "We just need to make it up, then it's ready to go."

I attempt to help him make the bed, but he waves me away. So I gather up the box and packing materials, taking them out to the Dumpster. When I return, Cory has packed away the tools and placed my bags on the end of the bed. Pretzel is curled up next to them.

"I thought you might like to unpack your stuff onto the shelves, so you're not living out of a bag for the next three weeks," Cory says.

I look at my new bed—made up with fresh sheets and a new comforter, surrounded by shelves for my things. He's gone to all this trouble to ensure I'll be comfortable, and it makes my heart swoop. His mom and sister are right—he'd make an amazing husband and father.

"Is it... okay?" There's a line on Cory's brow as he watches me expectantly, and I fight the overwhelming urge to hug him.

"Cors, it's..." I shake my head, trying to dial down whatever is happening in my chest. "Thank you. I love it." My voice comes out hoarse, and I swallow, glancing away. When I finally look back, he's studying me with tiny creases around his eyes.

"Good." His gaze rests on mine for a long moment, and I stand there, pinned to the spot. With each passing second my heart rate climbs, until it's a steady *boom boom boom* inside my ribcage. I don't dare move. I don't breathe.

The sound of a car horn somewhere outside seems to snap Cory out of it. He sucks in a breath and snatches up his jacket. "I'd better get to the bar," he mutters, spinning on his heel.

I watch his back as he disappears down the hall, the front door clicking shut behind him. Then I stand alone in his apartment, wondering how the hell I'm going to make it through the next three weeks in one piece.

11

CORY

Living with Josie is torture. Not because she's a bad house guest—she's great—but because it's that much harder to resist her. I knew this going in, but I don't think I appreciated quite how much it would test my self-control.

Take the other day, for example. Seeing her in the soft morning light in my kitchen did something to me. I wanted to walk up behind her, slide my arms around her waist, and snuggle into her warmth. I wanted to lift her up onto the kitchen counter and capture her mouth with mine. I wanted to make her coffee and drink it together in bed. I wanted to tell her I was actually *excited* to wake up, knowing she was there.

But I couldn't do any of that, so I did the only thing I could to show her how welcome she is—I bought her a bed. I'd prefer she was in *my* bed, with her legs wrapped around me, but this will have to do.

She's different at home than she is at work, and I'm noticing all these little things I never really noticed before. Like the way she constantly apologizes for being in my apartment, as if I didn't *invite* her to be there. It's as though she feels the need to justify simply being alive, or something. And now that I've noticed it at home, I can't help but see it at work too—in the way she lets Eddy walk all over her, the way she always felt bad about me walking her to the train, the way she chose to sleep in the back room at work rather than ask me for help. I don't know who or what made her feel like she doesn't have a right to have needs, but it kills me to see that side of her.

I close the front door behind me and step inside, unclipping Pretzel's leash. I asked Josie if I could walk him this morning, because I needed some fresh air to clear my head. And, I'm not going to lie, I'm enjoying this dog's company. I never realized how quiet my place was before he and Josie showed up.

Pretzel goes to his water bowl and takes a deep drink. Josie is standing in the kitchen with her back to me, and I pause in the doorway, feeling an odd sensation in my chest as I gaze at her. She's exactly the type of woman I'd pictured myself settling down with—back when I let myself imagine such things.

But I'm not the sort of guy a woman can rely on. I was never shown how to be that man, and the one time I tried, I fucked up badly, hurting someone I cared about. I'll never forgive myself for it.

And I'll never let it happen again.

I shove the thought away and step into the kitchen. "Hey," I say, and Josie turns to face me. "You won't believe what Pretzel—" My words halt when I notice tears streaming down her face. "Oh my God, Joze." I stride over and, without thinking, pull her into my arms. "What happened?"

She freezes at the sudden, intimate contact, and I

inwardly curse myself. But then I feel her soften against me, and every cell in my body lights up like a neon sign. I forget I'm her boss, that I'm not supposed to touch her; all I can think about is what's caused her to feel this way and how I can make it right.

I draw back enough to examine her face, wiping a thumb over her cheek. In all the time I've known her, I've never seen her cry. I feel like someone has punched me in the heart, and I'm aching to lower my mouth to hers and take away her pain.

She gives a shaky laugh and gestures to the counter. "It's the onions."

The... what?

I look over her shoulder at the knife and half-chopped onion on the counter. There's a bunch of other ingredients, and a pot sitting on the stove. My neck heats with embarrassment. How did I miss that? What the hell is wrong with me?

"It happens every time. I've tried everything to stop it, but nothing works."

I drop my arms and step back, huffing a self-conscious laugh. "Oh, shit." I rub a hand over my forehead, looking away. "Sorry. I don't know what—"

"That was really sweet," she says, touching my arm. "You thought I was upset."

I bring my gaze back to hers and nod, forcing my mouth into a smile. "Guess I don't need to kill anyone today, then."

She laughs, and the sound makes me relax a little.

"Do you have more to do?" I ask, motioning to the onion. She nods and I step over to the counter, picking up the knife and dicing the rest for her. I focus on my task, trying not to think about what a monumental dick I just made of myself.

"Thank you," she murmurs as I finish up.

"No problem, Buttercup." Without looking at her, I head to my bedroom and close the door with shaking hands.

I collapse back onto my bed and stare at the ceiling, trying to make sense of what just happened. I didn't know she was chopping onions—I thought something terrible had happened, and all I could think of was protecting and comforting her. It was innate. Primal.

And stupid.

But when I replay the moment in my head again, I can't imagine any scenario other than one where I pull her into my arms. And that only tells me one thing.

I'm in big trouble.

WHATEVER SHE'S cooking smells really good. I'm not sure if she's planning to share it, but I've spent the past hour and a half smelling it through the door and growing hungrier by the second. I had plans to go to the gym, but now I just want to eat.

I'm contemplating asking Josie if she's made enough for two when I hear a shriek, followed by the sound of shattering glass, and Pretzel barking. I leap to my feet, throw open the door and race out to find Josie standing on the counter, looking down at the glass-strewn tiled floor. Shit, has she hurt herself?

"What happened?" I ask breathlessly. "Are you okay?"

"I'm fine," she says, sounding anything but fine.

Pretzel is barking at full volume and I lift my fingers, blowing a loud whistle to silence him. Then I turn to Josie, shaking my head. "What's going on?"

Her wide eyes dart to mine, then back to the floor. "There was a spider..."

Oh, God. I'm so relieved, I laugh. "Is that *it*? I thought you were—"

"It's not funny! You didn't see it! It was huge!"

"Okay." I bite back my smile, trying to calm her down. "I'll just—"

"Don't come any closer," she says, throwing her hands up. "I knocked a glass off the counter. It's all over the floor."

"Yes, I can see that." I grab my boots from the front door and jam my bare feet into them, then I go to the hall closet and pull out a broom and dustpan, carefully sweeping up the glass. Pretzel sniffs beside me as I work, and I have to keep nudging his nose away. When I've disposed of the glass, I hold out a hand to help Josie down, but she looks at me incredulously.

"Are you kidding? I didn't see where the spider went."

I double check the floor. "It's not here, Joze. Are you sure it was—"

"Yes." She glares at me. "I didn't *imagine* it."

"I'm sure you didn't," I say, folding my lips in to hide my smile. "But if you come down, you can help me find it." I hold my hand out again and she relents, carefully climbing down. "Where did you see it?" She gestures to the floor. Pretzel is sniffing at a corner by the cabinets, and I try to push him out the way, but he dives back in. "Pretzel!" I scold, tugging on his collar until his head pops back up.

There, on his snout, is a small spider. I'd even go so far as to call it *tiny*.

Josie lurches away from him and I give a small chuckle.

"It's not that big," I say, reaching for Pretzel. But he ducks out of my grasp and Josie shrieks. That's a big mistake, because the dog thinks it's some kind of game and lunges at her, barking, the spider scrambling up onto the top of his head.

"Fuck!" Josie screams, stumbling back into the living room.

Oh my God, I've never seen her so freaked out. It's adorable. And *hilarious*.

My shoulders shake with mirth as Pretzel chases after her, delighted. She clambers up onto the back of the sofa, throwing cushions to keep him away, and I have to clutch my stomach to contain my laughter.

"Pretzel, stop!" She throws her last cushion at him and looks around frantically. I watch as she launches herself off the end of the sofa, snatching up the broom. Pretzel barks and jumps toward her, but she stabs the broom at him, trying to keep him back.

Oh, fuck. I can't help it—a laugh shoots out of me. I know women don't like to be called hysterical, but there is no other word to describe Josie right now. You'd think Pretzel had a live grenade on the end of his nose with the way she's acting.

"Cory!" she pleads, and guilt zips through me. "If you don't help me right now, I swear to God—"

"Okay, okay." I wipe my eyes and stride across to Pretzel, grabbing him by the collar. The spider tumbles onto the floor and I lift my boot.

"No!"

I stop with my leg mid-air, looking at her. "What?"

"Don't hurt it!" She throws the broom aside and swipes an empty coffee mug off the counter, slamming it down over the spider. Then she stands there with her hands on her hips, trying to catch her breath.

I lower my foot, confused. "I thought you *wanted* me to kill it?"

"No." She looks upset. "I'd never kill it."

I open my mouth, glancing down at the mug, then back at her. "Josie, you can't seriously—"

"It's not the spider's fault that it's terrifying. Just because I don't want it anywhere near me doesn't mean I think it deserves to die."

I shake my head in disbelief. She was close to hyperventilating because of that thing, yet she doesn't want to hurt it. That is so Josie. I smile to myself, turning to slide a piece of mail under the mug and carry the spider outside. I deposit it onto a shrub at the end of the garden, feeling bad. I shouldn't have laughed at her. Okay, it was hilarious, but I also feel like a dick.

I step back inside, setting the empty mug down. "Sorry. I shouldn't have laughed."

She turns from where she's stirring the pot on the stove. "No, you shouldn't have," she says, jabbing the dry end of the wooden spoon into my chest. "You can't have any of my chili now."

Disappointment seeps into me. Dammit, that smells *so good*. I'm dying for it.

I give her my best hangdog expression. "I'm sorry, Joze. Don't punish me with the chili, please." I lean over to peer into the pot. Fuck, it looks delicious. "I'll make it up to you."

She studies me for a second through narrowed eyes, then a smile creeps across her mouth. "Fine. I was making this for you anyway."

She was making it for *me*? I shake off the funny feeling that gives me as she shuts off the stove and looks around.

"Do you have any big bowls?"

"Top shelf," I say, inspecting the fresh guacamole she's made. I can already tell she's a good cook without even tasting the food. This could be very problematic for me.

"Shit," she mutters, stretching up onto her toes to reach into the cabinets, but the bowls are too high.

"Here." I step behind her and reach the bowls with ease. It's not until my fingers close around them that I realize what position we're in—me pressing her into the counter, her ass nestled snugly against my crotch.

Holy hell.

I nearly groan at the sweet pressure of her ass against me right there. And then I do something completely uncool; I lower my head just enough to breathe in the smell of her hair. God, just another inch and I could touch my lips to her temple, drag my teeth over the shell of her ear. I could hike up this little skirt of hers, dig my fingers into her hips, and fill her to the hilt.

I'm not sure if she's thinking the same thing, but I swear I feel her press back into me. The friction against my fly makes my jeans grow tight, and I know that if I don't move away from her this instant, she'll feel *exactly* what kind of effect she has on me.

I snatch the bowls from the shelf and step back, plonking them down onto the counter with more force than necessary.

"Thanks," Josie mumbles, turning to the stove and ladling chili into the bowls, avoiding my gaze. My pulse is thumping as I stride over and sink down onto the sofa.

What the hell was I thinking, lingering behind her like that?

Get your fucking head in the game, Porter.

I breathe in and out through my nose, mentally reciting The Pledge of Allegiance to dial down the situation in my pants. This is what I mean about living with her. *Torture.*

She carries two bowls into the living room and settles down on the sofa, holding one out to me. I take it, my mouth watering at the generous serving of chili, guacamole, and corn chips.

"Thanks," I murmur. I raise a spoonful to my mouth and —oh my God, I nearly black out from pleasure. "Holy—" I close my eyes on a moan, not even caring if it's inappropriate. "Fuck, this is amazing." I stuff another spoonful into my mouth, savoring the rich flavors. "This is the best chili I've ever had."

She beams, finally taking a bite herself. "You know there's no meat in it, right?"

"Wait, what?" I pause with a loaded corn chip halfway to my mouth, and glance down. "Seriously?"

"Yep. It's vegan."

I take another mouthful, chewing more thoughtfully. I guess the texture is different from chili I've had in the past, but if she hadn't told me, I don't think I would have noticed. "Maybe if all vegan food tasted like this, I'd consider cutting down on meat."

"I'm so glad you like it," she says, grinning. "I was worried when I became a vegan that the food would be boring, but I love it. This is my favorite recipe."

I study her over my bowl, remembering what she once told me—that she likes meat, but she gave it up because it was important to her. And just now, with the spider, not letting me kill it. She cares so much about stuff. She's so sweet, so caring, so... *good*.

"You kind of amaze me—how much effort you go to for the things you care about." I look down at Pretzel, waiting patiently for one of us to give him some food, and smile.

She shrugs. "If you care enough about something, it's not that difficult."

I nod, letting my gaze return to hers. I know what—*who*

—I care about, and I wish I could show her how much. "Maybe I should try giving up meat."

"Ha!" She scoops a corn chip through her guacamole, giving me a teasing smile. "I bet you couldn't go two weeks without it."

"What?" I say, mock offended. "I could totally go without it."

Josie arches an eyebrow. "I bet you need it more than you think." There's a playful, almost flirtatious lilt to her words, and I wonder if we're still talking about food. Her gaze rests on me, her perfect mouth curved in a smile as she crunches her corn chip. Then she swallows, lifting a finger to suck some guacamole off the end without breaking my gaze, and I have to look away.

Jesus Christ. What is she trying to do to me?

"I'll do it," I say thickly. "I can go without."

12

JOSIE

I've never had so much free time. The shelter has been closed for a week now and it's taken some getting used to. For years I've woken up almost every morning and gone straight there. Helping the animals has always made me feel like I'm making a difference, and now that's just... gone. I have to distract myself from missing that. Taking Pretzel on long walks out by the East River and stopping in at Game of Scones before work has helped. As for work; Cory and I decided not to tell anyone about our living arrangement because we didn't want shit from people—Eddy, mostly—so everything there is pretty much business as usual.

I wish I could say the same about things at home. There, I'm a ball of sexual frustration. The problem with living with my boss who I also have the hots for is that it's not always easy to get *private time*, if you catch my drift. I only seem to need it when he's home—especially when he's walking around in those sweatpants like a freaking snack. I've found the bathroom is my best spot, and usually end up sitting on the end of the bathtub with the shower running and the door locked, imagining he's in there with me.

Things are a thousand times worse since I cooked for him the other day. Well, it wasn't the *cooking* so much that was the problem—it was the way I shamelessly rubbed myself against him when he was reaching for the bowls. God, I know, but I couldn't help myself. He was so close, so warm against me, and I just wanted to feel more of him. *All* of him.

Instead, all I did was freak him out. He threw the bowls down on the counter and ran away from me as fast as his feet could carry him. I think the only reason he didn't tell me to leave is because he liked my food.

At least that's something.

Anyway, the most important thing is that Pretzel is happy. He seems to feel right at home at Cory's place, happily staying here in the evenings while we go to work. It probably helps that I take him for long walks to wear him out, and that—against my better judgment—I let him sleep on the bed with me. But I figure it's all temporary, and it's the least I can do to make sure he's comfortable.

A week after moving in, I settle in to do a session of yoga. It's helping to keep me sane during this time when I feel a bit... adrift. Cory has been amazing at accommodating us, but no matter what he does, I'm struggling to relax. Yoga has been grounding and centering when I feel scattered and tense.

I wait until Cory leaves for the gym before rolling out my yoga mat, then I put in my Bluetooth headphones and set up my iPad, pressing play on my favorite yoga video. I lose myself in the movements, flowing between warrior pose, tree pose, and bridge pose with ease. I'm thirty minutes into it, and just settling into downward dog, when I spot a pair of feet between my legs, behind me.

"Ahhh!" I collapse forward and roll onto my side, curling into a ball. So this is how I'm going to go—by a home invasion, in Cory's apartment.

When I open my eyes and glance up, Cory is hovering over me, concerned. He's saying something I can't hear and I yank my earphones out, trying to catch my breath. When I glance around for Pretzel, he's snoozing on the bed, as if I wasn't about to be brutally murdered.

I mean, okay, I wasn't. But he could at least *pretend* to care.

"Shit, Joze, I'm sorry." Cory drops to his knees beside me. "Are you okay?"

I sit up and pull in a lungful of air, willing my sprinting pulse to calm down. "I—fuck. I thought you were at the gym."

"There was a fire alarm and we had to clear out. I was halfway through my workout, but I didn't want to wait around."

I run my eyes over his damp shirt and flushed face. I've never seen him post-workout; usually he showers at the gym and goes straight to work. But here he is—hair all tousled, smelling strongly of sweat as it mingles with his earthy, musky cologne. Smelling like... I can't describe it. Like hot, fuckable *man*.

Dammit, this is just what I need: more sexy versions of him for my shower sessions.

I push up to stand and he does the same. I want to continue stretching—God knows I need to relax, now—but I can't with him home. A thought occurs to me. He was standing right behind me... while I was in *downward dog*.

Christ.

I cringe. "I wasn't expecting you home or I wouldn't have"—*greeted you ass-first*—"done yoga out here."

Cory's gaze drifts down my body, over my yoga gear: a crop top and form-fitting pants. My skin prickles with awareness, as if it can feel the way his eyes skim over me. They come back to my face, darker than before, and he tries to shrug but it looks wrong. "That's... fine. You can do yoga wherever you like." There's a raw edge to his voice and he clears his throat, as if he hears it too.

I stare at him, my pulse rushing in my ears. The air between us seems to thicken and crackle with something I can't quite describe as we stand there, looking at each other. He's never seen me in my yoga gear, either, come to think of it. It feels like we've crossed some weird, invisible barrier I didn't know was there, and neither of us knows what to do about it. God, it's starting to feel like that every time I'm in the same room with him at home—like no matter what we do, there's no way for us to live together and for it not to be awkward.

I step back, desperate to avoid embarrassing myself in some new way. "I'm going for a walk to Harriet's cafe," I mumble, looking for my sneakers. I shove my feet into them and grab Pretzel's leash, dashing out the door before Cory can respond.

Thank God.

That was odd, back there. It felt like something shifted, something I wasn't aware of. Well, I'm always aware of him, but for the first time it almost felt like *he* was aware of *me*—in a way I've never experienced before. I don't want to get my hopes up, but it kind of felt like he was checking me out. The way he looked at me in my yoga clothes and just kind of... stood there. It was almost as if he didn't want to look away. As if he *liked* what he saw.

I glance down at Pretzel and shake the thoughts from my head.

You're imagining things. He's giving you a place to crash because he feels bad for you. Don't turn this into something it's not, like you did with Paul.

I wrinkle my nose, thinking of my ex. He gave me all kinds of signs that things between us weren't the real thing. I just chose not to see them.

I force out my breath and turn down the street, breaking into a jog. I feel all antsy and unsettled, and I just need to burn it off. I jam my headphones back in and turn up my music, putting one foot in front of the other.

I only get half a block before I realize I need to turn back. My yoga top, while great for stretching, is not good to jog with. I don't have huge boobs, but they're big enough that I need a sports bra.

I reluctantly turn on my heel and head back to the apartment. I'll just pop in and slip on a bra, then head out. Cory will probably be in his room and won't even notice. If he is there and tries to talk to me, I'll keep my music on and just say I can't hear him.

I tie Pretzel to the railing where I can see him through the front window, and poke my head into the apartment, checking down the hall. No sign of Cory. I head for the living room, but remember I left my sports bra in the bathroom after my walk yesterday. I spin back and push open the bathroom door.

And there, in the shower, is Cory.

Holy shit.

He didn't pull the shower curtain all the way around, and he's standing with his back to me, one hand braced on the wall in front of him, the other... well, I can't see where that one is. I yank my headphones out, silently cursing myself. I didn't hear the water running or I would *not* have come in here.

I can't resist trailing my eyes over his tall, muscular, *naked* form. I know I should leave. I should not be looking at my boss in the shower, but I'm riveted to the spot. Fuck, he's beautiful. His shoulders and back are pure muscle, tapering down to a narrow waist. His ass is more perfectly sculpted than Michelangelo's David, and I want to take a bite out of his thick, solid thighs.

I stare at the back of him, my body pulsing with desire. I thought I wanted him before, but this is... this is too much. I might be dying. How can I want someone this much? How can I live with this burning need?

A groan snaps me out of my thoughts. I watch his head drop, one hand still braced on the wall above him, the muscles in his back flexing as his hips pump forward, then back, then forward.

Oh my God.

I stumble backward through the door, falling against the wall opposite. Then I stare at the half-closed bathroom door, trying not to self-combust at the knowledge that Cory is in there, touching himself in ways I can only dream of doing.

My brain offers up the same suspicion from earlier: maybe he's thinking about me. He just saw me in downward dog, and the way that he looked at me... Is it completely absurd to think that maybe—

"Fuck, yes. Just like that, Buttercup." Cory's rough voice floats through the partially open door and my breath freezes in my lungs.

What.

The...?

Did he just say *Buttercup*? Am I hearing things?

My heart is thundering as I step forward and press my ear to the crack in the door.

"You're so perfect," I hear Cory rasp over the sound of the water. "I've wanted you for so long."

I should leave. I should not be listening to this. He deserves privacy. He thinks he's home alone, not being spied on by his sexually deviant roommate with no sense of boundaries.

But my feet won't cooperate. My ears strain to hear more over the sound of the shower—strain for confirmation that I heard what I did. It's quiet for a while, except for the occasional grunt and the sound of water hitting the tub, then finally I hear Cory let out a long, quiet moan of release.

Holy hell. My mouth goes dry and my thighs squeeze together at the sound. I'll replay that on a loop in my fantasies forever. I drop my head against the wall and try to catch my breath. I haven't even done anything and he's got me panting.

Suddenly the shower shuts off, and my heart vaults into my throat.

Shit. He cannot know I was listening to him.

I tiptoe at lightning speed to the front door and slip outside, pulling it shut as quietly as I can. My mind is in free-fall as I turn back to Pretzel and untie him from the railing, fleeing from the scene of my crime.

I try to calm my whipping pulse as I make sense of what I heard. Did Cory really say Buttercup, or was it my imagination? I want him so badly; I'm desperate enough to hallucinate it. Even if he did say it, I don't know for sure it means *me*. Okay, I've never heard him call anyone else that, but then he doesn't call *me* that around other people either. For all I know, he has hundreds of Buttercups across the city. A freaking field of them. It wouldn't surprise me.

But then, maybe it would. The more time I spend with him outside of work, the more I peel back the layers of who he is. He bought and installed a bed for me. He's given up meat, for Christ's sake—I never thought I'd see that day. And things have felt different, ever since I moved in; like there's some sort of tension or electricity bubbling just under the surface between us, and we're both doing our best not to get too close to it.

I don't know what to think. I can't exactly ask him, can I? How would I explain that?

Guilt slams through me as I think about what I've done —listening to him when he thought he was alone. What a horrible invasion of his privacy.

But if he *was* thinking of me...

That changes everything.

13

CORY

I'm hanging on by a thread. It's like everything Josie does is designed to turn me on. The worst part is, she doesn't even seem to realize she does it. Like yesterday, when I came home early from the gym to find her bent over in the living room, and nearly fucking exploded on the spot. It took every ounce of strength not to grab her hips and grind into her from behind.

Thank God she went out for a walk. I know she caught the way I was looking at her in that tight little yoga outfit, but *fuck me*—I'm losing this battle, I can feel it. I had no choice but to get in the shower and picture what I wanted to do: throw her over my shoulder, carry her into my bedroom, tear off that Lycra and worship every inch of her. I've resisted jerking off to the thought of her since she moved in, but yesterday I snapped.

At least I didn't touch her. After getting way too close in the kitchen the other day, that's one line I can't cross again. It doesn't matter how much I want to—she's my employee, and she's too young for me.

As long as I keep telling myself this, everything will be okay.

"Ready?" I ask, holding open the front door. For some reason I found myself coming back home after finishing my workout and hanging around until it was time to walk to work. With her.

Fuck, I'm a mess.

"Yup." She steps through the door without meeting my gaze and I follow behind, locking the door with a sigh. She's been weird ever since I walked in on her doing yoga and I don't blame her. Between my behavior in the kitchen and the way I ogled her yesterday, I'm surprised she hasn't bolted. I need to get my shit together.

At least I got a decent workout in today. I've been pushing myself harder and harder this past week, to release all the built-up tension from my body. Between that and jerking off in the shower, maybe I can make it through the next two weeks in one piece.

We walk for several blocks, and even though I attempt conversation, Josie doesn't seem interested. I try not to over-think it. There's always something going on inside a woman's head and it's probably got nothing to do with me. As we head along Clinton Street, crossing at the foot of the Williamsburg Bridge, I force myself to focus on my surroundings instead of the quiet woman beside me.

I like this part of Manhattan. Rob and I used to share an apartment around here before he moved out to Jersey. It might not appeal to most people, but I love the gritty charm of it—graffiti and garbage and that acrid New York street smell, but there's also trees casting dappled shade from the afternoon sun onto the redbrick apartment buildings and stores that line the one-way street. The thing I love about this city is how everything you could ever need is right here, all the time. Laundromat. Chinese food. Gym. Bars. Drug stores. Delis. It's all only a few steps away.

A young guy walks toward us, head down as he looks at his phone. He nearly walks right into Josie, but I grab her shoulders and tug her out of the way. She looks up, startled, but I'm staring after the asshole who almost crashed into her.

"Hey!" I call after him. "Watch where you're going, man."

Nothing. Fucking youth.

I turn back to Josie. "You okay?"

She nods, and I consider saying something about how she needs to stand up for herself more, but when I notice her body is rigid and she's staring at the sidewalk, I sigh. Everything feels so off with her and I hate it.

Is this my fault? Have I made things too weird for her at home? Of course I have, leering at her in the living room when she's only trying to work out. What the fuck is wrong with me? I'm a selfish jerk, letting myself look at her like that. I promised her somewhere she would be comfortable and all I've managed is the complete opposite.

"Joze?"

She finally glances up, blinking against the afternoon sun. "Yeah?"

"Can we talk?"

Concern flits across her brow. "Uh... sure."

I gesture to a bench opposite Lederman's Deli, and we sit. At least this street isn't too busy, and we've got a few minutes before we need to be at the bar. This is going to be awkward as hell, but I can't stand the way she's been tiptoeing around me.

"Look, I—"

"I'm sorry," she says, wringing her hands on her lap.

I stop, surprised. "What? Why are you sorry?"

She grimaces, glancing away, and there's a sinking feeling in my stomach.

"Hey," I say gently. I resist the urge to touch her arm, trying to be patient. "You can talk to me. What's wrong?"

She turns back, but her eyes are pressed tightly closed. "I did something, Cors, and I feel so guilty. I have to tell you but..." She slumps forward, lowering her head into her hands. "Don't hate me."

"Okay, I promise I won't hate you."

She straightens up, glancing at me, then quickly drags her gaze away. "I can't look at you while I say this. God, I'm so embarrassed."

I feel the urge to chuckle. "Whatever it is, I'm sure—"

"I saw you in the shower," she blurts, and I freeze.

"What?"

She covers her face with her hands, speaking from behind them. "When I went out for a walk yesterday, I had to come home to grab my sports bra. I still had my head-phones in and I walked into the bathroom to find you, um..."

Oh. *God*.

I drop my gaze to the ground, feeling my face heat. She *saw me* in the shower? How the hell did I not notice *that*? My pulse thumps in my temple as I try to think back, but I don't remember much. I was lost in the moment—and I assumed I was home *alone*.

I steal a quick glance at her, wondering if she knows what—*who*—I was picturing at the time, but she seems oblivious. I blow out a long breath, trying to shake off the awkwardness, unsure how to proceed. There goes any chance I had of making her feel more comfortable at home. At least she doesn't know it was *her* I'd had on my mind, but is it wrong that a tiny part of me is disappointed? What would she think if she knew the truth?

"Joze," I begin. I'm so close to just confessing everything, to telling her how impossible I've found this past week, how desperate I am for her. But when her eyes meet mine, clouded with uncertainty, I stop. I can't put her in that position. It's not fair.

I clear my throat. "I'm sorry you saw that."

"No, *I'm* sorry. You thought you were home alone, and I didn't mean to intrude." She smooths her hands over her skirt and I force my gaze away from her legs. "If it helps, you're not the only one who thinks the shower is a good spot for that."

Holy fucking *hell*.

I look up at the sky, praying for strength. "You've done that in my shower?" I say roughly, trying to control the swelling I can feel in my pants.

"Um, yes?" She emits a sheepish laugh and I let my gaze slide back to her. She cringes. "Sorry, I thought it would make you feel less awkward knowing you're not the only one, but that obviously didn't work."

I stare at her rosy pink cheeks, wondering what she imagines when she's alone in there. *Who* she imagines. What his name is and if I could take him.

It's none of your damn business who or what she thinks about. You need to fix this now.

"Okay." I drop my head into my hands, pushing them up through my hair. "We agreed this would only work if we didn't let things get awkward, and this is about as bad as it gets."

She chuckles quietly. "Yeah."

"Maybe we need some kind of house rule," I suggest.

"Like a sock on the doorknob?"

A laugh rumbles in my chest, despite myself. "Something like that." I look at her again, and while she's still a little embarrassed, she's also smiling. At least now I know why she's been weird around me lately, and it's such a relief to laugh with her again. "I want you to feel comfortable in my house, and I'm sorry I haven't made that easy for you."

Her head jerks back in shock. "What? You've done everything possible to make me feel comfortable. You bought me a *bed*, for crying out loud. You helped me carry all my pots and pans over. And you've been so accommodating, especially with Pretzel."

"Right. But I don't want you to have to worry..." I pause, thinking. "Maybe we should have a rule that as long as we're living together, we don't do... that."

"Do what?" She looks confused, then understanding dawns on her face. "*Oh*."

It's a stupid fucking suggestion, I know that much. I doubt if I can go another two weeks without jerking off, especially not if I see her in that tight little yoga getup again, but I want her to feel comfortable. And at least if I know *she* isn't doing it, I won't be tempted to smash the bathroom door down the next time she's in the shower.

"The thing is"—she shifts her weight—"I don't know if I can agree to that. I might need to, um..."

Christ. She's trying to kill me. My breathing is so rapid and shallow I'm surprised I haven't passed out.

I might need to...

Need to what? What does she need? To come?

Fuck! Don't think about that!

Her eyes tentatively find mine and she chews on her lip, biting back a shy smile.

A shaky laugh slips out of me. "Yeah, I might, uh, need to... too."

Oh my God. Why did I say that? What happened to trying to make things *better*? I've lost complete control of this conversation and I shouldn't have let that happen. I can't let this—*anything*—happen.

I push to my feet, tearing my gaze away. "I guess we just need to be more careful."

She stands beside me. "Yup," she agrees, sounding a little breathless herself.

I glance over to find her gaze resting on mine, her bottom lip trapped between her teeth as she ponders me, like she's considering saying something more. But I know that if I stand here any longer, staring at her flushed cheeks and thinking about her touching herself in my shower, I'm going to throw her down on that park bench and take her right here.

"We'd better get to work," I mutter, turning down the street. It's not until we're halfway to Bounce that it occurs to me that if she *saw* me in the shower, she probably *heard* me, too.

Shit. She knows *exactly* who I was thinking about.

14

JOSIE

I can't believe I told Cory I've masturbated in his shower. He just looked so *embarrassed* by the whole ordeal and I felt the overwhelming urge to make him feel better. Part of me thought that maybe if I volunteered that information, he might divulge some secrets of his own —like who he was thinking of when I caught him in there.

He was frustratingly silent on that front, though. I'm glad I confessed what I did, and I feel better for apologizing —the guilt had been eating me alive—but I still don't know if the Buttercup he was referring to is me; if he may, perhaps, be interested in me. The longer I sit with the possibility of that, the more desperately I want him.

And the more I want to know the truth.

He's been quiet and broody since we arrived at work, but that's pretty normal for him here, especially when Eddy is working. And work is hardly the place to confront him about everything, although it would probably be even more awkward at home.

But, whatever. I'm trying not to overthink it. I'm definitely not going around in mental circles, thinking one minute that he wants me, the next that I've imagined the whole thing. Because that would be ludicrous.

Ugh, I don't know. Maybe it's time for me to get over him —find somewhere new to work, and someone to actually, you know, *date*. Move on with my life.

A guy approaches the bar, interrupting my thoughts as he asks for a Guinness. I fill a glass, handing it over with a faint smile. I try to imagine myself dating someone like him —medium height and build, dark hair, brown eyes, and I'm pretty sure I caught a British accent. He's objectively good-looking, but I feel nothing. I watch as he goes to join some friends in a booth, willing myself to be attracted to him.

Still nothing.

When I turn back to wipe the bar, Eddy is beside me. "You're quiet tonight."

I shrug. Cory comes out from the back room and I watch him, waiting for him to look my way, but he's got his head down as he replenishes the garnishes and cocktail napkins.

"So, listen." Eddy leans lazily against the bar. "Do you think you could open up for me tomorrow night?"

I frown. He's always asking me for favors, and the one time I asked him to cover for me months ago, he refused.

"You've got to be kidding me," Cory says. I glance over to find him glowering at Eddy. "Stop asking her to do shit for you."

Eddy gives a dramatic eye-roll. "Fine. Whatever." Cory's scowl deepens and Eddy slides out from behind the bar to carry a tray of drinks over to a booth.

I take some glasses to the sink, trying to untangle the mess of emotions inside me. Having Cory stand up for me used to feel nice, but tonight it's more confusing than anything else. It makes me think of how he's always stood up for me—always acted more like an older brother than anything else, because he hired me when I was young and vulnerable. Having him look out for me now makes me think he still views me that way; as that young girl who just arrived in the city, who just had her heart broken, who didn't have a clue.

And you don't jerk off to someone in the shower if you think of them like that.

Cory appears beside me at the sink. "Don't let Eddy push you around," he murmurs. "You need to speak up for yourself more. Say how you really feel."

I look up, and my heart bounces at the way he's leaning in close enough for me to touch, the way his eyes are riveted to mine. In the dim light of the bar the brown flecks of his irises glint with that dark porter color I love. I let my gaze move over his strong jaw, covered in thick, sandy-blond bristles, his messy hair, his unreasonably lush lashes. My mouth is dry from the nearness of him, and I run my tongue over my bottom lip, watching as his breathing quickens.

Say how you really feel.

Is that a challenge? An invitation? Has he figured out what I heard him say in the shower? There's something swirling in his eyes, a dark intensity I've never seen before, and it's on the tip of my tongue to ask him if it was *me* he was thinking about. If he thinks about me at other times. If he thinks about me like that at all.

But before I can, he swallows and leans back, shaking his head. "Just... think about it." Then he steps away to serve a group of women at the end of the bar, and I stare after him, wondering what the hell just happened, if maybe I imagined that whole thing, if I'm actually losing my mind a little.

"Excuse me?" I spin around to see the British guy from earlier smiling, and I lean on the bar.

"Sorry. What can I get you?"

"Another Guinness, thanks." He watches while I pour him a fresh glass. "Are you okay? I've been trying to get your attention for a few minutes."

"Oh, sorry." Heat stains my cheeks and I give him an apologetic smile. I'm no better than Eddy. "I've got something on my mind."

He takes the glass with a nod of thanks. "Want to talk about it?"

I breathe an uncomfortable laugh. I can hardly unload my problems to him with Cory right there—not that I would, anyway. "Thanks, but it's okay."

"I'd offer to buy you a pint, but I don't think it works if you're the barmaid." He gives a little chuckle as he lifts the glass to his lips. "Do you have a pen?"

"I... yes?" I reach behind the bar and hand it over. Then I watch as he scrawls a number on a cocktail napkin.

"If you want to go for a drink when you get off tonight, give me a text." He holds out the napkin, then hesitates. "Sorry, that probably sounded sleazy, but I really mean for a pint, or a brew, or... whatever." He drops the napkin on the bar with an embarrassed laugh. "I'm bloody shit at this."

I laugh as I take the napkin. At least he had the balls to actually *ask* for what he wants, unlike me. "You're not so bad." I look down at his number, wishing I could be interested in a nice, uncomplicated guy like him, instead of hopelessly infatuated with my boss.

"Well, I hope your night gets better."

"Thanks," I say, watching him go back to his friends.

Speak up for yourself more. Say how you really feel.

I turn Cory's words over in my head and make a decision. I'm going to find out how Cory truly feels about me.

And if he feels even a fraction of what I feel, I'm going to do something about it.

I CLOSE the door behind the last customer of the night and rest my head against the glass, buying for time. It was all fine and good to declare I'd get to the bottom of this, but now that I'm alone with Cory, I'm beyond anxious. Things felt almost alright between us by the end of the shift, and I'm not sure if opening up this can of worms is such a bright idea.

With a sigh, I trudge to the back of the bar and pull out the mop, focusing on cleaning up.

Procrastinating, in other words.

Cory and I clean side by side in silence for a while. I mop the floor, wipe down all the tables, and restock the beer fridge while he loads the dishwasher, lost in thought.

"So…" Cory's voice shatters the silence, making me jump. "Do you think you'll go out with that guy?"

I glance at him from where I'm wiping the counter, but he's focused on stacking glasses. "What guy?"

"That British guy."

Huh. Interesting. I wasn't sure he'd seen that interaction —and this sudden interest from him definitely gives some weight to the argument that he could be interested in me.

I decide to test this theory.

"Maybe." I turn and lean a hip against the bar. "He was cute." I watch a muscle flex in the side of Cory's neck, and feel a flicker of triumph.

So far, so good.

He shrugs. "I don't know if he's good enough for you."

Right. *Not good enough for me.* That's a point in the *big brother* column, for sure.

"Yeah, maybe you're right," I mumble, deflating. I glance around, deciding I've had about enough of tonight. "You ready to go?"

"I'll just refill the beer fridge."

"Already done it."

Cory looks at me, surprised. "Oh. Thanks, Buttercup."

The nickname hits me hard in the chest and I suck in a breath. He hasn't called me that since I heard it in the shower, and as he hastily yanks his gaze away now, I wonder if he's thinking the same thing.

Fuck, yes. Just like that, Buttercup.

A shiver runs through me as I replay his gravelly voice, and before I can talk myself out of it, I take a leap. "Cors?"

"Yeah?" He turns his back to me, refilling the cocktail straws.

"How many people do you call that?"

"Call what?"

The way he's being deliberately evasive feels like a solid point for the *interested in me* column, but I need to ask. I want to hear him say it, so I can't keep talking myself out of believing this.

"Buttercup. How many people do you call that?"

He's quiet for a moment, as if considering his answer, then finally says, "Only you."

My heart leaps, the air vanishing from my lungs. I knew it—he *was* thinking about me. He was thinking about me, *while he was touching himself.*

"Why?" Cory asks, keeping his back to me. "You don't... like it?"

Fuck, yes. Just like that, Buttercup.

Oh, God. A little whimper escapes my mouth and he spins around, eyebrows raised.

"Um, yeah," I choke out. "I do."

I watch his Adam's apple dip as he swallows. I can see his pulse hammering in his neck, and my fingers tingle with the urge to reach up and touch it.

He has to know what I'm thinking, surely. He has to know that I know.

His brow dips and he scrubs a hand over his beard, contemplating me. "Why are you asking?"

Speak up for yourself.

"Because I think—" I try to gulp in some air. *Do it. It's now or never. You have to know.* "I think I heard you say it when you were in the shower."

He stares at me for a beat, then huffs out a resigned breath. "Yeah. You did."

"Wow." My head spins as I process this. "So... you were imagining *me* when you were..."

He nods.

"Why?" And then, because I want to make certain I get the answer I need, I clarify, "Why were you thinking of me?"

"Why?" His dark eyes bore into mine. "Because I'm attracted to you."

"Really?"

He moves in close, hesitating before pressing the warmth of his palm against my cheek. "Yes."

Oh my God.

His touch sends goosebumps scattering over my skin, and even though I don't want to break the mood, I have to ask, "Why do you act like my big brother, then?"

He frowns. "What?"

"I always thought you saw me like a little sister—looking out for me all the time, trying to stop guys from checking me out at work. You won't even let me walk to the train station alone."

He strokes his thumb gently over my cheek. "I do those things because I *care* about you. I want you to be safe. But..." Fire ignites in his gaze as he slides his hand into my hair, his fingers tangling in the strands. "There is *nothing* brotherly about the way I want you, the things I imagine doing to you."

Oh. *Fuck*.

Heat floods through me. If I didn't believe him before, I do now. I'm shaking under his touch, my legs pressing together with need. The feel of his hand in my hair—both gentle and rough at the same time—is so good I could almost combust.

"I can't believe you didn't figure it out earlier," he mutters, his voice little more than a rough scrape. "The way I look at you, the way I've been acting... I'm dying here, Joze."

My bloodstream fills with static, buzzing and electric and holy shit, I can't believe he's saying this. "How long have you felt this way?"

He sighs and, as if coming to his senses, drops his hand and steps away. "It doesn't matter. I'm not going to—"

"How long, Cory?"

"A while," he admits with a grimace. "A few years."

"A few *years*? How many?"

He opens and closes his mouth, glancing at me then away, apparently having some kind of internal debate with himself.

"Please be honest," I whisper.

He brings his gaze back to mine, softening. "Since I hired you."

My jaw sags as I try to process this revelation, because...

oh my God. He's wanted me since he *hired* me? He's wanted me this *entire time*? I could cry for all the years that have passed where neither of us was brave enough to confess this.

"*Five years*? You've felt this way since you hired me and you haven't said anything?"

"I didn't want to make you uncomfortable. I love having you work here. I value you as a friend. I thought if you knew, you'd... want to leave." He shrugs, but his face, so deeply etched with worry, tells me he's anything but relaxed.

God, I want to kiss his brow and smooth those furrows away. I want to show him he's not the only one who's been fighting their feelings all this time.

"I'd never leave," I say, reaching inside for my courage. "Because I've wanted you the entire time, too."

15

CORY

"You've... what?"

She nods, stepping closer. There's a slight arch to her back as she looks up at me, and the nerve endings in my body are suddenly on high alert. The only problem is, I can't tell if they're screaming *DANGER* or *FINALLY.*

"For *five years* I've wanted you, Cory."

I stare at her in disbelief. How did I not know this? She's never *once* done anything to make me believe she feels this way.

It doesn't matter, because you'd never act on it. You're not going to act on it now.

She closes the distance between us. "Five years of wishing I could kiss you, fantasizing about you when I'm alone, imagining what it would be like to be with you."

I swallow hard, my heart beating wildly in my throat. She's so close, gazing up at me with those wide, beautiful eyes. She lifts a hand to my arm, slowly grazing my bicep, leaving a trail of fire in her wake. Heat spills through my bloodstream and my jeans grow tight. All she's done is touch my arm, and I'm so hard I can't think straight.

You can't act on this. You're not the guy to give her what she needs.

"Joze—" I begin, but my voice is shredded and I can't get the words out.

"Five years," she repeats, her own voice a husky purr. "And you've wanted me this whole time?"

I'm powerless to do anything other than nod. The stroke of her finger over my bicep is almost enough to make me pass out.

"So what happened in the shower yesterday..." She pauses, searching my face. Her pupils are blown out, the green in her eyes almost gone. "You've done that before? Thinking of me?"

I should lie. I should tell her that was the first—and will definitely be the *last*—time.

But I can't.

"Yes," I grate out.

Josie huffs a breath. She's restless, squeezing her legs together, shifting back and forth on the spot, and it takes me a second to figure out why.

She's turned on. She's so fucking turned on at the thought of me jerking off to her, that she can't stand still. I stifle a groan, fighting the urge to adjust the fly of my jeans.

Her gaze falls to my mouth. "Living with you has been a nightmare. Every time you're in the room I want you. It's bad enough at work, and now at home..." she trails off with a little whimper that goes straight through me. "It's killing me, Cors. I need you."

I lock my jaw, desperately grasping at my last reserves of self-restraint. I'm not going to act on this, I'm not—

"I've needed you for too long," she whispers. "I've spent

every night wishing you would throw me down on the bar and"—she pauses, biting her lip—"fuck me senseless."

Holy. Shit.

A hard breath shudders out of me. I've never heard her say anything like that. *Never.* The sound of such filthy words from her beautiful mouth severs the last thread of my self-control, and I take her face, slamming my mouth onto hers.

She stumbles at the sudden, unexpected contact, then her hands fist in my shirt and she melts against my body. Her soft, sweet mouth opens in invitation and I push my tongue inside, loving the vibration of her moan against me.

God, I am so weak. I am so selfish, taking this from her. I should not be kissing her.

I pull away, cursing myself. She could sue me for sexual harassment for God's sake. What am I thinking? "Shit, I'm sorry."

"I'm not." She yanks me back until our mouths collide again. The silken slide of her tongue over mine is the best damn thing I've ever felt, and my walls crash down in surrender.

I grab her hips, hoisting her up, and she winds her legs around my waist as I set her on the counter. Her hands move into my hair, tugging. It makes my hips pump forward, and she grinds back into me with a groan. The sound of her —the *feel* of her—sends lightning shooting through my veins.

I'm falling and I can't stop. I don't *want* to stop. I plunder her mouth, taking everything I can like the greedy asshole I am. I have never been as selfish with her as I am in this moment, letting my hands touch her back, graze the sides of her breasts, plunge into my hair to hold her head at just the right angle to take the assault of my tongue.

Still, I want more. I want her spread naked before me,

panting and lost in pleasure, but I need to know she wants it too.

"If you tell me to stop, I will," I rasp against the soft skin of her neck.

"Don't stop." She takes hold of my face and kisses me again, hard. It's a messy, desperate tangle of tongues and lips and teeth and I never want it to end.

My hand cups her breast, finding her nipple hard and waiting for me. When I brush my thumb over the peak, she quivers. I lean down and bite it through her shirt and she arches forward, nails digging into my shoulders.

"Yes," she breathes.

Her skirt has bunched up her legs and I can't stop my hand from moving to the bare skin of her thigh, stroking, squeezing. She's so soft, so perfect. In all my fantasies about her, I never imagined how amazing it would feel to touch her—how *lucky* I'd feel.

"Fuck, Cory." Her thighs squeeze against my hips as I move my hand up her silky skin. She hooks a finger through my belt loop, pulling me into the heat of her, and the throbbing below my belt becomes an ache. I have to stop myself from ripping my jeans down and plunging inside her.

But I can't do that. I won't let myself have that.

When my fingers reach the edge of her panties, I pause, knowing that once I cross this barrier I won't be coming back. My voice shakes as I beg her one final time, "Tell me to stop."

She grips my chin, tipping my face so I'm gazing directly into her eyes—so there's no mistaking what she wants. "Don't you dare stop."

I look at her, so perfect in this moment—glassy eyes, flushed cheeks, swollen lips—and finally give up the fight.

I slip a finger into her panties, watching her eyes roll

back. And when I feel the effect I've had on her—the wet, pulsing heat of her core—I turn feral. "Fuck," I growl, sweeping my fingers through her slickness. She spasms against my shoulder, her lips seeking mine. I slant my mouth across hers, lapping at her tongue as my fingers stroke her in slow circles. She makes broken, mewling sounds against my mouth, her body shaking with each circle I draw over her throbbing flesh. "You like that, Buttercup?"

"Yes," she moans, drawing back to look at me with hooded eyes. "And I *definitely* like when you call me that."

I give her a filthy grin, dipping down to kiss her neck, the hollow of her throat, that tiny heart-shaped freckle below her ear. She smells like cotton and fresh flowers and sex. It's intoxicating. I grip her panties and slide them down her legs, then pause, reminding myself to make sure she wants what I'm doing.

"This okay?" I ask, and she nods breathlessly. I slide a hand into her hair and cup her cheek, tilting her face up to mine. "I want to taste you, Josie." Her eyes are wide and I falter, but then I feel her hand brush the aching bulge in my pants and a moan slips out of me.

"Okay." She touches me again. "Then I want to taste *you*."

"Fuck," I rumble, dropping to my knees in front of her. I push her skirt to her hips, my mouth watering at the sight before me. I force myself to take a second to savor this moment—the perfection of her creamy-white thighs, spread open by my hands, her blushing pink center, waiting for me.

Then I do what I've been wanting to do for *five fucking years*—I lower my mouth onto the wet heat of her.

Christ, she tastes like heaven. Like honey. Like everything I could ever want.

I lick her again, loving the way she writhes under my tongue, the way her thighs squeeze against my hands.

"You taste so fucking sweet," I rasp, kissing her inner thigh. "My sweet little Buttercup."

She throws her head back and yelps with pleasure, and I smile, beginning my work in earnest. It doesn't take me long to figure out what she likes. Slow sweeps of my tongue. Sucking in just the right spot. Pushing two fingers inside her, right up to my knuckle, until she's bucking against my hand and my mouth.

"Yes, Cory. Fuck, yes."

I can feel her wetness on my chin and it makes me delirious. I've never felt something so good in my life. I could die right here and I'd be happy—tasting her, making her feel good.

I hook her legs over my shoulders and reach up to her breasts, pinching her nipples through her shirt. She pushes her hands into my hair and rocks her hips, riding my mouth. I fasten my gaze on hers, not wanting to miss the moment when I bring her to the peak of her pleasure. This orgasm will be as much for me as it is for her.

"Oh... yes..." Her body tenses, then shudders and spasms as she groans in release. Her thighs squeeze around my ears in a viselike grip, but I don't stop the pressure of my mouth until I know she's wrung every last drop of ecstasy from her body. When she finally goes slack, I rest my cheek against her inner thigh, feeling her body quake with aftershocks.

"Cors... oh my God."

I rise to my feet with a chuckle, wiping the back of my hand across my mouth. I'm not sure if I should kiss her after that, but she grabs my neck and pulls my lips onto hers. Then she rests her forehead against mine, gazing up at me.

"You're amazing," she murmurs. Her words twist sharply through me, forcing me to confront what I know deep down —that I'm not amazing, I'm just a greedy guy who can't keep his hands to himself.

Jesus. I really am my father.

I lean back, looking around the empty bar, feeling uneasy as the reality of what I've just done hits me. I went down on Josie—at *work*, of all places—because I have no fucking self control. What is wrong with me? She deserves so much better than this.

"I want to taste *you* now." Josie's hands stray to my belt and I step back, shaking my head.

"Not here," I mumble. Her brow dips and I wince. I'm such a jerk. I touch her cheek gently. "Let me take you home."

She hesitates, eying me, then nods. I hand her panties to her and she slides them awkwardly up her legs. I follow her to the door, flicking off the lights and pushing the bolt through once we've stepped outside.

After walking for a block, I hail a cab. Usually I'd be happy to walk home, but not tonight. I don't want extra time alone with her, alone with the knowledge of what I've done. What I can't undo.

She's quiet in the cab and I know she's wondering what I'm thinking. I don't have the words to tell her, and I should definitely *not* touch her, but I can't seem to stop myself from reaching across the backseat and taking her hand. She glances at me in surprise and I swallow, looking away.

When we get to my building, we enter the apartment wordlessly. I kick off my boots, watching her greet Pretzel and let him out into the courtyard. She turns around, as if she wants to say something, then seems to think better of it.

Guilt crawls over me as she shrinks under my gaze. I

stride across and pull her into my arms, pressing a kiss to her hair. "I'm sorry," I whisper, and she softens against me. "What happened at the bar..."

"Do you regret it?"

"No. No way. But..." I don't know what to say. I don't know how to explain that it can't happen again, but that I also don't want to stop holding her like this. "Can we talk about it tomorrow? I need to sort out my thoughts."

She gazes up at me for a long moment, trying to read my face, then steps away with a deep sigh. "Yeah. Okay."

I fight the urge to tug her back into my arms as she shuffles off to the bathroom. My feet itch to follow after her, but I force myself to walk into my bedroom and close the door.

I yank the comforter down with shaky hands, tug my shirt and jeans off, and fall into bed. Then I lie in the dark, wondering what the hell I've just done.

JOSIE IS STILL ASLEEP when I rise early the next morning. I lean against my door frame, watching her, feeling my chest ache. She's so beautiful with the morning sun filtering in through the blinds. It makes her skin glow, makes me want to crawl into that bed with her and finish what we started last night.

But I know I can't do that.

I glance at the French press she brought from her place, wondering if I'll be able to make coffee without waking her. I hardly slept at all, replaying the events of last night, and with every passing moment the guilt I felt grew exponentially. Guilt about acting on something I swore I'd never do. Guilt about doing something with her I have no intention of repeating. Guilt about taking her on the counter at work like a fucking animal.

It didn't matter that I was hard all night, thinking about her sweet thighs around my head—I didn't let myself have the release I didn't deserve. Part of me wonders if maybe I should have just fucked her and gotten it out of my system, but even I know I'm not that much of a scumbag. I also know it probably would have had the opposite effect.

Pretzel's head pops up, spotting me, and he bounds off the bed.

"Hey," I murmur, crouching down to pet him. He nuzzles into my hand and I stroke his soft ears. I hate to admit that I'm growing attached to having this little dog here. Josie too. It's going to hurt when they leave in a couple of weeks.

I open the courtyard door for Pretzel, and when I turn back, Josie is sitting up in bed, looking at me uncertainly.

"Sorry, I was trying not to wake you." I glance at the kitchen. "Do you want coffee?"

"Sure," she says with a tentative smile. It hits me in the solar plexus and I glance away, going to the counter.

"Why don't you, uh..." I gesture to the bathroom, indicating for her to get dressed. I can't have this conversation while she's still in bed. "The coffee will be a few minutes."

She nods, pulling the covers off. I focus on filling the French press and when I hear the shower turn on, I breathe out. I hate that I need to have this conversation—with Josie, of all people—but I do.

Ten minutes later she emerges from the bathroom, dressed and smelling like some kind of flower that I just want to bury my face in. I don't know what that scent is, but it's so her—so fresh and pretty and sweet.

I pour the coffee and we settle on the sofa. Pretzel climbs onto the cushions and curls up beside Josie with his head on her knee. She strokes his tawny fur absently and, fuck, I just want the ground to swallow me whole. I'm not used to having tough conversations with women the morning after; my entire sex life is built around avoiding exactly that.

But Josie isn't just some woman I met at the bar. She's my employee and my friend. I need to tread super carefully if I have any chance of salvaging this.

I take a deep breath. "So, about last night."

"You regret it," she states simply, holding her mug. "I know you said you didn't, but it's pretty obvious you do."

"No. It shouldn't have happened, but I don't regret it." God, I'll be dining out on the memory of last night for the rest of my life—as soon as I can get over how shit I feel about it.

She frowns. "That's... confusing. You don't think it should have happened, but you don't regret it?"

I nod, blowing on my coffee. No wonder she's confused. "I meant everything I said, everything I *did*, but it can't happen again."

She nods and remains quiet, and even though she hasn't asked, I feel the urge to explain.

"I'm your boss, and... you're a lot younger than me."

There, that's it. I've given her two good reasons why I need to keep my distance: there's a power imbalance because she works for me, and she's too young. Maybe she isn't *that* young, but I can't let myself admit that. Because if I do, I'll be forced to confront the fact that it's not so much about her age and my position as her employer, as it is about a deeper, more complicated reason I can't clearly articulate.

"You don't want me, Joze." Fresh guilt twists through me as I think about my actions last night. "You don't want the kind of guy who feels up his employee on the bar. You deserve better than that."

"What?" she says, looking shocked. "You didn't *feel me up* —I was an active participant. I wanted everything you did. And you were actually pretty selfless. Everything you did was about making *me* feel good. You wouldn't even let me return the favor. And as for sex—"

"It wasn't selfless," I say bluntly, needing her to know. "Everything I did was for me. It was because I wanted you, but I shouldn't have taken that. I won't be selfish with you. It's not right."

She rubs her forehead. "I don't understand. So you *do* want me?"

"Don't ask me that," I mutter.

"You're the one who told me to speak up for myself, Cory. I think I have a right to know."

I look at her from under low brows. "Yes, I want you." *I want every single part of you.* "But I'm not going to act on this again. We can't sleep together. We just... can't."

"So, let me get this straight: you *want* to sleep with me, but you're going to pretend you don't?"

I stare down at my coffee, going cold in my hands. "Yeah. Please trust me when I say that I'm staying away from you for your own good."

She scoffs. "*For my own good*? Now you really *do* sound like my big brother."

I grimace. "I'm trying to look out for you." I sigh, looking away. "I'm sorry. About everything. I know I'm an asshole. This is exactly why we can't do this." I set my coffee down and push to my feet. "I'll take the dog for a walk, give you some space." I whistle, and Pretzel leaps off the sofa, his tail wagging frantically when I reach for his leash.

As I leave the apartment, I realize the ache in my chest has only gotten worse.

16

JOSIE

I close the door to Game of Scones, looking for Harriet. She's at the back, stacking some board games, and glances up as I enter.

"Hey, Joze!" Her gaze slides to my feet, then back up. "You didn't bring Pretzel?"

I shake my head, slumping into the nearest free chair. Harriet's brow creases and she wordlessly goes behind the counter to the coffee machine. A few minutes later she drops into the seat opposite me, sliding a soy latte and brownie across the table.

"What's going on?" she asks gently.

I stare at the table, not sure where to begin. "Cory kissed me last night." Well, he did a lot more than kiss me, but one thing at a time.

Harriet emits a little squeal, which is quickly cut short when she catches my expression. "Oh, no. Tell me why that's bad."

"It's not. It wasn't. He told me he's liked me since he hired me—which is basically the entire time I've liked him. Then he kissed me, and…"

I let myself replay the way he took my face and melded his mouth to mine as if it was the last kiss he'd ever have. My eyes flutter closed as I remember the way his hands felt on my skin, the way his lips tasted, the way his mouth felt as he dropped to his knees and spread my legs.

My sweet little Buttercup.

God, the way his tongue moved over me, like a man falling upon an oasis in a desert. The sounds he made, the way he made light shatter and refract behind my eyelids as he brought me the most intense, divine pleasure I've ever felt.

And I never got to give that back to him. How on earth can he think he's selfish?

Harriet clears her throat and my eyes fly open. Heat slaps my cheeks. "Sorry," I mumble.

"Tell me what happened," she says, wide-eyed.

"He kissed me, then he"—I drop my voice—"*went down on me*, after we closed up at work last night." I cringe at that last detail. I can see why he wouldn't be happy about that part. "Then he kind of freaked out and we went home and went to bed. Separately."

"What do you mean, he freaked out?"

I cast my mind back and sigh. "He was... he was amazing. The way he kissed me, the way he was with me... like he saw me as a *woman*, if that makes sense."

Harriet nods. "I remember you saying it sometimes felt like he saw you as a little sister."

"Yeah. But when he was kissing me, and touching me, all of that was gone. Then..." I recount his words from this morning, trying to understand them as I explain them to Harriet.

He's my boss and I'm too young.

He wants me, but he won't let himself have me.

He shouldn't have "felt me up" on the bar, because that was "selfish."

That's what bothers me the most, I think. The way he talked about what happened between us... he took away all my power. He made it seem like something he did *to* me, like I wasn't an equal part of it. It's like in the cold light of day, he suddenly realized I'm *not* a woman after all, and that made me feel small.

It's for your own good.

I mean, what the fuck is that? Clearly, he doesn't view me as a woman with my own agency—a woman who can be trusted to make her own decisions—if he feels the need to protect me like that. It's infuriating.

But why am I surprised? He's been like this since the day he hired me.

I mean, yes—I am younger than him. And I guess I haven't dated a lot in the time he's known me. I've basically been celibate since things ended with Paul. Cory probably views me as inexperienced—which compared to him, I most certainly am—and that's why he feels... what, like he took advantage of me? But I'm twenty-seven, for Christ's sake, not seventeen. Why does he feel the need to protect me so much?

"Maybe," Harriet says, interrupting my thoughts, "you need to show him you're not young and innocent, like he seems to think you are. You want him to think you're a woman who knows her own body and mind? Show him."

I lift my eyebrows. I very much like the idea of showing him that, but I'm not sure how. I think back to last night, to the thing that made him snap—me telling him I wanted him to fuck me senseless. At that moment he saw me as a woman, and I want him to see me like that again.

My phone buzzes in my pocket and I whip it out, hoping

it's Cory, but it's Gerard from the shelter. "Sorry," I say to Harriet. "Is it okay if I take this?"

She nods and rises from the table. I wouldn't normally take a call during a conversation, but I haven't spoken to Gerard for a while. I get a nervous twinge in my middle as I answer. If he tells me the shelter is ready and I have to return Pretzel now, I'm not sure I'll cope.

"Hey, Josie. How are you? How's Pretzel?"

"Pretzel is wonderful," I say, unable to stop a little smile from forming on my lips. All the shit with Cory aside, Pretzel seems to be really happy and settled at Cory's place. He's loving our morning walks—even though Cory took him before I had the chance today—and he's always happy to see us after work.

"That's great. Listen, I have some bad news about the shelter."

My stomach tilts. "What is it?"

"We've hit a bit of a snag with our funding. The repairs are coming along well, but we've just found out that in order to pass compliance we have to pay a fine backdated from ten years ago."

"A fine?"

"Yeah. Apparently, the shelter was in violation of some code or something for years. No one seemed to know anything about it—must have been something the previous manager let slip."

"Shit," I mutter.

"Yeah," Gerard agrees. "It's seventeen thousand dollars, and until we pay that, the shelter can't open. And if we can't find the cash, then..."

"Then what?"

He sighs. "Then we'll have to close for good."

My chest hollows out and I drop my head into my hands,

fighting the sudden rush of tears to my eyes. Here I was hoping to one day work full time at the shelter, and instead it might have to close for good. "Is there anything else we can do?" I ask desperately.

"We'll have to apply for extra funding, but that could take months."

"What if we could somehow come up with the money?"

"Sure, but I don't see how—" His voice is muffled as he talks to someone in the background, then he returns to the phone. "Sorry, Josie, I have to go. I just wanted you to know. I'll keep you posted, okay?"

"Yeah. Okay."

"I'm assuming you can continue to look after Pretzel while we figure this out?"

"Yes," I say, without hesitation. My life feels like it's been flipped upside down lately—especially after last night—and I can't let go of Pretzel just yet. As I end the call with Gerard, it occurs to me for the first time that maybe I need Pretzel more than he needs me.

"Everything okay?" Harriet asks, wiping off a table nearby.

"No." I look down at my coffee and brownie, untouched on the table. "The shelter might close for good unless they can find the funds to pay for some kind of code violation, or something."

"Oh. Shit." Harriet slides into the chair opposite me again. "Is it a lot?"

"Seventeen thousand."

"Oof." She rests her chin on her palm, her brow creased in thought. Then she bolts upright, her face alight. "What if we have a fundraiser? We could do it here one night. Charge people to come and play games, Paula could sell her dog treats, and we could have a dress-up theme and prizes."

I gaze at her in surprise. "I could never ask you to do that, Harri."

"You're not asking; I'm offering. We'd love to help."

I rub my temples, overwhelmed. "I don't know," I mumble. But I know one thing—I can't lose the shelter.

17

JOSIE

I'm soaked to the bone by the time I get home. What started as a light drizzle when I left Game of Scones became a torrential downpour as I reached our street. I squelch through the front door, nervous about seeing Cory again—especially because I now have to ask if Pretzel and I can stay here longer—but his boots are gone and there's no sign of Pretzel.

Shit, are they still outside? In *that*?

I kick off my wet shoes and pad to the bathroom, peeling off my clothes and hanging them over the shower rail. I dry and wrap myself in a towel, heading into the living room, where I pull on a tank top and denim cutoffs. I start a batch of chili in the slow cooker, glancing out the window at the rain, which only seems to be getting worse. I keep thinking about the shelter, and what will happen to Pretzel if it has to close for good. Then I wonder if Pretzel and Cory are okay. It's been a couple of hours since they left, and—

The front door crashes open and I startle, turning to see Cory and Pretzel tumble in, noisy and soaking wet and... covered in mud.

"No, Pretzel. Stop. I need to clean you up." Cory holds Pretzel's collar, attempting to restrain him, but the dog won't cooperate. He's bouncing and trying to throw himself onto the floor. I've seen dogs do this a hundred times at the shelter when they're wet—they love to roll around to help them dry off. It doesn't help that Pretzel's whole left side is coated in mud. And Cory...

I run my eyes over him, suppressing a laugh. There's mud everywhere—the side of his jeans, spattered up the front of his damp T-shirt, caked in his hair. It's also smeared across his face, along with a thunderous expression.

Crap, I should help.

I bolt across the room, trying to contain Pretzel's wriggling body. "What happened to you guys?"

"We cut across Seward Park to come home when the rain started, and this guy"—he glowers at Pretzel —"seemed to think it would be hilarious to roll in a puddle and cover himself in mud. I tried to pull him out, then I slipped—"

Cory's words come to an abrupt halt when he hears a giggle squeak out of me. I know I shouldn't be laughing, but there's something so funny about a grown man looking pissed off while he's got mud in his beard.

"It's not funny, Josie. And *you*—" Cory scowls down at Pretzel, who yelps and scampers behind my legs. When I frown at Cory, he sighs, softening, and crouches down to Pretzel's level. "I'm sorry, buddy. You're just doing what dogs do. It's not your fault." He rubs at his forehead as he straightens up again. "This morning has been shit."

I know I'm an asshole.

I think of his words from right before he left, and compassion tugs at me. I've been so wrapped up in my own feelings this morning, but as I look at his exhausted, miserable face, it occurs to me that he's struggled with this as much as I have.

He toes off his boots, then finally lets his gaze meet mine. "Do you still hate me?"

"I never hated you, Cors." Even though I probably shouldn't, I put my hand on his arm, needing him to know. "And for the record, you're not an asshole." I watch his jaw work while he stares at me, breathing hard. When the moment becomes too much to bear, I force my gaze down to Pretzel. "I need to give him a bath. Can I do that in your tub? Otherwise—"

"Yeah. I'll help."

He scoops Pretzel up in his arms, and I follow them through to the bathroom. My damp clothing is still hanging on the shower curtain rail, including my bra and underwear, and I sweep them out of the way, mumbling, "Sorry." Then I quickly fill the tub with warm water while Cory tries to contain Pretzel. "Do you have any old towels?"

"Hall closet," Cory says, lifting Pretzel into the tub. I step out of the room as I hear him say, "Alright, buddy. Let's clean you up."

I grab a bunch of towels from the linen closet and I'm just heading back to the bathroom when I hear an almighty splash. I round the corner to find Cory's top half leaning over into the tub and Pretzel out on the bathroom floor, dripping wet and still muddy. "What the—"

"Pretzel!" Cory bellows, yanking himself up out of the water. His shirt is completely drenched and he grabs the hem, pulling it off over his head.

Oh. Fuck *me*.

I want to smack him for doing something so carelessly sexy right now, but I'm too busy ogling his torso. Solid pecs, with a dusting of dark blond hair that trails down over his trim stomach, disappearing below the waistband of his jeans. And here's something I didn't know—he has a tattoo: three stars in outline, each about an inch and a half wide, on the left side of his ribcage. It's simple, surprising, and unbelievably sexy.

Thankfully I'm distracted from the spectacle of Cory's body by Pretzel, who chooses that exact moment to shake off, showering us in water and mud.

Shit.

"Pretzel, no!" I cry, but it's way too late.

Cory straightens to his full height, lunges at the dog and hoists him back into the tub. "You are not coming out again until you're clean," he says firmly. Pretzel makes another dive for the edge, splashing Cory in the face, and I have to bite back a laugh. His gaze swings to me as he wipes a hand across his eyes. "Is something funny?"

"Nope." I turn to hide my smile and reach for my shampoo to use on Pretzel. It's a sensitive, soap-free formula that will be fine for him. "Here. Use this."

Cory grabs the bottle and removes one hand from Pretzel, who takes that as a sign to attempt another escape, charging at the side of the tub and sending a wall of water onto Cory's jeans.

"For God's sake!" Cory cries, glaring at Pretzel. "I couldn't get you *out* of the damn water at the park and now you don't want to be here?"

A laugh rises in my throat and I try to disguise it as a cough, helping to hold Pretzel back. Cory's eyes narrow at me as he pops the top off the bottle with his teeth and kneels beside the tub.

"You'd better not be laughing, Buttercup, or there will be trouble." His attention turns back to Pretzel as he pours half the bottle of my shampoo across his back. I should probably point out how expensive that stuff is, but I'm a little distracted by the fact that he called me Buttercup, especially after last night. He must realize the same thing, because he focuses intently on washing Pretzel in silence for a few minutes.

It's all going well until Cory tries to wash the shampoo out of Pretzel's fur. He has one of those shower heads that can be taken off the wall, and the pressure is surprisingly strong—I know because I've, um, *used it*, if you know what I mean—and when Cory turns the shower on at full pressure, Pretzel tries to launch himself out of the tub again. It knocks the hose out of Cory's hand, sending it dancing around the room, spraying water everywhere.

"Shit!"

Cory springs to his feet, scrabbling to catch the shower hose while Pretzel thrashes in the tub. I hold him down while Cory grapples with the hose, laughter quaking through me. My stomach muscles ache from holding in my mirth as I watch Cory flail wildly.

He finally grabs hold of the shower head and I turn away as he hoses Pretzel off, my shoulders shaking. He just looks so *mad* that he's been bested by a little dog in his own bathroom.

When the shampoo is finally washed out of Pretzel's fur, Cory drains the tub. He lifts Pretzel out and bundles him up in a towel, patting him dry as best he can. He's still frowning at the dog who defeated him, and as he lets a clean Pretzel out into the hallway, he blows out a breath, turning back to find me giggling.

His eyebrows rise. "You think that was funny?" He narrows his eyes, but I can see a tiny smile flickering at the corner of his mouth. "You're going to pay for that." He snatches up the shower hose, turning it on and aiming my way. I shriek, ducking just in time so it hits the tiled wall behind me. "Not so fast!" he says, aiming for me again. I leap out of the way, giggling as I stumble backward into the empty tub, and I realize he's got me cornered.

"Don't shoot!" I cry, raising my arms over my face, and Cory laughs.

"You're not getting off that easy, laughing at my misery. You have to pay."

And then I feel the warm water spray right across my chest. I yelp in surprise, waiting for him to aim it at my face, but the water shuts off and the shower hose drops into the tub beside me. I lower my arms to find Cory staring at me, breathing heavily.

That's when I remember I'm not wearing a bra. The only clean bra I have was hanging up to dry, and all I threw on was a white tank top when I came in earlier.

I watch Cory's eyes roam shamelessly over my breasts. I'm sure he can see them through my shirt, and I'm not even a little bit sorry. I let my gaze traverse his beautiful body— the solid muscle, that freaking hot tattoo, the bulge that's grown below his belt buckle—and I realize that maybe this is my opportunity to do what Harriet suggested; to show him that I'm not some young, vulnerable little girl who needs protecting. I'm a woman who knows her body—who knows what she wants and isn't afraid to ask for it.

I take a faltering breath, channeling my inner sex goddess, and fix my gaze directly on Cory's. "You made me wet," I say, intentionally imbuing my words with innuendo.

His eyes flare, his bare chest heaving with his rapid breathing. I wait for him to leave or tell me to stop, but he doesn't. It emboldens me more.

"You took your shirt off, so it's only fair…" I grab the hem of my tank and pull it up over my head, tossing the soggy fabric onto the floor. My nipples harden as his hungry gaze drops to my chest, and it spurs me on. "In fact, I'm wet all over." With trembling hands, I slide my shorts and panties down my legs and kick them off. Then I straighten up, completely naked, and challenge him with my gaze.

What's he going to do? Will he walk out, or will he join me?

I replace the shower hose on the wall and flick the water on, dropping my head back under the spray, arching my back as I lift my hands to run them through my hair. My heart is pummeling my ribs. I've never done something so daring in my life, and I'm not sure how this is going to pan out.

Cory is silent, and when I dare to glance at him, his hazel eyes are darker than I've ever seen them. "I need to clean the mud off me," he grits out, a muscle ticking in his jaw. "Will you get out of the shower?"

If this was work, I'd do what he asks. He is my boss, after all. But he's been pretty clear that those rules don't apply at home.

I bite my lip, shaking my head at him, and reach for the soap.

He stares at me for a long moment, nostrils flaring and brow furrowed as I soap up my body, then finally mutters, "Fine."

Disappointment burrows through my stomach, because I think he's going to turn and leave. Instead, I watch in disbelief as he reaches down and unbuckles his belt. The clink of metal against leather is the most obscene sound I've ever heard, and my breathing quickens when he unzips his fly.

Is this really happening?

Yes. Holy crap.

His jeans and underwear land on the floor and he steps out of them, one hand on his crotch. But let me tell you, one hand is nowhere near enough to hide what he's got there.

I rinse the soap from my body, watching as he hesitates and knowing how badly I don't want him to change his mind. "Go on then." I take a seat at the end of the tub and gesture to the water. "Clean up."

God, I'd *never* talk to him like this at work. But the fact that he obediently steps under the spray makes me wonder if he likes the role reversal.

He turns his back to me, dipping his head under the water to scrub the mud off his face and hair. Then he turns around and slowly soaps up his torso, keeping his gaze locked on mine, just as I did to him. I can't stop my eyes from straying to the massive erection jutting from his pelvis, and almost reflexively, my legs fall open. Maybe it's because I'm used to sitting in this very spot, taking care of myself.

Only this time, I'm not alone.

Cory's gaze drops between my thighs, and the pure want on his face makes heat swarm through my veins. I think of how he used his mouth on me last night, and while I'd love for him to do that again, I want to give *him* something this time.

I let my hand drift between my legs. He puffs out a hard breath as I swipe a finger through my slickness, so I do it again.

"I owe you a show," I say, moving my fingers in slow circles. "I got to see you in the shower. Now it's your turn."

Christ, what am I doing? I've never done anything like this and yet I can't seem to stop.

Cory's jaw goes slack as he watches me touch myself. Every stroke of my fingers sends pleasure coursing through me, and knowing Cory is watching makes it so much more intense. When I dip two fingers inside myself his length twitches, and I can't help but let out a whimper.

"You told me what you were thinking about in the shower," I say breathlessly. "Do you want to know what I think about when I'm alone in here?"

Cory swallows, his eyes half-lidded. He gives a tiny nod.

"You," I whisper. "Always you."

He presses his eyes closed like he's in pain, and I expect him to take hold of himself and join me, but his hands tighten into fists at his side.

"Watch me," I say, when he doesn't open his eyes again. He brings his gaze back to me, jaw clenched hard. I'm panting now, working my fingers over my most sensitive spot, keeping my eyes pinned to his. Heat builds below my navel and my lips part on a moan. When Cory lets out a low growl, I tip over the edge. Pleasure washes through me, shaking my core, and I hold Cory's gaze as long as I can, until my eyes close in surrender.

I expect him to be gone when I open them, but he's still there staring at me, like he can't believe what just happened.

My gaze moves to where he refuses to touch himself. He's so hard it looks painful. "Are you going to do something about that?"

His jaw is like granite, hands still in tight fists, and he shakes his head. It's like he's forgotten how to speak. Either that or he doesn't trust himself to do so.

"That's okay." I take a deep breath. "I owe you something else, too, after last night." I fall to my knees in the tub and wrap my fist around him.

God. He's so hard, so *big*. So perfect.

I expect him to push me away, but he doesn't. He just stares down at me as I stroke his length, throbbing in my hand. I hear his breath hiss out through his teeth, one hand moving to the tiled wall, the other taking hold of the shower curtain rail. He still won't touch me.

I waver, wondering if I should stop. He did say we wouldn't sleep together, and while technically this isn't sex, I don't want him to feel forced into anything.

I think of what he said to me last night and decide to give him an out. "If you want me to stop, I will." I look up at him, the water from the shower flowing over his shoulders and chest. His hooded eyes watch me touch him, but he doesn't respond.

I hesitate, then lean forward, giving a long, slow lick over the tip of him. His knees buckle and he steadies himself on the shower rail. I run a hand up his muscular leg. His thighs are so solid, so strong. I can't help it—I bite the muscle gently, and it flexes under my mouth. Then I move back to the hard heat of him and lick again, loving the way his salty taste hits my tongue, loving the way it sounds like he can barely breathe right now.

I glance up at him, needing to know he's okay with this. "I'll stop if you want me to, Cory."

He closes his eyes and drops his head back, and I'm so afraid he's going to ask me to leave. But he looks down at me again, making a low, gravelly sound in his throat. Then he says the first thing he's said to me since he climbed into the shower.

"Don't you dare stop."

18

CORY

When Josie takes me into her mouth I nearly pass out. The number of times I've jerked off in here, imagining her in this exact position...

I don't care that I swore I wouldn't do this with her again. Right now, all I care about is the wet slide of her tongue, the heat of her mouth, the way she's moaning like she's enjoying this more than I am.

Not fucking possible.

When she started touching herself, Jesus Christ, I nearly picked her up, slammed her against the wall, and buried myself inside her. I figured if I just didn't move, if I didn't say anything, maybe I'd be okay. I was wrong.

I've never been so glad to be wrong.

Heat swirls through my abdomen as I watch her work me. My limbs are tense, trying to stay in control. I feel like I could explode inside her mouth at any second.

"Fuck, that feels good, Joze."

"Call me Buttercup," she whispers, looking up at me with round, green eyes. She looks so sweet down there and it makes me hesitate.

"Are you sure?"

"Call me Buttercup," she repeats, jerking me with her hand a few times before stopping and giving me a sly look. "Or I'll stop."

Holy shit. I don't know who this filthy little thing is staring up at me, but I'm hooked. She's never been quite so bossy and demanding before. It's turning me on like nothing else.

"Okay." I caress her cheek, then slide my hand into her hair, nudging her closer. I need her mouth on me again. "Suck me, Buttercup."

Her lips curl into a dirty grin and she takes me back into her mouth. She wraps her fingers around the base of me at the same time, and I tighten my hand in her hair, thrusting my hips forward without thinking.

"Shit, sorry," I grit out, releasing my hand.

"Don't be." She gives me a long, hard suck, and I see stars. "I like it."

"Yeah?"

"Mm," she manages, her head bobbing as she moves back and forth on me. She's so much dirtier than I expected and I love it.

I tighten my hand in her hair again and push myself deeper into her mouth, testing. Her eyes fall closed on a groan and she adjusts her mouth to accommodate more of my length.

Fucking hell. She's going to be the death of me.

"Yes," I rasp. "Like that, Buttercup. Just like that."

Using that name spurs her on, and she moans and increases her pace. Watching this woman on her knees, getting off on getting me off, pushes me to my limit. Heat rushes up my legs and I try to pull away.

"I'm going to—"

She grabs my ass and pulls me all the way into her mouth, holding me there. And I can't do anything but give in to her, pressing my eyes closed and riding the waves of pleasure as I spill onto her tongue.

"Oh, God." I lean one arm against the shower wall, catching my breath. My body is shaking, my legs weak.

Josie pushes to her feet in front of me, wiping her hand across her mouth.

"That was fucking amazing," I murmur, touching her cheek.

Her lips tip into an indulgent smile. "Well, after what you gave me last night, you deserve it."

You deserve it.

Her words pierce through my blissed-out state, dousing me in shame, and I drop my hand from her face.

I don't deserve anything. I certainly don't deserve her.

Shit.

I try to take a step back, but collide with the shower wall. What was I thinking, getting in here with her?

I wasn't thinking. I was hard as fuck, looking at her naked body. I was high from laughing with her about washing Pretzel. I was so relieved she didn't hate me after this morning. I was just desperate to be near her again.

None of that makes this okay.

"Don't say that," I mutter, turning around to rinse off under the still-running shower. Then I step out and wrap myself in a towel, not looking at her. I can feel her gaze on me as she shuts off the shower and climbs out of the tub, but I glance around the bathroom, taking in the mess left from Pretzel's bath.

Dammit, I forgot about this. As soon as Josie's clothes came off, nothing else in the world existed.

"I'll clean this up," she murmurs. Her quiet voice tells

me how disappointed she is by me pulling away again, and I curse myself.

"No, you won't." I grab some towels and begin mopping up the water on the floor.

"It's fine," she says, collecting our wet clothes and dumping them in the tub, avoiding my gaze. "You can go."

She was wrong, earlier. I *am* an asshole. I'm the biggest asshole on the planet. Why do I keep letting myself give in to her? She's so much better than this—me losing control with her on the bar, in the shower.

"I'm not going anywhere."

We work in tense silence, cleaning up most of the water, then we both leave the bathroom to get dressed. When I come out of my room, Josie is in the kitchen stirring something in the slow cooker. I sink down onto the sofa, petting Pretzel, hating myself more than I ever have.

"Do you want some chili later?" she asks, as if nothing has happened. While I'd normally jump at the chance for more of her chili, I'm itching to clear the air with her. I can't just pretend I'm okay after that, because I'm not.

I'm not okay at all.

"Joze—"

"It's not ready yet, but after our shift tonight—"

"Josie." I press the pads of my fingers to my eyes. "Please come here."

She sighs, setting the wooden spoon down. But she keeps her back to me, standing at the counter. "What is it?"

The irritated tone of her voice makes my mouth pop open in surprise. She's never spoken to me like that before. "Are you okay?"

"What do you think?" She spins around and stalks over, frowning. "You just fucking *came* in my mouth, then you"—she waves her hands in the air vaguely—"I don't even know what happened. This is what you did last time. You want this, I know you do, and you let yourself give into that, but then you just... shut down. I don't know why."

"Why? Because it shouldn't happen. It shouldn't have happened at the bar, and it shouldn't have happened just now."

She rubs her forehead, dropping down onto the sofa beside me. "But *why*, Cors? If we both want this, why can't we have it?" She holds up a hand before I can answer. "And don't patronize me with more of that 'it's for your own good' bullshit. I'm a grown woman who can make her own damn decisions, and I'm tired of being treated like a child."

I stare at her in disbelief. I don't know what I'm more shocked by—her words, or the way she's standing up for herself. "I..." I shake my head, wiping a hand down my face. "Fuck. I don't mean to treat you like a child. I'm sorry if that's how it came across."

"Yeah, that is how it came across. I know I'm younger than you, but you're acting like I'm a teenager or something. I'm in my freaking late twenties."

"I know."

"Then what is it?"

I furrow my brow, trying to put my tangled thoughts into words. It's not really about her age, I guess I know that on some level. She *isn't* that young—but she *seems* young, because of how sweet she is, how good she is.

Like Alice.

The thought comes out of nowhere: Alice, the girl next door to me, growing up. Josie is so similar to her—same dark hair, same wide smile, same big heart. Alice trusted me with her heart, and I did nothing but hurt her. I feel that same sense of shame as I think of what I did, all those years ago, and finally let myself acknowledge the real reason I've been keeping Josie at arm's length this whole time. It's not about being her boss, about being older than her—it's about wanting to protect her.

From myself.

"It's not about you. It's... I don't want to hurt you."

She shrugs, refusing to accept that answer. "Then don't."

I try to brush her off. "Come on. You know what I'm like, sleeping around—"

"Seriously?"

"I don't do commitment."

"I'm not asking for commitment. I'm asking to explore what we feel and see where it goes. I know you care about me."

"Of course I care about you!" I snap. "That's why I don't want to do this!"

She jerks back, shocked at my tone.

"Shit. Josie, I'm sorry." I reach for her hand, but she pulls it away.

"I just don't understand why you'll sleep with basically *any* woman in Manhattan except me."

"What?" I say, disgusted. "I'm not going to treat you like a one night stand. You deserve better than that."

"So it's okay for you to have sex with random women from work, but not with someone you actually have a connection with?"

"The connection *is* the problem. Don't you see that?" I wait for her to understand, but she looks hurt, and my chest cracks open. "Please," I beg hoarsely. "I care about you more than..." Shit, how did I not realize this until now? "I care about you more than I've cared about anyone. And I can't... I won't..."

She shakes her head sadly, pushing to her feet. "I thought you were better than this."

I watch her grab her keys and storm out the door, swallowing against the lump in my throat.

Because that's the thing; I'm not better than this. The girl who lived next door all those years ago knows that better than anyone.

19

JOSIE

I slam the glass down, lifting the soda gun and filling it to the top. Then I slide the drink across the bar and it sloshes over the sides. "Sorry," I mutter, mopping the spill with a napkin. The customer takes it with a frown and I take their cash, unsurprised there's no tip.

I shouldn't be taking my bad mood out on customers, but ever since I walked out of Cory's place this afternoon I've been so *angry*. I'm angry with Cory for being so damn pigheaded about everything. I'm angry about his ridiculous logic that we can't get together *because* we care about each other.

What the fuck?

And I'm angry because I know he's better than this. He is. All that shit he was trying to feed me about sleeping around and not being able to commit to women, his excuse that he'll only hurt me—as if it's inevitable, as if he has no control over his behavior... I'm not buying any of it. I don't believe that he's refusing to take responsibility for his actions, for himself as a man, because that's not who he is. There's so much more depth and complexity to him than he's letting on. He's not the shallow, shitty guy he's making himself out to be, and that pisses me off—that he's trying to pull that shit with me. That he thinks I'm going to buy that.

I know he feels what I feel. When he lets his guard down with me, I see it. Hell, when I really stop to think about it, I can see how much he's cared for me this whole time. I see that he wants this as much as I do, but he's refusing to admit it. And that's frustrating as hell.

I blow out a long breath, wiping the bar clean. I'm working with Camila and Levi tonight, which is a nice change from Eddy. Cory's spent most of the night "doing paperwork" in the back room, which is fine by me, because I don't want to look at him. I'm trying not to think about what it will be like when I go home tonight.

"Hey."

I glance up to see Cat and Myles slide onto bar stools in front of me. "Oh, hey." I fight the urge to ask Cat why her brother is so damn useless, and reach for their usual drinks. "How are you guys? I haven't seen you in here for a while."

"We went on a little honeymoon," Cat says, exchanging a grin with Myles. "To Montauk."

"Wow." I hand their drinks over. "Where's your tan?"

Myles bites back a smile. "We didn't spend much time outside of the bedroom."

"Gross." Cory appears beside me out of nowhere. "I don't want to hear that."

I stiffen, glancing away from him. "Well, at least you had fun," I mumble to the others.

Cory sighs. "It's good to see you guys again."

Cat watches me wiping vigorously at a spot on the bar with my back to Cory, and narrows her eyes. "Okay, what's going on here?"

"What?" I hear Cory ask.

She gestures between the two of us. "I'm picking up some strange vibes. Spill."

Heat creeps up my neck and I look away.

"It's nothing," Cory mutters, turning for the back room again. "I have work to do." He heads through the door, pulling it closed forcefully, and I breathe out.

"That was weird," Myles says, and Cat nods.

Her gaze swings to me. "What's going on? Did something happen with you guys?"

Suck me, Buttercup... Just like that.

His rough words from the shower come back to me and my cheeks warm. I bite my lip, trying to push away the image of him towering over me, his hand in my hair, the taste of him on my tongue.

Did something happen? Uh, yeah.

"No," I say, focusing on refilling the cocktail straws.

"I don't believe you at all." She chuckles as she pushes to her feet. "But I have to go to the bathroom, so you're off the hook. For now."

I watch her push through the crowd, her pretty floral dress floating around her as she goes. When I glance back at Myles, his eyes are shimmering with mirth.

"You okay?"

"I..." I exhale slowly. "Myles, you're a guy."

"Last time I checked, yes." He chuckles as he reaches for his whiskey with a tattooed arm.

I glance down the bar, making sure that Levi and Camila can manage without my help for a moment, then fix my attention back on Myles. "Why is it that men *say* they care about you, but then give you bullshit excuses?"

His eyebrows hit his hairline. "Okay... Well, actions speak louder than words. If he's not *acting* like he cares, he probably doesn't."

My stomach knots. Is that what's happening here? Am I that naïve?

"But when it's Cory," Myles says, more gently, "it's probably something else."

Damn, I forgot how intuitive Myles is. I glance at the door to the back room, still firmly closed, then lean in closer to him. "What do you mean?"

"Heya." Geoff climbs onto a stool and leans into the little huddle Myles and I seem to have formed, his eyes twinkling behind his glasses. "What are we gossiping about?"

Myles looks at me in silent question and I nod. "Josie wants to know why Cory is stringing her along."

"What? I never said—"

"Am I wrong?" Myles asks smugly, and I roll my eyes. I also forgot how cocky he is.

"No," I mumble.

Myles sips his whiskey. "How much do you know about his dad?"

I frown, thinking back. "He told me his dad died, but that's all. Why?"

Geoff and Myles exchange a look, then Geoff sighs. "Cat and Cory's dad walked out on them when they were kids. I know Cat was about eight, so that would make Cory... what?"

"Eleven?" Myles guesses and Geoff nods in agreement.

"Oh." Sympathy weaves through me. "That sucks. He just walked out? They never saw him again?"

Geoff nods.

Myles glances down the back of the bar to make sure Cat is still gone. "Do you remember how hard things were when Cat and I first got together? She fought me every step of the way. I didn't know about her dad, that she hadn't processed what happened. Maybe Cory's the same?"

"Yeah, and maybe his dad leaving is why he's weird about commitment," Geoff guesses. "Like, he doesn't want to end up feeling trapped."

"Maybe," Myles agrees, "but there's probably a lot more to it than that."

"Oh, shit." I rub my face, seeing everything in a new light. In the space of a week, Cory's entire life has changed: I've moved into his house—with a dog we both seem to be looking after—and now I'm cleaning and cooking for him. It's become *very* domesticated, when he's used to his space and freedom. Add to that us admitting we have feelings and me pushing for him to explore that with me... No wonder he's freaking out. He's probably feeling cornered. Which wasn't my intention *at all*, but it makes complete sense.

I spot Cat threading back through the crowd toward us. "Thanks, guys," I murmur, stepping away before Cat can continue her questions. I head to the other end of the bar, helping Levi and Camila with customers, trying to process this new information. It explains so much about Cory, about why he lives the way he does. And it makes me sad, because he's missing out on having something meaningful. Something real.

It also makes my heart break for little Cory, only eleven years old, realizing his dad was never coming back. I spend most of the evening trying not to think about that, because it makes me want to cry.

When Cat and Myles leave a few hours later, I offer Geoff a refill.

"No, thanks," he says. "I'll leave soon too."

"Are you feeling any better since last week?" I can't believe it was only a week ago that Geoff was in here, heartbroken. So much has happened with Pretzel and the shelter and Cory. It feels like another lifetime. Thinking about

Animal Oasis again makes a weight settle in my gut. I still haven't figured out what I can do to help save it—if I even *can* do anything—but it's too much for me to contemplate right now.

"A little," Geoff says. "The more space I get from every-thing, the more I can see we weren't right for each other. It still hurts, but at least I know that I'm not wasting my time on something that isn't going anywhere."

I huff an uncomfortable laugh. Geoff's words cut a little too close to the bone. "Maybe I need to take that advice for myself," I mumble.

He studies me over his wineglass. "What exactly happened between you and Cory? If you don't mind shar-ing, maybe I could help?"

I hesitate. I'm not one for unloading my problems onto others, but then I think about how good Geoff was at listening to me talk about Pretzel last time. I check that Cory is still in the back room—and there are no customers who need my attention—then I lean across the bar, drop-ping my voice. "We hooked up, twice. And it was... amazing."

A grin breaks across Geoff's face. "I'll bet."

"I've liked him for years, and he told me he's liked *me* for years, and I thought something real might happen, but he keeps..." I shake my head, realizing for the first time how much this situation reminds me of my ex, Paul. "He gives in and we hook up, then he puts his walls up and tells me it's not going to happen again. Then it does, and... this is feeling a little too familiar for my liking."

"Familiar?"

"My ex used to do this. He'd be all in, and I'd think *finally, it's happening*—then he'd tell me he needed space and pull away. I'd have to crash on a friend's sofa until he sorted his shit and asked me to come back. I waited around for him for a year while he did that."

"You're living with Cory at the moment, right?" Geoff asks, and I nod. "Your feelings for him... are they just physical?"

"No. I mean, he's hot as hell, but no. I care about him so much. And he *says* he cares about me, but apparently he'd rather sleep around than be with someone he actually cares about, so I don't know what to think."

Geoff grimaces. "I'm sorry, honey. Do you want my honest opinion?"

I nod, chewing my lip anxiously.

"I think he does care about you—even I can see that. But you can't make someone do something they don't want to do. You can't change someone who doesn't want to change. And given all the emotional scars he probably has after what happened with his dad..."

I look down at the bar, feeling my heart plummet. Geoff's right. Cory won't change unless he wants to, and now that I know about his dad, things are a lot more complicated than I thought.

Geoff reaches for my hand. "You have real feelings for him and he's acting hot and cold. I don't know how healthy it is for you to continue to stay at his place. Especially if this is like what you went through with your ex."

Crap, that's a good point too.

"Is there somewhere else you could go?"

"Not really. I've still got Pretzel for the foreseeable future, and he's so happy there. I was actually going to ask Cory if I could stay longer because there are problems at the shelter."

Geoff squeezes my hand. "Your dedication to that dog is amazing. But what's happening with Cory is messing with your head and there is a real chance you could get hurt if you let it continue. It might be time to put *your* well-being before the dog's." He pauses, as if thinking about something. "You can crash on my sofa for a while if you need."

"Oh," I say, taken aback. "I can't ask you to do that."

"You're not; I'm offering. I've been where you are and it sucks—and I didn't have to live with the guy. I'm happy to help." He drains his merlot and rises from his stool. "Give me your phone and I'll put my number in. You don't have to use it, but it's there if you need. You can text me anytime."

I hand my phone over, surprised to feel tears nudging my eyes at Geoff's kindness. "Thanks," I murmur as he hands it back. He leans over the bar to hug me goodbye. I watch him go, thinking about his words.

We close up shortly after and I ask Levi if he can clean up without me. He agrees, and I sneak out the front before Cory can see me, taking a cab home.

When I let myself into the apartment, Pretzel bounds over to greet me, tail wagging like mad. I crouch down to cuddle him, tears stinging my eyes. I don't want to let Pretzel down, but maybe Geoff is right. Staying here with Cory has been difficult from the start because of how I feel about him, and things have only gotten worse since the lines between us have blurred. Maybe if we can go back to just being boss and employee, things will be easier.

I trudge into the living room and let Pretzel out into the courtyard, then quickly pack my things. I was so angry when I left, but now I'm just sad. Sad for Cory, who's been through a lot and is obviously still hurting from it. Sad that he didn't tell me. Sad that living here didn't work out. Sad that I'll never get to have something real with him.

Once I'm packed, I set my bags by the door and turn to the kitchen. I'll have to get the rest of my things later. The slow cooker is still on and I turn it off, inhaling the fragrant smell of the chili. I'm not in the mood to eat, but Cory will be hungry when he gets in from work. I serve him a bowl and quickly make some guacamole to go with it, because I know he loves it. He won't be home for an hour at least, but hopefully it won't go too brown.

Then I turn to Pretzel and sigh. "Want to go on a little adventure, sweet boy? We're going to stay somewhere new tonight." I pull my phone out to text Geoff and let him know we're coming, but before I can send it, the front door opens and Cory enters, looking pissed.

20

CORY

"Why did you take off early?" I close the front door and kick off my boots. My eyes land on Josie's bags in the entryway and panic zips through me.

Shit. Is she *leaving*?

"I had some things to do, sorry. Levi was happy to cover for me."

I forget my previous question, gesturing to her bags. "What's this?"

She sets down whatever she's doing in the kitchen and turns to look at me. "I think it's best if Pretzel and I find somewhere else to stay."

Fuck. She can't leave. I can't wake up in the morning without her here.

I stride down the hallway into the kitchen. "No. We'll work things out. I know we argued, and that was shit, but—" My eyes land on the bowl of chili on the counter, and I force myself to calm down, to not crowd her. "Do you want me to leave you to eat, then we can talk?"

She shakes her head. "That's for you."

I blink, looking between her and the chili. She stormed out of here, hasn't said two words to me all night, and now she's made me food? "Why?"

She shrugs. "I figured you'd be hungry after work."

"You made this for me, even after everything that happened?"

She nods, not meeting my gaze, and something hot tangles in my chest. How is she this selfless, this caring?

"Please don't leave," I say, hearing my voice crack. She looks at me in surprise. "I don't want you to go. Please."

She wraps her arms around herself. "It's for the best. I care about you too much and it's starting to hurt. I need to look after myself, too." Her gaze falls to the floor. "I love staying here, Cors, but I think it's too much for you. You're used to living alone and having freedom. Then I moved in with Pretzel, and started cooking for you, and cleaning, and... I think you might be feeling a bit cornered. Especially since we, um"—she scrunches her nose—"hooked up. I don't want you to feel like I'm trying to trap you into a relationship."

I stare at her in shock. "You think I'm worried about you *trapping* me? What, waking up beside you every day, introducing you to people as my girlfriend, planning a future with you? Hell no. Any man would be lucky to have that with you."

Her wide eyes meet mine. "If that's what you believe, why don't you want that with me?"

"I *do* want that with you. Of *course* I want that. But..." I rub the back of my neck, trying to find the words. Thinking about being in a relationship with her—planning a *future* with her—has brought things clearly into perspective. "You deserve so much better than me, Joze. I'm not a good guy."

"What? Why would you think that?"

"Because..." I turn and sink down onto the sofa, dropping my head into my hands. "I am just like my dad."

She lowers herself beside me. "What do you mean?"

"My dad walked out on us when I was a kid. It destroyed our family."

"I'm so sorry." She's quiet for a moment, then adds, "But... how does that make you just like him?"

I study the carpet through my fingers, debating how much to share. I've never told anyone about this, because I'm so ashamed. Only my mom knows, and that's because she was close with Alice's mom. But when I glance up at Josie's caring, concerned face, I know I have to tell her. It will change how she sees me—hell, she won't want me at all after this—but she deserves to know the truth.

"Well, there's more to the story." I lean against the back of the sofa, folding my arms across my chest and dropping my head back to stare up at the ceiling. "My dad cheated on my mom. I caught him. It was such a cliché. I came home early from school one day and caught him with some woman who worked for him. When you're eleven and you discover your dad having an affair, you don't have the maturity to make sense of that."

I hear Josie inhale sharply. "Oh my God, Cors. That's horrible." Her hand touches my arm and I close my eyes, focusing on the warm feeling of her fingertips.

"He left shortly after that and it messed me up big time. One minute I had a dad who took me to basketball games, who taught me how to cook, who filled the house with his off-key, drunken piano playing. And then... that was all gone. I didn't know who I was without him. I went off the rails in my teens and did some stupid shit."

"Like what?" she asks gently, and I shrug.

"Playing hooky from school. Smoking pot. I stole a car

once. I slept around a lot. But then..." I swallow, feeling my heart race as the memories come back to me. "When I was nineteen, I got together with the girl next door, Alice. She was just like you; really sweet and kind and caring. I liked her a lot. But—"

Shit, I don't know if I can do this. Josie will never look at me the same way again.

Her hand squeezes my arm and she sits quietly, patiently, waiting.

"I cheated on her."

There. I said it.

I wait for Josie to pull her hand away, to tell me how disappointed she is, to walk out, but she stays right there, her fingers still warm on my skin. So I take a breath, forcing myself to continue.

"She walked in on me with some girl at a party. God, I was so fucking stupid, so selfish to do that to her. I broke her heart. And my mom—" I stop speaking as my throat gets tight, Mom's face flashing into my mind.

We were in the kitchen in our house on Long Island. I can still remember the old orange and brown linoleum, the Formica counter, the smell of Mom's meatloaf cooking in the oven. Alice's mom had called her because Alice was upset, and Mom got so mad. I knew I'd fucked up. I felt like shit for what I'd done—and for the fact that Alice had witnessed it—but I couldn't take it back. I was drowning in guilt and regret with no one to pull me out.

Mom turned from the stove when I entered the kitchen, grabbing me by the shoulders and making me look at her. "What the hell were you thinking?" she said, her eyes wet. That's how I knew my mistake hadn't just hurt Alice, it had hurt Mom, too. "You, of *all* people, should know better than this."

I tried to make excuses, because I couldn't handle the truth of how I'd let down the people I cared about the most, but Mom wouldn't accept any of them.

"No, Cory." Her eyes were hard and cold as she looked at me. "You need to face what you've done." And then she said the thing I'd heard my entire childhood, but instead of it being a compliment, it was a bitter, scathing remark that came from a place of overwhelming disappointment. She looked me in the eyes, and said, "You're just like your father."

I didn't want her to see me cry, so I turned away. When I looked back she had left the kitchen, and she didn't speak to me for an entire week after that.

"What did your mom do?" Josie asks quietly, snapping me out of the memory.

But it's too late. It's as raw and real as if it's just happened, and I feel tears prick my eyes. "She told me I'm just like Dad." My voice breaks and—fuck, a tear escapes down my face. I reach up to wipe it away, but Josie's hand is there, tenderly stroking my cheek. I open my eyes and lift my head to look at her. Her own eyes are wet and she swipes the back of her wrist under them.

"Cory," she whispers.

I sniff, trying to pull myself together and man the fuck up. I don't know how I can feel *this upset* twenty years later, but it still stings. "I decided I'd never let another woman get hurt by me like that again. And you, Joze—" I draw a shuddering breath. "You're too precious to me. You're not some random woman from the bar, you're the most important person in my life, and I can't risk hurting you like I did Alice..."

"Twenty years ago?" She shakes her head, gazing at me in disbelief. "You made a mistake when you were a teenager

—like *everyone* does—and you've been beating yourself up this whole time?"

I exhale, looking away. She makes it sound so simple, but—

"Cory." She takes my face in her hands, gently turning me back so I look at her. I try to hide the pain that's gripping my chest like a vise, but I know she can see it in my eyes. "You've spent the past twenty years believing you don't deserve love." She strokes a thumb down my face, over my beard, touching me in the most tender, loving way, and my heart aches so much I can't bear it. "But you *do*," she says fiercely. "You're not that stupid kid anymore. You're generous, and kind, and caring—you don't even know how much. You deserve everything."

Fresh moisture hits my cheeks. Goddammit, I'm crying again.

"Hey," she says softly, tugging me close. "Come here." Her arms wrap around my shoulders, tucking my head onto her chest, and she rubs my back in slow, gentle circles. "I'm so sorry you've believed that all this time and no one has told you the truth, but I'm telling you now. You're a good man, and you deserve love. You deserve everything."

I press my eyes closed, letting myself hear her words. Words I've never heard from anyone. Words I didn't even know I needed to hear. Part of me wants to fight it, wants to tell her she's wrong. But another part of me wants to believe her; the part of me that is *so tired* of living like this.

She holds me on the sofa for a long time, rubbing my back. I can't describe it, but I've never felt so understood. Accepted. She knows my biggest, most shameful secret, and she hasn't walked away. She's shown me nothing but love.

But of course she has. That's Josie. Josie with her big heart. Josie who made me dinner tonight even after I was such a jerk. Josie who never gives up on even the most miserable, grumpy, ungrateful bastards.

I pull myself up on the sofa, turning to look at her. Really look at her. Her eyes are red-rimmed from crying with me—crying for the pain *I've* felt. She's sitting close, still touching me, still determined to comfort and be there for me, even after all the times I've pushed her away, all the times I've let her down.

I glance down the hallway at her bags, knowing without a doubt that I can't let her leave tonight.

I can't lose her.

I reach out to touch her cheek and she sighs, closing her eyes against my hand.

Fuck. This girl means everything to me, and it's time I damn well start acting like it.

"Come to bed with me," I whisper.

Her eyes fly open and she pulls her head away. "What?"

"Don't leave. Please. Come to bed with me."

Uncertainty flickers across her brow. "I won't leave. It's okay. But you don't need to—"

"I've made a mess of everything with us and I'm so sorry."

She softens. "It's okay."

"It's not okay. I want to be with you, Joze. I want this." My heart is in my throat as I watch her consider my words.

Then, as if testing me, she leans forward, tentatively touching her lips to mine. I wrap my arms around her, pulling her onto my lap, and she rests her forehead against mine.

"I want this too," she whispers. "So much."

I press my mouth to hers, gently at first, making sure she's okay with it. She parts her lips, and when I feel the soft lick of her tongue against mine, the aching in my chest eases.

"Okay," she murmurs, kissing my cheek, my jaw. "Let's go to bed."

My eyes fall closed as I take a moment to savor Josie saying those words to me, to savor how lucky I am. Then I scoop her up in my arms and carry her to my bedroom.

21

CORY

My pulse drums in my ears as I set Josie down on the edge of the bed. I turn to flick on the bedside lamp, casting a warm glow over the room. I can't believe this is happening. After all this time, all this fantasizing about it, I hope I don't disappoint her.

Shit, what's wrong with me? I'd never normally worry about that. At the risk of sounding arrogant, I'd say I'm pretty damn good at this.

But this is *Josie*. This is the woman I've wanted for *five years*. It means something.

Hell, it means everything.

Josie reaches for my hand, and it's not until I hold it out that I realize it's shaking. She stands from the bed, concern bending her brow. "Hey, are you okay?"

"Yeah." A small laugh chuffs out of me. "I think I'm a little nervous."

She gives me a reassuring smile. "I am too." She pushes up onto her toes, brushing her mouth over mine, then tugs my bottom lip between her teeth and gently bites it.

Fuck.

Heat spreads along my limbs and I let my hands slide down to grip her ass, squeezing her soft curves. She turns us around so my back is to the bed, nudging me until I sit. Then she pushes my knees apart and steps between them, grabbing the hem of my shirt. I lift my arms, letting her pull it over my head. She dips her head to drag her lips across my shoulder, and I close my eyes, reveling in her attention. Every caress of her mouth sets off tiny fireworks across my skin.

"You're so sexy. I've always thought so."

God, hearing that from Josie is like nothing else. "So are y—"

"Shhh." She places her finger over my lips. "It's my turn right now. I just want to enjoy you."

I chuckle, feeling myself relax. "Okay, Buttercup." I watch the way she explores my chest and stomach with her fingertips, her eyes wide and eager, like she can't believe what's happening. I try to touch her, but she pushes my hands away, so I lean back on my arms and let her have her fill. If she's feeling anything close to what I'm feeling right now, I understand. Because when it's my turn, I plan to take my time.

When her hands reach the bulge threatening my zipper, her gaze flicks up to mine, dark and hungry. Then she pushes me down onto my back. "Move up there," she says huskily.

I shuffle up so I'm lying back on the bed, waiting for her next move. I love how she takes control of me. It's so unexpected—and such a fucking turn on.

She climbs on top, straddling me, her breath huffing out when she feels how hard I am. A slow roll of her hips sends lust rocketing through me, eliciting a groan. She's still wearing her clothes and I want them gone, but I try to be patient. I ball my hands into fists to keep myself from reaching for her.

She must be able to read my mind because she smiles seductively, pulling her tank top over her head. She's wearing a white lace bra and it's so sweet—so *her*. She looks like a virgin on her wedding night, and for some reason that turns me on even more.

Her next move reminds me she's not as innocent as she looks: she reaches behind and removes her bra, keeping her fiery eyes fixed on mine. Then she takes her breasts in her hands, pinching her nipples with her forefinger and thumb, rolling her hips over me again. It's the naughty smile on her lips that makes me snap.

"I'm touching you now," I growl, sitting up to take one of her rosy-pink buds into my mouth. I use my thumb to stroke the stiff peak of her other breast, loving the way she shivers on my lap. I tease her nipple with my tongue, grazing my teeth over it to make her moan. That sound goes right through me until I'm throbbing hard against my fly. I grind up into her and she moans again.

"Fuck," I mutter, lifting my head to take her mouth in a hot, ravenous kiss. The feeling of her tongue sliding over mine is too much to take, and I flip her onto her back, climbing over her. "My turn."

She gives a playful roll of her eyes. "*So* impatient."

"Five years," I grunt, dipping down to press a firm kiss to her lips. "I've waited long enough."

She grins, laying back to let me touch her. But I force myself to pause and appreciate the moment—the way she looks lying on my bed, her dark hair mussed on my pillow. She looks so good there. I always want her there now.

I lavish her breasts with more attention, loving the way she responds so easily to my touch. Every flick of my tongue has her quivering and tugging on my hair. I pay attention to every sign she gives that she likes what I'm doing; I hoard every moan and whispered *yes*. I've never felt as high as I do right now, getting to touch her like this.

"You're so beautiful, Joze. Fucking perfect." I kiss my way down the soft curve of her stomach, pulling off her jeans and panties. But before I can put my mouth on her, she sits up and tugs at my jeans.

"I want these off."

"But I want to—"

"Off," she says again, unbuckling my belt.

I chuckle. "So *demanding*." But I comply, shucking my jeans and boxers, until we're both lying naked on top of my comforter. "Come here." I roll onto my side, pulling her into my arms. Her soft skin feels so good against mine, and I close my eyes and drop my face into her hair, enjoying the warmth and closeness. "I've wanted you for so long," I murmur, breathing in the sweet, flowery scent of her. "I can't believe this is actually happening."

"Me too," she whispers, turning her head to kiss my ear. Her hot breath over my earlobe sends desire shivering through me, and when she hooks a leg up over my hip, it takes every ounce of my willpower not to thrust into the heat of her. Instead, I reach down and around between the back of her legs, until my fingers find her wet, warm center.

"Oh—" She spasms against me in surprise. And when I push two fingers inside her, her breath hitches.

"I owe you an orgasm," I say roughly, feeling her clench around me. "I don't like that you had to give yourself one in the shower."

"You didn't like it?"

"Well, it was hot as fuck." I withdraw my fingers and

slide them up, over her most sensitive spot. "But it should have been me doing it."

She whimpers under my touch. "If it helps," she says breathlessly, "I was thinking of you."

"Then I definitely owe you one." I stroke my fingers in a circle, then stop so I can look at her, so she can see how serious I am. "I owe you one for anytime you had to do it yourself when you wished it was me instead."

Her lips quirk into a filthy smile. "Then you owe me thousands."

I groan, dropping my head into her neck, feeling myself ache with need where I'm pressed against her thigh.

"By that logic, how many do I owe you?" she asks.

I draw back to meet her gaze, softening. "Thousands, Buttercup. Fucking thousands."

She swallows, her breath quickening as I begin the movement of my fingers again. I capture her mouth with mine, her moans vibrating through me as I stroke her slick center faster, rougher, until she collapses and shudders against me.

"Only a few thousand to go," I murmur, kissing her ear, and she giggles.

As soon as I remove my hand, she dives on me, grasping my painfully stiff length in her fist. "You're so hard," she breathes, stroking. A moan shoots from my mouth as she swipes her thumb over the moist tip of me. She bites her lip, gazing down, and her brow knits.

"What is it?"

"It's just…" She pauses her movements. "I haven't had sex in a long time. And you're not small."

"I'll be gentle." I kiss her forehead. Then I ask, "How long is a long time?"

Pink stains her cheeks. "Um, five years."

"Wait." I push up onto my elbow. "You haven't had sex with anyone the entire time I've known you?"

She nods, and I frown, confused.

"Why not? Guys hit on you all the time."

"I've been on dates and stuff, it's just…" Her gaze flits to mine, then away. "I don't know." She shrugs. "I guess I only wanted you."

Her words crash into me like a wave, stealing my breath.

I only wanted you.

I can't believe it. Here I was, bringing women home from work to distract myself from the one woman I really wanted, and she was just… waiting. For me.

You deserve everything.

Her words from earlier roll through my mind, and when they're followed by the automatic self-loathing I've come to expect, I have to fight hard against the urge to pull away from her. That's what I would have done in the past, but not now. Not after tonight. I might not feel worthy of her yet, but she believes I'm good and I want to believe it too. I want to be the man she thinks I am.

"Holy shit." I take her mouth in a passionate, bruising kiss. I'm dizzy at the thought that she's been waiting for me, that she hasn't been touched by another man in all that time. It awakens something primal and possessive in me, something that makes me want to bury myself between her thighs and claim her as my own.

I guess I'm still the same greedy bastard I was before—but now I'm going to earn it. Because if anyone deserves the world it's Josie, and I'm going to be the one to give it to her.

At least, I'm going to try.

I roll her onto her back and kneel between her legs, reaching a hand over to my nightstand and snatching a condom from the drawer. She breathes hard, her lips parted as she watches me roll the condom down my length. I lower myself between her parted legs, pausing to remember this moment because I know I won't be the same man when we're done.

My voice shakes when I ask, "You okay, Buttercup?"

"Fuck yes." Her mouth curves into her wide, beautiful smile, and emotion flares hot inside my chest.

Then I thrust into the tight, wet heat of her, and I feel like I've fucking come *home*.

My head falls forward onto her shoulder and I stay there, filling her to the hilt, afraid to move in case everything ends right now. She gasps at the sudden invasion and I curse myself, remembering my promise to be gentle.

"Shit," I mutter, pulling away. "I'm sorry."

She grabs my ass and tugs me deeper. "Stay."

"Did I hurt you?"

"A little, but it's okay."

"It's not—"

"Cory, stop." She wraps her legs around me. "I want to feel it all. I know you said you'd be gentle, but I don't want you to be. Don't hold back."

I give a slow, cautious roll of my hips and she shakes her head.

"Please. I haven't been touched in so long. All I've thought about is you wanting me. You losing control with me." She ghosts her lips over mine, then whispers, "You fucking me until I can't walk."

Oh my God.

My hips snap forward in a deep, involuntary thrust, and she throws her head back on the pillow.

"Yes." Her nails dig into the skin on my back. "Like that."

I haven't been touched in so long.

I give another brutal thrust and her moan echoes off the

walls. Fire wraps around my spine at the way she wants me to fuck her, the knowledge she hasn't let anyone touch her since she met me.

I only wanted you.

Another thrust and her eyes roll back, her nails sinking deeper into my flesh. I like the sting, like knowing she's leaving her mark on me. I drop my head to suck her neck, wanting to mark her too, wanting her to be branded as mine.

I come to my senses, though, and pull away. I'm behaving like an animal.

"No." She pushes my face back into her neck. "Don't stop. Leave a mark on me."

Holy—

I growl into her skin, biting her as I pump my hips again. I feel her moan under my lips, feel her pulse beating against my tongue.

"You're making me lose my mind, Joze." My breath is shallow; my hands are trembling. I've never felt this kind of raw, carnal passion before, and I'm not sure I can stay in control for much longer.

"I feel the same," she rasps. "But I love it. You fill me so perfectly."

She's right, I do. Every inch of me is gripped within her tight, slick heat, like I was made for her. I think about the fact that she's been waiting for me this whole time and grind into her hard, desperate for her to think it was worth it. When she whimpers and tells me, "I've never been fucked like this," I lose it. My body takes over, turning me into a beast. I capture her mouth in a punishing kiss, my hips slamming in rough, erratic thrusts, my body consumed by fire and need.

"Oh, yes, Cory."

Hearing her call my name only spurs me on, and I pin her hands above her head as my tongue continues to ravage her mouth. I'm so close and I can only hope—

"Ohhh," she cries, her legs clamping around my waist, her body writhing under me. She throws her head back and moans my name as she's swept away in release, and I'm right there with her. Heat explodes through me and I dissolve into waves of pleasure, my body jerking, a harsh groan falling from my open mouth.

When I finally peel myself up to look at Josie, her eyes are tightly closed and her chest is heaving with her rapid breaths.

"Joze—"

"Just give me a minute," she says, pressing her fingertips to her eyelids.

Oh, fuck. Was I too rough? I bet I was, taking her like that—like the world was ending and this was all we had left. What is wrong with me? Why can't I stay in control around her?

She lowers her hands, finally meeting my gaze. When I see her eyes are wet, my heart stops.

S hit, shit, shit.

Do not cry right now. Crying after sex is the absolute worst thing you can do.

I blink quickly, trying to clear the moisture from my eyes. I couldn't help it; the minute Cory went still on top of me, emotion rushed up inside. I'm not even sure what from —the sheer disbelief that I actually had sex with him, the man I've wanted for so long, or because I was simply over-whelmed by how unbelievable it was.

Because it was... I have no words. It was everything.

"I'm sorry, Buttercup." Cory rolls off beside me, his face lined with concern as he reaches to touch my cheek. "Did I hurt you?"

"*No.*" I shake my head and turn onto my side to face him.

"Then why are you upset?"

"I'm not. I'm—" I give a funny little laugh. "You know how when you want something really badly, you imagine what it will be like and build it up in your head, then when it finally happens, it's never quite as good as you hoped?"

The lines on Cory's forehead deepen. "Yeah?"

"This was... not that. This was the opposite of that."

"Oh." His brow smooths. "Really?"

"Yes. Like, all my fantasies were complete and utter crap. Because this was—"

"The best sex I've ever had," he finishes, nodding. Then he stops, looking worried. "Wait, that is where you were going with that, right?"

I laugh. "Yes. That was *by far* the best sex I've ever had." I chew my lip, thinking about it. I haven't had that much sex in my time, but I know he has. "Was it really that good for you, too?"

"Uh, yeah." His eyes smolder as he nods. "Nothing else even comes *close*." We stare at each other for a long moment, processing this, until he finally sits up and leans over to kiss my head. "I'm just going to the bathroom. Be right back."

I let out a dreamy sigh as I watch his tall, muscular form wander out of the room. God, his ass is so perfectly sculpted, and the power in those thighs... How did I end up here, in Cory's bed, having what we've both openly agreed was the best sex of our lives? *How*? I must have been Mother Teresa in another life or something.

The door pushes open and I see a little black nose, followed by the rest of Pretzel as he wriggles through the gap. I smile, sliding off the bed and pulling on my underwear. "Hey, boy. Want to go outside?" I pet his head, then step out of the room and let him into the courtyard. I wait in the doorway, feeling the cool night air on my bare skin. My gaze drifts over to my bed, folded up on the other side of the living room, and I pause, wondering if I should sleep there. I don't want to push Cory into anything he's not ready for.

Pretzel finishes his business and I close the courtyard door behind him. I go over to the bags I'd packed by the front door and drag them back over to my bed. Then I pull out my pajama shorts and tank, slipping them on. Cory exits the bathroom, smiling to himself, but stops short when he sees me hovering beside my bed.

His brows slant together. "What are you doing?"

"I, um, wasn't sure..." I shift my weight, glancing between my bed and his room.

"I am." He steps close and pulls me into him. "Come back to my room. Please?"

Relief trickles through me. "Yeah?"

He nods. "And if it's okay with you, I don't want you using this bed anymore." I open my mouth to clarify, and he adds, "I want you with me, every night. If that's what you want?"

My heart feels like it's going to burst, looking at his hopeful face. "Yeah, Cors." I touch my lips to his in the softest kiss. "That's what I want."

THE SUNLIGHT FILTERING through the blinds wakes me. I blink in the morning light, realizing I'm not in my own bed.

Oh. Right.

My mouth tugs into a wide smile as I remember the events of last night. Coming home and deciding to leave. Having that heart-breaking conversation with Cory about his past. Then having mind-blowing sex until the small hours of the morning. The evidence of that is in the beard burn all over my skin and the delicious ache between my legs, where he made sure I felt *everything*. So intense. So all-consuming. So *good*.

I still can't believe it happened. Not just the sex—the connection with him, the way he shared something he obviously hadn't shared with many people, the way it felt like I finally saw who he really is. The way he pulled me onto his lap and said, *I want to be with you, Joze. I want this.* Happiness hums through me at the thought.

With a yawn, I roll over to see if Cory is awake yet, but his side of the bed is empty, the covers pulled up neatly, and my stomach drops like a stone.

I sit up, glancing around the room for clues as to where he's gone and why, but there are none. My chest tightens. Is that it? Has he changed his mind, just like that? I know last night was a lot, but after everything, I thought—

"Morning, Buttercup." The bedroom door opens and Pretzel bolts in, followed by Cory with two steaming cups of coffee. Pretzel leaps up onto the bed and I stroke his head, feeling guilty. Of course, Cory didn't change his mind. I'm just paranoid because all of this feels too good to be true.

"Morning," I murmur, focusing on Pretzel, suddenly hyper-aware of where I am. I've woken up in Cory's bed— my *boss's* bed—and even though last night was amazing, in the light of morning things feel a lot more real. I mean, it's Cory, and I know him. But that's also what makes this kind of awkward.

Cory doesn't seem to think so, though. He sets a mug of coffee on the nightstand beside me, dropping a kiss on my head, then climbs into his side of the bed like we do this every morning. Seeing how relaxed he is makes the tension inside me ease. I think it's just been *so long* since I've been in this position that I've forgotten how to act.

Well, I've never been in bed with my boss, but you get what I mean.

"Thanks for the coffee," I say, smiling. Damn, Cory looks good in the morning. His hair is all ruffled, his eyes are sleepy and tired—hardly surprising after our late night sexfest—and he's not wearing a shirt, so I can shamelessly ogle his shoulders and pecs and that sexy tattoo on his ribs.

He reaches for me but Pretzel is between us on his back, head lolled to the side as I scratch his belly. Cory half laughs, half frowns. "I'm never going to be the number one guy in your life, am I?"

I chuckle, patting the other side of the bed and nudging Pretzel, who reluctantly climbs over me, out of the way. Then I wriggle over to Cory and snuggle into his waiting arms. He's so warm and strong and perfect. I never want to leave this exact spot.

"I'll have to give him back eventually," I say with a sad sigh. Ever since I got Pretzel I've been trying not to think about this. I want to keep him—almost as much as I want to keep Cory—but I just don't see how I can make it work with my apartment.

Thinking of this reminds me of the news I got about the shelter yesterday, in the middle of everything happening with Cory. I need to ask him about sticking around with Pretzel for longer, and I can only hope that doesn't disturb this delicate new... relationship? Situation? Arrangement? Whatever it is, I can only hope that asking to stay longer doesn't disturb this new *place* we seem to find ourselves in.

"Cors," I say, sitting up and reaching for my coffee. "I have something to ask you, and you can totally say no if it's too much."

He grabs his own coffee and takes a sip. "What is it?"

I explain what Gerard told me about the fines and the shelter yesterday. "So that means..."

"You and Pretzel need to stay longer," he says with a shrug. "Sure. That's fine."

I eye him over my mug. It's not quite the enthusiastic

Thank God you're not leaving that I was hoping for, but it's definitely better than *No, get out*.

"Are you sure?"

"Of course. I'd never kick you guys out."

I release my breath in a long stream. "Okay. Thank you. I —*we*—really appreciate it."

"What about the shelter? Will it have to close if they don't find the money?"

I nod, feeling that same heavy weight of dread in my gut. "Harriet suggested holding a fundraiser, but I don't even know where to start."

"That's a cool idea." Cory scrubs a hand over his beard in thought. "We could do it at the bar."

I glance at him, surprised. "You'd let me do that there?"

"It's a good cause, so from a business point of view it's great publicity. But more importantly, it matters to you. Which means it matters to me."

"Oh." Warmth fills my chest. That's the sweetest thing he's ever said. "But I know nothing about hosting a fundraiser. I wouldn't know the first thing to do."

"Maybe not," Cory says, sipping his coffee. "But I bet you know someone who does. Between all our friends, there's bound to be someone who knows what to do."

I look down at my coffee, nibbling on my lip. "That's probably true, but it's a lot to ask."

Cory silently takes my mug, setting it on the nightstand with his. Then he slides an arm around my shoulder, pulling me close again. "Have you ever noticed how much you worry about burdening others?"

I frown, considering his words. I don't like to be a bother, but—

"You do," he says gently. "You apologize a lot—about things you don't need to apologize for. You never stand up to

Eddy. Hell, you only even started standing up to me recently. You put everyone else's needs before your own, no matter the cost to you. Case in point." He gestures to Pretzel, snoozing on my side of the bed. "Your generosity is amazing. You are incredibly selfless, and I love that about you. But... it's problematic when you won't also ask for what *you* need."

I open and close my mouth, unsure what to say. No one has ever pointed it out to me like that before, but I wonder if he's right. I think of Geoff last night, telling me it was time to "put my well-being before the dog's" and cringe.

"I've seen a change in you, though," Cory continues, crinkles forming around his hazel eyes. "A good change. You got fed up with me and stood up to me in a way you never have, and it was fucking awesome. It was the kick in the pants I needed." He chuckles and it makes me smile. "Maybe now it's time to push yourself further, and get some help with this fundraiser idea. It's a great cause; I'm sure people would love to help. And I think it would be good for you to *ask* for help, for once."

I exhale slowly. He's right—I did get fed up with him and stand up for myself. It was his words that helped me to do that. And look where that got me—into his bed, and if I'm lucky, into his heart. Maybe this would be good, too.

"Does this matter to you?" he asks.

"Yes. The shelter is one of my favorite places in the city. It helps so many animals."

"Well, there you go. If you want to save it, you need to ask for help."

"Okay," I say, nodding. "But who should I ask? It was Harriet's idea, so I could start with her."

"I bet Cat would help." Cory leans over to the night-stand, grabbing his phone. "I'll text her now."

I almost ask, *Are you sure?* but stop myself. This is going to feel uncomfortable, reaching out to people, and it will take some getting used to.

Cory's phone buzzes five seconds later with Cat's response, and he grins. "She's in. She said Myles wants to help too." He sends off another text, and it's followed by another buzz. "They'll come into the bar tonight to discuss ideas." He looks up at me, his eyes alight. "That okay?"

I smile, touched. "Yes. That's... yes. Please thank her." I reach for my phone and, with a deep breath, I text Harriet to tell her we're going to meet to discuss the fundraiser idea at Bounce tonight if she can make it. She replies less than a minute later with an enthusiastic *Yes!*

"Harriet's in, too." I set my phone down and Cory slips his other arm around me, tugging me into his warmth and kissing my forehead.

"See, Buttercup? People love you and want to help. This is going to be great."

I nuzzle into his bare chest, inhaling his musky, earthy smell. This is what I mean about Cory. He's not just hot— and, as I now know, *amazing* in bed—he's sweet and kind and good. I'm going to keep reminding him until he believes it about himself.

"Thank you for pushing me. I wouldn't have even considered this without you." I press my lips to his chest, meaning it to be sweet, but he smells too good and it makes heat unfurl low in my belly. We don't have to be at work until much later today, and I'm hoping we can stay right here until then.

Thinking about work sends a nervous ripple through me. The last time Cory and I were at the bar together, we were barely speaking, and now... everything has changed.

I try to imagine kissing him at work, but the image won't form in my head. He's not the same Cory at work—he's

Grumpy Boss Cory, dealing with Eddy and all the shit at the bar. Besides, I know he had his concerns about the fact that he's my boss. I can't imagine he wants to broadcast this.

It's not just that, I realize, as I trail my fingers through the patch of hair on his chest. This thing between us—whatever it is—it's so new. After everything Cory told me about his past last night, it feels... fragile. I don't want it ruined by our coworkers making jokes or gossiping. I want to protect it and stay in this perfect bubble where Cory looks at me like I'm the only thing that matters in his world.

"Hey," I say carefully, drawing away to look at him. "Do you think we could keep... *this*... just between us at work?"

His brow knits. "*This*, as in, you and me?"

"Yeah. I mean, you're the boss, and you know what Eddy is like. He'll give you a ton of shit."

Cory is quiet, drawing a tiny circle on my arm with his finger. I study his pensive expression, feeling anxious. Was that the wrong thing to say? Does he *want* to tell our coworkers?

He lets out a long breath and leans in to kiss my shoulder. "Okay, we can keep it quiet," he says, skating his hands down to squeeze my butt. "I guess it's a good thing we're not at work right now, because I wouldn't be able to keep my hands off you." He tugs me until I can feel his hardness against my hip, and I give a little whimper of need.

"It's a very good thing," I say breathlessly, grinding against him.

He lifts his head and whistles at the dog. "Pretzel. Out."

I watch in shock as Pretzel obediently climbs down off the bed and slinks out of the room. *How* does Cory manage that?

He turns back to me with a sexy grin, and I slide my hands under the covers, taking hold of the hard heat of him.

He grunts and his eyes fall closed as he crushes his mouth to mine.

Fuck. It was all fine and good to decide to hide this at work, but now that I know what it's like to touch him, how on earth will I keep my hands to myself?

23

CORY

God, I want to kiss Josie. We've been at work less than two hours and already I need to have my hands on her.

Why did I say I was happy to hide this at work? I guess she had a point about how it would look, with me being the boss and all. I think she was trying to protect me, in a way, and that's sweet. But I don't really give a shit what people think—least of all Eddy.

I care about what *Josie* thinks, though, and if she's not ready to tell people, I have to be okay with that. She had her bags packed and ready to leave my house less than twenty-four hours ago, and I don't blame her after the way I acted. I need to earn her trust, her commitment. I need to show her that since we've decided to do this, I'm going to make a real go of it. I need her to know I'm not going anywhere, and that's going to take time.

But the thing is, I'm feeling fucking impatient all of a sudden.

I spot Cat and Myles climbing into a booth across the bar and give them a wave. They're here for Josie, but she's busy mixing mojitos, so I grab a vodka soda and whiskey, and head over.

"Hey, guys." I set their drinks on the table. "Thanks for coming in to talk about this fundraiser idea."

"Of course," Cat says, taking a sip of vodka. "We'd love to help. You know Stevie was a rescue. Oh!" She waves to someone over my shoulder. "Hayes! Over here."

I turn to see Cat's employee and friend, Hayley—a British woman who's worked with her for years, first in her vintage store and now with Cat's clothing line in the local market. She's tall and curvy, with strawberry-blond hair she always wears in some wild style. Tonight it's in a long braid with flowers woven through it.

"I hope Josie doesn't mind," Cat says as Hayley threads through the crowd toward us, "I invited Hayley. She's fantastic at this kind of thing."

I smile. "That's great."

"Hey." Hayley drops onto the vinyl seat beside Cat, pulling out a notebook. I'm about to ask what she wants to drink when someone else joins the booth.

"Are you guys here for the fundraiser thing?" Harriet asks, and Cat grins.

"Yes!" She shuffles around the booth, followed by Hayley, so Harriet can join them.

I grin at the little group assembled to help Josie. She was so worried about "bothering" everyone with her idea, and yet they all seem excited to be here.

"Thanks for coming. Joze was nervous about asking for help, but I think this is a good cause. I know she appreciates it." I glance over at the bar, smiling to myself as I watch her pour a line of shots. When I turn back to the group, Cat is eying me suspiciously.

Shit.

"Uh—" I clear my throat, gesturing to Hayley and Harriet. "What can I get you?" They give me their drink orders and I scoot off to the bar, away from my nosy sister. I pour a glass of whiskey and a gin and lemonade, placing them on a tray. Josie has a break between customers and I slide the tray toward her, motioning to the group. "Here, you take this over."

"Oh. Uh..." She looks from the tray to the booth, hesitating.

"Joze, go. Everyone is waiting for you. They're really excited."

She gestures to the line of customers at the bar. "I'll go soon. We're too busy."

"We're fine," I say, sensing she's procrastinating more than anything else. When she looks at me, chewing her lip, I nudge her gently. "Go." I bite back a playful smile. "Do I need to remind you who the boss is here?"

Her eyebrows rise and she slowly moves away from the bar. There's a mischievous sparkle in her eyes as she steps past me, murmuring, "Okay, *Boss*."

Whoa.

My blood heats as I stare after her. She's never called me that before and... *fuck*. There's something about the way that word sounds coming from her mouth that goes straight to my groin. It's a good thing we have that not-at-work rule, because I'd be tempted to pull her into the back room, pin her against the wall, and...

I drag my mind out of the gutter, turning back to the bar. Eddy is trying to juggle bottles of spirits, and I know it's only a matter of seconds before one hits the floor. "Hey," I say, irritated. "Quit it. Clear some tables, will you?"

I serve a line of customers, keeping one eye on Eddy, the other on Josie's table. Hayley is scribbling ideas in her notebook while everyone talks enthusiastically, and I can't help but smile. A little while later Josie comes up to the bar to make another round of drinks for everyone, grinning.

"How's it going?"

"So good. Cat and Harriet have some great ideas," she says as she mixes the drinks. "We're going to have a themed animal dress up night with a cover charge. Hayley suggested getting local businesses to donate things like dog walking and grooming services for a raffle, and Myles is going to set up a Go Fund Me page." Her green eyes are bright and her cheeks are rosy with excitement. It takes all my strength not to pull her into my arms.

"That's great." I check that Eddy can manage the bar, following her back to the booth. She slides onto the vinyl and I hand out the drinks. "Sounds like you guys have come up with some great ideas over here."

"It's going to be cool." Myles reaches for his whiskey. "I thought I might create a signature cocktail for the night, if that's okay with you?"

"That's an awesome idea," I say. He created and sold a cocktail app a while back and is a master mixologist. "I'll match every dollar that drink makes in donations."

Josie turns to me in surprise. "You don't have to do that."

"I know I don't. I want to," I say. She gazes at me for a beat, trying to quell her smile, and I force myself to step away. "Let me know if you guys need any more drinks."

I wipe down some tables and clear a few empty glasses, dumping them in the sink. When I turn back, Cat is leaning at the bar, giving me a knowing look.

"Are we going to talk about this?"

"About what?" I ask, dragging a dishcloth over the counter in front of her.

"About the fact that you're sleeping with Josie?"

"Shhh," I hiss, checking that no one heard. "And we're not... Nothing is happening."

She lifts her eyebrows smugly. "You think I haven't noticed the way you're mooning over her? Jeez, Cors. And what, exactly, is that mark on her neck?"

I feel my cheeks color. That's the mark I made while I fucked her like an animal last night—the one she begged for while crying my name in pleasure. I made another one on her breast and her hip this morning. She might not want me telling everyone she's mine yet, but *I* know she is.

I'm not sure I'll be able to keep this from my sister, though. She knows me better than anyone.

"Fine," I mutter, lowering my voice. "But don't say anything, okay? It's new and we're just"—I hike up a shoulder, trying to play it cool—"seeing where it goes."

Cat snorts. "Bullshit. You've got it bad."

"I do not—"

"*Don't* fuck this up. She's great."

I frown. "I know she is. She's amazing." *Too good for you*, that familiar voice reminds me. It's followed by the usual punch of self-doubt as I gaze across the bar at Josie, but I breathe out and shove the feeling away. "I'm not going to fuck it up," I say firmly, though I'm not sure if I'm telling Cat, or myself.

"Seriously, though, this is awesome. I've wanted you guys to get together for ages."

"Me too," I murmur without thinking, and Cat grins.

"I knew it. You have got it *so bad*." She laughs, poking me in the ribs. "Ask her to come out to Mom's for the Fourth of July weekend."

"It's way too early for that." I watch Josie across the bar, knowing that if she's not ready to tell people about us, she's definitely not ready to come to my mom's house for a holiday weekend. But now that Cat's put the idea in my head, I can't imagine going without her. I want her there with me—eating with my family, watching the fireworks, even showing her my childhood bedroom.

Shit, Cat's right. I've got it bad. I think I always did. The only difference is that now I'm letting myself admit it. I'm letting myself believe I could be good enough for her.

I only wanted you.

God, I still can't believe Josie hasn't been with anyone since she met me. That she thought I was worth waiting around for. I could kick myself for all the time we've wasted apart, and it's making me want to dive into this thing headfirst.

I suck in a lungful of air. *Cool it. Pace yourself. Don't freak her the fuck out.*

"Well, I won't say anything." Cat reaches over to squeeze my hand. "I'm really happy for you, Cors. This is awesome." She heads back to the booth, and I turn to serve some people, unable to stop myself from grinning like a fool.

Not long later, the group wraps up, and Cat and Myles say goodnight before they head off. The crowd has died down for the night, and Josie clears some empties on her way up to the bar.

"Sorry, that took longer than I thought," she says, stacking dirty glasses in the dishwasher.

"Don't apologize. It still counts as work."

"It does?"

"Sure." I shrug. "It's an event taking place at the bar."

Josie laughs. "Well, thank you." She places her hand on my arm—an innocent action to everyone around us, but her touch makes my entire body tingle with awareness. "And thank you so much for making me do this. I think we can actually make the fundraiser happen."

"You're welcome." I swallow hard as she strokes her finger in the tiniest movement over my skin. Then I dip my head closer to her ear and say in a low voice, "Are you going to call me Boss again?"

Her eyes flare. "Did you like that?" She leans into my ear. "*Boss*."

Holy Christ.

I tear myself away from her and clear my throat, gesturing to the back room. "Josie, can I please have a word?" I aim for a neutral tone, but it comes out a little gruff and her mouth pops open uncertainly.

"Uh... sure."

I lead her into the back room and close the door, locking it. When I turn back, she looks worried.

"I'm sorry—"

"Buttercup." I let out a heavy breath, stepping close to her. "I need to kiss you."

"Oh." She gives a relieved laugh as I draw her body into mine. "I thought you were mad at me for speaking to you like that."

"Fuck, *no*. That was hot." I brush her lips with a soft, restrained kiss. Then I go to pull away, but she winds her arms around my neck and pulls me in. When I feel her tongue sweep over my bottom lip, need rushes my bloodstream and I groan, pushing her up against the back of the door. "God," I rasp, dropping my hands to her ass and lifting her up onto me. It's only been a few hours since I was last inside her, but it feels like forever.

She makes a little whimper as I grind into her, and I know that if I don't stop now I'll end up fucking her right against the door. While that would be insanely hot, that's not what I want.

Okay, that's not *all* I want.

I want this to be real, and that means I need to do things the right way. Going down on her at work and receiving a blow job in the shower is basically the opposite of how things should have started with us. I cringe when I think about it, because as much as I—and she, I'm pretty sure—enjoyed it, she deserves so much more.

With Herculean effort, I pull my mouth off hers and set her down on the floor. "Sorry," I say, adjusting the stiff front of my jeans. "I didn't mean to maul you up against the door."

"Maybe I wanted you to." She gives me a sly smile and I chuckle.

"How would you like tomorrow night off?"

Her brows flick together. "What?"

"I'll cover both of our shifts. I was hoping to take you out for dinner." It must be at least a decade since I last took a woman on a date, usually because I prefer to skip straight to dessert, but with Josie, I want all the other stuff. I want to take her out somewhere in the city, to share a meal, to talk and just... be with her.

Then we can go home for dessert.

"Really?"

"Yeah." I tuck her hair behind her ear. "If we're going to do this, I want to take you on a proper date. Is that okay?"

"Yes," she says, but the word is unnecessary because her face tells me everything. It's the way she bites her lip, like she's trying to bite back her huge smile. That simple expression makes me feel like I've won the damn lottery.

As I watch Josie turn and happily head back into the bar, a thought occurs to me.

Where the fuck do you take a vegan to dinner?

24

JOSIE

I'm going on a date. With my boss. With *Cory*.

I'm dizzy as I get ready, still on a high from the events of last night and today. I spent several hours with Hayley and Harriet, reaching out to local businesses about the fundraiser, and it's been incredibly positive so far. Now I'm blow drying my hair and spending more time doing my makeup than I normally ever would, my stomach full of butterflies. It's silly, I know—I've known Cory for years, we're living together, we've already had sex so many times I've lost count—but I can't help it. I'm nervous.

If we're going to do this, I want to take you on a proper date.

I was desperate to ask him what he meant by "if we're going to do this," but managed to resist. It's barely been forty-eight hours since this whole thing began, and as much as I want to know how he's feeling about everything—about *me*—it's way too early to ask. My ex always told me I was needy, and I don't want to be like that with Cory.

When I finally emerge from the bathroom in a short sundress with a daisy print and tall wedge sandals, Cory is on the sofa, wrestling with Pretzel. He looks up and his whole expression changes.

"Fuck," he says, slack-jawed. "You look so beautiful."

I grin as he walks toward me. These are the tallest sandals I own, and I love that even with these on, he's still so much taller than me.

His hands thread into my hair and he crushes his lips to mine, ruining my lipstick. "I can't believe I get to take you out tonight," he says in a gravelly voice, eying me like I'm his meal. He sucks in a breath and forces himself to take a step back. "I'm going to have a shower and then we'll go, okay?"

I nod, unable to contain my silly smile. "You might want to remove the lipstick," I say with a giggle, gesturing to the crimson red smeared on his lips.

He wipes his wrist across his mouth and laughs as he turns for the bathroom. "I won't be long."

I touch up my lipstick and try to distract myself from my nerves by playing with Pretzel. I haven't been on a date in a while, and it's weird having to get ready in the same house as my date. Especially when Cory emerges from the bathroom shortly after, wrapped in just a towel as he pads to his room. He gives me a wink on the way past and my God, I nearly follow him in there and forget the date altogether.

My patience is rewarded, though, because when he steps out of his room looking more handsome than I've ever seen, my mouth goes dry. He's in dark jeans, dress shoes, and a button-down shirt with the sleeves rolled back to the elbows. His hair is actually styled, instead of just messy like it is at work, and his cologne... utter perfection.

My thighs squeeze together on the sofa when his mouth kicks up in a grin and he asks, "You ready, Buttercup?"

No. No, I'm not ready for this. I'm not ready for how intensely I feel about you, so quickly.

"Yep," I say, standing and grabbing my purse. I resist the urge to kiss him and ruin my lipstick again, instead running a hand down the front of his dress shirt. "You look..." A rough exhale seems to be enough to tell him how I feel, and he chuckles.

"Thanks."

We say goodbye to Pretzel, promising to be home soon, then Cory takes my hand and we head out into the balmy spring evening.

Holy crap. I can't believe I'm on a date with Cory Porter.

THE CAB DROPS us off on a bustling little street in the West Village. Cory gestures to the restaurant across the road, placing a hand on the small of my back as we cross. He was quiet on the drive over, and his hand was all clammy in mine on the backseat. I think he's nervous too, and it makes me want to kiss his face off.

"I chose this place because it's vegan," Cory says as we step up onto the curb. "I thought you'd like it, and since I'm trying to lay off the meat..." His smile is hopeful and I beam back.

God, my heart is overflowing with how sweet this man is.

"I love it," I say, even though we haven't stepped inside yet. "It's—"

"Josie? Josie Lennon, is that you?"

I freeze, the familiar voice washing over me like a bucket of ice water.

No. Please don't let it be him.

But it is. It's my stupid fucking ex, walking toward me on what is supposed to be the best night of my life.

"I thought it was you," Paul drawls, strolling over with

his hands in his pockets. His golden-blond hair is perfectly coiffed as it always was, his ice-blue eyes zeroed in on me.

I feel Cory's hand tighten on my back and I press my eyes closed, praying this isn't happening. My heart claws up my throat and my shoulders instinctively curl in.

"Come here," Paul says, in that arrogant way he always had, where what he wants matters more than anything else, and I feel like I have no choice other than to simply get this over with.

"Hi, Paul," I mutter, letting him pull me into an embrace. I'm stiff as a board, patting him limply on the back. I don't want to talk to him, let alone touch him, but that's Paul—it's easier to go along with it.

Cory clears his throat and I pull away from my ex, stepping back into Cory's side. His arm encircles my waist, and I finally breathe out.

"Cory Porter." Cory extends a hand, like the grown-up he is. Paul seems to straighten up, as if to make himself taller as he takes Cory's hand.

"Paul Wayward."

My pulse pounds in my skull as they stare each other down. The tension on the sidewalk thickens until I feel like I'm choking on it.

"So how do you two know each other?" Cory asks tightly.

"Oh, we go way back, don't we, Josie?" Paul's eyes glitter. "And how do you know her?" The question is directed at Cory, but his gaze is still on me.

"Cory's my boss," I blurt, instantly regretting it. I forgot how unsettled Paul made me feel. I haven't seen the guy in half a decade, but I'm right back to being the person I was when we were together—timid, insecure, uncertain.

Cory's hand falls from my waist and I glance at him. His

brows draw together in a frown, and when his gaze meets mine, the hurt there makes my chest tighten.

"I mean, um—" I shake my head, wanting to backtrack, but when I see the amusement in Paul's eyes, I shrivel.

"You okay there, Joze?" His voice is almost taunting, reminding me of the way he spoke to me all those years ago. The way he *always* spoke to me.

I grimace, glancing away. It's safe to say tonight is effectively ruined.

"She's fine," Cory says, his tone a warning. "If you'll excuse us, we're going to continue with our evening." Before Paul can say anything more, Cory's hand lands on my back again, and he gently steers me into the restaurant.

My mind is reeling as the hostess takes us to a booth near the back. It's not until I'm sitting opposite Cory with a napkin across my lap, that I let myself look at him. "I am so sorry."

"It's okay."

"It's not okay." My heart is still walloping. "I didn't mean... When I called you my boss, I didn't—"

"I know." Cory softens. "I could tell you were uncomfortable with that guy. And, you know, we haven't exactly defined this yet."

I swallow. Shit, I did not mean to bring this conversation up on our first date of all times. "It's fine," I say, waving a hand. "We don't need to label it. Let's just... keep it casual." I hope I come off as nonchalant instead of anxious. Seeing Paul has brought back all my old insecurities, and I feel like Cory can see right through me.

He opens his mouth to say something, then closes it, frowning as he looks down to adjust his place setting. "Okay. If that's what you want."

The waitress appears and insists on reciting the

specials. I try to listen but I'm all out of sorts. Paul stole a year of my life, and while I thought I'd done a good job of moving on, running into him just ripped that wound right open again.

I manage to order a glass of wine and Cory requests a beer, asking if we can have a few moments before ordering our food. Then he turns back to me, his brow knitted as he studies me over the table.

I pin on a smile, desperate to shake off the encounter with Paul and the ensuing awkwardness. "So, Hayley and Harriet were really helpful today. We approached some local businesses about the fundraiser, and—"

"Joze." Cory takes my hand, not letting me change the subject. "What happened out there? Who was that guy?"

I blow out a long breath. "My ex."

He blinks. "You mean..."

"Yeah. The guy I moved here with, right before you hired me."

Cory's hand tightens on mine. "I thought I noticed an accent. Shit." He scrubs a hand over his beard, his expression murderous. "I should have decked him."

I snort a laugh, taking my glass of wine as the waitress arrives with our drinks.

Cory takes his beer, then looks at me without humor. "You've never told me the story about that. What happened to you guys?"

"Oh, it was just..." I trail off as I stare down into my wine. I don't want to get into this right now, but Cory looks so concerned, and I guess he deserves an explanation for my odd behavior and change of mood. "We dated for a year, back in Austin. It was... messy. He'd declare his love for me, then he'd get all distant and weird. Then he'd want me back, and we'd go through the cycle again."

Cory is quiet and I force myself to look up at him. His jaw is hard as I keep speaking.

"Then he got this job at NYU, and asked me to move to New York with him, but when we got here, he made it out like I'd begged to follow him and he'd never wanted it in the first place." I shake my head, remembering how young and stupid I was. "I packed up my whole life, even after he'd spent a year stringing me along, because I was naive enough to think that if we moved to a new city, things would be different."

"Why didn't you leave him?" Cory asks, hand clenched tight around his beer.

"You said it yourself, I never put my needs first." I mean it to be a joke, but Cory doesn't so much as crack a smile, and I sigh. "I think I believed he was someone I could fix. I was convinced that if I just tried harder, if I loved him enough, things would be good." I take a long sip of wine, thinking back to Geoff telling me you can't force someone to change. "In reality, he just wasn't a nice man. When I told him about my mom, he talked about how hard it must have been for her, giving everything up for me. I'd never thought about it like that, but he kept pointing out all the things *she* sacrificed. It made me feel like shit."

"Oh, Buttercup." Cory reaches across the table to touch my cheek, and the tenderness of the gesture makes my throat grow tight.

"When he finally ended it, he said a lot of nasty things. He told me I was needy, and he said that my mom was better off without me since I'd left Austin, and—" I stop as I feel tears press at my eyes.

Goddammit, I really know how to ruin a date.

I raise my hand to shield my face, trying to get my emotions under control. Paul used to hate it if I showed emotion in public—he always said it was embarrassing. He'd be rolling his eyes right now.

But Cory slides out of his side of the booth and joins me on my side, gently taking my face in his hands. "Hey. That guy is an absolute asshole, okay? None of that is true."

I swallow, taking a deep breath before I meet Cory's gaze. "I know. I mean, I know that on an intellectual level, but sometimes..."

"Yeah," he murmurs. "You can't help but believe the worst about yourself. I know the feeling."

Oh, this man. Comforting me in such a raw, honest way while I have an emotional meltdown in the middle of a restaurant on our first date. He should be running for the hills, but he's right here with me.

"Have you ever considered that his words might be the reason you feel like you shouldn't stand up for yourself or ask for help?" Cory says. "That he's the reason you always feel like you're a burden to others?" His tone is gentle, but his words hit me like a tsunami.

Oh my God. He's right.

You want too much, Josie.

Paul's words from years ago suddenly come back to me —words I'd forgotten, but I think they've always been buried in there. Every time I asked Paul what was happening with us, where I stood with him—a perfectly reasonable request in a long-term adult relationship—he told me I was clingy and needy. He belittled me and eroded my confidence, and over time I believed him.

And the things he said about my mom... I haven't been home to Austin since arriving in New York, telling myself she was better off with me giving her space. But is that true? I'd love to go home for a visit. She asks me to come home for Christmas every year, and I've made excuses, thinking I was doing her a favor. But really, I've been hiding up here in the city, worrying about getting in anyone's way.

"You're right," I say, staring at Cory in shock. "He made me feel so crappy about myself, made me feel like people would be better off without me burdening them." I think about the fundraiser meeting last night and the time I spent with Hayley and Harriet today, how—far from being *bothered* by me asking for help—everyone has been enthusiastic and eager to support me. That's all because Cory pushed me to speak up, to ask for what I want, because he cares about me and wants to lift me up, rather than push me down like Paul did. I've been speaking up more lately and it feels good. I can't let one shitty run-in with my ex erase all the progress I've made.

I think of Cory's words in the bar the night we first kissed—*say how you really feel*—and straighten up. "Cors... I was wrong, earlier. I don't want this to be casual."

He lifts his eyebrows. "You don't?"

"I..." My pulse spikes. *Say how you really feel.* "No. We don't have to label it, and I'm not trying to rush things, but I like you more than a casual amount. This... You... This is a big deal to me."

A smile slowly builds on Cory's mouth. "Fuck," he murmurs, taking my hand. "I am so glad you said that. I'm trying not to rush things too, but the past forty-eight hours have felt surreal. Like a dream. I've wanted you for a long time, and now that we're here I don't want this to be casual, either. I want this to be *something.*"

Then he slides his hands into my hair and draws my mouth to his for a kiss. The soft brush of his lips over mine is like a balm to all the old wounds Paul opened this evening, and I sigh, feeling a hundred times better.

"That's the best thing I've ever heard you say," I murmur

against his lips. When we finally pull apart, I notice the waitress hovering nearby, and I remember our surroundings. "I think we should probably order," I say with a giggle.

Cory laughs too, drawing away from me. "Yeah. Are you sure you want to stay? Because if you'd rather go, that's okay."

"I want to stay." I squeeze his leg under the table. "It's our first date and you brought me to a vegan restaurant. That's... Yes, I want to stay."

Cory grins, waving the waitress over. We order our food, then he grabs his beer, turning his full attention to me. "Now. Tell me about the progress you made with the fundraiser today."

25

CORY

The next three weeks pass in a blur of work, sex, and getting the fundraiser ready. Josie is incredibly busy and while I wish she had more free time, I know it's only temporary.

I'm so proud to watch her make this thing happen. She's a fucking badass when she wants to be, and I'm going to do everything in my power to help her remember that.

Josie is so swamped with the fundraiser that I've started cooking more, so it was one less thing for her to worry about. I've resisted getting back in the kitchen for years because it always reminded me of Dad, but now that I'm using Josie's recipes and cooking for her—for *us*—it feels different. It feels good.

Everything about life feels good lately and I have her to thank for it. I never realized how much I was going through the motions before—work, gym, mindless sex with women whose names I never had to learn. Life was easy, sure, but it meant nothing. I was stuck in a rut that I thought was fine, but now that I've seen what life can be like with Josie... Shit, I can't imagine anything else.

Tonight is the fundraiser and we've been at the bar all afternoon, making sure everything is ready. Guests will be charged a cover fee to enter, and they've been asked to come in an animal costume in support of the shelter, with a prize for best dressed. Myles has a signature cocktail planned for the evening: a vodka Greyhound, with a couple variations in the form of a Salty Dog and Dalmatian, to keep everything on theme. There are raffles to win everything from dog walking and grooming services, to custom-designed animal outfits (courtesy of Cat), organic dog treats (courtesy of Harriet's friend Paula), pet portraits (courtesy of Hayley), and I stopped listening after that because there were so many things.

Josie and I are in the back room, getting into costume before guests arrive. I'm wearing this lion thing she told me would look "adorable," which is basically a tan colored tank top with a fur-trimmed hood, lion ears, and a tail that hangs over my black jeans. When she first came home with it, I wasn't convinced, but then I saw the delight on her face when I tried it on and, well, that was that.

But it's fine, because she's wearing this sexy as hell deer costume; a full-body jumpsuit hugging every inch of her curves, with a white, fur-trimmed neckline that sits low, exposing her shoulders and collarbone. It's got a matching headband with little antlers and ears, and I swear, I never thought I'd want to fuck Bambi, but seeing Josie in this gives me some very questionable thoughts.

"I don't think we thought our costume choices through," Josie says, reaching for her knee-high brown boots. She bends at the waist to pull them on, glancing back at me as she slowly zips them up.

Fuck *me*.

"Why's that?" I say roughly, turning to look at the wall so I don't destroy her costume before anyone even sees it.

"Well, you're a lion and I'm a deer. This would never work. You'd eat me."

I give a dark chuckle, turning back to her with a smirk. "I'm going to fucking *devour* you later, Buttercup. This works perfectly."

She laughs; a warm, husky sound that makes me wrench my gaze away from her again. Eddy, Levi, and Camila are out in the bar, along with half our friends who came early to help set up. I've told Cat about me and Josie, and I'm pretty sure Harriet knows, but we still haven't shared what's going on with anyone else. She's been so consumed with planning this fundraiser over the past few weeks and it didn't seem fair to pressure her about this, but now the fundraiser is here, and I'm dying to walk out in front of our friends and coworkers and show them how I feel about her.

I glance back at Josie, opening my mouth to say something, but stop when I see her anxious expression. Tonight isn't about me, it's about her. It's about the shelter. I need to respect that.

"You ready?" I ask, checking the door is closed before stealing a quick kiss.

"Yeah." She smooths a hand over the lion's mane on my hood. "I'm kind of nervous."

"I get that, but I don't think you should be. It's going to be awesome. You've done an amazing job." She beams up at me, and I realize something. "But your costume *is* wrong. I mean, it looks fantastic, but... you're not a deer—you're way more powerful than that. More powerful than you give yourself credit for. You're a lioness."

She stares at me for a second, speechless. "Wow. That's... thank you. That's the nicest compliment I've ever received." Her lips tip into a naughty grin, and she leans in to kiss me again. "I want you to wear this for me later," she purrs, tugging on my tail.

I haul her against me and kiss her hard, nipping at her bottom lip. "I want you on all fours for me later."

Her breath comes out in a stutter against my mouth. "Yes, Boss."

I groan, dropping my face into her neck, sinking my teeth into the exposed skin on her shoulder.

Tonight is going to be torture.

"NINE THOUSAND, SO FAR," Myles says, looking up from his laptop. He's sitting behind the bar, keeping a running tally of donations and totals from raffle sales, updating us every so often.

"Okay," I say, holding out a beer. "Nine thousand is good, but it's still a way to go."

"It's over halfway, plus it's still early." He rolls back the sleeves on his Dalmatian onesie. "Shit, it's way too hot for this," he mutters, taking the beer from my outstretched hand and holding the cold bottle to his forehead.

I laugh, suddenly grateful that at least my costume is a tank top. Summer in New York is no joke.

I look across the room for my sister, spotting her in a booth with her friends, and I wave her over. "Hey," I say, when she reaches the bar. "We're only at nine thousand. We need to pick things up. Can you encourage more people to buy raffle tickets?"

Cat nods. "Sure thing."

"Where's Geoff? I figured he'd be here."

"Oh, he is." She points across the bar to where two

grizzly bears are standing side-by-side. God, those costumes look hotter than Myles's onesie. "He brought a date, and apparently he's super rich. He owns a bunch of hotels or a retail chain, or something—I wasn't really listening. I'll go lean on him for money."

"Great." I chuckle as she spins on her heel and strides off with purpose. My gaze drifts around the bar, looking for other familiar faces. I invited my buddy Rob—the guy I used to run this place with—but he couldn't make it. He's got a wife and three kids in Jersey, so I'm not surprised. He donated to our Go Fund Me page, though. He's a good guy. I should really make more of an effort to visit him and his family; I haven't been out there in years.

When I turn back to the bar, my eyes land on a redhead in a *Playboy* bunny outfit. I eye her costume, mentally debating whether it counts as being on theme. I guess *technically* it's a rabbit.

"Hi, Cory," she says, leaning across the bar. "I was hoping you'd be here tonight."

Oh, right—I thought she looked familiar. I cast my mind back, trying to remember the last time I saw her. It was the night Josie needed a place to crash. She was trying to get me to take this woman home, and instead I took her and Pretzel.

The rest was history.

"Hey, uh..."

"Rachel," she supplies, looking a little annoyed.

"Of course." I reach for the Prosecco. I might be shit with names, but I never forget a drink. "Thanks for coming to support the fundraiser."

"It's a great cause."

I set the bottle of Prosecco down. "I hope you'll buy

some raffle tickets." I hold out the glass and her hand closes over mine.

"And I hope you'll call me," she says, holding my gaze. It's exactly the type of forward, ballsy gesture I would have loved in the past, but right now it's making unease swirl in my stomach.

"Uh..." I pull my hand away with a grimace, glancing around for Josie. What can I say? I can't exactly tell her I have a girlfriend, because Josie and I haven't had that conversation yet. And even if we had, I'm surrounded by people who don't know about us.

I catch Josie's eye where she's ringing up a sale further down the bar. She glances between me and Rachel, who's leaning unnecessarily close, and her brow pinches. When she tears her gaze away, my chest feels hot and tight.

Fuck it.

"I won't, sorry," I say to the redhead, then I back away from the bar and stride over to Josie. "Hey, I need to talk to you."

She hands the customer's credit card back and turns to me. "Now?"

"Yes. Now."

"Okay..." She follows me into the back room and I close the door behind her, locking it.

"I can't keep doing this, Joze."

She freezes. "What?"

"This isn't working for me."

"But—"

"I'm sick of not touching you here, not being able to kiss you in front of everyone. It sucks."

"Oh, God." She puts her hand on her chest, visibly relieved. "I thought you meant..."

"Shit, no." I gather her into my arms. "Sorry, that wasn't

the best way to say that. I just..." My pulse ramps up and I take a deep breath. "I'm crazy about you, Buttercup. I don't want to hide what we have anymore. I want everyone to know you're mine."

She looks up at me with wide eyes, the tiny stud in her nose catching the light. "Are you sure? What about Eddy and—"

"Fuck him. Fuck everyone. All I care about is what you think."

"I think... I feel the same." Her lips quirk into a shy smile. "I'd love to tell everyone you're *mine*." She says the word reverently and it makes my heart swell. As if she thinks *she's* the lucky one.

But she's not. It's me. I'm the guy who gets to call this incredible woman mine—this woman who's spent the past three weeks working her ass off to save this shelter, because she cares so much. Because she's that good.

That familiar self-doubt eats into my gut, but I quickly shake it off. It's getting easier to do that the more I'm around Josie.

"I'm glad you feel the same," I say, sliding my hands down to grip her butt through her deer costume. "Because when we hit our target, I'm going to kiss you so hard, right in front of everyone."

She giggles. "*If* we hit our target."

I shake my head, touching my lips to hers. "You're going to do it, Joze. I have no doubt."

26

JOSIE

"We're almost there," Myles says, looking up from his laptop where he's tucked behind the bar.

My mouth pops open. "Really? How?"

"Cat's friend Claudia made a huge donation, and Geoff's date was pretty generous, too."

"How much more do we need?"

Myles glances back down at his screen. "Roughly seven hundred, then we'll hit our target."

"Oh my God," I say breathlessly. "We're only seven hundred away? I could donate a few hundred, then—"

"I'll take care of it," Cory says, sliding his arms around my waist from behind and nuzzling my neck.

I watch Myles's eyes crinkle in amusement at seeing us together. "Are you two finally admitting this is happening, then?"

"Yes." Cory kisses my ear and his words suddenly click in my brain.

I spin around in his arms. "What do you mean, you'll take care of it?"

"I'll donate the rest."

"But you already matched the cocktails—"

"I know." His hands drop to my hips and squeeze. "I want to do this, too."

"That's…" I shake my head in disbelief at this man and his generosity. "Thank you, Cors. That means so much to me." I glance back at Myles. "So, we've done it?"

He nods. "Yep. If Cory gives us seven hundred, that brings us up to…" He types something, then turns the screen around to show me. There it is in black and white:

Total donations: $17,014

Elation bursts bright in my chest and I turn to Cory, bouncing on the spot. "We did it! Oh my God."

"*You* did it, Joze. Come with me." Cory tugs me out into the crowd, to the front of the room. "Excuse me, everyone." He taps the microphone on the sound system, quieting the room. "Thank you all for being here to support Animal Oasis tonight. We've just checked the tally of our raffle sales and donations, and I'm pleased to tell you"—he pauses for dramatic effect—"we have now *met* our fundraising target of seventeen thousand—"

The crowd erupts into applause and cheers. My whole body is buzzing as I try to process this. We did it. We saved the shelter I love so much.

Cory laughs, waving his hands to quiet the crowd. "We wouldn't be here tonight if it wasn't for Josie Lennon." He reaches for my hand, pulling me closer. "Josie is one of those people who cares about things many people ignore—especially animal welfare. I've never met anyone as selfless and generous as her. It's because of Josie's hard work, along with that of my sister and our friends, that you're all here. I'm so proud of what Josie has achieved tonight, and I'm also very proud—and lucky—to call her my girlfriend."

My heart stops in my chest.

His *girlfriend*.

He's never called me that before. Emotion wells inside me and I swallow hard. God, I know it's just one word, one tiny word, but... it's not tiny at all.

It's everything.

Cory Porter—my boss, my crush of forever, the sexy bartender that every woman wants—is my boyfriend.

And now the entire world knows.

"Let's raise a glass to thank Josie for all her passion and hard work to make tonight happen." He holds his beer in the air and the room follows, cheering and clapping.

My throat is tight as I look around at all these people here to support me and the shelter. Harriet is in a booth, whooping and cheering, and beside her I spot Cat, grinning like mad.

Cory leans into my ear, speaking just for me. "I'm so proud of you, Buttercup. I knew you could do it."

Then he tugs me into his arms, pressing his lips to mine, and the crowd cheers even louder. He laughs against my mouth and I laugh back. I feel drunk, in this moment; drunk on the fact that we saved the shelter, on Cory being so openly affectionate with me in front of everyone. On him being mine. On this being real.

"Thank you," I say, gazing up at him. "I wouldn't have done this without you pushing me."

The music comes back on and the crowd slowly turns back to mingle and chat. Somebody waves Cory over to talk and he leaves my side with a reluctant look. I step back behind the bar and watch him laugh with a group of people, my chest warm and full.

"So..." Cat sets her empty glass down on the bar in front of me with a mischievous smile. "You and my brother, huh?"

"Yeah," I say, chuckling at her excited expression. I reach for the vodka to refill her glass. "You seem happy about it."

"Are you kidding? I've been waiting for you guys to get together." She glances over her shoulder to where Cory is talking to Geoff and his date, who I can't properly make out because of the giant, furry bear costume. "You know, I've never seen Cory like this before."

"What do you mean?"

"He's practically giddy. I think he really likes you."

I chew my lip to try and hide my ridiculous grin. "I really like him, too."

She turns back to me. "Yeah?"

I nod.

"I'm glad. I know he often comes across as an overprotective grump, but it's because he cares so much. He's a big softie inside." Her expression shifts. "Just... don't hurt him, okay? He hasn't had a girlfriend in... shit, I don't know how long. Twenty years?" She laughs, but it's without mirth.

"I won't," I say quietly, thinking of all the things he told me the night we got together.

"This time of year is difficult for him, with the anniversary of our dad's death coming up. It always seems to hit Cors pretty hard." Cat turns to watch him again, and a smile touches her mouth. "But it's nice to see him so happy."

My heart squeezes. He's done so much for me; all I want to do is make him smile, make him forget everything that hurt him.

"You two talking about me?" Cory asks, sliding onto a barstool beside Cat.

"Of course." Cat picks up her drink, taking a casual sip. "Josie was just telling me about all the weird sex stuff you're into."

Cory's cheeks color. His gaze swings to me and I raise a hand to muffle my laugh.

"What?" he huffs. "It's not *that* weird—"

I chuckle. "She's kidding, Cors."

His gaze cuts to Cat, who's laughing into her vodka. "You want to start paying for your drinks?" he asks, and she laughs even harder.

Myles climbs onto the stool beside Cat. "What's so funny?"

"Nothing," Cory mumbles, rising to his feet.

I step around the bar and push up onto my toes, kissing him. "Ignore them." He looks so damn sexy in this lion costume, with his gorgeous sculpted biceps on display and the cute little fur-trimmed hood. I wasn't kidding when I said I wanted him to wear it later. And I've seen the way he's been looking at me in this deer outfit—I believe him when he said he wanted to devour me in it.

Huh, maybe we are into some weird stuff.

I notice Gerard pushing through the crowd and I turn to him, grinning. I was hoping he'd make it. "Gerard! Did you hear? We did it!"

"I did." He shakes his head, looking around us in awe. "I can't believe it."

Cory slips his hand into mine and I gesture to Gerard. "Gerard, this is Cory. He owns the bar, and..." I sneak a glance at Cory's smiling face, adding, "He's also my boyfriend."

God, it feels *unbelievable* to say that.

Cory's hand squeezes mine, then releases it to shake Gerard's. "Cory Porter. Glad you could come."

Gerard clasps Cory's hand in both of his. "Thank you so much for doing this, both of you. You've raised enough for us to stay open. I can't thank you enough."

I beam. "I'm so glad we could help. You know how much I love that place."

"I do." Gerard chuckles. "I bet you'll be relieved for the shelter to take Pretzel off your hands again. I know he can be a handful."

Oh.

I stare at Gerard, letting his words sink in. Shit, of course. Why didn't I think of that before? Now that we've made the money we need tonight, the shelter will open again. With the shelter open, there's no need for me to keep Pretzel.

And if I don't have Pretzel, I don't need to stay at Cory's.

Unless he wants that? So much has changed since this whole thing began; maybe the old arrangement doesn't apply anymore?

I think about what he said earlier tonight—*I'm crazy about you, Buttercup*—and glance at him, searching his face for a sign. He's gazing across the bar in thought, a frown etched into his forehead, and my stomach sinks.

You want too much, Josie.

Paul's words play through my mind, bringing me to my senses. What's wrong with me? It's barely been five minutes since Cory called me his girlfriend for the first time; I can't ask if I can live with him permanently in the next breath. We've only been dating for three weeks.

"Yeah," I murmur to Gerard, trying to ignore the hollowness I feel behind my ribs, because I don't want to give Pretzel back—and if I'm being entirely honest, I don't want to leave Cory's. Everything feels so perfect and I don't want it to change.

"Excuse me." Cory smiles politely at Gerard. "I'm just going to clear some glasses." His fingers brush my lower back before he steps away, and I feel uneasy as I watch him go.

"There's something else I wanted to mention," Gerard says. "Once the shelter opens again, we're going to need a new animal enrichment and rescue coordinator."

My pulse jumps. Full-time, paid positions at the shelter come up once in a blue moon—if that.

"I have to advertise the role and go through all the proper channels," Gerard continues, "but given all the time you've spent with us, I think you'd be perfect. Would you consider submitting an application?"

I'm surprised to feel myself hesitate. I've wanted a paid job at the shelter for years, but that's not what I'm thinking about right now—I'm thinking about how everything is changing so quickly. If I have to move out of Cory's and give up Pretzel, I can't face the thought of leaving Bounce as well. It's too much.

Gerard is looking at me expectantly, so I nod. "I'll think about it."

He smiles, thanking me again for everything I've done, and I force myself to breathe in slowly as I head back to the bar. Tonight's been a lot to process and all I can think about now is getting home—well, Cory's place. I guess it won't be my home for much longer.

"I knew it." Eddy appears beside me, wiping the bar.

I turn to him warily. "What?"

"You and the boss. I knew there was something going on."

I sigh. Here we go. "Look, it wasn't—"

"Nah, I knew. He's always had a thing for you. It's pretty obvious."

I stop, surprised. How is it possible that *Eddy*, of all people, could tell before I could?

"I'm happy for you guys," he says, and I'm taken aback by his genuine smile. "He's been in a way better mood lately, thanks to you. Just don't expect me to cover all your shifts when he gives you time off."

I roll my eyes. "Nothing is going to change, Eddy."

If only this were true.

27
—

CORY

We're both quiet on the cab ride home. It's late and I'm tired, but mostly I keep replaying what Gerard said to Josie as I walked away. I didn't mean to overhear him offer her a job at Animal Oasis, but his words stopped me in my tracks.

My insides knot as I think about it again. Would Josie really leave the bar to work full time at the shelter? I know how much that place means to her, but shit, I don't want to lose her from Bounce.

That's not the only thing on my mind. When Gerard suggested Josie return Pretzel to the shelter, I'd expected her to say she was keeping him. Those two are peas in a pod. I never thought I'd be jealous of a *dog*, but I am—at least once a day. She loves that mutt more than anything and I hate the thought of her losing him after they've grown so close. I've grown close to Pretzel too, and when I try to imagine my apartment without him there now, it feels wrong. I can't even *begin* to picture the place without Josie.

Being with her at the bar tonight, in front of our friends and coworkers, made everything between us feel so much more real. Calling her my girlfriend felt amazing. I've never felt this way about a woman and it's making me want to take things to the next level—to ask her not to move out. Ask her to spend the holiday weekend with my family.

I haven't taken a woman home to Long Island before, and the thought sends nerves flickering through me. Cat and Myles will be there, and I know my mom already loves Josie after meeting her at the wedding, but my extended family is a lot to take.

It's not just that, though. This is the house where I grew up—where my dad walked out, where I broke Alice's heart and learned how easily I can hurt others. That world is separate from this one I share with Josie, and the thought of mixing the two together makes me uneasy.

I close the door behind us and kick off my boots, pulling down the hood of my lion costume as I watch Josie's nightly ritual of greeting Pretzel. Every time she returns home, she crouches down to tell him how much she missed him and what a good boy he's been.

Seriously. That's one lucky dog.

It's not the same tonight, though. Pretzel's as enthusiastic as always, but she just pets his fur before silently letting him out into the courtyard. Then she heaves a sigh and turns back, giving me a strained smile when she sees I'm watching.

"Hey," I murmur, crossing the room to her. "You okay?"

"Yeah."

I reach out to stroke a hand over her hair. She's still in her deer costume, but the antlers have been tossed onto the coffee table. "Tonight was amazing. What you did for that shelter—for all those animals—is incredible."

Her gaze flicks to me and back to the floor. "Thanks," she mumbles. "It felt good."

"So why aren't you happy, Buttercup?" I watch her pick at a nail, wondering if she's thinking about Gerard's offer and wants to talk about it. Part of me hopes she doesn't, because I can't guarantee I won't beg her not to leave the bar. "Joze," I say gently, taking her hand. "Please talk to me."

"Okay." She inhales. "I was thinking about what Gerard said about giving Pretzel back. Once the shelter opens, I'll have no reason to hold on to him, and..." she trails off with a shrug.

"Yeah, I was thinking about that. What if you didn't give him back?"

She examines the carpet. "I can't have dogs in my apartment, remember?"

"I remember." I place a finger under her chin, tilting her face up to mine. "But that's not what I meant. What if he stayed here? What if *you* stayed here?"

"Like we are now?"

"Yes, but, you know, without an end date."

"You mean..." Her eyes widen. "Are you serious?"

I nod, chuffing a laugh. "This place wouldn't be the same without you guys here."

She stares at me, her mouth opening and closing as she absorbs this. "You don't think it's too soon?"

I lift a shoulder. "We're already living together. Maybe if we hadn't known each other for years it would be too soon, but I love what we have now. I don't want to take a step backward." I study her face carefully. If she doesn't feel the same way, I'll do my best to respect that.

But it might fucking kill me.

"I understand if it's too fast for you," I add. "I know tonight has been a lot."

"No." She lunges at me, taking me by surprise as she kisses me hard on the mouth. "I really want to stay."

Oh, thank God.

"Yeah?" My heart is racing. I didn't realize quite how desperate I was for her to want this.

"Yeah. I love what we have now, and I was afraid... I don't know. That it was going to change."

"I was afraid of that, too."

Hell, I'm still afraid. I'm afraid of how fast I'm falling for this woman—how incredible she is and how even after several weeks of trying to convince myself I'm enough for her, I still don't quite believe it. I'm afraid that if I take her home to Long Island, into that other part of my life, she might figure that out for herself.

But as she looks up at me with the most adoring smile, I realize that if I want this to be real, I can't hide parts of myself from her. It wasn't until I told her about my past that we got this close, and I don't want to lose that closeness by putting up walls to keep her out again. I want to let her all the way in, and trust that she'll still want me enough.

"Joze, there's something else." I take a deep breath. "I was thinking maybe you could come out to my mom's place on Long Island with me for the Fourth of July weekend."

I don't get a second to worry about her feelings on this, because she nods immediately. "Yes! I'd love to— Oh." She stops, rubbing her forehead.

"What is it?"

"Well, the shelter..." She pulls her bottom lip into her mouth, worrying it between her teeth. My stomach plunges as it occurs to me that she might have already decided to take Gerard up on his job offer. I wait for her to say as much, but instead she says, "I usually volunteer over holiday weekends."

Relief washes through me, and I chuckle. This is classic Josie, always putting the needs of others before herself. I'm tempted to say this—to remind her that her happiness matters too—but she speaks again.

"You know what? I will come. I really want to and I'm sure Gerard will understand. Besides," she adds, grinning up at me, "I must have earned a weekend off, given I saved the shelter and all." Her eyes shimmer as she laughs. God, I could get used to this woman who owns her power and knows what she wants. It's fucking sexy.

"You've definitely earned it," I agree, lowering my hands to her waist and walking her backward toward the bedroom. "And you'll get it. But right now, I want you in bed."

She giggles, reaching to unzip her costume and I shake my head. "Nope. Leave that on." I grab the antlers from the coffee table and hand them over, pointing to the bedroom. "Put these on and wait for me in there. On all fours."

Her eyebrows hit her hairline.

"I'll make it worth it, Buttercup." I give her a wicked grin, pulling my lion hood back up. Her pupils dial out to an inky black as she looks me over, still in costume. She slides on her antlers and steps into the bedroom.

I call Pretzel back inside and close the door, settling him down in his crate for now. Then I turn and stalk into the bedroom, pleased to find Josie on her hands and knees in the middle of the bed. I grab her hips and drag her to the edge, still on all fours. She's the perfect height like this, which I confirm by pressing the stiffness in my jeans to her ass. It elicits a groan from her that makes me dizzy with need. This woman wants to live with me, come visit my family, *and* she'll get on her hands and knees when I ask? Fuck, how can she be real?

"Was this costume expensive?" I ask, running a hand over the round curve of her ass.

She looks back at me over her shoulder. "No."

"Good." I grab the fabric and tear it apart at the seam, exposing her backside. She gives a little shriek of surprise and I bring my hand down on her butt cheek, just enough to sting. Shit, I don't know what's gotten into me.

No, I do. It's her. It's everything about her.

She moans, pushing back against my palm as I smooth it over the red handprint I've left.

"Did you like that?"

"Yes," she breathes.

"You have the most perfect ass, Joze." I spank her again, earning another moan. She's wearing a lace thong and seeing it on her wriggling backside sends a bolt of lust right through me. I drop to my knees, unable to wait another second.

"Fuck, I need you." I grab her thighs and spread them, tugging the thin strip of lace out of the way, then bury my face in the slick heat between her legs. She whimpers, grinding back on my face, and it only makes me devour her more.

"Oh God," she rasps, dropping onto her elbows and pressing her face to the mattress. "Right there. Yes."

I work my tongue on her until she's quivering and calling my name in release. I'm so hard it hurts, but I don't stop until I know she's done. Then I push to my feet and shuck my jeans, desperate to be inside her.

"Keep the top of your costume on," she says, looking back at me over her shoulder. "I like you as a lion."

I grin, grabbing a condom and rolling it down my length. She's still on all fours on the edge of the bed—exactly how I want her. I don't even pause before thrusting into her tight, wet heat, releasing a low howl of relief. Her breath shudders out and she presses back onto me. I lower my chest to her back, wrapping my arms around her.

God, every single inch of her feels amazing. Everything about her is perfect.

I don't say anything as I pump into her, too afraid my words might give away too much. And I definitely don't let myself think about the possibility of her taking a job somewhere else and leaving Bounce. Instead, I kiss the back of her neck and slide one hand down to the slickness where I'm driving in and out, focusing on making her feel good, until we both collapse onto the bed, breathless.

After, we lie in the dark, holding each other close. It doesn't take Josie long to fall asleep—she must be exhausted after all the work she's put in these past three weeks—and I keep my arms around her, almost scared to let go.

Somehow, in the space of a month, it feels like I've gone from an empty, meaningless life to having everything I didn't realize I needed. Because I do need her. I need her to stay with me at the bar. I need her in this bed with me every night. I need her waking up beside me every morning. I've never needed anything more.

And now, Josie is coming to spend the weekend at my childhood home with my family. She's going to see firsthand into that part of my world.

I just hope it doesn't turn out to be a mistake.

28

JOSIE

A week later, we pull up outside Cory's mom's house in Nassau County, Long Island. It's two stories, with white wooden siding and a sloping roof, set back from the road behind an enormous oak tree that dominates the front yard.

Cory parks the truck up the driveway, beside the house. He rented a pickup for the drive, because it was easier to bring Pretzel and our stuff than trying to cart it all on the train. We were going to share a car with Cat and Myles, but they brought his daughter, Amber, and it would have been too cramped.

I was glad to not be around the others, though. Cory spent the drive tapping the steering wheel and not saying much, and I was too nervous to fill the silence. I've never gone to a boyfriend's parents' home before—I never even *met* Paul's parents, which in hindsight was a huge red flag.

Still, I've already met Cory's mom and she's lovely. A fact I'm reminded of when we arrive at the front door and Gail drops straight down to make a fuss over Pretzel. My nerves fizzle out when she stands and pulls me into her arms.

"Hi, Josie. I'm so glad you're here." She squeezes me hard for a long moment until Cory makes an exasperated noise.

"*Mom*," he mumbles, and she releases me with a sheepish laugh, turning to her son.

"You too, Cors. Come on in."

We follow her through to the living room, with me trying to restrain Pretzel as Cory sets our bags down. Cat is on the sofa with Amber and they look up when we enter.

"Hey, guys!" Cat says.

"Hey." Cory glances around. "Where's Myles?"

"In the kitchen." She looks at me, gesturing to her step-daughter. "You remember Amber from our wedding, Joze?"

I nod, smiling at the little blond girl. She gives me a shy smile in return, but before I can say anything, Gail pops into the living room, handing me a treat for Pretzel.

"Thanks." I take the treat and offer it to Pretzel, making sure he feels calm and safe in this new environment. Amber watches curiously from the sofa and I smile. "Amber, this is Pretzel. Do you want to come say hello?"

She glances at Cat, who nods and takes her hand. "He's really nice," Cat assures Amber, guiding her over. Pretzel hesitates as they approach, but after a little coaxing, his tail is wagging again.

"Do you want to let him out in the yard?" Cat asks me. "It's fenced. Stevie is out there now."

"Yeah, he should stretch his legs after the drive."

Amber looks up at me. "Can I take him?"

"Sure, he'd love that. Thank you." I lead Pretzel over to the sliding glass door and unclip his leash, watching as Amber follows the dogs out onto the grass. When I turn back, Cory is standing across the room, watching me with little creases around his eyes. I wander over and he slides an arm around me.

"Can I see your room?" I ask. He's still a little tense, and I want a moment alone to check in with him.

He eyes me, considering my request. When I smile up at him angelically, he gives a reluctant smile, kissing my forehead. "Alright. This way." He leads me up the stairs, his hand snug in mine. I pause to look at family pictures on the way, soaking everything in. My heart is already so full, being in this house. I'm not sure if it's from Gail's warm welcome, the way I already feel comfortable here, or that I'm seeing into this whole other part of Cory's world—that he's actually letting me in.

We turn the corner at the top of the stairs and Cory pushes open the door to his room. He hangs in the doorway while I wander around, taking it in. There's not a lot to it—a bed with a plaid comforter, a few Giants posters on the wall, a sofa in the corner. When I turn back to him, he's lost in thought.

"Everything okay?" I ask. "You seem a little off."

He exhales slowly. "I probably should have said something sooner, but... I overheard Gerard offer you the shelter job."

"Oh." I shift my weight. "Well, he didn't *offer* it to me. I'd have to apply."

Cory scrubs a hand over his beard, nodding. "Are you going to?"

I shrug. I've been thinking about this all week and I still don't know what to do. I love working with Cory, and no matter how much I want to be paid to work with animals at the shelter, Bounce feels like home.

"I know how much the shelter means to you, Joze. If you want to take the job, I'd totally support you. You know that, right?"

"Yeah," I murmur. He's saying the right things, but the

line between his brows gives away his anxiety, and I'm over-whelmed by the urge to reassure him. "I love working at the bar, though."

His lips curve in a rueful smile. "It's hard to imagine it without you."

"It's hard to imagine leaving," I say truthfully. I hold out my hands and Cory steps forward, taking them. "Will you please stop worrying?"

His expression softens. "Yeah."

"Good." I push up onto my toes to kiss him. When I pull away, I spy his bookshelf and cross over to it, examining the titles. One item in particular catches my eye and I can't resist plucking it from the shelf. "Is this your yearbook?"

His brow scrunches when I hold it up. "Don't look at that," he groans, attempting to swipe it from my hands, but I drop onto the bed, laughing.

"Please? I want to see."

"Fine." He sinks down beside me, taking the yearbook and flipping to his page before handing it back. "Here."

Holy crap. Even in high school he was a total babe.

I grin, holding the photo next to him to compare. His face was skinny and I imagine he was kind of lanky, compared to the muscular frame he has today. His jaw is fuller now, covered in a short, sandy-blond beard, unlike the clean-shaven guy in the photo. His face is a little more weathered now too, with a few lines on his forehead and crinkles around his eyes.

But he's perfect. I wouldn't change a thing.

He watches as I compare eighteen-year-old Cory to the man he is today, and I'm relieved to see he's entertained more than anything.

"You know, there's a smaller age gap between me and this guy"—I point to the page—"than me and you."

Cory rolls onto his back on the bed with another groan. "Don't remind me."

I laugh, tossing the yearbook aside and swinging a leg over to straddle him. "Want me to make you feel young again?"

"I'm very tempted," he says, sliding his hands down to cup my butt through my denim cutoffs. I squeeze my thighs around him and he grunts, pressing up into me. He might not be eighteen anymore, but his body responds to my touch like he is.

I brush my mouth over his, then—thinking of his mom and sister downstairs—I reluctantly pull myself to my feet. "Will we be sleeping in here?"

"No." He hauls himself off the bed. "I usually let my cousin's kids crash in my room and I take a tent in the backyard. Is that alright?"

"Of course," I say, smiling. Yet another example of how generous and caring he is. It amazes me he can't see this about himself. "I haven't been camping since I was in Austin."

"It'll be fun." He steps close and sighs, sliding his hands into my hair and stroking my cheek. "I'm so glad you're here, Buttercup."

"Me too," I whisper, reaching up to kiss him.

Cat's hovering in the doorway as we break apart. "You two are so cute." She wanders into the room, amusement flickering over her brow as she looks at Cory. "Did you just call her Buttercup?"

"I..." He frowns at his sister, folding his arms over his chest. "That's none of your business." His brotherly irritation makes me laugh, especially when Cat ignores him, turning to me.

"How long has he called you that?"

"Um..." I cast my mind back. "Since, like, my second month at the bar, I think."

"So basically this whole time?"

I nod.

"Innnteresting," Cat says, drawing the word out as her gaze swings to Cory.

"It is *not* interesting," he mutters, attempting to push her out of the room. "Will you please—"

"Wait." I grab Cat's arm, tugging her away from Cory. "Why is that interesting?"

Her lips curl in a Cheshire grin. "I'll show you. Come with me." She spins on her heel and I follow, intrigued.

"Cat," Cory calls in a warning from the bedroom, but she pretends not to hear, striding down the stairs. Cory appears behind us, taking the steps two at a time until we all pile into the living room.

"Here." Cat snatches a DVD off a cluttered shelf in the corner, holding it out to me. "Have you ever seen this? It's Cory's favorite childhood movie."

I take the DVD, examining the title: *The Princess Bride*. "No," I say, turning it over. "Is that the actress from *Forrest Gump*? She looks so young. How old is this?" I flick a teasing glance to Cory and he rolls his eyes.

"You're forgetting we're from a different generation than her," he mutters to Cat, who snorts a laugh.

"Well," she continues, gesturing to the DVD, "her name is Buttercup. Cory had a huge crush on her growing up."

"I did not—" Cory begins, but Cat silences him with a knowing look. "Yeah, okay," he mumbles, cringing with embarrassment.

"Aw." I squeeze him. "You gave me the nickname of your movie crush? That's cute."

Cat laughs, and Cory stares at the ceiling with impatience, refusing to indulge her.

I turn the DVD over in my hand. "What is this about? It looks like a love story."

"It totally is," Cat says, grinning gleefully. "In fact, Buttercup is this princess who gets captured, and it's all about how he's trying to rescue her because she's his one true lo—"

"*Alright*," Cory says at last, his face red as he glares at Cat. "She gets the idea."

I hand the DVD back to Cat, laughing. Then I step up to press a kiss to his hot cheek. Poor Cory.

Cat tosses the DVD onto the coffee table with a smug grin. "So now we know he's basically been in love with you since you started working for him."

"Jesus," Cory mutters, sinking down into an armchair with his head in his hands.

I laugh, but my insides are in a frantic flurry over Cat's words: *in love with you*. My heart is jumping all over the place, my mind in free-fall. God, the thought of Cory being in love with me... I want that so bad.

Cat flops onto the sofa opposite Cory, regarding me curiously. "How long have you liked *him*?"

"Cat." Cory glances between her and me, shaking his head. "You don't have to answer that, Joze."

I grin. "I don't mind. Um... honestly? I liked him the moment I saw him." I shrug, perching on the arm of Cory's chair, leaning over to press my lips to the closely-shaved hair on the side of his head. "I mean, he's pretty easy on the eyes."

"Yeah, women seem to think that. But"—Cat wrinkles her nose, giving him an exaggerated once-over—"I just don't see it."

"That's probably a good thing," Cory says dryly, and we both laugh.

"It wasn't just that, though," I continue. "I was going through a hard time when I met him, and he kind of took me in. He gave me a job and just... made everything better." I stroke his hair as he gazes up at me, his hazel eyes warm with affection. They're the color of brown ale in this light. "I've always felt like I belong, at Bounce. He's always looked out for me."

"Yeah," Cat says quietly, watching us. "He's very protective of the people he loves."

I swallow at Cat's use of that word again, tearing my gaze from Cory. He clears his throat, going to say something, but Amber comes in through the sliding glass door. Her cheeks are flushed from running around with the dogs outside, and Cat stands from the sofa.

"Hey, sweetie. You want a drink?"

She nods, glancing at me and Cory shyly as Cat ducks into the kitchen.

"Having fun?" Cory asks. "I think Pretzel likes playing with you."

Amber's mouth pulls into a broad smile. "He's so cute."

"Yeah, he is," Cory agrees, giving me a squeeze.

Amber drops onto the sofa and her gaze falls to the *Princess Bride* DVD on the coffee table. Her eyes light up as she scans the cover. "What's this?"

"It's a movie about a princess. Do you want to watch it while we wait for the food?" Cory offers and she nods eagerly. He reaches for the DVD, then pauses. "Actually, I should probably check with your dad."

"I'll ask him." Amber springs to her feet, calling, "Dad? Can I watch a movie?"

I observe this interaction, fascinated. I've never seen

Cory around kids before and it's doing something weird to my insides.

Myles pokes his head in from the kitchen. "What movie?" He finally notices me and Cory, and smiles. "Oh, hey."

"It's about a princess," Amber says, which makes him chuckle.

"That doesn't exactly narrow it down."

Cat enters with a huge glass of lemonade, handing it to Amber. "It's *The Princess Bride*."

"I haven't seen that in years." Myles wipes his hands on a dish towel and wanders into the room, taking the DVD case from Cory and inspecting it. "Is this okay for an eight-year-old?"

"It's fine," Cat says, kissing him. He nods and wanders back into the kitchen as Cat puts it on.

We watch the first half of the film together, laughing about the little boy whose grandfather insists on reading him a love story when he's home sick from school. I'm immediately captivated by the girl in the story—Buttercup—and the farm boy, who's secretly in love with her, and tells her by responding to her every request with, *As you wish*. My heart skips as we watch, wondering if Cory has ever felt that way about me. I can't recall a single time he's ever said *As you wish*, but then I never ask him for anything, so—

"Cat, honey." Gail pokes her head into the living room, interrupting my racing thoughts. "Your husband is in here doing all this work and he's supposed to be a guest. Maybe you could come help?"

"I'll help," Cory says, pushing to his feet.

"I can help too," I offer, trailing after him. "I brought stuff for the grill."

Cory turns to me in the doorway. "I'll take care of that.

You relax, Butter—" he bites off the rest of the word, glancing over my shoulder at the TV with a frown.

My heart pinches. I lean in close, dropping my voice. "Are you going to stop calling me that now? Please don't."

His eyes meet mine, clouded with uncertainty. "You still like it?"

"Even more than I did before." I reach up to stroke his cheek, relieved when his expression softens. "I love the way you call me that. I love—"

Holy crap on a cracker. *Hold it right there.*

My hand shakes as I slowly lower it to my side. What the hell was that? Was I just about to blithely tell him I love him for the first time in the doorway to the kitchen at his mom's house? Where did that even come from?

Oh, who are you kidding? You know where that came from. You're completely in love with him and have been for years.

Well, okay. Yes.

But this feels different. This isn't some infatuation with my hot boss, wishing he'd see me differently. This is so much more intense, so much more real. This is visceral, buzzing through my bloodstream from head to toe. This is based on knowing him so much more now—knowing his good and bad, knowing his mistakes and missteps, knowing who he really is. Because who he really is—it's not any of the things from his past. It's the kindness in his heart. His generosity. His protectiveness and fierce determination to look after those he cares about.

God, he's everything.

I swallow, pushing my thoughts away and trying to regain my composure. Cory's eyes linger on mine, as if he knows what I was about to say and is considering how to proceed. My heart stammers as I wait for him to back away, for the inevitable awkwardness.

Instead, he lowers his mouth to my ear and murmurs, "Okay, Buttercup. *As you wish.*" Then he steps into the kitchen with a little chuckle, pulling open the fridge and grabbing two bottles of Corona. I stare at him as he pops them open and wedges pieces of lime into the top before handing one to me. He clinks his bottle against mine with a wink, then turns to the counter and picks up a knife.

What.

The...?

He just said, *As you wish.* Does that mean—

Nope. You're reading way *too much into that. It's a stupid line from a movie, and you're just excited about being here with him.*

I lift the bottle to my mouth and take a long sip of the cool liquid, telling myself to *calm the fuck down.* I should just enjoy this weekend for what it is and stop trying to make it into something more.

And I should definitely *not* tell him I'm in love with him.

Gail motions to the stools at the breakfast bar and I take a seat, watching Myles and Cory work side by side at the kitchen counter. Gail watches Cory too, her eyebrows raised.

"You feeling okay, Cors?"

"Of course," he says over his shoulder, slicing peppers and threading them onto skewers. "Why?"

"I just haven't seen you cooking in... oh, I don't know, decades?"

"What? I do the grill every year."

"Yes," Gail admits, "but you stand there with a beer, silently brooding about having to do it. Now you're happily chopping vegetables. I didn't even ask you to."

He shrugs like it's no big deal, but the expression on Gail's face tells me it is. I remember what Cory told me about his mom, how she accused him so coldly of being like his father, and I sneak a look at her as I sip my beer. Her face is kind and warm, filled with love as she watches her son work. It's hard to imagine her saying something so hurtful to Cory, but we all say harsh things when we're angry. I wonder if she remembers saying that—if she knows how much those seemingly insignificant words hurt him and shaped who he became.

Pretzel comes barreling inside at that moment, and I set my beer down, ready to scoop him up, but Gail gets to it before me. She drops to his level and showers him with attention, which only winds him up more. She doesn't seem to care, though, and it makes me smile.

I reach for my drink, looking around the kitchen at the scene, feeling fuller and happier than I have in a long time. Usually I spend holidays working at the shelter, or home alone with Netflix. I keep thinking about what Cory pointed out on our first date—that Paul's unkind words are the reason I've withdrawn from life, the reason I've felt like a burden more than anything else. Yet here I am, surrounded by people who care, in a home that's so warm and welcoming it reminds me of my mom and the place I grew up. Sure, there are a few more people here, but the feeling is the same. It's *palpable*. It's the feeling I want to create in my own home one day.

Cat wanders in to grab a beer from the fridge, then joins Gail and I at the breakfast bar, watching the boys work. "Aren't these two well-trained?" she jokes, motioning to Cory and Myles. "Actually, hold on." Her brow furrows and she glances at her mom. "I've never seen Cory in here prepping food." She walks over to examine her brother as he works. "What are those?" she asks, pointing to something on the counter.

"Vegan burger patties," he says, and Cat's jaw unhinges.

"*You're* going to eat that?"

"Yeah. They're good."

Her gaze swings to me and she strolls back across the kitchen, a funny smile on her face. "Is this your doing?"

I laugh, stroking Pretzel's ear. "What?"

"He's in the kitchen. He's"—she blinks rapidly, as if still processing it—"*not eating meat.*"

I glance at Gail and she looks equally flabbergasted. "Okay, yes," I admit, "but it was his idea. I'm not trying to change him, I swear."

Gail shakes her head, touching my arm. "These are good things, honey."

Cory looks at me over his shoulder, chuckling. "Yeah, she's good for me."

"I'll say." Cat reaches for a potato chip from a bowl on the counter, crunching loudly.

"It's so nice to see him happy," Gail murmurs, watching her son chat with Myles. "I was beginning to think he'd never settle down."

Cat nods in agreement. I should probably point out that we've only been dating for a month and "settle down" feels a little premature, but I'm too busy getting swept up in the fantasy she's created with those two words. I think back to the conversation we had at Bounce the night of Cat's wedding, when Gail and Cat talked about how Cory would make a good husband and father. God, I know I'm getting so far ahead of myself, but my heart won't listen. And now that I've let myself acknowledge how utterly in love I am, I can't seem to slow down. My head fills with images of us coming here every year, of our own kids playing in the backyard with the dogs, of Christmases together in Gail's living room. It's a heady, intoxicating feeling, letting myself imagine that with Cory. It's everything I could ever want.

"Nah, I knew he would," Cat says, gazing at me with a

secret smile. "He just took some time to finally do something about it." My face warms as she leans closer. "I hope you're prepared to have lots of kids. Mom is still mad that I don't want to start a family. Well, we have Amber of course, and I love her to pieces, but I don't want babies." Cat leans away, sipping her beer casually. "Do you want kids?"

"Cat!" Cory spins around, his brow low. "What is your deal today?"

I laugh. "It's okay." I know she has good intentions, and the truth is, being here in this lovely home, feeling so warm and happy... I can't help it. I can't keep the words in. "I do. I want a big family. Not right now," I add quickly, glancing down at my beer. "But one day, I'd love to have kids of my own, and I'd like to adopt, too."

There's silence in the kitchen, apart from Myles chopping something at the counter, and I pick at the label on my bottle, wondering if I said too much, got too carried away. I look at Gail and Cat, who are both beaming, and when I finally let myself glance in Cory's direction, he's staring at me. His gaze is penetrating, unblinking and fierce, and it makes my pulse scramble. A noise from the movie in the other room seems to snap him out of it, and he glances away.

"I'm going to set up the grill," he mumbles, striding out of the room.

I 'm going to kill my sister.

First with all that *Princess Bride* shit, and now with her asking Josie about kids?

Jesus Christ.

I stalk out onto the patio, throwing the cover off the grill. My heart is thudding as I check the propane tank is secure, then lift the lid to inspect inside. Mom doesn't use it often, so I focus my anger on cleaning the grill, while trying to figure out why I'm so mad at Cat; not for putting those ideas in Josie's head, but for putting them in *mine*. I'd always ruled out marriage and family as a possibility for me. I'd decided I would never let a woman get close enough to want or expect that from me, and I sure as hell never let myself imagine becoming a father.

Somehow, Josie got through all those defenses. She broke down all my walls and strode right into my heart, and the closer she gets, the more I want to imagine a future with her. A future that sounds a lot like what she described to Cat. I'm pretty sure Josie was about to tell me she loves me earlier, and it wasn't until that moment that I realized just how hard I've fallen for her. My first instinct was to shut that feeling down, but I'm powerless against it. I'm high on this woman, on the way she makes me feel like there's something good inside me, even if I can't see it. Having her here with my family, talking with my mom and laughing with my sister like she's always belonged here... she's made this place feel lighter. She's transformed all the memories I had of Dad and Alice and everything—all the heaviness I've felt when I come back here—she's replaced them with her smile, her presence.

She's doing that inside me, too. She's filling me up with love—filling the dark corners I tried to ignore, all the broken parts I didn't know needed healing.

Despite myself, I smile as I think of her saying she wants to adopt. Of course she does; that is so Josie. My chest tangles with emotion as I picture her holding a baby, and I try to shake the image from my head.

These are dangerous thoughts to entertain.

"Cors?" Josie steps out onto the patio, eying me uncertainly. "You okay?"

"Yeah," I mumble, turning back to the grill. "My sister is driving me nuts."

Josie chuckles, coming over. "She's just winding you up." She leans against the table, chewing her lip. "Listen, um, I'm sorry if that was too much, back there."

I glance at her. "What?"

"What I said about kids and stuff. I didn't mean to freak you out."

"You didn't freak me out." I crouch down and examine the propane tank, afraid that if I look at her, she'll see the truth on my face. That, far from being freaked out, I'm right there with her.

"Oh." Her voice is quiet and I know she doesn't believe

me. "Okay, then." I hear her turn to go and I force out a breath, pressing my eyes closed.

"Joze, wait." I can't stand her thinking I'm pulling away when what I'm really feeling is the opposite. "I mean it," I say, pushing to my feet. I turn back to her, taking her hand. "You didn't freak me out. *Cat* is annoying me," I add, trying to lighten the mood with a laugh, "but there's nothing wrong with what you said. Nothing at all."

She looks up at me with round eyes, and I slide my arms around her, pulling her close. When she gives me a little smile and murmurs, "I'm glad," my heart trips over itself.

Fuck, this woman. How could I not want everything with her? How could I not want to spend the rest of my life trying to be the man she sees inside me?

MY COUSINS ARRIVE with their kids and we move out to the backyard to eat and drink and relax. I get roped into multiple games of cornhole with the kids, but I don't mind. It gives me time away from Josie to process what I'm feeling. I watch her, sitting on the patio with my mom and uncle, talking and laughing. Her cheeks are pink from the heat and beer, and every time her gaze wanders over to me and she waves, my heart somersaults like I'm a fucking teenager. This is what she does to me.

"Uncle Cory! It's your turn!" My nephew tugs on my arm, bringing my attention back to him. He's not technically my nephew—he's my cousin's kid—but all the kids call me *Uncle Cory.*

"Sorry, Lex." I adjust the Giants cap on my head and take a swig from my beer, trying to focus on the game. These kids take their cornhole seriously.

The afternoon drifts on in that hazy, hot, beer-filled way it always does on this holiday, and by the time the sun sinks toward the horizon, I've set up the tent for me and Josie, and laid out an air mattress and two sleeping bags. The kids are all gathered on the back lawn, excited for the fireworks to start, and I look around for Josie, wanting her with me to watch them. We never have fireworks ourselves, but we're only a few blocks from a local place that does a big display, and Uncle Lou always gets sparklers for the kids.

I find Josie inside with Cat, cuddling Pretzel on the sofa.

"Hey," I say, stepping in through the sliding glass door. "Come outside, the fireworks will start soon."

Josie glances up anxiously. "I don't know if I should. Pretzel will probably flip out when they do. Fireworks are really distressing for animals."

"Yeah," Cat says, nodding. "Stevie hates them. I usually stay in here with her."

"Oh." My shoulders slump in disappointment. I thought it would be romantic as hell to sit out on the slope in our backyard and watch the fireworks together, but I'd never ask her to leave Pretzel.

"You know," Cat says, glancing between me and Josie, "I'm going to be in here with Stevie anyway. Why don't you go out with Cors? I'm happy to look after Pretzel."

Josie hesitates. "Are you sure?"

"Of course. Come here, boy." Cat pats her knee, motioning for Pretzel to climb onto her lap. He nestles in beside Stevie and Cat tucks her other arm around him. "See? He's happy. You go enjoy the fireworks."

Josie's gaze swings to me and a smile tugs at her lips. "Okay. Thanks, Cat." She climbs off the sofa and wanders over, slipping her hand into mine. "Let's go."

I glance back over my shoulder as Josie leads me

outside, mouthing a "Thank you" to my sister. She grins and gives me a wink, flicking on the TV as she settles down with the dogs. Maybe I won't have to kill her after all.

It's almost dark when we step outside, and I grab my sleeping bag from the tent and spread it out on the ground, creating a soft spot for us to sit. The kids are at the bottom of the garden with the sparklers under the watchful eye of my uncle, writing their names in the air, their shrieks and laughter drifting up to us.

"This is so lovely," Josie says as she settles down beside me. A firework goes up overhead and Josie gasps, gazing up at the burst of blue and red. "Wow," she breathes.

I wrap an arm around her shoulders and she nestles into my side. It's the first moment I've had alone with her since this afternoon, and my head—actually, my heart—is bursting with all the things I want to say to her. But now that we're finally here, I don't know where to start.

We watch the fireworks for a while, neither of us saying anything. Just having her with me is enough—is so much more than I ever dared to dream possible. This woman who walked into my bar five years ago and changed my life. God, she said I took her in and made everything better, but she's the one who's made *me* better, in every way.

Josie turns to catch me gazing at her and nudges me. "You okay?"

"I was just thinking about what you said to Cat earlier, about when I hired you. You said I took you in and made everything better."

Her lips turn up at the corner. "You did."

"I remember what you were like when I hired you. You were—"

"A mess." She cringes, looking down at her hands. "I know."

"Well, you weren't the same person you are now. You were quiet, and sad, and..."

"Broken," she whispers. "That day I came into Bounce, I wanted to get wasted and forget everything. And you were there"—her gaze lifts to mine and she smiles—"all tall and handsome and charming. You distracted me from everything and ended up offering me a job."

"I wasn't even hiring," I say, chuckling.

"And I had no bartending experience. Why did you hire me?" She laughs, not expecting an answer, but it's a question I've thought about a lot over the past five years. Because the truth is, I'd been kind of a mess myself when I met her.

"I was really intimidated my first week," she admits. "But you were patient and kind. You made me laugh and feel better than I had in a year."

I smile, tracing a pattern on her arm where my hand rests.

"You brought me back to life," she murmurs. "That sounds dramatic, but... I was so shattered and damaged after my relationship with Paul. You gave me a job, you were so nice to me, and just hanging out with you every night..."

"I can't take all the credit, Joze. You're a lioness, remember?"

"I didn't feel like it. I felt like a deer who'd been hit by a truck and left for dead on the side of the road. I didn't become a lioness until you helped me see my strength."

I recoil at the violent, vivid picture she paints. I know what she means, though. She was so different from now, and damn, it feels good to know I helped her find her power.

She chews her lip. "I know it's weird that I never got together with anyone after that, but you were honestly all I wanted."

I lean in, kissing her softly. "You were all I wanted too,

Buttercup. I know it wasn't obvious, because"—I shift uneasily—"I did the opposite, but I'd promised myself I would never touch you, and I just wanted to be distracted from it. I wanted everything to feel meaningless, because the only person I wanted anything meaningful with was you." I stroke the soft skin of her arm, thinking about her words. "You should know, you brought me back to life too."

"What do you mean?"

"When you walked into the bar that day, I wasn't in a great place. It had only been six months since Rob left and work wasn't the same." I sigh, thinking back to the way things felt after Rob moved out to Jersey. It wasn't just that I missed the fun we had—it was that I felt like I'd been left behind. I couldn't shake the sense that while he was growing up and moving on with his life, I was stalling.

Josie slides her arm around me and squeezes. "That's tough."

"And I was dealing with my dad's death," I say, forcing the words out even though they hurt. I want her to know. "I hadn't seen him since I was a kid and I guess I'd always assumed that one day he might find me, maybe apologize for everything and make amends, I don't know. But when he died, I realized that would never happen, and... I went into a dark place. I was there for a long time. Then one day"—I tilt my head to brush my lips over her hair—"you walked in, so beautiful but so sad, and I just wanted to wrap you in my arms and protect you from the world. I wanted to make you smile. I knew you were too good for me, but that didn't stop me from wanting it all anyway. It was selfish, me hiring you, knowing I couldn't give you what you deserved. But I wanted to be around you. You made me feel good."

Even now, thinking about the fact that I swore I'd never touch Josie—and that I failed to stick to that vow—makes me tense. But her expression softens and I push the thought away, watching as red and blue light from the fireworks above shimmers over her in the dark.

"And more recently, since you and Pretzel moved in with me. And that night, when we talked about my dad and Alice, when you listened to me and told me..." My voice cracks and she squeezes me tighter. "You told me I deserve love."

"You do," she whispers, leaning in to press a kiss to my cheek. "You deserve everything. Especially love."

My breathing is shallow as I hold her gaze. Every fiber of my being wants to tell her I love her. I twist on the sleeping bag to face her properly, but before I can open my mouth to speak, Josie lifts a hand and traces the line of my jaw. She looks so incredibly vulnerable—afraid, almost—and I dip my head, kissing the inside of her wrist.

"Cors?" she whispers.

"Yeah?"

"I..." She pulls in a shaky breath. "I love you."

Oh, fuck. I close my eyes, letting those words wash over me. I'd hoped I might be lucky enough to hear them from her at some point, but I never expected to feel so utterly wrecked when I did.

"I don't mean to scare you," she adds quickly, looking worried. "But I'm working on speaking up more, and I wanted you to know. You don't have to say it back—"

"Joze..." A bright firework booms overhead, highlighting the uncertainty in her eyes, and I swallow, trying to speak around the emotion thick in my throat. "I've fallen so hard for you."

Her breath catches. "You have?"

"Yeah." I can't help but chuckle at how astounded she looks. As if I wouldn't feel the same. As if I could feel any other way. "I'm so fucking in love with you it's not funny." I lean in and capture her mouth with mine, trying to show her just how much my heart feels like it's going to beat out of my chest.

"I can't believe it," she whispers between kisses, her hands sliding up my neck into my hair. "I wasn't sure you'd feel the same."

"Fuck, yes." Before I can stop myself, I roll over on top of her, crushing my mouth to hers. "Of course I feel the same." The sound of my niece's laughter from down in the garden reminds me we aren't alone and I pull myself away, muttering, "Shit."

She giggles, sitting back up on the sleeping bag. I'm still close enough to drag my mouth over that little heart-shaped freckle below her ear, and I feel her shiver under my touch. I know I can't take her right here on the back lawn with my family nearby, and that's a real fucking problem. Because I've never needed this woman more.

I glance at the tent, but the kids are still nearby and that wouldn't be romantic—or appropriate—at all. I can't take her up to my old room, because it's filled with all the kids' stuff and they could walk in at any point.

Wait. I know.

I lurch to my feet, tugging Josie up with me.

"What are we doing?" she asks, wide-eyed.

I slide my arms around her waist and draw her close, pressing my firm crotch to her belly. "I need you, Joze."

She gives a muffled groan into my chest. "Where can we go?"

I grin. "Follow me."

30

JOSIE

Cory grabs another sleeping bag and our pillows from the tent, then we sneak around the side of the house. He tosses everything into the back of the pickup and hauls himself up there, holding a hand out to help me up. I laugh as I climb onto the bed of the truck, watching Cory arrange the pillows and unzip the sleeping bags so they're open like blankets. Does he really think this will work?

As he motions for me to lie down beside him, I realize how private it is, tucked between the side of the house and the hedge, hidden back from the road behind the huge oak tree. When I lay my head back on the pillow and look up, I can see the stars—tiny pinpricks of light, occasionally obscured by a bright, booming firework.

Cory snuggles in beside me, tucking an arm around my side. I can feel his heart thumping in his chest as he draws me close.

I can't believe this man loves me, that he feels what I feel. I know I'd promised myself I wouldn't tell him but I couldn't help it. I spent the afternoon on the patio talking to his mom and uncle and sister, hearing stories about him as a boy and falling more in love by the second. I couldn't take my eyes off him as he played cornhole with the kids, running around the backyard in denim shorts, a white T-shirt clinging to his muscular chest, a Giants cap casually thrown on his head. His skin and beard were golden in the afternoon sun, his ass looked fucking perfect in those shorts, and his loud laughter made my body hum. I'd never seen him like that—free and easy, playing in his backyard, high-fiving kids when they made the shot in cornhole. I knew I couldn't dial down my feelings if I tried. And the more I sat with that realization, the more I knew I had to tell him.

Boy am I glad I did.

Cory leans up onto his elbow, gazing down at me. "I love you, Buttercup." He touches his lips to mine in the softest kiss, and my heart fills my chest. Hearing those words from him... it's like I'm living inside a dream.

I tug him until he's right on top of me, pressing me into the bed of the truck. Even though I've got a sleeping bag underneath me, it's not as forgiving as a mattress, and it makes him feel heavier. The weight of him reminds me that this isn't a dream—it's real.

"Joze," Cory groans as I wrap my legs around him. "I'm crushing you."

"I love it. I love *you*." I graze my lips over the salty, sun-kissed skin on his neck, relishing the way it feels to have him pin me down. He said he needed me, but I need *this*—him covering me, filling me, making me ache. "Take your clothes off."

He lifts himself up to peel off his T-shirt, then unzips the fly of his shorts, rolling onto his side to wriggle awkwardly out of them, followed by his underwear. It's dark out here, but my eyes have adjusted enough that I can make out the hard slabs of his pecs, the tattoo on his ribs, the sharp jut of his erection telling me he needs this as much as I do.

I strip as quickly as I can, desperate to feel his skin on mine. With a glance over his shoulder to make sure we're alone, Cory grabs the other sleeping bag and drapes it over us, settling his weight on me again.

He lets out a long sigh as our skin comes into contact. "You feel amazing," he whispers, ghosting his mouth over my ear. It sends goosebumps dancing over me and I shift restlessly, needing more of him. The heat of him in the sticky summer air should be too much, but it's not. It's not nearly enough.

I slide my hands down to his ass, stroking and squeezing the muscle. I can feel his rigid length nestled between my thighs at my entrance, and molten heat floods through me. I know he's not wearing a condom and part of me doesn't care —wants him to thrust inside and fuck me exactly like this, consequences be damned. The thought is so dangerous— and so thrilling.

He moves his hips carefully, not entering me, just sliding back and forth through the slippery channel at the apex of my thighs. The sensation is incredible and I moan, digging my fingernails into his ass, urging him on. When our mouths collide, his tongue sweeps over mine, hungry and urgent and searching. His hips continue to rock, rubbing his throbbing hardness over my most sensitive spot, and my breath falters.

"God, Cory," I pant, meeting his movements with my own. I feel frenzied, delirious as the pleasure builds in my core. But I can't get there because I'm hollow, aching with the need to be filled by him.

He lifts himself up onto his arms to look down and

watch where he's sliding up and over my entrance, like an arrow that keeps missing its target. "Fuck," he growls, the movement of his hips becoming more frantic. "This is killing me." He lowers himself back down, one hand teasing my nipple as his mouth crashes into mine again. Between desperate, messy kisses, he rasps, "I wish I could fuck you like this."

"Me too." I can't help myself; I do some quick menstrual math. I know it's not a reliable form of birth control, but... "We could. I'm due for my period in a couple days, so it would probably be okay." As for the conversation around sexual health; we had that the first week we started dating.

"Oh, God," he groans into my neck, his ass flexing under my hands.

"But it's not a hundred percent..."

"I don't care." He draws away to look at me. "I mean, unless you don't want—"

"Yes," I whisper. "I want to." I've never wanted anything more.

He swallows, pausing to caress my cheek. We gaze at each other in the dim light, both of us breathing heavily as he shifts his hips. I feel him nudge my entrance and my pulse trips in anticipation.

"Are you sure?" he asks, searching my face.

"I'm sure."

He slides a hand down, hooking it under my thigh and spreading me open for him. With one deep thrust, he fills me.

"Ohhh..." My eyes roll back at the silky sensation, the knowledge that he's finally fucking me the way he's always been meant to—raw and unrestrained.

"Jesus," Cory growls into my ear. He stays like that,

planted inside me, unmoving. "Nothing has ever felt this good. Nothing."

"I know," I breathe, staring up at him in awe. A firework bursts overhead, the glittering light illuminating the emotion in Cory's eyes.

"I don't want to move. I don't want this moment to end."

I sigh, brushing a soft kiss over his cheek. "I know what you mean. But also..." I clench my pelvic floor, grinning when he emits an involuntary moan. "I need you to fuck me. I need it more than I need air right now."

"Yeah." He expels a heavy breath, his eyes inky black in the near-darkness. "I need that too." His hips pump forward, driving him deeper. When he sees the pleasure on my face, a dirty grin curls along his mouth. "Like that, Buttercup?"

"Yes," I whimper, wrapping my legs around him to get him deeper still. He draws out and slams back in, knowing that's exactly how I like it. His eyes are hooded as he does it again, building up a steady rhythm designed to make us both come undone.

Everything feels different, knowing he's not wearing a condom—and it's not just that there's nothing between us. I watch the sky above as we become one, feeling like we're the center of the universe. The heat between us burns brighter than the hottest star.

"I love you so much," he rasps, leaving wet, open-mouthed kisses on my jaw, my neck. "You're everything I could ever want."

A firework shoots up above, sending a shower of glittering, golden sparkles over the neighborhood, and the same thing happens inside my chest.

"Me too, Cors." My voice is a broken, helpless mewl. "Me too."

He wraps his arms around me and rolls us over so I'm on

top. Then he holds me tight against him as he rocks into me. Pleasure builds at the base of my spine and I try to meet his rough, erratic movements, but it's no use.

"Oh, Cory—" Heat erupts inside me as I fall apart in his arms. He presses his face into my neck to muffle his moan, shuddering and bucking underneath me, filling me with his liquid warmth.

And I know that, as long as I live, no moment will ever be this perfect again.

31

CORY

I can't stop staring at Josie across the breakfast bar. She's talking to my youngest niece, Maddy, while sneaking pieces of bacon to Pretzel under her chair. Josie's cheeks are a rosy pink, her eyes a vivid, sparkling green, and even though her face is a little tired after our late night, she's never looked more beautiful.

Last night was unbelievable. Once all the kids were in bed, we went back to the tent and made slow, passionate love—again without protection. I can't believe we did that, but I trusted Josie when she said there was no chance of her getting pregnant. I also find myself thinking, as I sip my coffee and watch her laugh with Maddy, that it wouldn't be the worst thing in the world if she was wrong.

I shake my head, dropping my gaze to the bitter brown liquid in my cup. What the hell has happened to me? Who am I to be having these thoughts? Josie is so fucking perfect, whereas I—

"She's really something, Cory." I glance up to find Uncle Lou leaning against the door frame beside me. He nods across at Josie, smoothing his thumb and index finger over his thick brown mustache. "How did you two meet?"

I shift my weight. Uncle Lou is my mom's brother, and he always gives me shit. I know he's going to have a field day with this. "She, uh, works for me."

His eyebrows hit his hairline and he lets out a whistle. "You dirty dog," he says, with a low laugh that makes me grimace.

I glance at Josie, relieved she can't hear us from across the room. Maddy is showing Josie her American Girl doll, and when I catch Josie's eye, she sends me a smile that makes my chest expand.

God, I love that woman.

"Well, she's real keen on you," Uncle Lou adds. "Was asking me all kinds of questions yesterday."

My stomach dips as I glance back at him. I have no secrets from Josie, but I'm not entirely sure I'd like the way my uncle would portray my teen years, given half the chance. The apprehension must show on my face, because Lou laughs.

"Ah, don't worry. I only told her the good stuff. Mostly." He tweaks his mustache again, watching Josie. "She's a real sweetheart. Heart of gold."

"I know." I grip my mug tight, itching to step away from this conversation.

Lou's gaze swings back to me. "It's good to see you finally settling down." He gives a hollow chuckle. "Try not to screw everything up, like your old man did."

My gut lurches as I glance over at Josie.

"You've got your father's genes, son. You can't change where you come from." He gives a sad shake of his head. "Heaven knows that son of a bitch left a trail of destruction in his wake. Your mother was a wreck for years."

Bile rises in the back of my throat. It wasn't just Mom that Dad hurt—it was Cat and me, too.

"Ah, well." Lou claps me on the shoulder, startling me. "You can only try, right? It's not your fault your old man was a screw-up." He steps into the kitchen, swiping a plate off the counter and piling it with bacon.

I glare after him, my pulse thumping in my temple. Why the fuck did he have to say all that? Like I didn't know Dad was an asshole—and that I'm more like him than I want to admit. As if I haven't been stewing in that knowledge for years.

I drain my coffee and set the empty mug down on the counter, whistling to Pretzel. He leaps up from his place under Josie's stool and follows me through the glass door. I slide it closed and stalk out onto the lawn, forcing myself to take a deep breath.

Pretzel sniffs around the yard, finding the best spot to pee, and I watch him absently. What am I doing here, with Josie? Telling her I'm in love with her, letting myself imagine a future with her—having sex without protection, for fuck's sake. I should *not* be—

Stop, some tiny, self-protective part of me says. It's the part that Josie has been nurturing, the part that's trying to convince me I'm good enough for her. I want so badly to believe it, but—

"Cory?"

A female voice interrupts my thoughts and I turn around, my eyes landing on a brunette by the fence. My breath freezes in my lungs.

"Alice," I say in disbelief. I knew her folks still lived next door, but last I heard she was in Canada. I haven't seen her back here in... what, seventeen years? The last time I saw her, she'd come home from college for a long weekend and I tried to apologize for what had happened between us. She'd told me to go to hell.

I glance over my shoulder, desperate to run back inside, but I know that wouldn't be cool. Jamming my shaking hands into my pockets, I try to calm my rapid heartbeat as I wander over to the fence. I think of Josie's words—that it's been twenty years since I did what I did, that I'm not the same man anymore, that it's time to stop beating myself up. But Uncle Lou's comment from seconds ago keeps running through my mind—*you can't change where you come from*—and nausea washes through me.

"I thought that was you," Alice says, leaning her forearms on the fence. Her dark hair is pulled back into a ponytail and, even though it's been two decades, I can still see the same girl I hurt all those years ago.

"Hey," I say wearily. "How are you?"

A grin breaks over her face, surprising me. "I'm great! Just sold my company up in Toronto and decided we'd bring the family back here to figure out our next move. Plus the kids have never seen where I grew up, so..." She shrugs, cocking her head as she examines me with a smile. "What about you?"

"I..." I blink, trying to catch up with the unexpected turn this conversation has taken. I know I should say something benign, like "work's good" or whatever, but I can't stop the next words from flying out my mouth: "Alice, I am so sorry."

Her expression softens. "It's okay."

"It's not," I say, as images from that night come back to me. The look on Alice's face when she walked into the room at that party, when she realized what I was doing with someone who wasn't her. "What I did—fuck, that was not okay."

"Cory." She reaches over the fence, touching my arm.

"We were both really young." A wry laugh slides from her lips. "I'm not holding it against you."

I stare at her for a beat, absorbing this. "Shit," I mutter, wiping both hands down my face.

"Mom!" a voice calls from beyond the fence, and Alice glances over her shoulder.

"Sorry, I have to go, but it was really great to see you. Take care, okay?" She gives me a genuine smile before turning on her heel and heading back into the house.

My head spins as I watch her leave. She's exactly as I remember—kind and sweet, just like Josie. And now, she's forgiven me for the worst thing I've ever done. I can see Josie doing exactly the same thing.

Unease crawls through me as I consider this. I think of all the times Josie forgave me for pulling away from her at the start of our relationship, and something twists in my chest.

I'm going to end up hurting her. I know it. Uncle Lou is right, I can't change my genes. All my life I've been told that I'm just like my dad—the proof was right here, talking to me over the fence two seconds ago. The worst thing of all is that I can see myself, years from now, having the same conversation I just had with Alice, but with Josie instead.

Fuck. I feel sick.

32

JOSIE

I wipe the bar, smiling across the room at my friends crammed into a booth. Cat, Myles, and Geoff are wedged in beside Harriet and her boyfriend, Luke. The table is joined by Harriet's sister, Alex, and her husband, Michael, a few minutes later. Harriet waves me over and I nod, glancing around to find Cory. I spot him serving a drink to a familiar blond at the end of the bar.

We arrived back from his mom's yesterday afternoon. He's been off ever since, though I'm not sure why. He spent the entire shift last night in the back room and when I asked if he was okay, he kissed me and told me he loved me and squeezed me so tight I almost couldn't breathe.

Later, I texted Gerard to tell him that I won't be applying for the job at the shelter. I love working at the bar, and after that amazing weekend away, I can't imagine not spending my nights serving drinks next to Cory at Bounce.

Besides, I know something is up with him and I need to focus on fixing that right now.

Cory and the blond both turn to look at me. Oh wait, I recognize her—Stacey, I think her name was. She frowns when Cory points in my direction, and I glance between them curiously. I'm about to go over when a loud cheer goes up at Harriet's table. She catches my eye and waves again, so I slide out from behind the bar and wander across. Harriet is bouncing on the spot, spilling her lemonade, and I laugh at her excitement as I reach her table.

"What's going on?" I ask, my gaze sliding to Luke. He looks equally thrilled.

"Tell her!" Alex squeals, eliciting a chuckle from her husband.

I meet Geoff's eye and he laughs too. "Enough with the suspense, Harri."

"Okay." Harriet sets her lemonade down and fixes her full attention on me. "I'm pregnant."

Surprise jolts through me and I grin, reaching forward to pull her into a hug. "Wow! Oh my gosh, I'm so happy for you." I squeeze her tight and turn to Luke. I don't know him that well, but I can't stop myself from hugging him too. "Congratulations."

"Thanks," he says, his cheeks pink as we part. He tucks an arm around Harriet and presses a kiss to her forehead.

"How far along are you?" I ask. Harriet motions for me to squeeze into the booth beside her and, after checking Cory and Camila can handle the bar, I do.

"Six weeks," she says, reaching for her lemonade again. "Some people think you shouldn't tell others until twelve weeks, but I couldn't wait."

"So—" I glance at her sister, Alex. I know Alex is pregnant, because she changed her regular drink order from wine to seltzer a few months back. Plus Geoff can't keep a secret to save himself.

Alex nods, reading my mind. "Yep. We're having babies together!" The sisters share a happy look and envy nudges my middle. I always wanted a sister. It must be amazing to have someone close to share this with.

"Let's talk baby shower," Cat says, and Harriet shakes her head.

"I don't need a baby shower. Besides, Alex is busy with work, and—"

"I could do it," I hear myself say.

Harriet glances at me in surprise. "You don't have to do that."

"I know I don't have to; I want to." I smile, realizing for the first time how often people have said those words to me, and how I've always felt guilty. But I get it now; they've *wanted* to help me, because they care about me. This is what true relationships entail—give *and* take. Now it's my turn to give. I've never planned a baby shower before but it's the least I can do to thank Harriet. It was her fundraiser idea that saved the shelter—not to mention all the hours she put in to help me make it happen. Besides, she's my best girlfriend. She's the closest thing I've ever had to a sister. I *want* to do this for her.

Cat spins to face me. "Can I help?"

"Sure." I catch Cory watching me across the bar, and jump to my feet. "I'd better get back to work," I say, smiling at the table. "Congrats again, you guys." I head back across the room, hoping for a moment alone with Cory. I want to clear the air with him so things can go back to feeling like they did on the weekend.

"I told her I have a girlfriend," he blurts when I reach the bar.

My steps falter. "What? *Who*?"

"That blond. The one I... months ago—" he breaks off with a grimace.

I cock my head, baffled by his nervous rambling. "Are you okay?"

"Yes." He nods quickly. "I just saw you watching us earlier, and I didn't want you to think..."

"Oh." I huff a laugh, stepping forward to take his hands. They're strangely clammy, and I glance over his shoulder before tugging him into the back room and shutting the door. "You're allowed to talk to other women. You know that, right?"

He opens and closes his mouth, looking unsure. I frown, wondering what I might have done to make him think I'm not okay with that, then it hits me.

I sigh, stepping close enough to slide my arms around his waist. "I don't care what happened in your past. I know the man you are now and I trust you." I step up on my toes to kiss his bearded cheek. "I love you."

His body stiffens in my arms. I don't know why, but my touch—my words—only seem to make this worse.

I step back, dread rising in my gut. Cory's gaze is riveted to the floor, and I study him, trying to read his body language. He's been weird ever since breakfast yesterday, and for the first time it occurs to me what might be bothering him.

We had unprotected sex, and I haven't got my period yet.

Shit, why didn't I think of that before? No wonder he's been distant. I should never have talked him into it. What the hell was I thinking? Okay, the odds of me getting pregnant at that point in my cycle are next to nothing—I know because Paul hated using condoms and I hated the way the pill made me feel, so I learned to pay very close attention to my body—but it was a stupid, risky thing to do nonetheless.

But... I think back to the way Cory said *I don't care* when I warned him it wasn't foolproof, and confusion swirls through me. In the moment it almost felt like he *wanted* something more to come of it, so why is he...

No. I shake the thought away. Men will say anything during sex. Reading into that is ludicrous.

I clear my throat, wanting to reassure him. "Look, Cors, I know we didn't use a condom on the weekend, but—"

The door to the back room opens and Cat sticks her head in, grinning. "Did she tell you?"

Cory glances over my shoulder at the door. "Tell me what?"

Oh, fuck. *Not now, Cat.*

"Harriet's pregnant!"

I wince, avoiding Cory's gaze. Her timing could not be any worse.

"And," Cat adds, grinning, "Josie and I are going to throw her a baby shower."

Goddammit, Cat. Stop.

I risk a glance at Cory. He's examining me with an expression I can't decipher. "Isn't that something her sister should do?"

"Yeah, but Alex can't do it. And, you know"—I shrug —"Harriet is one of my closest friends. It's an honor to do this for her."

He nods, his face still unreadable. What is he thinking right now? Between the conversation in the kitchen at his mom's, the sex, and me jumping at the chance to organize a baby shower, he must think I have baby fever.

"It'll be fun!" Cat says. Her lips quirk into a mischievous grin as her gaze slides to me. "Besides, Harriet will return the favor when it's your turn." She leans forward to playfully poke me in the arm, adding, "You never know, that might be soon..."

Oh, fucking hell.

Cory's eyes zip to mine, ringed with panic, as Cat slips out of the back room.

Fuck, fuck, fuckety-fuck.

"She didn't mean—" I shake my head, trying to stem the nausea rolling through me. Any second now Cory is going to throw open that door and run for his life. "She was just being silly. I didn't tell her we—"

"I know." Cory blows out a weighted breath, dragging a hand over his face. "Ever since we got together, my sister has been a pain in the ass."

I give a strained laugh, desperate to put his mind at ease. "I'll get my period tomorrow, okay?"

Cory frowns. "I'm not worried about that, Joze. I trust you know your body."

"Right," I say, not feeling comforted in the slightest. "Well, I'm sorry for talking you into doing... that. It probably wasn't—"

"Whoa, whoa, whoa." Cory's hands fly up in defense. "You didn't talk me into anything. I wanted it *just* as much as you. Probably more."

I gnaw on my lip, eying him uncertainly. If that's true, and he's not worried about me being pregnant, then what on earth is going on? One minute things between us are magical and the next he's pulling away. Why?

Unease ripples through me as I realize how familiar this scenario feels, and I try to shake the feeling off.

Cory isn't Paul. You're just being insecure.

I inhale deeply, attempting to break through Cory's weird mood one final time by stepping closer and touching his cheek. I search his eyes, looking for the carefree guy I saw on the weekend—the one who played cornhole, laughing in the sun. The one who was over the moon when

I bared my heart to him. With a shaky exhale, I say, "I love you, Cors."

He gazes down at me, looking pained. Then his eyes soften and he draws me close, pressing me into his chest. I should be relieved, but I can hear his heart beating a mile a minute. "I love you too, Buttercup," he murmurs. And I could be wrong, but I swear I hear him whisper, "I wish that was enough."

33

CORY

My father's grave is in a cemetery on Staten Island. It takes me thirty minutes to find it, because I've never been here before in my life. The day of his funeral I locked myself in my apartment and got blind drunk, refusing to pay tribute to the man who destroyed our family.

Now, I weave through the rows of tombstones, some weather-worn over the years, some still undisturbed by the passing of time, until I finally find my father's resting place. Then I stand and stare at the words *Joel Porter* etched into the slab of stone, unsure what to do.

I couldn't sleep last night. I kept thinking of Josie in the back room at work, trying to tell me how much she loves me and trusts me, trying to reassure me that she would get her period soon, as if her being pregnant with my baby is the last thing I'd want.

As if I haven't been thinking about how fucking amazing that would be.

The problem is that every time I let myself indulge in that fantasy, my uncle's words play through my head: *try not to screw everything up, like your old man did.* They've been playing over and over, like a broken record, since we left Long Island.

I dragged myself out of bed early this morning, leaving Josie fast asleep with Pretzel tucked into her side. I spent two hours in the gym, hoping it would make me feel better, but what a joke that was.

When I finished up, I found myself in a cab heading over here instead of home. I don't know why. Maybe it's because on this day six years ago Dad died of a heart attack and it felt like the rug was pulled out from under me. I hadn't realized I'd spent my entire life waiting—hoping—he'd show up one day and apologize, try to make amends, somehow repair the damage he'd done all those years ago. And when I *did* realize, the absurdity of that became clear. There's nothing he could have done to make up for the time I spent without a father, the hurt he caused me and my sister and my mom, the way he put his own needs above those of his family.

I jam my hands into my pockets and kick at a clump of grass in front of Dad's grave. I don't know what to say to this asshole. All I know is that the things I hate about him are the same things I hate about myself, too.

You're just like your father.

I grit my teeth, recalling what my mom told me after I hurt Alice. She was right—I am who I am because of this man, and it was stupid to pretend otherwise. It was stupid to let Josie get close, to let myself believe I could be the man she needs.

My phone vibrates against my leg and I pull it from my pocket. Rob's name flashes on the screen—same time on this date, every year. We can go months at a time without talking, but he always knows to call today.

"Hey, man," he says, when I raise the phone to my ear.

"Hey," I mumble.

"Just wanted to check in. I know today can be rough."

I stare at Dad's name on the tombstone, nodding silently in response.

"How've you been?"

"Good." My answer comes automatically, with no real thought, because things *have* been good. This past month with Josie was like something out of a dream. The problem is, I feel like I've been startled awake. Try as I might, I can't seem to close my eyes and slip back into the spell. "How's the family?" I ask, itching to change the subject.

"They're good. Brad's starting school soon, and Anna has just learned to walk, but only by holding onto the dog. It's hilarious."

I stare at the ground, feeling a sharp tug in my chest. I want the life that Rob has, and I want it with Josie, but I just don't see how I can become that guy; the kind of guy who can give Josie—give our *kids*—what they need.

The kind of guy who won't fuck everything up.

"How did you know you were ready?" I hear myself ask.

"For what?"

I glance across the rows of tombstones. "A family. Kids. Whatever."

"Oh. I guess... you don't, really. You just do it and hope for the best."

I frown. "What if you screw up?"

"You will." Rob chuckles. "Every parent does. But, you know, you try to learn from your mistakes and hope your family will forgive you."

I snort bitterly, knowing there's no way in hell I'll ever forgive my father for what he did. I think of Alice forgiving me—forgiveness I don't deserve. People are too damn quick to forgive things that are unforgivable.

Rob sighs in my silence. "I know your dad messed up big time, and I don't think there's any excuse for what he did, but at the end of the day... you have to realize your parents are human too. They make mistakes, just like everyone else."

I clench my jaw. It's easy for Rob to say this because he had a perfect childhood. Even now, his parents are blissfully happy together. He still goes fishing with his dad in the summer, and they have these huge family Christmases every year with lots of quirky traditions. He's seen love and stability and trust first hand, so he knows it's real. He knows how to be that man, because his father is. It's all he knows.

"I should go," I mutter. I rub the heel of my hand in my eye, feeling like a jackass. "Sorry. I'm just not in a good space right now, man. Thanks for calling, though."

"All good. If you need to talk or anything, I'm here."

I nod, even though he can't see me, and end the call. I stare blankly at Dad's tombstone, thinking of Rob's words: *you try to learn from your mistakes and hope your family will forgive you.* That's the thing; I *did* learn from my mistake. I learned not to let myself hurt someone again. It doesn't matter what I *want* with Josie, what matters is what I can give her, and I don't trust myself not to let her down. Alice might have forgiven my mistake, but I couldn't live with myself if I did something to Josie—not to mention if we had kids...

I shake the thoughts from my head. My throat burns as I turn from my dad's grave. I shouldn't have come here.

Iᴛ's mid-afternoon when I finally arrive home. I sat in a sports bar on Staten Island for a few hours, drinking luke-warm beer and going over and over this in my head. I don't see any way forward that doesn't end in Josie getting hurt.

Pretzel greets me at the front door, tail wagging and eyes bright. I crouch in front of him and pet his head, trying to ignore the twisting in my stomach, the way my heart slams against my ribs like it knows I'm about to slash it to shreds.

Josie's pacing the living room when I enter. I drop my keys on the counter and wipe my hands down my face, unable to meet her gaze. I know she's been worried about me being gone all day. I should have answered one of her calls this morning, or at least texted her back. But I didn't, because I'm an asshole.

An asshole who doesn't deserve someone as wonderful as her.

"Hey," Josie says tentatively.

"Hey," I mutter, raking a hand over my scalp.

Just do it. Tell her this needs to end. She'll thank you one day.

I glance up to see Josie wringing her hands, her features engraved with worry. Then she sucks in a deep breath and attempts to plaster on a smile. "Do you want some lunch? I can make you a sandwich, or there's leftovers—"

"Joze." I hold up a hand to halt her nervous rambling. God, I can't stand to see her like this. I've been nothing but a dick to her since we came home from my mom's place, and she's been walking on eggshells around me the whole time. I motion for her to sit. "Let's talk."

She drops backward onto the sofa, her face white. I don't join her. If I get too close I'll end up pulling her into my arms, and that's the last thing I need. I lean back against the counter, folding my arms over my chest and dropping my gaze back to the floor.

Shit, I don't know if I can do this. She'll never forgive me. She's going to hate me forever and I won't blame her.

But this isn't about me. I can't keep being selfish with her.

I clear my throat. "I don't know how else to say this, so I'm just going to say it."

"Okay..."

"I can't give you what you want."

There's a beat of silence. "What?"

I examine the carpet, my jaw hard as I force the words out. "The future you want. The commitment, the family... I'm just... I'm not that guy."

After a long pause, Josie exhales wearily. "I never asked you for any of that. Those things I was talking about, I meant way, *way* down the road."

"I know. But—"

"And I got my period this morning," she continues in a rush, "so there's nothing to worry about there. Okay?" I look up to see her mouth tilted into an apprehensive smile.

"You did?"

She gives a swift nod.

I can't explain why my chest hollows out at this news, why something akin to disappointment seeps through me. Did some part of me *want* her to be pregnant with my kid? How fucking selfish is that?

But that's me, isn't it? Taking too much and hurting people in the process. Wanting things I have no business wanting.

You've got your father's genes. You can't change where you come from.

I glance away, hardening my heart. The sooner I cut her free from me, the sooner she's better off.

"Josie, I think..." I grind my molars, waiting for the

emotion in my throat to pass. *Say it. Tell her it's over.* "I think we need to end this."

She's silent. When I finally drag my gaze up from the floor, she's staring at me. She tries to fold her hands on her lap, and I notice they're shaking. "Why?"

I don't know what else to tell her besides the truth. "I just... don't see this working out, and I think we should end it now, before someone gets hurt."

Her brow wrinkles. "Don't do this, Cors. Please. I know the weekend was a lot, but—"

"It's not that. It's—" I let out a low growl of frustration. "Don't make this harder than it needs to be."

"I'm not... I don't mean..." She shakes her head, scrambling for the right thing to say. "Can we please talk about this? Because—"

"There's nothing to talk about." Fuck, I am the biggest prick on the planet. I have to shove every cruel word from my mouth, because it's the only way to push her away from me. "This is over."

"But..." She blinks rapidly. "You said you loved me."

I grimace, wrenching my gaze back to the floor. "I know."

"Did you mean that?"

"I..." I swallow, ignoring the pain lancing through my chest. I want so badly to tell her that of course I fucking meant it—I've never loved anyone like I love her, and I'm quite certain I never will again.

But I can't say that, because I'm this close—*this close*—to breaking down and throwing myself into her arms, telling her I can't do this, telling her I need her more than anything. I can't keep doing that. I can't keep putting my needs before hers.

If I really loved her, I never would've let myself do that in the first place.

I lift my shoulders in what I hope is a careless shrug, keeping my gaze fixed on the carpet. I can't bear to see the look on her face, because the shame welling up inside will pull me under. It will fill my lungs and drown me.

Josie huffs out a disbelieving breath. "Wow. Okay then."

There's silence for a few seconds, then I hear a sniff and make the mistake of glancing up. Josie dashes a hand over her cheek and it's then that I realize she's crying.

Oh, fuck.

No.

My heart cracks right down the middle. Every cell in my body wants to pull her close and stop those tears, wants to kiss them away and stroke her hair and make her smile again.

But how can I do that when I'm the one who caused them?

I grip the counter behind me so hard that my hands ache. Anything to stop myself from reaching for her as she wipes her eyes.

I've never hated myself more.

It's for the best, I repeat to myself numbly. *She'll thank you one day.* Because a few tears now are nothing compared to the devastation I'd cause further down the road.

Pretzel notices Josie's distress and nuzzles into her side. She looks down at him, her face lining with panic.

I glance between her and the dog, and it takes me a second to realize what she's thinking. She's thinking about what to do now—where to go if she can't stay here, and where to take Pretzel. She still has her apartment, because she was waiting for the lease to come up for renewal next month, but I know she can't take him there. Either way, I'm not going to dump her and kick her out on the same day. I couldn't live with myself.

"You guys can stay here," I blurt before thinking it through.

She looks up at me, confusion clouding her eyes. "What?"

"I'll find somewhere to crash for a while. I'm not kicking you and Pretzel out, okay? You can stay here."

She opens and closes her mouth, at a loss for words. I don't blame her. God, I'm such a fucking mess.

"I mean it, Joze," I say hoarsely. "I'll grab some stuff after work tonight and crash at a friend's place." I have no idea where I'll go—the only place I'd feel comfortable is Rob's, and he's miles away in Jersey, but I can't worry about that now. "You guys can stay here as long as you need."

Something like gratitude flashes in her eyes and my throat tightens. I can't stand it. I can't stand to see her looking at me with anything but contempt right now. It's all I deserve.

I shift my weight and Pretzel turns to me, jumping off the sofa to come and nudge his nose into my leg, as if he can tell how miserable I am. Goddammit, I'm going to miss this little guy almost as much as I'll miss Josie.

I stroke his soft ear, pushing those thoughts away. I don't get to think that. I don't get to feel sorry for myself. I'm the one who made this mess.

Josie looks between Pretzel and me, her eyes filling with tears. "Cory, I just... I don't understand what changed. Why you—"

"Nothing changed," I say, reaching for my keys on the counter again. I need to get the hell away from her before I take back everything I just said and beg her to marry me instead.

Jesus Christ. I've never felt more unhinged in my life.

"I told you I was an asshole," I mutter, shoving my keys into my pocket with shaking hands. "You just didn't want to listen." Then I stride down the hall and out the front door, trying to tell myself that I haven't just made the biggest mistake of my life.

34

JOSIE

The door closes behind Cory and I stare down the hall, feeling strangely numb. I bring my knees up to my chest and wrap my arms around them, waiting for the reality of what just happened to hit me.

I shouldn't be surprised—not after the way Cory's been acting since we came home from Long Island. I guess I thought if I played it cool and didn't pressure him the old Cory would return, but now he feels more distant than ever. The guy who stood in front of me in the kitchen just now— with his rigid shoulders, the cold furrow in his brow and the iron clench to his jaw—that's not the same man I spent the past month with.

What happened to him?

I fight hard against the tears I can feel building, but it's no use. I just don't understand how things can go from so amazing to so shit—how he can go from so loving to so cold —in the blink of an eye.

And when I asked him if he loves me... Pain carves through my chest as I picture the way he just stared at the floor and shrugged. He *shrugged*. The more I replay that moment, the more confused I feel, because the thing is, I don't know if I believe him. I was so sure he felt what I did, that things between us were real. Is it possible I imagined it? Or did I do something to make him change his mind? I think back to the conversation with his mom about kids, how I told him I loved him under the fireworks, how we had sex without protection and then had to wait to be sure I got my period... It's a lot, I get that. Enough to scare any man.

But... when I think back over the weekend with him, everything just felt so *right*. It felt like *finally*, this is what I've been waiting for all this time. It felt like he'd been waiting for it, too.

I blink away the tears silently streaming down my face. Because it doesn't matter, does it? Regardless of how it seemed, or what I think he felt, he obviously doesn't *want* to love me anymore. It almost felt as he told me we needed to end things in such a cold, unfeeling way, like he was *trying* to be hurtful. I don't even know what to make of that. Maybe I really did overestimate his feelings for me—because he can't care that much if he can go from *I love you* to *it's over* in just a few days.

And what a few days it's been. Ever since we returned from his mom's I've been so careful, tiptoeing around and trying not to be too needy. I cringe as I recall the way I curled in on myself when he came home this afternoon, desperate to play it cool, to smooth things over, to not do anything that would freak him out.

The more I think about this, the more I realize I've been a different person after the weekend away, too. I recognize that girl—it's the same small and powerless version of myself from five years ago.

I don't like her at all.

What the hell happened to the woman who learned to

speak up for herself? Even now, as Cory gave me a bunch of weak, vague excuses about why we couldn't be together, I was afraid to push too hard.

Fresh tears spring to my eyes as I think about the fact that I gave up the chance for a paid position at the shelter—the thing I've wanted for years. Sure, it was partly because I wanted to stay at Bounce, but I also wonder if I was afraid to apply for the job because things with Cory felt too precarious after we got back from Long Island. If I was afraid to rock the boat.

Fuck. How could I let a man make me feel like this again?

I wipe my cheeks and push to my feet, anger igniting in my veins. You know what? *No*. Cory doesn't get to do this to me. He doesn't get to make me feel small and hurt and confused, like Paul did. After all we've been through together, if he can't even *try* to find the words to explain how he's feeling to me—if he'd rather just cut and run—then yeah, it *is* over. And there's no way in hell I'm staying here.

Pretzel jumps off the sofa to sit expectantly at my feet, and I look down at him.

Shit. I can't just leave. What will I do with Pretzel? He's my boy now and, with or without Cory, I'm not letting him go.

I drop to my knees in front of him, pulling him into a hug. He licks my ear and it makes my heart ache. He's so happy here at Cory's, with the courtyard space for him to play and get outside. I don't want to drag him away from the only real home he's had since the shelter.

I think of what Geoff told me a month ago—that I needed to put my well-being before the dog's—and sigh. As much as I want to stay for Pretzel, it's only going to hurt me. Everywhere I look, I think of Cory: of the cooking we've done in his kitchen, the time we've spent in his bed, the conversation we had on this sofa when he broke down and let me in.

God, thinking about that puts things in perspective. It was me pushing from the start, wasn't it? Me pushing him to kiss me at the bar, me pushing him in the shower, me pushing him to talk and finally give in. Why didn't I realize that before? It was me who said I love you first, me who talked about kids and the future...

You want too much, Josie.

Tears mist my eyes at the memory of Paul's words. I try to shove them away but as much as it stings, they feel true right now.

Fuck, I'm so tired of thinking about all this. I'm tired of worrying about what's happening with Cory, of wondering if I messed everything up, of trying to figure out why he changed after the weekend. I'm tired of how *familiar* this whole thing feels, like I'm reliving the worst parts of my life from five years ago.

One thing is crystal clear: I can't stay here.

I take a deep breath and fire off a text to Geoff, asking if his offer to crash at his place last month still stands. I hate having to ask, but I also know that Geoff is kind and generous, and—most importantly—right. It's time to put my well-being first.

I set my phone down and curl back into the sofa to wait for his reply, Pretzel snug against my side. "Guess it's just you and me now, buddy," I whisper, closing my eyes.

PRETZEL WAKES ME. I hadn't planned to fall asleep, but after the stress of the day I must have been completely drained.

When I blink my eyes open, it's almost dark out. I reach for my phone to check the time and there's a message waiting from Geoff.

Geoff: Of course, you're welcome any time. Come over whenever you're ready. There's a key under the mat for you.

Grateful tears prick my eyes and I pull myself up to stand and stretch. I let Pretzel out into the courtyard to pee, turning to look back across the apartment while I wait. My chest fills with sadness as I think about the past month I've spent here—what I thought I'd found with Cory, and what I've lost.

I shake the feeling away and stride over to my shelves beside the Murphy bed, pulling out a bag and stuffing clothes into it quickly. The sooner I can get out of here, the better. Maybe I can send someone back to get my kitchen things later, because I can't bear the thought of having to face Cory anytime soon.

Actually, that's a good point. What am I going to do about work? I'm lucky I've got tonight off, but I'm due in tomorrow. I can't stand the thought of going into the bar and trying to pretend I'm okay, putting on a smile for customers. Eddy will no doubt have some things to say—things I'm sure I don't want to hear right now.

I gather my stuff from the bathroom and dump my bags by the front door, going to get Pretzel in from the courtyard. Just as I'm closing the door, my phone buzzes in my skirt pocket. I expect to see some instructions from Geoff, but when I pull it out I see a message from Eddy, of all people. I swipe my phone open to read.

Eddy: Hey can you come into the bar? Cory is being super weird.

I frown down at my screen, ignoring the way my heart

jumps at seeing Cory's name. I don't care if Cory is being weird, this isn't my problem anymore. He made sure of that.

Josie: It's my night off.

My phone immediately buzzes with a reply.

Eddy: Seriously, something is really wrong with him.

My stomach begins a slow, uneasy descent. I know I'm supposed to be mad at Cory, but my anger is quickly eclipsed by concern.

Josie: What kind of wrong?

Eddy: I think he's drunk.

I stare at the screen, rereading Eddy's words. Cory's drunk? At *work*? Shit, that is bad. I've never seen him drunk —especially not at Bounce. Something about that seems really off.

I know it makes no sense, but part of me feels guilty— like somehow, I'm responsible. More than that, though, I'm worried. He might have been a dick to me this afternoon but I still care about him. I don't want anything to happen to him.

Josie: Can you call him a cab?

Eddy: I tried, but he won't let me or Levi near him.

Dammit, Cory.

I huff out a breath and send off a quick reply.

Josie: Fine. I'll be right in.

I stuff my phone in my pocket and tell Pretzel I'll be back soon, then turn for the door. A strange cocktail of nerves and panic swirl in my gut as I stride down the street, and I send off a text asking Cat if she can meet me at the bar. I have no idea what Cory will be like in this state and I could use the backup.

Cat: Of course. Everything okay?

Josie: Not sure. Apparently Cory is drunk.

I manage to flag down a cab on East Broadway,

watching as the dots appear and disappear on my phone while Cat composes her response. Finally, it comes through.

Cat: Shit, I didn't realize the date. Okay, I'll be there in ten.

The *date*?

I lock my screen and turn to look out at the passing lights of Essex Street as I try to make sense of Cat's words. What does the date have to do with anything?

Cat and Myles are jogging toward the bar when my cab pulls up. I shove some money at the driver and lurch out the door, catching them at the entrance.

"Man, I'm out of shape," Cat says, doubling over with her hands on her knees. She takes a few deep breaths and straightens up, turning to me before I can enter the bar. "I should tell you—today is the anniversary of Dad's death. I completely forgot it was today. And Cory..." She grimaces, looking at Myles then back at me. "He never handles today well. I thought this year things might be different, but I guess not."

Oh, fuck. That's *today*? Any anger I felt for him earlier melts away, and compassion blooms in its place.

"Come on," Myles says, gently nudging Cat toward the door. "With Cory down, the place will be overrun. I'll jump behind the bar and you guys see if you can get him into a cab, okay?"

Cat looks to me for agreement but I chew my lip apprehensively. I'm guessing she has no idea what happened between Cory and I this afternoon, because she tries to reassure me by saying, "He'll feel better once he gets a hug from you."

I grimace, looking away. "I don't know about that. He... ended things with us today."

Myles turns from the door back to the conversation, his brow low. "He what now?"

"Oh, shit." Cat rubs her forehead.

"What did he say, exactly?" Myles presses.

"Just..." I swallow down the lump forming in my throat. "That he can't be the guy I need, and he doesn't see a future with us."

"Fuck, fuck, fuck," Cat mutters, turning to Myles and pressing her face into his T-shirt. "This is my fault."

Myles smooths a hand over her pink hair. "It's not your fault, baby."

"Yes, it is! I got so excited about him and Josie, and—"

"Cat, this was always going to happen," Myles says calmly.

I raise my hands to my hips with impatience. "What are you talking about?"

Myles shrugs, stepping aside to let a group pass us on the sidewalk. "Well, basically, you've forced him to face his demons and he's terrified."

"His demons?" I echo. I always forget that underneath Myles's scruffy, tattooed exterior, there's a wise, intuitive guy who's really good at reading people.

"Yeah, you know—all the stuff we talked about with his dad leaving. He's never had a solid male role model, so he doesn't know how to be a husband or a father. You guys were getting serious and his dad's death probably just reminded him how"—Myles rolls his hand, searching for the right word—"ill-equipped he is to step into those roles. So, he panicked and ran."

Oh my God.

I glance at the door to Bounce and back to Myles, letting his words sink in. That makes so much sense. And there's something Myles doesn't know, too—all the stuff with Alice;

the words his mom said that made him think he was just as bad as his father, made him think he didn't deserve to be loved.

God, how did I not realize this? How could I have been so stupid as to think one conversation on his sofa a month ago would heal the pain he's been carrying for twenty years? That *I* could heal that pain for him?

How could I not realize this isn't about me at all?

"Come on," Myles says again, gesturing to the door. "Let's try to get him home."

Cat and Myles walk into Bounce and I trail behind nervously, my eyes taking a moment to adjust to the low lighting. Man, it's hot in here, and Myles was right—the bar is slammed. My first instinct is to step back there and start serving people, but Myles points across the crowd to a booth near the back, mouthing over the din that he's spotted Cory. Then he jerks a thumb toward the bar to indicate he's going over to help Eddy and Levi.

Cat threads through the crowd, pulling me by the hand, until we arrive at Cory's booth. The table is littered with empty beer bottles and he's got his head in his hands, staring down at the table top. I stand and watch as Cat slides into the booth next to him, gently touching his arm. He immediately swats her away, but when he lifts his head to see it's her, he softens. His eyes are swollen and red, and the sight hurts my heart so much I want to cry. I've never seen him look so wrecked and hollow.

Cat leans in to say something I can't hear, sliding an arm around his shoulders to give him a squeeze. She manages to coax him out of the booth and onto his feet, and it's not until he sways and nearly topples over that he notices me. I prop myself under his right arm, one hand around his back to help steady him. His eyes meet mine in the dim light, hazy and unfocused, and he blinks down at me. Then his brow knits, like he can't understand why I'm here.

Why *am* I here? Didn't he make it clear where I stand? This was a mistake.

I drop my hand from his back and go to step away, but the arm he has over my shoulder curls around me and pulls me in tight to his chest. I feel his nose press into my hair, his heart pounding through his sweat-moistened T-shirt.

"Come on," Cat yells over the crowd. "You're getting in a cab, Cors. *Now*."

Together, Cat and I help Cory lumber out of the bar and onto the sidewalk. There's a few cabs idling at the curb and we steer him over to one, pushing him onto the backseat. His hand finds mine and tugs me toward the door.

"Cat—" I call, looking over at her.

"I'm going to go in and help Myles," she says, glancing back at the packed bar. "Can you get him home?"

I hesitate, but she's already striding back into the bar. With a wary sigh, I slide onto the backseat and pull the door closed. I give our address to the driver and turn to Cory as the car peels away from the curb. He's lying with his head back on the seat, his eyes closed, and relief seeps through me. I'm not even sure where to begin with him.

I mean, yes, today is the anniversary of his dad's death and that's hard, especially given Cory's complicated relationship with his father. But why didn't he just *tell* me? Why didn't he reach out to me for support? I thought he'd finally let me in, but—what did Myles say? That I forced Cory to face his demons and he's scared?

"You didn't have to come," Cory slurs beside me on the backseat.

I glance at him, feeling a prickle of frustration. Of course I didn't have to come. I was *worried* about him. But before I can express this, his face crumples and he drops his head into his hands.

"I'm not worth the trouble," he mutters, grinding the heels of his hands into his eyes.

My heart softens. Fuck, how did I not realize just how broken this man is?

I reach a tentative hand out to touch his arm. "I want to make sure you're safe, okay?"

He shakes his head, his face buried in his hands. "Why? If I were you, I would've left me for dead."

His words make something burn sharp and hot in my chest. "Cory—"

"But you'd never do that, would you?" He glances up, his eyes meeting mine as streetlights flash through the car interior. "You're so good like that, Butterup." He hiccups, his brow creasing as he tries again. "Butter...*cup*."

I draw a breath to speak, but he's not done.

"She forgave me, d'you know that?"

I squint my eyes in confusion. "Who?"

"Alex."

"*Alex*?"

"ALICE," he enunciates with great effort. He frowns in annoyance, as if he'd said it correctly the first time and I'm the one making this conversation hard. "I saw her on the weekend. She"—hiccup—"said it was all gooood." He drags out the O on good, ending with a bitter snort.

I gape at him. He *saw* her? When? How did I miss *that*?

"But tha's jush not true, 'cause I hurt her. And now"—he turns to me, his face contorted with regret—"I hurt you."

"Cors," I whisper, reaching for him. "You didn't—"

"I did. I made y'"—hiccup—"cry."

I open my mouth to protest, then close it again. Because he's right. He did.

He nods sadly, looking down at his hands. "I'm just like him, Joze." He doesn't have to mention his father—we both know who he means. "I'm no good. Look at me. Look at what I've done to us."

My vision blurs with tears as I take in his slumped, defeated form. I wish he could see the man I've seen over this past month—hell, over the past five years. He's sweet and kind and generous and caring. He's nothing like the man who abandoned his family without so much as a backward glance.

Why can't he see that? Why isn't my love enough to show him that?

The cab pulls up to the building and I pay the driver, wondering how the hell I'll get Cory out of the car. But when I walk around to open his door, he stumbles out onto the sidewalk. With half his weight on my shoulder, we make it to the front door. I can feel his eyes on me as I fumble single-handedly with the key, finally getting the door open. We tumble into the apartment and Cory slumps against the wall, about to slide to the floor, but I swoop under his arm again.

"No, big guy. Let's get you into bed."

Pretzel joins us in the hall, jumping up at Cory in excitement as I direct him toward the bedroom. When I deposit him on the bed, Pretzel leaps up too, licking Cory's face as he flops back to stare at the ceiling.

"Hey, Pretshell," he slurs, rolling onto his side to cuddle the dog. He pulls Pretzel in close and spoons his wriggling body, gently saying "Shhh, it's okay, boy," into his ear. Pretzel relaxes against him and I have to look away in case I start blubbering.

I crouch at the foot of the bed and focus on untying Cory's boots, tossing them over by the door. Then I stand

and assess his jeans and T-shirt. "Can you get your own pants off?" Cory looks up at me with a lop-sided grin and I hold up a hand. "So you can *sleep*, Cors. Don't even joke about that."

His smile dims and he rolls onto his back, attempting to undo his button fly. Why did he have to wear such complicated jeans, tonight of all nights?

He gets two buttons undone then flops back again, exhausted. "Ish fine, Butterup. Leave 'em on."

"It's not fine," I mutter, stepping closer. It's a million degrees tonight and he'll boil in his sleep. I reach down to undo the buttons, desperately trying to keep my fingers from brushing against his junk. Not that anything is happening in there—he's so drunk I'm surprised he hasn't wet himself.

Cory leans up on his elbows to watch me slowly remove his jeans—leaving his underwear firmly *on*—and when I motion for him to sit up properly, he does. I peel his shirt off and toss it aside, refusing to look at his body. His perfect, delicious, almost-naked body.

"You're taking care of me," he murmurs as I yank the bed covers down under him and push him onto the sheets.

"Of course I am." I head out to the kitchen and fill two glasses of water, returning to the room. "Drink these."

He blinks at me, then takes each glass and diligently slugs it back. I head out again and return, this time with his toothbrush and another glass of water.

"Brush," I instruct, and he clumsily drags the brush over his teeth, rinsing with the water and spitting into one of the empty glasses. He drains the rest of the water and I take the glasses out to the kitchen, giving myself a moment to just breathe. Emotion wells up inside me but I tamp it down, knowing I can't lose it yet.

I expect him to be passed out when I head back into the bedroom, but he's sitting up in bed, arms hooked around his bent knees, his expression sad. Pretzel nuzzles into his side and he sighs, looking down and rubbing a hand over his head. I hover in the doorway, my chest aching as I watch the scene. It's one I've seen dozens of times, but knowing this is the last time makes it so much harder.

Cory's gaze flicks up to mine, his hazel eyes looking clearer than before. The water must have helped to sober him up. He reaches a hand out to me and, against all my better judgment, I go to him. I slide my hand into his, closing my eyes at the warmth and comfort of his touch. Even though I know better, I sink onto the bed beside him and pull him into my arms. His familiar musky, earthy smell envelopes me as he buries his face in my shoulder. I hear a snuffling noise and, shit—I'm pretty sure he's crying, but I can't bring myself to look because my heart is so close to breaking, so I just squeeze him tighter and rub his back. I want to tell him everything I know to be true—that he's none of the things he thinks he is and everything he thinks he's not—but now isn't the time. And would it even help? I've been telling him that for a month and he still doesn't believe me. It's not enough. I know that now.

"I *did* mean it," he murmurs into my neck, and I freeze. "When I said I love you... of course I meant it."

Something lodges in my throat and I press my eyes shut. "I know," I whisper.

"It's always been you, Joze. I think I've loved you since the moment I hired you. But you deserve the world, and I'm not—"

"Shhh," I say, because if he keeps talking I'm going to start bawling and I can't do that to him.

"I only stayed away from you because I've been so scared

that I'd hurt you. Because I'm not good—" He chokes on a sob and I press my face hard into his shoulder until I can't breathe. "That's why today... Shit, I fucked everything up. I'm so sorry. I don't want to lose you."

Oh, God.

He holds me tighter, his voice little more than a rough shred when he says, "I want to marry you. I want to have babies with you. You're everything to me."

Fuck.

There goes my heart. It fragments into thousands of tiny pieces, scattering out across Manhattan, because he's finally saying everything I want to hear, but it's all wrong. It's too late now. It took him getting blind drunk to say this to me, and he *still* doesn't believe he deserves it.

I lift my face away from his shoulder to suck in a deep, fortifying breath. I can't meet his gaze as I draw away, terrified that I'll burst into tears and tell him I want all those things too.

That wouldn't be good for either of us. It would only continue to paper over his pain—the pain that's so much deeper than I realized. We'd only end up going through this whole thing again, and that will only hurt me more.

"You need to get some sleep," I manage, shoving my emotions down inside so I can be strong for both of us in this moment. I glance at the door, knowing that even though I won't leave him home alone in this state, I shouldn't stay in the bed with him, but when I look back at his wretched, miserable face, I can't bring myself to leave.

I turn and pat the pillows, motioning for him to lie down. He lets out an exhausted sigh and collapses back, wiping his cheeks.

"Roll over," I murmur, waiting until he's facing away from me so I can flick the light off. Then I kick off my denim skirt, leaving on my tank, and climb into bed and spoon him. Even though he's so much bigger than me, I can sense he needs to be the little spoon tonight.

I feel his chest shudder under my hand. When I realize he's crying again, I reach up to caress his moist cheek and press my lips to his back, breathing in the smell of his skin. It's bittersweet, being here comforting him, knowing I won't be this close to him again.

But he needs to heal these wounds, and I can't sacrifice myself in the process. In the past I would have, but I learned that lesson the hard way.

This time, I need to do what's best for me.

It's not until Cory is finally asleep that I let myself silently sob into the pillow.

35

CORY

I splash cold water onto my face and pat it dry, grimacing when I catch sight of my reflection in the mirror above the bathroom sink.

Jesus. I don't look nearly forty—I look nearly *dead*.

Last night was possibly the worst night of my life. As soon as I got to the bar without Josie I realized what a monumental mistake I'd made. I kept picturing her crumpled face, the way she looked so hurt and confused by how I'd acted. And even though half of me insisted it was the right thing to do, the other half of me was—there's no other word for it—heartbroken. I'd pushed away the most amazing woman I've ever known, and I was well aware of the irony: that by trying to *avoid* hurting her, I'd actually brought about the exact thing I feared.

So, I drank. There was nothing else to do, and it's how I usually handle that day each year anyway.

I didn't mean for it to get quite so out of hand, and I sure as hell didn't expect Josie to see me in that state, let alone come to my rescue.

The second I saw her in the bar, though, I knew it couldn't have gone any other way. I was almost disappointed to see her there, because after the way I'd treated her she should have been mad as shit. Instead, she was trying to make sure I was safe. She was trying to take care of me—so much so that she slept beside me, bringing me more water during the night and making sure I was okay.

Now she's in our bed, sleeping off what was probably one of the worst nights of *her* life, too. All thanks to me.

I study my reflection, my stomach churning with dread. I know I have to go out there and face her, have to own my behavior last night. I wish I was one of those people who can't remember shit when they get wasted, but I'm not. Never have been. I remember everything—how I broke down in the cab, pouring my heart out and wishing against all odds that she'd forgive me. I remember all the things I confessed to her as she tucked me into bed—how much I want a future with her, how much she means to me.

I also remember that she didn't say any of that back.

I step out of the bathroom with a deep sigh, noticing for the first time her bags packed by the door.

Shit. She was going to leave last night, but she didn't, because I was such a mess.

I get a flashback from the night we got together, a month ago. She had bags packed by the door then, too, because I pushed her away. And she stayed then, too—probably against her better judgment.

I shake my head, turning away. I really don't like the pattern I see here.

The courtyard door is open when I enter the living room, and I poke my head out to find Josie sitting at the outdoor table in the morning sun, gazing up at the sky. She's still wearing the same clothes from yesterday, rumpled from sleep, her hair fluffy and her face tired. Pretzel sniffs around the garden, then trots over when he sees me. I duck back inside, making sure he has food and water, and put coffee on to brew. Then I change into a fresh T-shirt and jeans, taking two mugs of coffee outside to join Josie.

"Hey," I murmur, tentatively sitting opposite her.

"Hey." She takes the mug from my outstretched hand and stares down at it, chewing her lip.

We sip our coffee in silence for a while, listening to the sounds of the city. It's only 8 a.m. and I'm already sweating in the stifling city heat. All that booze I put in my system last night probably didn't help.

Josie clears her throat and I look at her. She's gazing at me over her coffee cup, her nose stud catching the early light, her eyes an intense green, ringed with sadness.

Goddammit. I really wanted to keep it together this morning. But that flies out the window when I choke out, "I'm so sorry, Joze."

She nods, her face softening with compassion. "I know."

That's it. She doesn't get mad, doesn't demand why I did what I did. She doesn't stand and leave—she just continues to gaze at me. A tiny bud of hope unfurls in my chest. Is there any way that I can salvage this? That things can go back to the way they were before I—

"You know I still have to leave though, right?" She says it gently, but it may as well be a machete to my heart.

Heat presses behind my eyes as I look up at the cobalt sky. Of course she's going to leave. She deserves so much better than me. Always has.

"I'd judge you if you didn't," I mutter with a humorless laugh.

When I finally glance back, she's frowning. "Cors, I need

you to know—I'm not leaving for the reasons you think I should. Not because you're a bad guy who isn't worth loving. That's—" Her voice catches, and she takes a faltering breath. "That's never been true. I'm leaving because you don't believe me when I tell you that."

I look down at my coffee as a knot forms in my throat.

"You're carrying so much pain inside," she continues tearfully. "This stuff with your dad and Alice... I didn't realize how deep those wounds were. I should have, but I didn't. And I don't think my love is enough to heal it. I can't fix that."

I bring my gaze back to hers. "I don't *want* you to fix that."

"I know." She swipes her wrist under her eye and desperation flares in my chest.

"Why can't we just go back to how things were? I know last night was shitty, and I'm sorry, but things were good before that, right? It won't happen again—"

"It will. I know you want to believe it won't, but it will. How can you let my love in if you don't think you deserve it? My mom raised me to believe that there is nothing love can't heal, and I think she's right, but it has to start inside you. I can't love you enough for both of us, Cors." A tear spills down her cheek and she tries to wipe it away, but another one falls in its place. "I want to, I really do. But the last time I gave too much of myself in a relationship, I lost myself. I can't do that again."

I stare at her, knowing she's right. I picture the shell of a woman I met five years ago, the one who was so sad and empty. I can't let that happen to her again. I can't be the reason that happens to her.

Her shoulders shudder with a sob and, on instinct, I spring out of my chair and kneel in front of her, pulling her into my arms. She buries her head in my shoulder, the wetness of her cheeks soaking into my shirt.

"I'm so sorry," she murmurs. "I can't."

"I know." My throat burns as I fight to keep it together, to comfort her in the way she did for me last night. Even though it feels like my heart has shriveled up and will never beat again, I'm also proud of her. This is a woman who's done nothing but put the needs of others ahead of her own for years, and somehow she's found the strength to look after herself now. I don't want her to leave me and yet, I admire her for doing it. I spent so long telling myself she's too young for me, but she's more emotionally mature than I could ever be.

When we finally pull apart, she's composed herself. She gives me a weak smile, squeezing my arm, and it takes everything in me not to press my lips to hers and carry her into the bedroom.

Instead, I wrench myself away and stand, dragging a hand through my hair. "Are you sure you want to leave here, though?"

"Yes. I need to. I'm going to crash at Geoff's for a while until I figure out what to do. He's allowed dogs, so..."

I nod, relieved that at least she has somewhere safe to stay, but I can't deny the emptiness I feel at the thought of her leaving, of this place without her and Pretzel here. Grief overwhelms me, and I struggle to push it away. I can't let myself picture what my life will be like without them now. I can't do that, because I won't want to live it.

"Um..." I begin hoarsely, fighting with everything I have to keep my emotions in check. "I'm going to head out for a few hours. And maybe it would be best if..."

"Yeah." She nods, her eyes filling with tears again. I make myself look away. "I'll be gone when you get back."

"Okay. Yeah. Okay," I repeat lamely. There's nothing more for me to do than spin on my heel and leave. I don't dare say anything else, because I know I'll break down, and she's seen enough of that from me to last her a lifetime. So I grab my keys, forcing myself to ignore the way Pretzel follows me to the door, and step outside.

36

JOSIE

I burst into tears the moment I see Geoff.

"Oh, honey." He takes my hand, ushering me inside. Pretzel hesitates behind me, and Geoff fetches some cheese from the fridge to lure him in. He hauls my bags in too, then closes the door, turning to me. "Do you want to talk about it, or is it more of an alcohol-with-breakfast situation?"

I can't help a watery laugh. "I'm sorry. Thank you so much for letting me stay here. I promise I won't be like this"—I gesture to my tear-streaked face—"forever."

"Hey." He steps closer, taking me by the shoulders. "You take as long as you need, okay? Cat told me what happened." He motions to the sofa and I sink down onto the plush, raspberry velvet fabric.

"She did?"

"Yeah." He wanders over to the kitchen, peering into his cabinets. "I have coffee. I have vodka." He glances back at me, assessing. "Or maybe some chamomile tea..."

"Tea would be great, thank you." I pull my shoes off and set them beside the couch, curling my feet up under me. Pretzel looks about ready to jump into my lap, and I decide to set up his crate and keep him in there until we're settled. Geoff's sofa is way too nice for Pretzel to get his claws on.

Geoff sets a cup of steaming chamomile tea on the coffee table, then lowers himself beside me on the sofa. "I hope it's okay—Cat's on her way over. We go to a yoga class in the Village some mornings."

Crap. She's the last person I want to see right now. She made me promise I wouldn't hurt Cory and that's exactly what I've done.

Geoff eyes me over his coffee. "I can text her and cancel?"

I shake my head. "No, you don't have to do that." I'll need to face her eventually. I reach for the mug of tea and cradle it, blowing on the fragrant steam. I think about the last time I spoke to Geoff—really spoke to him—and it was when he first offered for me to stay here. When he suggested that Cory might have more baggage than I realized.

"You were right," I murmur, lifting my cup to my lips.

"What do you mean?"

"Staying with Cory wasn't the best idea, given all the stuff about his dad he needed to work through. I should have left when you told me to a month ago." I glance at Geoff and he tilts his head, studying me.

"Do you really wish you had, though?"

"No," I mumble. My heart might be bruised and battered right now, but I wouldn't give up the month I spent with Cory for the world. Even though it was short-lived... it was everything.

"Knock, knock." Cat pokes her head into Geoff's apartment. "Oh. *Dammit*," she mutters, the second she sees me and my bags. "I was really hoping you guys were going to work things out. Did he not apologize?"

"He did. But... Ugh." I rub my forehead. "Please don't hate me, Cat."

She slips the door closed behind her and crosses the room to us. "Why would I hate you?"

"Because you told me not to hurt him, and I..." I puff out a breath, somewhere between a sigh and a sob. "I didn't *want* to leave, really—"

"Hey, it's okay." Compassion shimmers in her brown eyes. "What can I do?"

I shrug, pretending I don't feel sadness press between my ribs. "There's nothing you can do. You guys should go to your yoga."

"Forget yoga." Cat waves my words away, wedging herself between me and Geoff on the sofa. "I need to fix this."

"I don't think—" My words catch in my throat and I set my tea down, trying again. "I don't think there is any fixing it."

Cat's face falls, but she nods in understanding. "Do you still love him?"

My heart tumbles over itself in an attempt to answer. "Yes," I say, pressing my fingertips to my sternum. "Fuck, I love him so much. I just... wish he could love himself. But he won't let me in. He doesn't trust himself not to hurt me. He thinks..." I swallow. "He thinks he doesn't deserve love."

"What makes you say that?"

I tug my bottom lip into my mouth, hesitating. I'm not sure if Cat knows about Cory's past, and I don't want to break his trust by telling her.

She sighs. "Is this about what happened with Alice?"

"You know about that?"

"Yeah." She sinks back on the sofa. "I overheard Mom confront him in the kitchen when it happened."

"Do you remember what she said to him?"

Cat thinks for a second, then shakes her head.

"She told him he's just like your dad. I'm sure she didn't mean it," I add quickly. "She probably only said it because she was angry, but Cory has clung to that ever since. He hates your dad for what he did, and he hates himself for being the same."

Cat frowns. "Why would him cheating on Alice make him just like dad?"

Oh, shit. There's an icy trickle down my spine as it occurs to me that Cat might not know their father had an affair. Oh, shit, shit, shit. I've really put my foot in it now. I didn't mean to dig up some long-buried family secret. I should have kept my big mouth closed.

Cat's voice is very quiet when she asks, "Dad cheated on Mom, didn't he?"

I raise my hands over my face, shaking my head. "I don't know. That's none of my business."

"He did," she says, more forcefully. "He did, didn't he? I always wondered, but Mom never actually confirmed it."

Fuck.

I lower my hands, giving her a miserable look. "I'm so sorry. I never meant to—"

"Whoa." She reaches out to take my hand. "That is *not* your fault. I always had a feeling he did. And knowing this… it explains so much about Cory."

"Also," Geoff adds, speaking for the first time in minutes, "it explains why Cory hates your ex-husband so much."

I look at Cat. "Your ex cheated?"

"Yeah. And you should have seen Cors when he found

out." She grimaces. "I had to hold him back from strangling Mark."

Despite myself, a half-smile touches my lips. That's Cory —so protective of the people he loves.

"Wow," Cat says, still processing all this. "No wonder he hates himself. He hurt Alice and then Mom made him feel like shit for it, when he was probably already feeling awful. But—" She turns to me. "Look, cheating is never okay, but it was a *mistake*, and he's not the same guy he was back then. You should have *seen* him as a teenager, Joze. He was off the rails after Dad left. Mom tried her best, but she didn't know how to help him. He was so lost. God." She sags back against the sofa, blowing out a breath. "I can't believe he's been holding this against himself for so long. Poor Cors."

I have to look away and take a deep breath at this point. It's all I can do to stop myself from burying my face in Geoff's pillow and wailing. When I've finally felt the tears in my eyes recede, I reach for my cold tea and take a huge gulp.

Maybe I should have taken the vodka after all.

"What are you going to do, then?" Cat asks. Pretzel whines in his crate and she goes over to pet him. "You're still keeping Pretzel, right?"

"Yeah. My lease is up next month and I want to find a place that lets me have pets."

"Oh!" Cat straightens suddenly. "Hayley's roommate just moved out, and she had a dog. Would you consider moving to Brooklyn?"

I bolt upright on the sofa. "Are you serious? Yes! My old apartment is in Bushwick. She wouldn't mind me bringing Pretzel?"

"No way." Cat pulls her phone out and hastily composes a text. "Hayley loves dogs. I'm sure she—" Cat's words halt as her phone buzzes in her hand, and she laughs at the screen.

She turns it around to show me, and all I can see is the word *YES!!!* in block letters. "You're in. Should I tell her you'll be over today?"

"Yes. Thank you so much." I press my hand to my heart, feeling a rush of relief.

"Aw." Geoff pokes his bottom lip out. "I was looking forward to a slumber party."

I give a grim laugh. "You don't want me crying on your sofa for a week, Geoff."

"Hey." He shuffles over and slings an arm around my shoulder. "I meant it when I said you're welcome here." He squeezes me and I blink away. The kindness these two are showing me is more than I can handle right now.

"Okay," Cat says, slipping her phone into the pocket of her yoga pants. "Hayley said to come over whenever you're ready."

I exhale slowly. At least that gives me something to focus on, rather than sitting here drowning in self-pity. Hopefully I can get Pretzel settled in there before I have to go into work...

Oh, God. My stomach rolls at the thought of going into the bar and seeing Cory, so soon. There's no way I can face him tonight.

"Um, Cat?" I shift uncomfortably. She's already done so much for me and I hate to ask more. But this is what friends are for, right? Helping you through a breakup. "Would you mind... could you tell Cory I won't be coming in tonight? I don't think I can bear to see him yet."

"Oh, hon." She glances up from where she's petting Pretzel in his crate. "Of course. I'm going to ask Myles to go in and work a shift tonight, just to help out. Cory won't be in a good state. I'll help where I can too. Don't worry about it."

"Thanks," I mumble, pushing away the guilt that tugs at

me. I just need to take tonight to pull myself together. Then by tomorrow...

But will I be ready tomorrow? Will I *ever* be ready? I can't rewind things back to the way they were before—where Cory was no more than my boss and friend, where I watched him hit on other women all night and pretended I was okay with it. He used to walk me to the train because he was worried about me—and, now I can see, wanting to spend more time with me—but I can't imagine he'll want to do that anymore. And worse—if he *did*, I can't imagine not wanting to hold his hand, not going home with him. I can't imagine being around him at *all*, without wanting those things.

I fight tears as realization slowly sinks through me like a stone. I'm going to have to quit Bounce, aren't I? *Fuck*. I love working there.

But it won't be the same now.

"Right." Cat pushes to her feet, unaware of my inner turmoil. "I think I need to go call my mom."

Oh, crap.

"*Please* don't tell her what I accidentally revealed about your dad," I beg. "I didn't mean—"

"I won't, I promise." Cat chuckles. "It wouldn't make any difference, anyway. You can't do any wrong in my mom's eyes. She loves you."

I wince. "I don't think she'll love me quite so much when she finds out I broke her son's heart."

Cat rolls her lips to the side in thought. "You know, I think she'll understand. She'll probably be grateful that you helped him to—what did Myles say? Face his demons?" She gives me a kind smile. "It might be rough going for a while, but I think she'll agree you did the right thing."

"You think I did?" I press, desperate for someone to reassure me. Because after talking this whole thing through, I can't help but wonder if I've actually done the *wrong* thing, leaving Cory when he needs someone the most.

"Yeah, I do."

I glance at Geoff and he nods. "I think you did too. You can't carry someone else's baggage for them, and you'd hurt yourself trying. He's the only one who can heal this stuff."

"Exactly," Cat agrees. "And now he can begin to do that."

Hope flickers inside me. "You really think he will? He won't just go back to the way his life was before?"

She gives an adamant shake of her head. "No way. He's in love with you, and he's never been in love with anyone that I know of. After experiencing that, he won't be able to go back to his old life. And if he tries—I won't fucking let him. Just... don't give up on him yet, okay?"

"Okay," I murmur. I'm not entirely sure what that means, but I do know one thing: I couldn't stop loving him if I tried. And who knows, if he begins to heal some of his wounds, maybe one day...

I shake the thought away, not daring to let myself dream. I did that over and over with Paul, and it only wore me down. It broke me.

I won't do that again.

I glance away, repeating Cat's words to myself. *You did the right thing.*

If that's true, why does it hurt so much?

37

CORY

I walk around the city for an hour before the heat nearly kills me. When I pass the Roxy Cinema in Tribeca, I decide to go in for the air conditioning, and end up watching two movies back to back. I didn't plan to stay so long, but I'm too afraid to go home in case Josie and Pretzel are still there. I don't even pay attention to the films —I just sit in the cool darkness, staring numbly at the screen, waiting for the time to pass.

When I finally let myself back into the apartment, I pause in the doorway, listening for the telltale sound of Pretzel's paws on the floor. It doesn't come. My throat prickles as I close the door, standing in the silence of my empty apartment. I don't want to be here. I don't want to do anything that doesn't involve me being close to Josie.

I force myself to kick my boots off and shuffle into the kitchen. I'm tempted to reach for the booze again, but I know that won't solve anything.

"Cory?"

I nearly jump out of my skin when Mom appears beside me, her brow lined with worry.

"There you are. I tried calling you, honey."

I pull my phone out of my pocket and blink down at the notification for three missed calls.

"I used my key, I hope that's okay."

I nod, turning away and dropping my own keys on the counter. My voice is rusty when I ask, "What are you doing here?"

"Cat called me. She told me what happened. She also told me..." Mom's hand touches my arm and I go rigid, too scared to move in case I collapse in on myself, swallowed whole by my misery. "Why don't you have a seat, honey? Let's talk."

She vanishes from my side and I lean over the kitchen sink, inhaling deep and slow. I don't want to talk to my mom about this right now—I don't want to talk to anyone. But she's come all the way into the city to see me and I'd never turn her away.

With great effort, I turn and join my mom on the sofa. She shuffles closer, reaching out for my hand, and that's all it takes.

A sob erupts out of me and I fall forward, into her arms, shaking.

"Oh, Cors. Sweetheart. It's okay."

"It's not okay," I rasp through my tears. "I've lost her, Mom."

"You haven't lost her." Mom strokes my back. I might be nearly forty, but in this moment I'm nineteen again. Only this time, I'm not in our kitchen back home, and Mom isn't turning her back on me.

When I finally pull myself together, Mom hands me a tissue from her purse with a gentle smile.

"I had a long talk with Cat this morning, and I need to apologize to you. I want you to know, I've always tried my best to be a good mom."

"You *are* a good mom," I say fiercely, gripping her hand. "I don't—"

"Shhh, honey. Please let me say this." She pauses, considering her words. "I've always tried my hardest, but I'm only human and that means I mess up sometimes."

I think of Rob's words: *Your parents are human too. They make mistakes, just like everyone else.*

"When I found out what happened with you and Alice, I reacted in a way that wasn't fair. I took my pain out on you. I'll always regret that, because even though I could see you needed me, my own pain was too strong to be there for you."

I press the tissue to my eyes. "It's okay. You were right."

"No." She twists on the sofa to look at me squarely. "I was not right. I was angry, and I was disappointed in the moment, but I was *not* right. You are nothing like your father."

"But—"

"No. You need to hear me on this, Cors. We should have had this conversation a long time ago, but I didn't realize you'd taken what I said literally. I didn't know you even remembered, but I should have, and I'm sorry."

"But I did what he did."

"Yes, you made a mistake, but that doesn't make you the same. Your father... he was a complicated man. He struggled to commit to things, struggled to stay the course. I'm sure you can recall how often he changed jobs, how many half-finished projects there were around the place growing up." She laughs. "Remember that time he decided he was going to landscape the back garden?"

"Yeah." I can't help a little chuckle. Dad wanted to redo our backyard in a Japanese-inspired design and stripped up the lawn and all the shrubs in preparation, then lost interest and moved onto something else. We had a barren, dusty dirt yard for an entire summer before Mom got out there and replanted.

"Unfortunately," Mom continues, "his commitment issues included us. He tried, I know he did. I'll never be okay with what he did, but ultimately, we couldn't make it work. I guess you could say he was prone to giving up." Her eyes move over my face. "But you're the opposite of that. You commit to something and give it your all. You fight for what matters and make it work. You don't give up on anything. Look at what you've created with the bar. You own your own business. You own your own apartment, in Manhattan! I'm so proud of everything you've achieved."

My chest swells. Mom has never outright said that to me before, and I didn't realize how badly I needed to hear it.

"It's not just that. Your father was impatient and stubborn. He could be selfish as hell. I'll admit, you've definitely inherited his stubbornness." She gives me a wry smile. "But you're not impatient or selfish."

"I am selfish, Mom. I should never have acted on my feelings for Josie."

"It's not selfish to fall in love, honey. You can't help how you feel."

Well, that much is true. Five years of trying to distract myself from her and I still gave in. I couldn't stop myself from falling for her, no matter how hard I tried.

Mom sighs. "You know, I saw Alice yesterday. She's staying with her folks for a little while, and she told me you two spoke on the weekend."

I grimace. "Yeah. I wanted to apologize again. I thought she hated me, but... she said she forgave me."

Mom nods, apparently unsurprised. "If Alice can forgive you, don't you think it's time you forgave yourself?"

"I can't do that, Mom, because if I forgive myself, it means I'm forgiving Dad. And I can't—" The words stick in my throat and I look down at my hands.

I expect Mom to push me more, but she's quiet for a long time. Finally, she says, "I understand."

I glance at her. "You do?"

"Yes. It took me a long time to learn how to forgive your father, and I couldn't do that without help."

"You *forgave* him?" I splutter.

"I did. There's an expression—I can't remember it exactly, but it goes something like, *holding onto anger is like drinking poison and expecting the other person to die*. I didn't want to keep that poison inside me. I wanted to be free of that."

Rage flares in my gut, but Mom places a soothing hand on my arm before I can erupt.

"Forgiveness doesn't mean condoning what was done. It means letting go of the anger you're holding about it. Anger can't change the past, but it sure as hell can hurt you in the present."

Despite her words, I give a furious huff, looking away. It's all fine and good to say that, but saying it and doing it are two different things.

"Your sister and I have had to find our own way to process what happened in our family, and you'll need to find your way too. We both found speaking to a therapist to be extremely helpful."

I glance back at Mom. "You went into therapy?" I knew my sister had been in therapy, but not Mom.

"I did. When you and Cat both left home, I found it harder to keep myself distracted from my grief over everything that had happened. It's easy to fool ourselves into thinking we're fine when we're busy and around others all the time, but once we're alone, once we're forced to stop, it's harder to run from our pain."

I think back over the years since I left Long Island, the time I spent working my ass off before I bought Bounce—and then worked even harder. I think of all the time I spend at the gym, the women I used to bring home every night, even when I didn't feel like it. Is that what I've been doing, all this time? Distracting myself from my pain? Running away?

"I think," Mom begins tentatively, "that maybe it's a good thing for you to be on your own for a while. I think you need to spend some time looking inward, Cors, and acknowledge the pain you're carrying. I really think seeing a therapist could help. I know someone in the city I could call—"

I snort. "Now you want *me* to see a shrink?"

Mom exhales patiently. "Things ended with Josie because of what you're holding onto from the past. That tells me that there's something in there"—she reaches forward to tap gently on my chest—"that needs healing."

I swallow hard. Part of me wants to listen to her, but the other part of me wants to go right back to how my life was before: long hours at the bar, punishing workouts at the gym, random women in my bed I don't have to care about.

Fuck. No. I don't want that. I don't want anything that isn't a life with Josie.

"Let me put it this way," Mom tries again. "If you put the work in here, there's every chance you could win Josie back."

God. Tears spring to my eyes and I blink them away. I'll do anything to make that a reality.

"Okay. Make the call."

38

JOSIE

"I'll see you tonight?" Harriet asks.

I stop at the door to Game of Scones and turn back to her. "Of course. Can't miss girls' night."

"Great. Although—" She chuckles. "Maybe we should stop calling it girls' night, given that Geoff is always there."

I laugh. "No way. He loves it."

She crosses the cafe to pull me into a hug, pausing to run her gaze over me. She thinks she's being subtle but I know what she's doing—she's checking if I'm okay. She's been doing this for months now.

I give a dramatic roll of my eyes. "Okay then, see you tonight."

She sighs as I head out the door. I know she worries about me, and even though I make a show of being annoyed, I'm actually grateful. If it wasn't for my friends, I don't know where I'd be.

I walk for a few blocks in the cool October air before turning down the steps to the subway, lost in thought. It's been three and a half months since I moved out of Cory's and quit Bounce. Three and a half months since he walked away from me in his courtyard without looking back. Three and a half months of fighting the urge, every minute of every day, to call him and tell him how much I miss him, how much I wish I hadn't left.

Leaving the bar hurt almost as much as leaving Cory. I went in when he wasn't working and handed a letter of resignation to Eddy, asking him to pass it on to the boss. Eddy was way more bummed out than I'd expected, even stopping to give me a hug before I left. I was so worried Cory was going to call and fight with me about the fact that I was quitting, but he texted saying he understood and the place wouldn't be the same without me.

I cried for two hours straight after that.

The next day I asked Gerard if it was too late to apply for the full-time position at the shelter, but he'd already filled it. Of course he had—it was an awesome job, and if I hadn't been so torn about leaving Bounce, I would have taken it in the first place. I think Gerard could tell I was upset, because he said he didn't want to lose me as a volunteer, and he'd definitely consider me for the next position that comes up. Whenever that might be.

I spent a week looking for jobs, and panic was just setting in when Harriet mentioned she could use extra help at the cafe. I told her she didn't need to hire me out of pity and she assured me it wasn't pity—she wanted to cut her hours back because her morning sickness was awful, and she trusted me to step in. Now that she's into her second trimester she's feeling better, but Luke's cut back his hours too and they seem to be enjoying their time off together before the baby arrives. I don't mind—I'm grateful for a job, especially because she let me fit my hours around the time I volunteer at the shelter. She's been amazing.

Not just Harriet; Hayley has been awesome too. Ever

since I moved in she's gone out of her way to make sure I'm comfortable and Pretzel is happy. She even took it upon herself to organize a girls' night at our place each week. She's never openly admitted it, but I think it's an attempt to distract me from everything, because even though I get up every day and go about my life, I just feel... empty.

God, I know I'm ungrateful even thinking that, because I have such wonderful friends, and a nice job, and a sweet dog, and a lovely apartment, but...

I don't have Cory.

That's my fault, I know that. I'm the one who chose to walk away. Cat told me he's been seeing a therapist for a while now, and I'm so glad he's found the courage to work through everything. I really want him to find peace—to find a way to stop being so hard on himself.

I guess a tiny part of me hoped he might, I don't know... fight for us? Not right away, of course, but once I knew he'd been seeing a therapist, I thought he might...

Ugh, I don't know.

Maybe he's just not ready yet. Maybe he had some kind of breakthrough in therapy and realized we weren't right for each other after all.

Or maybe he's come to see how much I let him down.

Because I did, didn't I? I walked away from him when he was at his lowest point. I chose myself over him. And while it felt important for me to do that in the moment, it came at such a great cost. To us—to *him*. I can't help but think he won't be able to forgive me for that.

I wouldn't blame him.

When the subway finally pulls into the station, I haul myself up the steps, noticing how the trees are losing their leaves. I usually love this time of year, with the changing colors and the drop in temperature, but I just feel numb. Part of me is even wondering if I should leave New York. Everything reminds me of Cory—walking Pretzel by the East River, going into the shelter he helped me rescue, even getting into the back of a cab. At the risk of sounding ungrateful, seeing his sister all the time doesn't help. She's been a good friend, but I won't lie; spending time with her makes me think of her brother—of the weekend we spent away together, which felt so magical, right before it all started to unravel.

Things were made even worse when, two months ago, I fell in love.

His name is Inigo Montoya. He stole my heart. I was *not* prepared for the day Cat showed up at girls' night with a black lab mix—and neither was Pretzel. He spent that entire evening wrestling with his new best buddy, and I basically watched his heart break when Cat had to drag Inigo home.

The name should have tipped me off, right? It's an iconic character in *The Princess Bride*. And when that didn't, the fact that Cat was being so damn shady about it should have. One week she told me it was her neighbor's dog and she was dog-sitting while he was out of town. The next she said something about it belonging to one of her clients.

When I finally begged her for the owner's details last week so I could organize a regular play date for Pretzel, she broke down and told me she couldn't give them to me, because I already had them. Because it was Cory's dog.

Cory's dog.

Apparently his therapist suggested it, and he went to a shelter the very next day. Cat said she didn't want to tell me because she thought I would find it hard, but she was watching him sometimes when Cory worked late and she was so sorry for lying and... I stopped listening after that because it hurt too much. Not her lying—that, I understood. But just picturing Cory with that sweet dog made me think of him and Pretzel, and my heart broke a little bit more.

I turn down our block, my chest somehow both hollow and heavy. When my phone vibrates in my pocket, I pull it out and smile faintly at my mom's name on the screen.

"Hi, Mom."

"Hey, Sugarplum. How's life in the big city?"

"It's..." I sigh, wishing for the millionth time I could just get over this and be happy again. I force a smile, hoping it comes across in my voice. "It's just dandy."

"Oh, Josie." Mom's voice softens. "Are you still having a hard time?"

I made the mistake of telling her about Cory when we were away on Fourth of July weekend. She got so excited and begged me to come home for Christmas this year—and bring him with me. When I eventually told her things had ended, she called and I broke down in tears, telling her everything.

"It hasn't been great," I mumble, pulling out my keys and letting myself into our apartment. Hayley glances up from the sofa when I enter, Pretzel at her side. I give her a tight smile, heading straight for my room, and Pretzel trails after me.

"I'm sorry," Mom says. "I don't suppose you'd consider coming home for Christmas anyway? I know you've got your life there and you're busy, but I'd love to see you. I miss you."

"I miss you too." I suddenly remember the conversation Cory and I had on our first date, all those months ago. I sink down onto the edge of my bed, absently stroking Pretzel when he jumps up beside me. "Mom, have you ever thought... Have I ever been... Was it a burden, having to raise me? Giving up so much for someone who wasn't your biological child?"

"Josephine—God, no. What's brought this on?"

I lie back beside Pretzel, loving the way he tucks himself into my side. "It's just something I've been wondering about."

"Well, I can tell you raising you was one of the greatest joys of my life. I can't say it didn't have its difficult moments, because of course it did, but I wouldn't change a thing."

"But... you gave up so much. You never dated, or fell in love..."

"Didn't I?"

"I never saw you with any men—"

"Who said anything about men?"

"I... what?" I bolt up on the bed, shocked, and she chuckles.

"You know how close I am with Marybeth, Sugarplum. I assumed you'd figured that one out years ago."

"Oh my God," I murmur, scanning back over memories containing my mom's best friend. She's been in our lives since I was about fourteen—maybe fifteen—and I'd never considered... Well. That explains a lot. And I can't help myself—I laugh. She didn't give up everything for me, then.

Mom laughs too. "Sorry to drop that bomb on you, but I really thought you knew."

"That's... no. That's fine," I say truthfully. "I'm relieved, actually. I thought you'd gone all this time, giving everything up for me."

"God, no. I've had everything I could ever need, don't you worry. More—because I got to have a little girl I never dreamed I'd get to have. And I'm grateful for every minute."

My eyes fill as I listen to her words. How could I have ever doubted that?

"I'd love to come home for Christmas, Mom. And I was actually thinking..." I take a deep breath. "I was thinking about moving back home for a while. If you wouldn't mind having me stay?"

"Oh, Joze. I'd love to have you here, but are you sure that's what you want? Things will get better, it might just take a little more time."

I pick at the comforter, thinking about her words. Do I want to leave the city? I don't know. I've always loved it here, but how much of that was because of Bounce—because of Cory?

"I'll put you down for a Christmas visit," Mom says. "But maybe you should take a little more time to think about moving, okay? Don't decide just yet."

"Okay," I murmur, but I think I've already made up my mind.

"I'd better go, Sugarplum. Marybeth and I have aqua aerobics soon."

I facepalm, wondering how on earth I missed the fact that Mom's in a relationship with that woman. Talk about oblivious.

"Give Pretzel a cuddle from me, okay? Love you."

"Love you too, Mom." I end the call and pull Pretzel into my arms, squeezing him tight as I stare at the ceiling.

"HERE WE ARE," Geoff says merrily, bringing a pitcher of margaritas into the living room and setting it on the coffee table. He heads back into the kitchen to fetch virgin margaritas for both Harriet and Alex, then flops down on the floor cushion beside Cat.

"Thanks, Geoff." I send him a grateful look as he pours

drinks for everyone, trying not to feel guilty. As the only bartender in this group, I always feel like I should be the one in charge of the cocktails, but when I tried to mix drinks on our first girls' night all I could think about was Bounce, and the margaritas that evening were half tequila, half tears. Geoff wordlessly took over the following week and I haven't touched a cocktail shaker since.

Hayley brings a charcuterie board in from the kitchen, shooing away Stevie who makes a beeline for the coffee table when she sets it down. There's no sign of Inigo tonight and I wonder if Cat made a point of not bringing him, to spare my feelings. That bums me out, because he and Pretzel bonded like nothing else, and it was nice to see Pretzel have so much fun after everything that happened with Cory.

I guess we've lost that now, too.

I glance at Pretzel, curled up in a sad ball on the floor. He's awfully subdued tonight, and I think it's because he misses his new buddy. With a sigh, I tug him onto my lap where I'm sitting on the floor and stroke his fur, trying to cheer him up. When no one is looking, I sneak him a piece of gouda from the table. No cheese is too fancy for my best boy.

"Is this a new pillow, Hayes?" Cat motions to the floor cushion she's sitting on and Hayley nods.

"I got it at the market last week," she says, settling onto the sofa. Hayley runs a booth at the East Village Market Collective, selling Cat's line of vintage-inspired clothing and accessories. "It's so dangerous, working there. I swear I spend half my paycheck before I even get out the door."

I smile, casting my eyes around our apartment. Hayley has held nothing back in decorating this place, her quirky style combining secondhand goods, bold colors, and fun prints. It feels like stepping into a flea market in here, and I love it. It's so her.

That's exactly how she dresses, too—her curvy figure always wrapped in something colorful and funky, her long hair in some unusual style I could never pull off. She's unapologetically herself, even as a British transplant in New York, and I admire her confidence.

And she's unbelievably kind. She found this gorgeous navy-blue Cath Kidston bag with a white and red rose print, and brought it home for me one day from the market, "just because."

I cried for two hours that night, too.

"I think it's a great addition," I say. "I love the way you've decorated this place."

"Thanks," Hayley mumbles. Her gaze meets mine, then quickly scoots away. She's been giving me weird looks all afternoon and I can't figure out why.

"Did you know Hayes studied interior design back in England?" Cat grins proudly. "That's why she always did such an amazing job merchandising, back when I had my shop."

"Wow." I smile at Hayley, trying to break the tension that seems to have formed between us. "That's so cool."

She nods, fiddling with the tassels on a throw rug over the arm of the sofa, and I sigh. I'm not sure what's going on, but I can't stand thinking I've done something to upset her.

"Um, Hayley? Are you okay? Did I... do something?"

She looks at me again, chewing on her lip as if debating what to say, then finally sets her drink down. "Please don't be mad at me."

I glance anxiously at the others, then back to her. "Okay..."

"I overheard you say this afternoon that you wanted to

move out, and I'm kind of sad. I thought we had a good thing here."

"Oh." I feel my cheeks grow hot as the entire room stares at me.

Geoff frowns. "I thought you liked it here. Have you found a new apartment?"

"No," I mumble, wishing I hadn't asked in front of everyone. I catch Hayley's hurt expression again and wince. "It wasn't that I wanted to leave you, or this apartment, Hayes. I love it. It was more that I was considering leaving, um, the city."

"What?" Alex nearly spills her virgin margarita. "You want to *leave* New York? Where would you go?"

"Maybe back to Austin?"

"But..." Hayley looks baffled. "Why?"

"You know, things haven't been... Ever since..." I shift uncomfortably, aware of Cat's gaze on me. "It's just not the same."

Geoff nods in sympathy. "Yeah, I get that. When would you leave?"

I lift a shoulder. I hadn't thought that far ahead, but honestly, what's the point in sticking around when everything feels so hollow? "Soon, probably. I think I need a fresh start."

Harriet exchanges a look with Cat, but I pretend not to notice. I wasn't planning to tell anyone until I'd finalized everything, because I figured they'd try to talk me out of it.

Instead, Harriet simply murmurs, "We'll miss you."

There's an awkward pause, then Geoff turns to Alex, asking her something about a book she's writing, and the conversation moves on. I can still feel the weight of Cat's gaze, and I'm relieved when Myles calls her about an issue with Amber at home and she has to leave early. I feel like she's disappointed in me or something, and I get it. She asked me not to give up on Cory, and I feel like that's what I've done.

But can you really give up on something that's already given up on you?

39

CORY

"She's leaving the city." Cat collides breathlessly with the bar and I chuckle.

"Well, hello to you too."

"Cory." She leans down to scoop up Stevie, then jumps onto a bar stool. "Didn't you hear me? Josie is *leaving the city*."

My pulse crashes. "She's what? How do you know?"

"I was just at girls' night and she told us. I faked a crisis at home so I could get the hell over here."

I drag the heel of my hand across my forehead, trying to stay calm. "Did she say when she was going?"

"Soon. She's heading back to Austin." Cat tries to still Stevie's wriggling body on her lap. "Cors, you have to do something."

"I..." Shit. I haven't heard two words from Josie since she quit months ago, and while Cat has been pressing me to reach out to her, I've hesitated. She walked away because I had a lot of shit to work through, and frankly, that hasn't changed.

I've been trying, though. I started therapy the week after

Mom came to see me. I'll admit I was reluctant at first. Dr. Sheridan is an older woman with a no-nonsense attitude who immediately called me out on my crap, and it pissed me off to be confronted like that—especially by someone who didn't even know me. Over time we've formed an unlikely bond, and I no longer dread the twice-weekly sessions. I flop into the chair in her office near Union Square and pour my heart out. It's been fucking hard, but it's helping.

So many times I've come out of a session and wanted to call Josie, to tell her about something that came up, or just hear her voice. I'm still such a work in progress, though, and I don't know how she'll feel about that. More importantly, I don't want to put her in a position where she has to compromise on doing what's best for her. I want to respect the fact that she put herself first, because I know she's struggled to do that in the past. Dr. Sheridan has told me over and over that I'm not responsible for anyone's feelings but my own, but when it comes to Josie, I'll never stop wanting to make sure she's okay. I'll never stop wanting to make sure she's happy and safe.

And, I'm pretty sure, I'll never stop loving her.

The first two weeks were the hardest. When Josie quit, I stopped going to the gym, stopped cooking—hell, I barely left my apartment once I'd convinced Myles to cover temporarily at the bar "for old time's sake." After a few therapy sessions, I found my feet and started taking care of myself again. I hired two new bartenders and I got back into the kitchen, even purchasing a new vegan recipe book, which I'm slowly working my way through. I told Dr. Sheridan that it wasn't just Josie I missed—it was Pretzel, too—and she suggested I visit a few animal shelters and get a buddy. I didn't expect to find anything, but then, as I was staring blankly into a cage and fighting back tears, a black lab mix came over and put his paw on my hand, as if to comfort me. It immediately reminded me of Josie and, well, that was that.

When Cat told me that both Josie and Pretzel love Inigo as much as I do... it took everything in me not to race over there and beg her—beg both of them—to move back in.

"Hello?" Cat waves her hands in my face, interrupting my thoughts. A few customers are waiting for drinks so I motion for Cat to sit tight and turn to serve them, stealing a moment to think some more.

What am I going to do, really? I don't want Josie to leave Manhattan, but what can I offer her? I know what I *want* to offer her, but what if she doesn't want that? What if she feels exactly the same as the day things ended? What if she's just completely moved on? What if—

"Jesus, Cory." Cat leans over the bar, pulling my thumb off the soda gun that's flooding Coke across the counter. "You should not be operating machinery."

I grimace, handing over the drink to the guy, on the house, before reaching for a dishcloth. "Sorry," I mutter, mopping up the spill.

Cat glances around and when she sees there's no one waiting to be served, she coaxes me out from behind the bar, into the back room.

I hate it back here. Every time I'm in here, I think of Josie worrying about Pretzel in his crate, Josie in her deer costume the night of the fundraiser, Josie pressed against the back of that door while I fought the urge to—

Enough.

Cat wheels on me the second the door is closed. "You can't let her leave New York."

"I can't stop her from leaving if that's what she wants to do."

"Of course that's not what she wants!" She glares at me like I'm totally dense. "What she wants is *you*. I've been telling you that for months now."

I release a weary sigh. "She's the one who ended things, remember?"

Cat rolls her eyes. "Yes, but only because you wouldn't deal with your shit. Look at you now! You basically live at your shrink's office."

I snort. "I see her twice a week."

"But you're *doing the work*. That's all she needed from you."

"I just—" I shift my weight. "I still have stuff to work on."

"Of course you do. We all do. Healing is a lifelong journey. It never ends." Cat stops abruptly, as if hearing herself, and scrunches her nose. "God, I sound like Myles," she mutters, shaking her head. She sighs, stepping forward to take my hand. "Seriously. She doesn't need you to be perfect —she's not perfect."

"She is," I counter immediately, and Cat rolls her eyes again.

"No, she's not. No one is, and she understands that. She always has. And she certainly doesn't expect you to be. Stop being so hard on yourself."

"I—"

Oh, crap. I think this is what they call a breakthrough, isn't it? Because Cat is dead right. I'm doing all this work in therapy, but here I am, yet again, straight back to my old habit of convincing myself I'm not enough for Josie.

"You're right," I murmur.

If there's one thing I've learned during my time with Dr. Sheridan, it's that I'm not a bad guy. I did something bad in the past, but it's not who I am—it's something I did. And I did it from a place of pain, much like how I acted with Josie. *Hurt people, hurt people*, is one of Dr. Sheridan's favorite sayings. And now that I'm healing my hurt, I know I can be the man Josie needs.

Fuck. I can't let her move back to Austin. If she still feels even a fraction of what I feel, I'm going to do everything in my power to keep her here. I'm going to show her I'm ready for her in every way, and I'm not going to hold back.

"You have to ask her to stay," Cat urges. "Call her now."

"No." My heart skips in anticipation. "I'm not going to call her. I need to do something bigger, because I'm going to ask her a lot more than to stay."

"Oh, Cors." Cat lunges at me, tugging me into a tight hug. "I knew this day would come."

I chuckle into her pink hair. "You did not."

"I did." She's practically glowing with excitement for me as she draws away. I've never loved my sister more.

"Do you think Josie wants that?" I ask hesitantly. "After everything..."

"Fuck yes. That girl is so in love with you."

I exhale. For the first time in months, my heart lifts hopefully.

"So what are you going to do?"

"I have an idea." I scrub a hand over my beard, thinking. "And I'm going to need your help."

40

JOSIE

I close the cage with a sad sigh.

"Sorry, Petal," I say, slipping a treat to the poodle. "I don't think it will work."

I've been trying all week to find a playmate for Pretzel, since Inigo seems to be a no-go now, but none of the dogs at the shelter are quite right.

Even if "Pretzel and Petal" does have a nice ring to it.

"Aren't you finished for the day, Josie?"

I turn to see Gerard cleaning out a nearby cage after one of our long-timers got adopted today. There wasn't a dry eye in the house when Buddy, a huge German shepherd we've had with us for a while, finally found his forever home. I was sad to see that big guy go.

"Yeah," I mumble, pushing to my feet. I was supposed to finish half an hour ago but I'm nervous about going back to the apartment. Hayley and I haven't had a chance to speak since I dropped the bomb about me leaving last night, and I don't know what she's going to say.

"Have a good night," Gerard calls as I grab my bag and turn for the door.

"You too, Gerard." I head out through the Seaport District, taking a moment to admire the old buildings as I walk. Now that I know I'll be leaving, the city has taken on an extra shine, as if enticing me to stay. It's not the city's fault —it's always been beautiful. It's just me who wasn't able to see it for the past three months. I pull my phone out to take a photo, and notice a missed call from Cat. With a frown, I lift my phone to return the call.

"Hey!" Cat answers, sounding a little breathless.

"Hey. Everything okay?"

"Yes. I was just thinking, um, did you want to bring Pretzel over for a play date with Inigo tonight?"

I stop abruptly. "Seriously? Yes! He'd love that."

"Great! Do you mind, uh, doing it at Cory's? I'm... dog-sitting at his place while he's out of town."

"Oh." I rub my forehead, feeling my stomach pitch. I don't really want to go over to Cory's. Being back there will stir up all kinds of memories. "Um..."

"I thought it might be nice for Pretzel to come back here anyway," Cat says in a rush. "See his old home again, you know?"

I pause, waiting to cross at Fulton Street. I guess that's a good point. I'm sure Pretzel would love to visit that place. Inigo would be comfortable too, rather than trying to take him somewhere new, which is always challenging with a rescue dog.

"Cory won't be here, if that's what you're worried about. He's... on Long Island for a few days." Cat clears her throat, and her voice comes out squeaky. "I mean, we could always go somewhere else, but—"

"No, that's okay." I step out onto the street and head toward the subway. *It's been three and a half months*, I chastise myself. *You can handle this.* "We'll come there."

"Oh, great! That's awesome, yay!" She sounds unusually excited for this dog date, and despite myself, I smile.

Maybe, just maybe, this will be okay.

THIS WAS A TERRIBLE IDEA.

I'm standing in front of Cory's building, adrenaline slicking through my veins as I wait on the dark sidewalk. It's stupid—I know he's not home, but I'm anxious all the same. Being inside his place again will hurt.

Still, this isn't about me. It's about Pretzel.

It feels weird when I knock. I've never knocked on this door before, and as my knuckles make three short raps, I realize just how much of an outsider I am to Cory's life now. He was my boss, my friend, my crush for so long—and now nothing. He was the one man who helped me to find my inner strength, who built me back up after Paul tore me down, the guy who cracked my heart open and made me love more fiercely, more deeply than I ever have, and now... I've lost him.

A tight fist closes around my heart, squeezing hard as Cat opens the door for me and Pretzel and lets us into the apartment. I barely make it into the living room before my throat is closing in with tears. How could I have convinced myself coming here would be okay? I want to curl up on the carpet and wail. Everywhere I look, I see reminders of me and Cory, of the things we shared, the love we had. I see how our relationship unfolded between these walls, how I got to know the real him outside of work, how he helped me find the real me, too.

"You okay?" Cat asks softly.

Her words snap me out of my reverie and I blink,

turning to her. "Yeah, sorry." My voice is scratchy with emotion and I try to clear it. Pretzel and Inigo are already rough-and-tumbling on the floor and watching them makes me want to cry, too. Everything here makes me want to cry.

I glance back at Cat. "I think I might just pop to the bathroom for a second to pull myself together."

She gives me a kind smile, looking over her shoulder at the back door. "Why don't you go sit in the courtyard and get some fresh air?"

I hesitate. The courtyard has the awful memory of when I ended things. But then the bathroom has the memory of our water fight, when we tried to wash Pretzel. I don't know which hurts more.

"Okay," I mumble, heading for the door outside. I glance back at the dogs. "Are you okay to—"

"We're good in here. Take your time."

Cat's mouth twitches with a smile she can't seem to fight, but I'm too emotionally drained to question it. With a deep, bone-weary sigh, I push the door open and step out into the cool evening air.

And there, standing in the middle of the courtyard under rows of bright string bulbs, is Cory.

My breath stills in my lungs.

Why is he...?

I take a faltering step forward, my gaze catching on the rows and rows of bulbs, strung above us. Did he do this? They look *amazing*, casting a warm, yellow glow over the entire outdoor space—the shrubs, the table setting... and the man I love.

I bring my gaze back to Cory, dressed in a navy-blue Giants hoodie and black jeans, his hands in his pockets. The light makes his hair and beard look golden, his hazel eyes almost glowing as they move over me, drinking me in. I feel like I've been punched in the heart, seeing him again—so tall, so gorgeous, so perfect. How could I have walked away from this man? How could I have thought that was the right thing to do?

His expression is tentative when he finally says, "Hey."

My pulse surges. "Hi," I whisper. If I say anything more, I'm going to burst into enough tears to flood the courtyard.

"I hope it's okay that I'm here." He swallows. "I wasn't sure if you'd want to see me."

Fuck it.

I stride the few remaining paces between us and throw my arms around him, pulling him into a fierce hug. "Of *course* I want to see you. I've missed you so much."

I feel Cory's breath whoosh out over my hair and his arms tighten around me. "Me too, Buttercup."

Oh, God.

I press my face to the soft fabric of his hoodie, inhaling his familiar scent, listening to his heart as it pummels against his breastbone. I can't stop my hands from clinging desperately to his back, afraid to let go again.

I don't want to leave New York. I don't want to put this part of my life behind me and pretend I'm okay with moving on. Because I'm not. I don't think I ever will be.

"Can we talk?" Cory murmurs into my hair.

I nod, reluctantly letting go.

He tucks a strand of hair behind my ear, gazing down at me with a wistful smile. "These past three months have been really hard. When you left, I thought…" He breathes out unsteadily, dropping his hand. "I didn't think I could go on. My mom came to see me and we had a long talk, and it was her idea for me to go into therapy. That wasn't a whole lot of fun to begin with." He chuffs a laugh. "My therapist is a real pill. But she's also right about everything."

I stare up at Cory, my heart expanding with every word. I am so proud of this man, of him taking these difficult steps to heal. Most people would have given up and gone back to their old ways, but not Cory. He just dug in and did what he needed to do, no matter how hard and painful it was. Because that's who he is.

"I've been seeing Dr. Sheridan twice a week for the last three months. I've come a long way, but I need you to know, I'm not..." he trails off, his brow creasing as he searches for the right words. "I'll probably be going to her for a long time, working on this stuff." A wry smile touches his lips. "My sister tells me healing is a lifelong process."

I smile too, holding his gaze, but his expression turns serious.

"I'm sorry that you had to carry the burden of my pain while we were together. I didn't realize I had so much shit in there, but you helped me to see it. And while you walking away hurt, it was also necessary."

I shake my head, feeling the familiar sting behind my eyes. "I shouldn't have walked away, Cors. I let you down when you needed me the most, and I'm so sorry."

Cory reaches for my hands, taking them in his. "Of course you feel that way," he says with a tiny smile. "You always want to take care of others. The day you ended things... I could tell it was hard for you, but you stood your ground and looked after yourself for once. While I didn't want you to leave, I was also proud of you in that moment. Proud that you'd found the inner strength to do what was necessary."

"But—"

"It *was* necessary, Joze, because you were right. I wasn't letting your love in. I didn't believe I deserved it. If we'd stuck it out that day, it would only have been a matter of time before I pulled away again. You ending things forced me to confront the truth I'd been running from for years. It forced me to finally do something about it. And I am so grateful for that."

Relief trickles through me as I gaze up at him. I've been beating myself up for months now, thinking I should have tried harder, should have stuck it out with him, but hearing him explain how much it helped him... He's right. It was the right thing to do.

It's just that sometimes the *right* thing, is also the *hardest* thing.

"I'm grateful for you too. You're the one who helped me find that inner strength."

Cory smiles. "It was always in there. You're a lioness, remember?" He runs his thumb over the back of my hand, his expression shifting. "Cat told me you're moving back to Austin, is that true?"

My heart feels strangled as I search his face. Seeing him tonight has just made me love him even more, but he hasn't indicated... I mean, I don't know if he still feels that way for me. Not only that; I'm so proud of the work he's done in therapy, and I don't want to get in the way of that if he's not ready. Maybe that's all this is supposed to be—a chance for us to finally say goodbye.

"I'm thinking about it. I love New York, but..." I stare up at Cory, my chest aching at the thought of saying goodbye. Is this really it? "Without you, without Bounce..." My throat closes around the words and I look away as a tear rolls down my cheek.

Cory's hand comes up to brush my tears away. When I glance back, he suddenly looks very vulnerable.

"Do you still love me?"

"Yes. I never stopped." I choke on a sob, but he doesn't reach for me.

Instead, he raises his fingers to his lips and blows a loud whistle.

I hear a sound behind me and glance back toward the door, wiping my cheeks. The last thing I want is for Cat to see me like this, but it's just Pretzel, nosing his way out into the courtyard, then lumbering over when he sees me. I pet his head, trying to reign in my emotions.

With a deep breath, I glance back at Cory. He unzips his hoodie to reveal his lion costume, from the night of the fundraiser. Tossing his hoodie aside, he pulls the fur-trimmed lion's hood up onto his head, and then...

Holy shit...

He gets down on one knee.

My heart stops.

"What are you doing?" I whisper. I think I know the answer but I'm too afraid to hope, in case I'm wrong. In case this is all a dream.

"You said I helped you find your strength, and I want you to know—you helped me find mine too. I thought I was strong before but I wasn't, not really, because I didn't know that true strength is vulnerability. Your love helped me find that."

Tears stream silently down my face as I absorb Cory's words. I wipe at my cheeks, wanting to remember every single detail in this moment. Pretzel nudges me but I ignore him, staring at Cory down on one knee.

"Check his collar," Cory murmurs, motioning to the dog.

I force my gaze down to Pretzel. He jumps up my leg and I reach to feel his collar. The only thing I can find on there is his dog tag, hanging under his chin, so I twist it around to have a look.

But it's not his usual tag—it's a red heart. I squint to read the words in the courtyard lights, and a gasp escapes me.

There, engraved in the red plastic, are the words: *Will you marry me?*

I can barely see through my tears as Cory takes my hand. "You're my lioness, Joze. I can't be a lion without you."

I'm shaking with sobs now. I can't believe this is happening. In a million years, I would never have let myself dream that we'd be here, but I'm in awe of Cory's growth over the short time we've been apart and I know he's only going to grow more. He's going to help *me* grow more.

I mop my cheeks with my sleeve, my heart drumming a wild rhythm as Cory smiles up at me, so handsome in his lion costume. This man, on one knee for me... how did I end up here?

"Will you marry me, Buttercup?"

I throw myself at Cory and he catches me, falling back as I land in his lap. Then I bury my face in his chest, crying so hard I can't breathe.

He cradles me in his arms, rocking me gently. When I've soaked his lion costume with every last tear I have, he chuckles nervously. "I hope that's a yes?"

"Fuck yes." I give a watery laugh as I draw back to meet his gaze. "I can't believe... I never thought... Yes. I'll marry you."

His eyes shine as he gazes at me. My face is a mess from crying but he doesn't care—he crushes his lips to mine, and I sink into his mouth, feeling like I'm finally back home. Pretzel tries to wedge himself in between us and we're forced to pull apart, laughing. Then Cory leans back to whistle again, and this time Inigo joins us in the courtyard with a gift bag in his mouth. He drops it when he sees Cory and I piled on top of each other on the paving, Pretzel dancing around us. When he bounds over to Pretzel, leaving the bag behind, Cory frowns.

"No, Inigo—" He shakes his head at the dog. "That's not what we rehearsed. You're supposed to bring the bag to *me*." But Inigo and Pretzel are too busy chasing each other around the courtyard now, and Cory half laughs, half sighs. "Fine, I'll get it myself."

Adjusting his arms around my back and under my knees, he pushes to his feet, carrying me as he heads over to the discarded gift bag. He bends down, instructing me to pick it up. I do, then he drops back into one of the chairs at the table with me across his lap. He takes the gift bag, his arms around me as he opens it. The first thing he pulls out is a women's lion costume.

"This is for you," he says, handing me the package. It's a full-body jumpsuit like my deer costume, but it's got a fur-trimmed hood like his, and cute little ears.

I giggle. "Are you going to destroy this one too?"

"Probably." He laughs, pausing to kiss me on the nose. Then he reaches back into the bag, this time pulling out a small velvet box. "This is for you, too." Cory pops the box open, and my breath catches.

Inside is the most beautiful ring I've ever seen. It's a huge, heart-shaped diamond, cradled between two smaller diamonds, set in a rose-gold band.

Cory examines my face. "I hope it's okay. I don't know if the heart is cliché, or whatever, but the moment I saw it I thought of you. You've got the biggest heart, Joze. It's the thing I love most about you."

"It's perfect," I breathe. "I love it." I watch a grin transform his face, and he pulls the ring from the box, sliding it onto my finger. It sparkles in the lights and I look up at him, my heart so full it's overflowing. It's a good thing I've got this heart on my finger now, too. I need more hearts to contain all the love I feel for this man.

I press a warm kiss to his mouth. "You've got a big heart too, Cors. Everything you've done tonight—" I gesture to the costume, the courtyard, the dogs. I expect him to argue, like he always used to when I told him he was good, but he smiles and accepts my words, and fuck, I have to press a hand to my chest to stop the love from spilling out into the courtyard.

"You're going to be my wife," Cory murmurs, almost reverently. "And I was hoping, in the not-too-distant future, you'd be the mother of my children, too. Biological, and adopted."

I stare at him in disbelief. How is it possible that I'm getting everything I could ever want?

I slide off his lap to reposition myself, straddling him. "I can't wait to have a family with you. You're going to be an amazing husband and dad. I always knew it." I dip my head to kiss the exposed V on his chest. Damn—the musky, earthy smell of him is like a drug. I want to overdose on him.

"Is that right?" Cory's voice has a rough edge to it and I grin, kissing up his neck, his cheek, ghosting my lips over his.

"Yes." I roll my hips, pleased to feel him already hard for me. "But right now, I think we need to practice."

"Practice?"

"Practice making babies. All night. Maybe tomorrow night too."

He gives a gravelly chuckle. "And the next." His finger-tips dig into my hips, holding me steady while he presses his arousal up into me.

"Do you want me to put the lioness outfit on?" I ask, smoothing my hand over the fur trim on his hood.

He laughs. "That was more of a gesture. Although I was thinking..." He hesitates, looking almost nervous, and I lean back, waiting patiently. "It's Halloween soon. What do you think about wearing them as a couple's costume at the bar?"

I smile. "That's cute. I'd love to do that."

"Cool. But I meant, uh, as an employee again. You know, if you'd consider coming back to Bounce."

"You want me to work for you again?"

"Yeah. The place isn't the same without you there. *I'm* not the same without you there. Is that something you'd—"

"Yes. Yes! Oh my gosh, yes." Surprise and delight and relief swirl through me in equal measures, and I kiss him hard. I might not have the shelter job, but Bounce has always felt like home. "I miss it there. I miss *us* there."

"Good. I can't wait to have you back at work with me. And... there's something else, too."

"What is it?"

"I want you to move back in with me, Joze. If you want that? You and Pretzel, me and Inigo..."

"A family," I whisper, and Cory gives me a huge, dopey grin. "Yeah. I really want that."

He slides his hands up under my sweater, pressing their warmth to my back. I drop my forehead to his, breathing in the perfection of this moment.

"Thanks for not giving up on me," he whispers.

I touch my lips to his. "Thanks for not giving up on *me*." I caress a hand over his cheek, his beard, his jaw. "I'm going to love you forever, you know that?"

He sighs, closing his eyes as if savoring my words. "I can't fucking wait."

41

CORY

"How did it go?"

Josie is waiting on the sidewalk when I step out of Dr. Sheridan's office. I press my lips to hers, and we fall into step together, heading for work.

"It was great," I say.

"She was okay with everything? She didn't tell you you'd made a huge mistake?"

I chuckle, threading my fingers through Josie's as I think back over the session. I didn't get the chance to talk to Dr. Sheridan about my plans to propose to Josie beforehand, and I'll admit, I was anxious about what she might say. She picked up on my nerves right away and said that as long as it felt right to me, and I was doing it for the right reasons, then that was what mattered. She also pointed out that marrying the woman who forced me to deal with my shit was a pretty good move, because I'd have to keep working on myself. Quietly, almost as if to herself, she added, "Love is the reason for everything, anyway." I never took her for a romantic, but maybe we all have that soft spot inside us.

"She was very supportive," I tell Josie, smiling down at her.

"I'm glad. I hope this isn't asking too much, but... I'd love to meet her sometime. If you'd want that."

God, this woman. I have never felt more loved, more supported, more accepted. "I'd love that. I think she would too."

We walk along Third Avenue in silence for a while, the cool October air reminding me of fall's arrival. When we turn down East 10th Street, the trees are a blaze of gold and copper, shedding their leaves onto the sidewalk, and it makes me smile. Everything in the city feels brighter and happier with Josie by my side.

I glance over to find her lost in thought. Today is her first day back at Bounce, and I've been looking forward to it all week. Josie and Pretzel moved back in a few days ago, but she didn't want to leave Harriet in the lurch at the cafe, so she insisted on working a full week before leaving. Thankfully, both Harriet and Hayley were understanding about Josie's change in plans. Josie said they were thrilled she was staying in New York, and had secretly been rooting for us to get back together.

I bump Josie's shoulder gently as we walk. "Nervous about your first day?" I joke.

"A little." She glances up at me, a smile twitching at the corner of her mouth. "I hear the boss can be kind of a grump."

"Oh yeah?"

"Yeah." She nods, pretending to look concerned, and I chuckle.

"Maybe you just need to do something to impress him."

"Maybe. I also hear he's hot as fuck, so..."

A laugh bursts out of me. "Hot as fuck, huh?"

"Oh, yeah." She gives a dramatic, dreamy sigh. "I'm pretty sure I'll be in love with him by the end of the day."

My chest fills with warmth and I squeeze her hand. "He'd be a fool not to fall in love with you the moment he meets you."

She bites back a smile, tugging my hand so I come to a stop. We pause in front of a redbrick apartment building, and a line appears between Josie's brows as she looks up at me.

"I wanted to ask you something, and if it's too much or whatever, that's fine."

I lean against the railing of the stoop. "Okay, Buttercup. What is it?"

She looks down at the yellow leaves at our feet, taking a breath. "I'm going to spend Christmas in Austin with my mom this year, and I was wondering—"

"Yes."

Her gaze flies up to mine and a surprised, hesitant smile nudges her mouth. "I didn't even ask you yet."

"Okay. Sorry." I laugh. "Go ahead."

"I was wondering if you'd like to come and spend Christmas—"

"Yes. I'd love to spend Christmas at your mom's."

She breathes out a relieved laugh. "Oh, good. I was so nervous to ask you."

I smile. As if I'd say no to that. As if I'm not super pumped to meet her mom and see where she grew up. "I've already asked you to marry me and have my babies. Did you really think Christmas with your mom would scare me away?"

"Well, no. But..." She looks down at her hands. "This is a

big deal to me, because I haven't been back to Austin since moving here."

"Then it's a big deal to me, too." I take her hand and brush a kiss over the back of it. "I'll be there."

She gives me a smile that lights up the entire East Village. I kiss her hand again, then we both continue to walk, our fingers intertwined. We arrive at the bar a few minutes later, and I unlock the front door, holding it open for Josie. She steps through and I lock it again, following her into the back room. I pause in the doorway, watching as she drops her bag on the sofa with a happy sigh.

"Welcome back, Joze."

"Thanks." She takes a second to soak it in, then turns to head out into the bar. "Come on."

"Wait." I reach for her, aching to touch my lips to hers. "Come here. I just want to kiss you for a few minutes."

She gives me a wry smile. "We need to open up."

"We have time."

She arches a brow. "Do we?"

I shrug. "So we open a few minutes late."

"I don't know if—"

"Josie," I say, feigning impatience, "as your boss, I'm asking you to come over here and kiss me right now."

She splutters a laugh. "Oh, that's how it's going to be, is it?"

"If I have to wield my power to get your lips on me, so be it."

"Okay." Her eyes darken as she rakes them down my body. "You can have my lips on you." Her husky voice makes heat pulse through my veins, and when she locks the door to the back room and drops to her knees in front of me, all the blood in my body rushes south.

I stare down at her as she unzips my jeans. "What are you doing?"

"Somebody suggested I should try to impress the boss on my first day." She cups my stiffness, dragging her hand up and down to jerk me through my underwear.

Holy hell, this woman is trouble. I can't believe I ever thought she was innocent.

"Consider me impressed," I say roughly.

"Oh, good." Her hand drops away. "So, I should stop?"

I growl. She's being such a little tease right now and I fucking love it. It reminds me of the first time she was on her knees for me, in the shower. I recall my words in that moment, how much they turned her on.

"Don't you dare stop."

Heat flashes in her gaze. She knows exactly what I'm thinking about. "Okay. Then say it."

I give her a wicked grin. "Suck me, Buttercup." I thread a hand into her hair, tugging gently, and she huffs out a hard breath.

"Yes, Boss." She yanks my underwear down and pounces on me, swallowing me down in one gulp.

I brace myself against the wall, watching as she brings me to the brink of pleasure with her mouth. Forget opening the bar anytime soon; I'm going to have to fuck her now. I don't know how I got lucky enough to be here with her in this moment, but I'm not going to waste it. I look down, marveling at how she always manages to surprise me. And when I think about how this sweet, dirty, gorgeous woman is going to be my *wife*, that's it.

I try to push her away, grunting, "Joze, stop—I'm gonna —" but she's not having it. She takes me back into her throat, sucking harder, and light bursts behind my eyelids as I lose myself in her.

I try to look mad when she rises to her feet in front of me, but mostly I'm just dazed. Dazed and horny and so, so in love. "I wanted to fuck you," I mumble, stroking her cheek.

She laughs, pretending to look appalled. "Cory, we're at *work*."

I huff in disbelief.

"We need to open up, and"—she motions to my pants, still around my ankles—"you might want to put those back on."

"Shit." I tug my underwear up and hastily zip my jeans.

"Seriously, though," she says, her brow dipping. "We shouldn't make a habit of getting it on in the back room during work hours."

I sigh. "You're probably right."

"But if you want..." She bites her lip, a mischievous light shimmering in her green eyes. "We could have sex on the bar after we close up."

"Yes," I say immediately, pulling her against me. "I very much want."

She giggles, sliding her arms around my neck. "I love you."

"I love you too, Buttercup." I press my lips to hers in the softest kiss.

"Okay," she murmurs, dragging herself away from me. "Let's get to work." She heads out of the back room and steps behind the bar, smiling to herself. She looks so happy to be back here, where she belongs.

My heart swells and presses against my ribs as I watch her. This girl walked into my bar—my life—five years ago, and I haven't been the same man since. I don't know what I've done to deserve her love, but I know now that I *do* deserve it—that we all deserve love, that it's not our mistakes that define us, but who we become because of them. I've become a better man because of what I've been through, and now, I'm going to become a husband and a father.

I've never been more excited for anything in my life.

EPILOGUE

Head to:
https://www.jenmorrisauthor.com/tlyd-epilogue
to read an exclusive *The Love You Deserve* epilogue!

Did you enjoy *The Love You Deserve*? Reviews help indie authors get our books noticed!

If you liked this book, please leave a review on Amazon. Or you can leave a review on Goodreads. It doesn't have to be much—even a single sentence helps! Thank you.

ACKNOWLEDGMENTS

I wrote most of this story during lockdown in late 2021. My mental health declined over this period, and Cory and Josie were my escape from the tedium and stress of being stuck in my house for months on end. I hope that, wherever you are and whatever is going on for you, this story will bring you the same joy and hope it brought me.

As always, my first thanks go to my partner, Carl. Every story I write has parts of myself woven through it, and *The Love You Deserve* is no exception. The truth is, I identify with Cory's struggle to believe he's loveable (though not for the same reasons). I'm lucky in that I have Carl by my side to help me see all the good I have inside me. Life would be so much harder without his support.

Like Cory's mom, I'm in therapy, working on my own healing. As parents we can only do our best, and we all screw up in our own ways. I'm grateful for every lesson my son Baxter teaches me, and for his love and kindness.

This book wouldn't be in your hands without my editor, Rachel Collins. She not only helped me refine and polish it; she 'got' the book and buoyed my spirits when I was drowning in self-doubt. Thank you, Ray. You're never getting rid of me now!

Huge thanks to my unpaid assistants and book-stabesties, Kira Slaughter and Tammy Eyre, for wholeheartedly supporting everything I do. You guys make me feel like an awesome writer, and are always there to lift me up when I doubt myself. I'm so glad to have you on my team.

Thanks to Sarah Side, who is at my beck and call for reading terrible drafts, offering emotional support, giving minor edits and feedback, making jokes, and general cheerleading.

To Samara, for checking in with me every day, offering friendship from the other side of the world, and letting me rant about everything from the Instagram algorithm to parenting. So glad we found each other.

Andi Cowan, for being there any time I need to bounce ideas around with someone.

Enni Amanda, for helping me polish the blurb and experiment with hilarious word variations until we find just the right one, which I ultimately don't end up using (sorry).

Big thanks to my critique partners: Loren Beeson, Julie Olivia, Jennifer Evelyn Hayes, Andrea Gonzalez, and Alicia Crofton. You each helped me to see areas I could improve and make this manuscript shine, and I appreciate your time, energy, and expertise.

My team of beta readers: Emma Grocott, Emilie Ahern, Michele Voss, Esther Reid, Kirsty Wong, Diana Bartlett, Angela Rehm, Laura Harris, and Antonette Hrycyk. Thank you for loving this book as much as I do, and pointing out the things I could improve with kindness. I love being able to share my work with people who are so positive and enthusiastic.

My cover designer Elle Maxwell always manages to

create something I adore. I'm so grateful for her talent, her attention to detail, and her patience when I ask for one more tweak, because I just love to be a pain in the ass. Thanks for putting up with me, Elle.

Thank you to all my advanced readers who shared their excitement over this story and helped to promote it. There are far too many to name, but just know that I appreciate every single review, share, post, comment, and mention. Your love for my stories brings me so much joy.

I want to say thank you to animal shelters worldwide, and anyone who volunteers their time to care for animals. The world is a better place because of people like you. Special thanks to Animal Haven in New York, which inspired Animal Oasis. You can check them out and make a donation, here:

https://animalhaven.org/

A big thanks to you, my lovely reader, for spending time with Cory and Josie. I love this couple and their journey of healing, and I hope you do too.

And finally, to anyone who has ever struggled with their self-worth. It's so hard to feel this way about yourself, and you are truly not alone (despite how it can sometimes feel). There's no shame in seeking professional help, because it's not always easy to heal these things without it. You deserve all the happiness in the world.

ABOUT THE AUTHOR

Jen Morris writes sexy romantic comedies with heat, humor and heart. She believes that almost anything can be fixed with a good laugh, a good book, or a plane ticket to New York.

Her books follow women with big dreams as they navigate life and love in the city. Her characters don't just find love—they find themselves, too.

Jen lives with her partner and son, in a tiny house on wheels in New Zealand. She spends her days writing, dreaming about New York, and finding space for her ever-growing book collection.

The Love You Deserve is her fourth novel, and the fourth book in the *Love in the City* series.

ALSO BY JEN MORRIS

Have you read book one in the series, *Love in the City*? Follow Kiwi girl Alex as she ventures to New York in search of her dreams, and finds a sexy bearded man along the way.

You might also enjoy book two, *You Know it's Love*. Join Cory's sister Cat as she tries to save her vintage clothing business—and fight her feelings for the cocky new bartender at her brother's bar.

Book three is *Outrageously in Love*. It follows Harriet, a nerdy bookworm, as she tries to break out of her comfort zone—starting with a little mile-high club action on her flight to New York...

Next up in the series is book five, Hayley's story!

Stay in touch so you don't miss anything:

Find me on Instagram and Facebook: @jenmorrisauthor

Subscribe to my newsletter for updates, release info, and cover reveals: www.jenmorrisauthor.com

See all the book inspiration on Pinterest: www.pinterest.com/jenmorrisauthor/